Something is ;...

In 1938, while work : site—a
paramount cradle of North ~~America~~ let John
Patton Jr. found the key to our darkest secret—an anomalous skeleton
neither animal nor man. Uncertain of its implications, Patton concealed
this secret for decades—until unveiling it to the world in a sensational
novel—with extraterrestrial speculations—that made him notorious across
the globe.

Nearly thirty years later, his grandson Gardner is forced to come to
terms with his grandfather's past, a man he never knew but in whose
footsteps he inevitably follows. When his cousin, controversial
documentarian Bart Thompson, arrives at Moundville for a seemingly
routine shoot, Gardner is eager to lend a hand. He soon learns,
however, that Bart isn't back just to shoot a movie. He wants to find the
skeleton their grandfather buried nearly seventy years before, and prove
once and for all what he claimed was true.

Flip the Novelization Over for Another Book!

A Genesis Found: The Film Companion is really two books in
one— *A Genesis Found: The Novelization* & *Buried in the
Mounds*.

Buried in the Mounds contains several behind the scenes features,
including a 40-page interview with the film's Producers, an anecdotal
essay from Assistant Director Markus Matei, the film's official shooting
screenplay, a comic, and the elusive first chapter from John Patton Jr.'s
Buried in the Mounds!

A Genesis Found

The Film Companion

A Genesis Found
The Film Companion

Wilson Toney and Lee Fanning

With an Introduction by Keith Penich

And contributions by
Markus Matei and Benjamin Flanagan

Wonder Mill Films
Huntsville, Alabama

This is a work of fiction. Names, characters, places and incidents are the product of the author's imagination or are used fictitiously. Any resemblance to actual persons, living or dead, is purely coincidental.

Publisher's Cataloging-in-Publication data

Toney, Wilson.
   A genesis found : the film companion / Wilson Toney & Lee Fanning ; with an introduction by Keith Penich ; and contributions by Markus Matei, & Benjamin Flanagan.
      p. cm.
      ISBN 978-0-615-35865-9

1. A Genesis Found (Motion picture). 2. Mound State Monument (Ala.) –Fiction. 3. Mississippian culture --Alabama --Fiction. 4. Civilian Conservation Corps (U.S.)– Alabama --History –Fiction. 5. Civilization --History –Fiction. 6. Archaeology --Fiction. 7. Extraterrestrial beings--Fiction. 8. Adventure fiction. I. Fanning, Walter Lee. II. Penich, Keith. III. Matei, Markus. IV. Flanagan, Benjamin. V. Title.

PS3570.O434 .G45 2010
813.54 -dd22   2010925515

First Edition

Wrap Cover Design by Jessica Twilbeck
Original Buried in the Mounds Cover Design by Samantha Hernandez
Photography by Samantha Hernandez except frame grabs and where noted.

agenesisfound.com
wondermillfilms.com

Printed in the United States of America

For the Pattons, the Toneys, the Wilsons and the Fannings.

Introduction

Being something of a cosmopolite, I had been puzzled by Lee Fanning's stubborn insistence on being a filmmaker in the South and on telling "Southern stories." I lived there, in northern Alabama, for two years—two years that I considered to be something like my time in the wilderness. The Southern attitude—very much a real and distinct phenomenon—I took to be born mostly out of ignorance. Little by little I've modified this opinion, as I've grown older, hopefully a little wiser, and perhaps more intuitive. The South, troubled though it is, has its own charms, and a unique cultural identity that is not otherwise found in this country. However, perhaps I am beginning in the wrong way. The film, *A Genesis Found*, on which this book is based, is set in the South, certainly. And it was filmed there, and what's more, by people who originate there and intend to remain there if at all possible. There are few who can boast so much; indeed, there are few who would want to. For all this, I won't say that *A Genesis Found* is a (much less *the*) quintessentially Southern story. Of course the South is present, and this is one reason, but not the only reason, that the story is valuable. We catch glimpses of the Southern attitude, of the Southern wilderness, and of course, of the ancient indigenous metropolis called Moundville. It is a monument (or rather, series of monuments) that many people today might be tempted to call mundane. As one character points out, the park tends to be deserted except for people who find it a convenient place to jog. Yet the mounds are deserving of some wonder—if burying aliens in them is the only way to stir up this wonder, that's more to our own discredit than it is a reproach of the mounds. However, apart from all of this, *A Genesis Found* is at bottom a universal story, dealing with such questions as might be asked by anyone, in any part of the country, and in any part of the world. It is furthermore a very good adventure-mystery and I hope that despite its limited means, many people will come to enjoy it.

The plot of the film, as well as the filmmaker himself, is in many ways preoccupied with storytelling as an art and as a profession, and also as a quintessentially human impulse. And so it is appropriate, and not simply gratuitous, that Wilson Toney has here adapted the film into novel form. You will find that the novel presents the same story and the same world seen in the film, but does so through a substantially different lens and with a substantially different voice. The Southern atmosphere is thicker here—Toney is almost the prototypical laid-back, wisecracking Southerner. He's not Mark Twain, certainly, but for that he's closer to his roots. He does not hesitate to break the fourth wall from time to time. The effect of this is to emphasize the plot's preoccupation with storytelling, and furthermore to make explicit the storytelling process with which the reader is directly involved. One might easily imagine, in reading this novel, that he has been transported temporarily to an archetypal Alabama back porch on a hot, humid, lazy afternoon with flies buzzing; and, with an old hound snoring at his feet, an old cat lying in his lap, an old man tells a story that he had some part in, however small. This creates an interesting contrast with the film: although the content of Lee Fanning's film is in many ways extremely personal, his direction is not. He rather seems to prefer an objective camera that lets the story tell itself. This is not a reproach, however; indeed, for a filmmaker, it is precisely this that often constitutes better storytelling in his medium. Yet this seems not to be a general trend in contemporary film—to this point, however, I will return shortly.

Although the manner of storytelling is quite different between the novel and the film, the content of both are very similar.

A GENESIS FOUND

Wilson Toney does not, for the most part, add superfluous elements to the plot to "fill" the novel. Rather, he adds nuances to the written story which are not possible or desirable in the visual medium: the personal asides I've already mentioned; another example is Toney's use of an omniscient perspective, through which we gain insight into the thoughts of even some of the minor characters, usually with a good deal of humor. With such obvious considerations aside, the book and the film are actually so similar that it might be easier to appreciate the book when one hasn't seen the movie; and presumably vice versa. However, even if this is found to be the case, the book you are holding is a full package and contains a good deal of material in addition to the novel. Scattered through the book are quotes attributed to the story's wittiest and most engaging character; most of these are humorous, some serious, and all actually quite wise. At the end of this half of the book you will find a collection of 'deleted scenes', which deal with plot events merely implied in the story proper, as well as with more distant extrapolations. Flip this book over, and you will find the first chapter of *Buried in the Mounds*, the book inside the book (and film), as well as Lee Fanning's original screenplay. You will also find an enlightening essay by Assistant Director Markus Matei, as well as an in-depth interview with Fanning and the film's producer, Benjamin Stark, by journalist and peer Benjamin Flanagan. All in all, anyone who has enjoyed the film should not be disappointed by the insights to be gained here both into the story of *A Genesis Found* and into the story behind it.

If you are reading this book, then quite likely you are either friend or family of someone who was personally involved in the making of the film. Or perhaps you became aware of the project less directly through its meager, grassroots distribution campaign. If neither of these is the case, however, then you are a rather remarkable indication of the film's success. At the time of writing this introduction, the extent of that success remains to be seen.

A GENESIS FOUND

Much devotion and hard work is going into the film's promotion; however, with all else being equal, this effort necessarily stems from a good deal of optimism and wishful thinking. The film, a product of Wonder Mill Films, represents a conscious attempt to succeed as part of a DIY/Regional movement—a movement of reaction to, if not replacement of, the current major industry as is—in simplistic terms, as an alternative to Hollywood. Thus there are many forces in the world hindering or at least doing nothing to help *A Genesis Found*, and very few things working in its favor. I count the following: first, Lee Fanning's own intense devotion to the film, its promotion and its success. Second, the hard work of friends and family, of which the present book is a shining example. Additionally, the merits of the film and of the story as art and as entertainment, which are not inconsiderable. And finally, the degree, however small, to which DIY is a viable way of making movies in contemporary society.

Regarding these last two points, I believe that *A Genesis Found* compares in general terms of quality rather favorably with other films of its socioeconomic bracket and even with many of the behemoths of the mainstream. The reason for this, without any doubt, is the film's emphasis on story. I don't believe that I exaggerate too much if I say that storytelling is dying out in our contemporary American culture, and not least of all in its movies. This is true of the great as well as the small in the world of film: when story is considered at all, it is usually considered merely as a vehicle to transport audiences in as much style as possible from the beginning of a movie to its end. The story is now often subordinate to the personal quirks of the filmmaker, and more generally to the purely visual experience. The movies, capable of doing so much for the eyes alone have downplayed the essentially linguistic aspect of storytelling, and with it the cognitive processes that are associated with comprehension thereof. In itself this is neither good nor bad; however, one should be cautioned that

A GENESIS FOUND

both Lee Fanning's film and Wilson Toney's novel require a little bit of thinking to be fully appreciated.

Whatever its success turns out to be, *A Genesis Found* will not be revolutionary, either in terms of the business model behind it or in the substance of its art. Lee Fanning and Wonder Mill Films have made the movie they wanted to make, and it is not in any way geared toward popular success. The indie scene, dominated by hipsters, wants quirkiness, or endless variations on Wes Anderson—and that will not be found here. The various cult scenes want zombies and gratuitous nudity, and perhaps aliens, but not aliens as they are dealt with here. The mainstream wants money, which certainly won't be found here. What little potential audience there is left will hear about the film or not hear about it, see it or not see it, and like it or not like it, all more or less as dictated by circumstances and personal tastes. The final determination of *A Genesis Found's* success will fall to luck, influenced to some unascertainable degree by the hard work put into it. This is a sad state of affairs, but in the end it is the only real one. However, if you are reading this, you are contributing to the future of Wonder Mill Films and its filmmakers—and, perhaps more importantly, you are in a small, symbolic way contributing to the future of the ideals represented by this film and others like it. With some luck, Wonder Mill will be able to produce many more films after *A Genesis Found* (and after the company's second film, *The Nocturnal Third*, which is due for release soon). With all this said and without further ado, I ask you to enjoy the book you are now holding.

KEITH PENICH

Davis, California
March 25. 2010

A Genesis Found
The Novelization

By Wilson Toney

We are all star offal. That explains a lot.

The Wisdom of Bart Thompson

The shovel moved slowly. The shoveler slower still. The man (maybe boy) stopped to wipe his brow. He reflected for a moment, "Days are endless, nights more so. But then, what do you expect? There's a depression on!"

John Patton Junior dumped a shovelful of rich red dirt into the ever-increasing mound behind him. Only the Government could find it practical to pay a person to empty one mound by creating another. A flash of white showed in the red dirt, almost translucent against its rich red background, yet another bone was found. Patton stopped his whittling of the mound long enough to sing out, with more excitement than he felt "Found another one!"

Patton's fellow workers, looking for an excuse to stop their own digging, stopped and looked over to him. Then they went right back to their daily bread winning. Gone were the days when they would all throw down their shovels and gather around. You get used to everything, even finding skeletons. Besides, their boss would just holler at them to get back to work. And the day was filled with enough hollering without encouraging more of it.

Tim Shaw looked at Patton and exclaimed, "How big you reckon he'll be?" Tim's voice was pure Mississippi, but Patton's Alabama ear had no trouble understanding him.

"What'ya mean?" Patton responded.

"I heard they found some out here ten feet tall. Giants! You know- supposed to have done the grunt work on building these things. They're even mentioned in the Bible for Christ sakes!"

The things Shaw was referring to were the man made mounds that these young boy men were being paid thirty bucks a month

1

(or at least that was what was sent home to Mama, the boys got a dollar a day spending money and room and board) to shovel from one place to another. These mounds were large hills of earth that some other, probably complaining, young men had built hundreds of years earlier, long before this part of the world had even heard of, much less seen a white man. There were a lot of them and the Civilian Conservation Corps was duly investigating them. For those of you that are historically challenged, the CCC was a child of the depression. A Government program that took young men off the street (or farm, mostly, in the South) and put them to work doing things the Government thought was useful, like desecrating this ancient American Indian graveyard. To the Government's credit, it wasn't malicious, just science.

"I doubt he's ten feet tall," Patton replied. "Probably only nine feet ten or so."

A Ford truck, black of course, came bounding over the rough terrain, dodging mounds like a pinball. Even from a distance you could see the big Fedora hat that the driver was wearing. Patton recognized the truck, he saw it most days, and knew the driver as well as could be expected. The driver was the chief scientist of the Moundville dig, as it was known. He was a doctor, but not the kind that can fix you if you get snake bit in this wilderness, but a doctor of archaeology. While Patton knew what that word meant, most of the others working the site were clueless. But they all called him Doc, either out of respect or laziness.

The Ford showed off its brakes, coming to a sudden stop. Doctor Walter Jones stepped out of the driver side, almost knocking his much loved Fedora off in the process, but with a deft move developed by long practice in the protection of his trademark, his hand shot up and steadied the hat. The commander of the camp stepped out of the rider's side. His name was DeJarnette, but he was an American all the same. He was older than dirt, sturdy military type, rough and not at all loved by his charges. But then few bosses are.

As the day was dwindling, and the efforts of the workers more so, DeJarnette found an opportunity to gain some good feelings from the boys and he announced, "All right boys, let's pack it in" loudly a good two minutes before the official quitting time.

Tim Shaw grinned, grabbed a wad of Double Bubble from his pocket unwrapped it carefully, looked at the comic, he had already seen this one before, which wasn't surprising, popped the gum into his mouth and let the comic and the wrapper slip from his fingers. They floated gently in the slight Southern breeze, and landed almost on the foot of DeJarnette.

DeJarnette looked like something unmentionable had been shoved in his face, a face that twisted into a grimace as he shouted, "Pick it up, Shaw." Wearily, DeJarnette shook his head, as if he was tired of telling the same thing to the same boys for way too many a time. Retirement in three years, he thought, just three more.

Shaw smiled and picked it up. Just then DeJarnette turned to talk with another boy and Shaw let the papers go again. This time a real wind caught the papers and they scampered across the flat earth showing colors of bright red and blue. You could still see Joe Blow for at least five feet before the gaudy strips disappeared into the pine forest that surrounded the mounds. "Find it now, Copper," Shaw said under his breath.

Doctor Jones approached the mound where John Patton was standing, stretching his long legs in a walk that looked more like a canter. Patton was looking down at the bone that was peeping out of the dirt. It looked like an eye socket, but at best that was a guess as Patton was hardly an anatomist. "Seen anything like this before Doc?" Patton asked the approaching older man. Patton spoke without inflection in a good, country Southern drawl. Jones, being city bred, did not know if Patton had spoken in jest or was serious;

even after years of interaction the subtlety of the speech patterns of rural people still sometimes evaded him. It was, after all, Jones' main job to have seen stuff like that many times before.

"Oh yeah," Jones replied, his voice was flat, different than Patton's, he wouldn't be dropping his G's, but still strong. "We've been finding these all over the site." It was a truthful understatement. There were relics all over the site, including skeletons, but they were all over the Southeast too.

Jones glanced down at the protruding bones, nodding his head, "Yes, looks like American Indian circa 1400- Moundville III to be precise, just at a glance of course. We'll find out more when we do real science on it." Jones transferred his gaze to Patton. Patton looked at Jones. Blue eyes staring at brown. Recognition showed in the aging brown eyes that were staring,

"You're in my Archaeology class, aren't you?"

"Yes sir," Patton answered, "John Patton Junior, sir."

Jones extended his sun brown if slightly aged hand and Patton grasped it with his sun brown but young hand. There weren't that many students interested in archaeology and Jones always made it a point to make over any he came into contact with. Teaching positions, after all, were hard to come by in this depression and harder still if you ran off any potential students before you squeezed a buck or two out of them. While it was true that the CCC provided the opportunity for these particular students to go to his archaeology class free of charge, it still didn't hurt if there were more of them there instead of less. Might hook one to come to his real University class if this damned depression would ever let up.

"There's not many of you," Jones said ruefully, "And that's a fact."

"No sir," Patton replied proforma; there were other things on his mind. "I was wondering sir," Patton continued, "You talked about how the site was possibly abandoned by 1400, um, I was wondering when you thought these were buried? They seem...."

"Shallow?" Jones asked and answered at the same time.

"Yes sir," Patton said. "I know erosion's a factor but they just don't seem as deep as other artifacts we've found here."

"I agree with you," Jones said. "These were buried well after 1400 A.D."

"What does that mean sir?" asked Patton. "That folks were here longer?"

Jones shook his head and stated, "There's no indication that anyone lived here, Mr. Patton, just that they were buried here."

"It turned into a graveyard, huh?" Patton asked.

Jones nodded. "I think this place was a spiritual sanctuary to the people that lived around this site. It was a pathway to the afterlife, maybe even to God, for a long time, even after the site itself was abandoned."

"What makes you say that sir?" Patton asked in earnest.

Jones wanted to say seven years of college and thirty years of experience but didn't. Again, teaching jobs were hard to come by and it didn't pay to insult prospects. Instead Jones stated, "Let's just say it looks that way, shall we, Mr. Patton?"

Jones threw his left arm out wide, motioning with his hand at the multitude of mounds about them. Patton for the first time really looked at the mounds. They were everywhere. On the top of one someone had arranged a group of skeletons in a circular pattern like a macabre ring around the rosy. On another mound a group of skeletons had been arranged into a pattern vaguely resembling a hand. In the middle of the large hand was a heap of bones that looked like a spot or a pupil. It could be a large eye looking right at you from a hand. Of course, Patton was young and the young always see differently than the old. Jones would have just seen skeletons, if he saw anything at all.

DeJarnette's bark of "Let's get a move on Patton" brought Patton's mind away from mystical patterns and back into the present.

Doctor Jones dipped his fedora at Patton and then ambled back to the truck. DeJarnette, strutting like a banty rooster, fell in behind Jones and strutted to the truck. The difference in not just their walk but also their body language was not lost on Patton. To one he was at least a human, to the other just a wart in the path of progress. The truck rumbled to life then began to dodge mounds on its exit.

Patton watched for a second then gave a slight nod of his head. He spoke aloud, although there was none left to hear as all of the other boy-men had departed, "Want a ride, Mr. Patton? No thanks Doc, I prefer to walk a half mile after a twelve hour day in the sun." Then he wearily picked up his shovel and rake and headed back to that paradise of sweating bodies and burping contests that was the barracks.

Life ain't like quantum physics. It's more complicated than that.

The Wisdom of Bart Thompson

Patton wiped the sweat from his face with a handkerchief that was already soaked. It was a tossup as to whether it removed as much sweat as it planted. The so-called bed he was lying on was harder than rock, the blasted light was shining right in his eyes and the bed bugs were threatening a riot. Another glorious night in the Hotel Moundville. Oh well, in hard times one puts up with a lot of crap and this temporary barracks (sure they will build a permanent one, sure they will) was marginally better than a cave somewhere. Probably.

A GENESIS FOUND

The book Patton was reading, *Certain Aboriginal Finds on the Black Warrior River Basin,* was hardly a page-turner but attempting to read it beat just lying there sweating. Besides, despite the archaic phrasing used by the author, it was beginning to make some sense.

Tim Shaw had the bunk next to Patton, either by accident or to repay Patton for some misdeed in a previous life. Shaw was always talking and Patton was often his intended victim. Patton did his best to keep Shaw from knowing that he was a bore and a pain, but his best wasn't always good enough. At this moment, Shaw was chewing gum rapidly, his jaw moving as fast as a piston, the ever-present bubble gum visible at about every third chew. Shaw was also reading, kinda. His selection was more sedate than Patton's; it was a pulp magazine with a pretty picture of a skeleton's hand shooting straight up from a grave. Every word in the pulp was probably true.

Shaw evidently found a particular passage somewhat less than scintillating as he tossed the magazine to the floor and growled, "All right, I'm not stomaching this no more." He turned to Patton and asked, "Whatcha reading?"

"You wouldn't like it Shaw," Patton replied truthfully.

Shaw shrugged and laughed at the same time. "Probably true," he said and continued, "That some kind of a school book?"

"Somethin' like that," Patton answered.

Shaw took a knife from his duffle bag without leaving the bed. He was close enough to the dirt floor to play mumbly peg. The floor being compacted dirt (if they were lucky it was just dirt, but there were a lot of farms nearby and God knows where the dirt came from) was less satisfying to Shaw for throwing his knife into; a nice wood floor would have satisfied his inner vandal more, but one must make do in these trying times.

"Sure do care about this stuff, don't you Patton?" Shaw asked.

Patton glanced wearily at Shaw before answering; it looked like it was going to be one of those nights. "And what's wrong with that?" asked Patton.

"Nothing, I reckon," Shaw reckoned. "Just creepy to me is all. Who'd want to dig up corpses, everyday all day long?"

"It ain't creepy," Patton returned, defending his potential profession, "it's science."

Shaw had the knife in his hands and was cleaning his nails. It didn't occur to him that given that the knife had just been pulled from the dirt that it might just be leaving more grit behind than it was removing. If one wanted a true picture of a Southern redneck they could do worse than to take a snapshot of Shaw.

"Science, eh?" Shaw said doubtfully, "So's Frankenstein. I just think some things oughtta stay in the ground."

"I thought you wanted to find a giant, Shaw," Patton said very seriously.

"Shoot," Shaw exploded, "I don't wanna find nothing. Next thing you know we'll be stumbling onto some kinda cursed tomb. Mummy will start chasing us all the way to Mobile." Shaw laughed. "Backwards place like this, I wonder if even God knows what's out there."

"Well He don't have to," said Patton, "It's our job, be it giants, cursed tombs or buried treasure."

Shaw's head jerked around. He gazed intently at Patton.

"Treasure?" he asked, "out there?"

Patton grinned at Shaw and said, "It's a local secret." Patton said it with conviction. "You being a North Mississippi yokel, I ain't so sure I should tell you."

Shaw took a second to let the sentence sink in, then a wide grin came onto his amiable face and he said, "Aw, you're pulling my leg."

Patton shrugged. He continued to look at Shaw.

"I heard we might be looking for it," Patton said, "It's just-" then Patton put his finger on his lips and winked.

"That would be nice," responded Shaw through a smile that showed the first ravages of chewing tobacco (with just a nice shade of yellow), "No sir, wouldn't mind stumbling onto that. As much of my pay they send back to the folks, it's like I'm working for free, can't even spare a dime for no new reading material. You sure you ain't got something else Patton?"

"You ain't got a Bible, Shaw?" questioned Patton.

"Come on, I can't read that good," Shaw said. "Sides, what else is a preacher for?"

Patton sighed, "It's against my better judgment," he stated wearily, "and that's God's truth." Patton reached under his mattress and pulled out a magazine.

Shaw watched Patton's movement with more than average anticipation. Visions of *Spicy Detective Stories* were galloping through his mind.

Patton tossed the magazine and Shaw scooped it mid-air. Lou Gehrig couldn't have made a better catch. Eagerly Shaw pulled the magazine cover up to eye level. It was a *Scientific American.* Shaw looked like he had just lost his life savings in the market. Shaw's eyes went from the magazine back to Patton.

"It's all I got," Patton said.

Shaw shrugged. He slipped his gum out of his mouth and slapped it under his bed rail.

Patton resumed his reading hoping that Shaw had his fill of talking for one night. As Patton turned the page he came upon a beautiful colored plate showing the Rattlesnake Disc. It consisted of a hand held upright with an eye in the palm; the hand was surrounded by a horned rattlesnake. Patton was jolted. He pulled his journal from beneath his bed and looked at the illustration he had drawn of the odd configuration of the skeletons he had seen with Jones earlier. Yep, take away the snake and the two looked a lot alike. Patton began to draw the photograph in his journal in free hand.

"Whatcha got there?" his buddy Shaw asked.

"You don't want to read this," Patton answered honestly, "It's just a buncha notes."

"As much as you study Patton," Shaw said with a shade of disrespect, "You shoulda stayed in school."

Patton shrugged. "I reckon it'll do me good someday," he responded to the jibe. "They find this and when I'm in the ground they won't have to dig me up just to know something about me."

"Well, ain't nobody gonna read it then," Shaw replied defending his position. After all, the way Shaw saw it, the CCC didn't pay nearly enough for the work they required, so only a fool would do more for free. "Ain't nobody gonna read it," Shaw repeated, "Not even your grandchildren."

Give a man a fish and he will eat for one day. Teach a man to fish, he'll learn to drink beer on his own; then he'll be totally useless.

The Wisdom of Bart Thompson

Some people would be surprised at the following statement. The University of Alabama consists of more than just a football team. The U of A has classes, students, scholars, a superb library, and yes, a football team. How good is the football team? Just try to get tickets!

Gardner Patton was one of the students that attended U of A. He cared little for the football team and less for any other sport, which probably made him an anomaly on the campus, but even if so, he wouldn't have cared. Mostly he cared about Kelsey. Then he cared about archaeology. Kinda. Then he cared about his good name, if he had a good name.

Gardner was all of twenty-one, which made him a man, or at least he chose to think that. He was short but sturdy and had more stamina than most. Stamina that he abused a lot when studying for finals. He looked like his grandfather but more on that later.

Speaking of Gardner's grandfather, he just happened to be looking over his grandpa's journal. It was worn and dilapidated. It was, Gardner supposed, a family heirloom. It wasn't as good as a nice fat trust but it was better than nothing. Maybe. Gardner was randomly looking at pages, killing time; then he closed the book and staring at him from the cover was the Rattlesnake Disc.

At Hoole Library you can get a copy made quickly and efficiently and Gardner was doing just that with his grandfather's journal. If you were lucky you would catch Charisse on duty and you could pass the time watching that good looking blonde casually toss her hair about as she made the copies for you. Gardner had not been lucky. His copy attendant looked like he could play defensive line for the mighty Tide. And he just might at that.

Gardner glanced up from his *War of the Worlds* book (how many times had he read it? Truthfully he had lost count) just in time to see the first page of the journal come out of the copier. It read "Journal of John Patton Junior Property of the University Libraries- Special Collections- Restricted Use Only- Do Not Circulate!"

The second page out of the copier was a map of the Moundville Archaeological Park and the surrounding Black Warrior River Valley circa 1938. Gardner got tired of looking at the copier after that and went back to his book. He figured any guy big enough to play for the Tide could handle a copier without assistance from him.

11

Gardner's phone rang. The copy guy gave him a look that Gardner ignored. He looked at the phone screen and it told him right away he wanted to take this call; it was from Kelsey.

"Hey," he whispered, "Nah," another whisper, "I'm at Hoole," just a little louder. The book slipped from his fingers and made a smack that could be heard in Tennessee when it hit the floor. The attendant, all 6 foot 4 inches and 300 pounds of him glared more insistently at Gardner. Gardner forced a smile, held up a finger and returned to his whispered conversation.

"I'm doing Bart a favor," he whispered some more. "Yeah, he got in a few days ago, just now called me though. He's camping at Moundville with his crew, special permission. Something about a documentary he's making. Yeah. Listen, I gotta head over there after class, you wanna go?" Gardner grinned at Kelsey's rather colorful explanation of why she didn't want to go and gave Gardner notice of an alternate destination she recommended for him.

"I gotta give him these copies," Gardner continued, "Just some of the stuff Grandpa donated to the University. Bart actually tracked it down. You sure you don't want to go? He said he got us a present."

Gardner heard again just how sure Kelsey was that she didn't want to go.

"Nah, it's cool," Gardner replied to Kelsey's onslaught. "I understand totally. By the way I finished our badges for Halloween. Mulder and Scully here we come." He hesitated as he listened to her reply then stated, "Naw, it's in re-runs, besides it's not that old. People will know who we are."

Gardner noticed a small photograph on the floor and quickly he stooped down and snagged it talking in a hushed whisper the whole time, "Yeah, I'll be there in a while. Just meet me at class. Love ya too." He closed his phone and turned the photo over and gazed at it. The picture was of a young, black haired man, late teens/early twenties, clean-shaven, fairly good looking, wearing a Civilian Conservation Corps uniform. The photo was black and white of course, aged and not as sharp as one would wish. It was Gardner's famous (infamous?) grandfather. The resemblance was strong, much to Gardner's dismay. Gardner slipped the photo into his backpack. He glanced at the copy attendant, but it didn't appear the guy noticed. In a few minutes his copy of the journal was complete. Gardner put it into a manila folder and headed across campus.

Ten Hoor is an Arts and Sciences building. Most of the archaeology classes were taught there along with Anthropology, Paleontology and probably other ologies no one but the students taking them cared about. Ten Hoor was named after a famous writer that nobody had ever heard of. It is the last building on campus and was right next to the road that runs right next to the Black Warrior River. Ten Hoor sat in a depression (down hill from the rest of the campus) and every time it rained, which was often, it flooded. Water was standing in puddles all around the building and of course mosquitoes just loved to breed there as there was often a bevy of warm blooded college students wearing very skimpy clothes because of the heat to feed on. Thus they had Ten Hoor and feasted on the arts and sciences crowd, much to the delight of the business students.

Kelsey West was sitting uncomfortably in a chair manufactured probably in the seventies; you know the type, hard rigid plastic held up by a stainless steel frame. The chair had been out of style even before it was bought. Kelsey's long brown hair was just a bit frazzled, like it hadn't seen a comb properly for awhile. This was highly unusual as Kelsey was typically immaculate from head to toe. Kelsey had a copy of the Crimson White (the U of A student newspaper for the uninitiated) in her slender hands and was attempting to read it without much success.

She put a hand to her forehead, felt for a moment, lowered her hand and lay the newspaper down on the top of her desk.

Gardner was sitting beside her in a sister chair, except this one had part of its back broken so that it poked him every now and then. It wasn't comfortable but it did help him stay awake. Even though he had been reading the *War of the Worlds* he had noticed Kelsey's hand on her forehead out of the periphery of his vision, "You okay?" he asked with genuine concern.

"Yeah," she replied off-handedly. "Just a bug I suppose." Kelsey picked up the paper again and said softly, "Damn, Gardner, look at this."

Gardner glanced at the headline. It was very large and it proclaimed 'Documentary Filming at Moundville: Tuscaloosa Native at Helm. A photograph of a gaunt faced young man wearing a baseball style hunting cap and a plaid shirt was smiling out at them. Beneath the photo was a caption that stated, "Bart Thompson- Director of *The Dogma War* which was a controversial favorite at the Sundance film festival."

"He'll love that," Gardner stated knowingly.

"You sure?" asked Kelsey. "The paper buried it in the back pages so's that hardly anyone can find it."

"Well they ain't-" Gardner stopped in mid-speech, he was supposed to be a college man and he really should use better grammar, "Haven't, I mean, mentioned him around here in years. It's worth something. Besides, Bart always says anything, even bad publicity, is better than no publicity."

"But not off the front page," Kelsey said.

Gardner shook his head slightly and said, "Give him a break Kels. He's still a Patton at least by proxy. Some things both good and bad go with that name."

Kelsey picked up the folder that was sitting on Gardner's so-called desk and started to leaf through it. "This what you're taking him?"

Gardner nodded. "Yeah. Background, he says. Grandpa's journal."

"You read it?" she asked.

"Why would I want to do that?" Gardner asked with just a hint of innocence.

"Well." She replied a bit more seriously than warranted, "It was your grandfather's."

Gardner shrugged. To him that was meaningless, there were a lot of things that were his grandfather's that he cared not a whit about.

Kelsey ignored the shrug. Her curiosity was up; after all, she thought she would want to read it if her grandfather had written it. "I'm really surprised you are not curious," her voice trailed upward, almost but not quite making the statement a question.

"Look, I'm going to state the obvious," Gardner stated obviously, "If I'm serious about this archaeology thing- if we're serious, then we want to stay as far away from this thing," he nodded towards the folder containing the copy of the journal, "as we can. Life is tough; it's tougher when you're stupid."

Kelsey shrugged herself, mimicking Gardner. "Well, that seems unfair," she said, "He wasn't always crazy, was he?"

"Kels," Gardner shook his head and said the word soft and very slow. She knew it meant not now and perhaps not ever do we want to talk about this subject. Naturally she ignored him.

"Is this him?" she asked, withdrawing the photograph from the folder.

"Unfortunately," Gardner replied with a nod of his head.

"You look like him," she said almost lovingly.

"I can't help that," he said flatly. "And if there is a God in Heaven, maybe one day I'll grow out of it."

Kelsey's reply, if she had one to that, was interrupted by Professor Kerry Sims entering the room. Sims was a large commanding man and the room seemed to shake as he walked.

A GENESIS FOUND

He was affable enough, at least on a good day, but he was a bit dotty about archaeology. But then he was a professor and we all know just how much off center they can be.

Sims turned on the projector screen at the rear of the room and lay down a map of a large mound with a big F circled on it. The legend stated "Mound F- Moundville Archaeological Park." Not that anyone had to be told where this particular mound was located, of course, as Moundville was the subject of this month's lessons and everyone knew they would be digging at Moundville sooner rather than later. None of that mattered to Sims, as he was a state the obvious kind of guy.

"We'll be excavating Mound F," Sims' voice boomed out, echoing off the concrete walls with the fading gray paint. If the students hadn't been used to it, the voice would have startled them. But this was mid-semester and all had heard that booming voice in both humor and anger.

"Mound F," Sims continued, "Is in the southeastern part of the site. If you are up to the challenge let me know and I'll give you a more detailed route to the site." He paused and smiled. The class did not laugh. Oh well, can't be funny all the time.

"According to modern theories," Sims continued, "This mound may have been used for ceremonial and burial purposes by one of the higher clans. Now our primary objective here is to learn about religion as a social system- not grave robbing. I don't care what time of the year it is, we leave that for the medical school."

The class laughed at that one. Sims smiled. Still have it.

Sims held up a red plastic flag. "Look at this," he said, "It is your friend, it is also your grade's friend. Any remains found will be recovered with dirt and flagged. Failure to do so will make me mad and you sad. Hope you caught the subtlety there." Sims waited a second to make sure his word had sunk in, at least as sunk in as words ever are to college kids with nothing but sex and beer on their minds, then he continued, "All right, now what do I mean by religion as a social system? Let's talk about that- this is very important so please, everyone that wants to pass, chin up, ears out."

Sims began the college professor drone. College professors excel at droning; it comes with seven years of sitting in classes hearing their predecessors drone, possibly. Gardner was barely listening; he was in his "let's-get-the-hell-through-with-this-class" mode. To pass the time he was drawing a tripod death machine instead of taking notes. He had inherited some of his grandfather's talents at least as the drawing was quite good.

Kelsey goosed him and gave him that special glare reserved between lovers, that states, stop being an idiot will you, people associate me with you and I want them to think I have a little class. Lovers can say a lot with a jab and a glare.

"It ain't like I can't hear," Gardner whispered and smiled his lovers signal of, come on you think anyone cares who you date? It was meant to pacify and ingratiate. It did neither. Kelsey continued to glare.

"Moundville was important," Sims was saying, "because it was one of the earliest significant communities established in prehistoric America. It's a recent example of how mankind progressed to civilization." Sims paused for a moment hoping to pull in those students, much like Gardner, that were busy doing just about anything but listening. And there were more than enough to make the pause worthwhile. Once Sims was sure that most were paying attention, including that damn Patton kid he continued, "What we don't know is why Moundville was built in the first place. There are many theories but none have yet reached consensus. I personally think we will find the answer when we can better understand their religion. This is very difficult and challenging work as we are dealing with essentially a lost civilization. All we have is the dirt they left and any clues they

17

happened to leave in that dirt. It's analogous to determining how an American household is run based on what one pulls out of a vacuum cleaner."

Sims changed slides. A photo of the Rattlesnake Disc was projected. Gardner changed his doodling to that figure.

"This is the Rattlesnake Disc," Sims said loudly enough to gather even more attention. "This is a prime example of one of the clues we must decipher. Now take a close look at this symbol here," Sims used a pointer to show the eye in the hand. "This eye in the hand motif is not exclusive to Moundville. It is found in many other Native American cultures in the Southeast and even beyond. It is often defined as the hand of the creator, or the eye of God. It's not necessarily perceived to mean that at Moundville. We have our own theories on that score. The most prevalent being that the symbol was a representation of the constellation we call Orion today. There are other interpretations of course, some less cosmic," Sims stopped talking for a second and glanced at Gardner, then continued "Some more so."

Gardner glanced away instead of meeting Sims eyes. It was much to his credit that his face didn't register the disgust he felt; after all, the theory wasn't his but his grandfather's. Never once had he even discussed the issue with Sims much less defended it. It was unfair. Kelsey gave Gardner another look that said, "Don't worry." Gardner wasn't, he had been a Patton far too long to let anything bother him related to his grandfather.

"Essentially guys," Sims remarked, "What we are looking for is the answer that archaeologists have been after for over a century. The key to the origin of the mounds. Find that and I guarantee not only an A but a scholarship." Again laughter. Music to his ears.

"Kels," Gardner whispered.

Kelsey either did not hear or wanted it to be thought she had not heard; she stood and walked from the room quickly, almost running. The folder in her lap, the one containing the journal of John Patton Junior slapped the floor with a loud "Whap." Gardner watched her leave and for once he wasn't just checking her out. Something was wrong but he was damned if he knew what.

He bent over and picked up the folder. The map to Moundville fell out. He noticed that his grandfather had circled Mound F on the map he had drawn. What it meant he did not know. If it meant anything besides the ramblings of an old man that may have been a few bricks shy of a load. As he returned the map to the folder he saw once again the eye in the hand drawing. A curious notation was at the top of the page, a number: 87343. What the hell did that mean? Just then his phone beeped. He knew who it was even before he looked. Sure enough, it was from Kelsey. "Can u take me home?" the message asked.

Sims was saying, "Now please, listen up guys and girls and everything in between, this information is essential. Passing essential."

Gardner smirked. Teach her to run off in a snit. But what did it say about him? He gathered his things and quietly walked out of the room hoping that Sims was exaggerating on the importance of what he was going to impart to them.

I have a God given right to be an atheist.

The Wisdom of Bart Thompson

Gardner pulled his beat up Ford truck into the Moundville Archaeological Park. Whether it was divine intervention or just good fortune, he arrived at the very moment that three lovely ladies were taking their daily jog. He saw both the front of them and the back of them and life was good for a few seconds. Then he focused on the mounds.

A GENESIS FOUND

The incongruity of the situation was not lost on Gardner. Here were ancient mounds, virtually lost for centuries, the labor of men as ancient as time, and yet people were so nonchalant about them that they used the area of this sacred place for a jogging path. The truth was most of the people did not have a clue as to what the mounds were. The shame of it was that they wouldn't care even if they did know.

To the uninitiated, the mounds were just big hills covered in dark green grass. Only someone trained in the arcane subject of mound building would know, without being told, that these hills were not natural but man-made. The hills looked no different than any other hill one might find anywhere in these United States. There were a lot of them and they resided in a particularly flat part of the country so one might suspect they were man-made, but it would only be a guess, even if a good one. It would take a professional to know they were really man-made, or a farmer knocking them down to clear the land and finding the stuff buried within them. That is, after all, how they had been discovered, not by science but by accident.

On the highest and widest mound in the park, the state had built a recreation of an American Indian village circa 1200 A.D. It was beautifully backlit by the sun. It looked as if it floated on the Black Warrior River, the river that had doubtless been the lifeblood of the original people that had built the mounds. Gardner remembered taking a field trip here as a mere lad. Seeing the village and stealing a kiss from Becky Schrimsher had been the highlights of that day. The village didn't look like it had changed much, if at all. Beck had definitely changed, or maybe it was Gardner. As we age, our tastes change and what we find attractive as a youth we don't always find attractive as a slightly older youth. Then again he had gotten glasses. Whatever the reason, he ran like hell when he saw her coming. Beck wanted to take Gardner down that particular memory path every time she saw him. Gardner... Gardner was sentimental about some things, but definitely not this.

Surrounding the large mound were many other mounds. Surrounding the mounds were trees, concrete and the river. There were several woodland trails one could hike through if smart enough to bring a can of *Off*; otherwise, one would come running like a bat out of hell from those trails after a few feet into them, and one would be surrounded by mosquitoes. Gardner had found that Archaeology taught you, if nothing else, to always have a can of *Off* in your car.

Gardner cranked his engine and pulled further into the park. Just on the hill opposite the village he could see a white travel trailer and a small tent pitched opposite of it. The trailer sat like a white jewel in the forest, surrounded by green; with the sun bouncing off of it, it almost twinkled. That was undoubtedly Bart's crew and Gardner's destination.

A knock on the flimsy white door resulted in a strange giant youth with bushy black hair and a bad complexion opening same. The young man stared at Gardner and did not speak. He had not only bushy hair on his head, but bushy eyebrows, and would doubtlessly have had a bushy beard if he had not been clean shaven. He did not smile, nor did he open the door more than a foot.

Gardner did smile, for all the good it did him, as the young man remained stone faced. Finally Gardner broke the silence and asked "Is Bart Thompson..." but before he could finish the sentence he was interrupted by a loud "There he is!" from somewhere inside the trailer.

The tall, redheaded, gaunt man that Gardner knew much too well came into view. A white towel was rapidly being rubbed in his hair. It was one of the few times Gardner had seen him without his signature hunter's cap. A large smile crossed the man's face as he said in pure Alabamian, "Pologize. Just got out of the bed and then out of a quick shower."

"I wouldn't have expected otherwise," Gardner said truthfully, "After all it's just two p.m."

"Same old Gardner," Bart said with a laugh. "Still got a stick up your posterior."

"Same old Bart," Gardner replied, "Still getting up at two p.m."

"Come here," Bart said and reached his arm out, grabbing Gardner's neck and pulling him towards him. "Where's your ring, kid? I've been gone five years, and you ain't hitched yet?"

"Naw," Gardner replied. "Still got a ways to go."

"Where's Kelsey anyway?" Bart asked.

"She's got some bug-thing," Gardner said. Well, it was half true.

"Yeah, sure," Bart responded mockingly. "No need to lie about it, I know she ain't much for me kid. Don't worry about it- just make sure I get an invitation to the wedding."

"You expect me to wait another five years?" Gardner asked innocently.

"I do at that," Bart replied with a laugh, "Least if you got any sense. Longer still if Kelsey's got any sense."

"Out of the mouth of babes," Gardner said seriously.

"Ain't that the truth," Bart defended himself. "If we're through insulting each other let's get on with the introducing. This here is Levi," Bart nodded to the giant that had opened the door, "Levi, this is my cousin Gardner Patton. He's here digging what we're filming."

Gardner held out his hand. Levi hesitated a second then took it and squeezed way too hard. Here was one big guy that wanted you to respect his bigness.

"You've got something in common," Bart said nodding his head toward Levi. Bart spoke in a deeper voice than usual as if he was about to betray a confidence.

"What's that?" Gardner asked.

Bart nodded his head towards Levi, "He's my cousin too."

Bart smiled and said, "He's my Dad's nephew."

"Condolences," Gardner said and without doubt meant it. "Levi, you from around here?" Gardner asked.

"You know it," Bart again answered for Levi. Gardner suspected it wasn't an accident. Some relationships were that way and Levi hardly seemed the loquacious type.

"Yeah," Bart continued, "Ole Levi and me grew up together, leastwise when I wasn't babysitting you."

Gardner smirked and said "Just tell Levi about the time I taught you to play poker. I ate ice cream for a week off that deal."

"Now, now," Bart replied, he outstretched his hand and made the stop sign, "Fore you know it Levi will begin to question my character. Not that it couldn't stand some questioning. Course Levi already knows me too well for any mud to take aholdt. We went to Sunday school together, played baseball together, Cub Scouts together; yeah, me and Levi quit about everything together."

"Now that I would believe," answered Gardner and smiled a real smile for a change. "Especially of you."

Levi had seemed to have his fill of the Lum and Abner show and had retreated to the small couch in the small trailer. He had picked up a book entitled *Orson Welles and the War of the Worlds Broadcast*. In smaller letters the book humbly announced, "Panic, Sensation, Invaders from Mars, It Really Happened Folks You Can't Make This Stuff Up." Well it seemed a real page-turner.

"Cool book," Gardner said hoping to start a conversation with his cousin-in-law; after all he was an expert on all things *War of the*

23

Worlds, from the good movie to the cheesy TV show. Levi just nodded. He perhaps thought it better to be thought a fool rather than open his mouth and remove all doubt.

Bart finished with his towel, tossed it to Levi and said, "Put that with the rest of our unmentionables, huh."

Levi caught the towel in mid air. He continued to give Bart and Gardner the stone face but he took the towel and walked outside. Bart smiled as his cousin ambled off, "Levi don't say much," he told Gardner, "But he makes up for it with his ever infectious smile." Bart reached onto the kitchen table and grabbed his hunter's cap; he placed it on his head and stated, truthfully, "Felt naked without it."

"Looked it too," Gardner said. "Levi dumb?"

"He ain't smart kid," Bart laughed.

"You know what I mean," Gardner insisted.

"That whole side of the family is dumb, but I think Levi can talk. Leastwise I heard him mumble afore. I do think he's sick but he usually ain't much better and that's the truth. Come on out and meet the rest of the crew. If you want talk they'll be glad to supply it and then some."

Gardner led the way out of the small trailer with Bart pulling up the rear. It was one of the few times Gardner had led the way with anything associated with Bart. Bart quickly got in front of Gardner, and it made Gardner wonder if there was something there for a psychiatrist. Probably was, anyone that could find meaning in inkblots could find meaning in anything. Bart motioned toward a dilapidated tent where two men sat, one reading, the other fooling with some electronic device.

The man fooling with the electronic device was a black guy in his mid-twenties, very muscular. The other man was an older white guy, say mid-fifties, he wore glasses that didn't seem to fit and he had a newspaper in his lap. The chairs the two were sitting in were as dilapidated as the tent or even more so if that were possible. They didn't seem to be Hollywood types, but then again Gardner didn't really know what a Hollywood type would seem like having never seen one.

"Ben, Doc," Bart said, "This here's Gardner. You know, my cousin I told you about."

Ben was evidently the black guy as he nodded first without looking up from his play pretty. Gardner thought it to be a Blackberry or a smartphone of some sort. Doc nodded second and smiled. Gardner noticed a copper bracelet on the Doc's wrist; he thought that had gone out with bell-bottoms.

"These two won the coin toss," Bart stated with just a touch of envy.

"The camper doesn't have air conditioning," Ben stated. Then he smiled at Bart.

"That's Ben Watson," Bart nodded towards the black man. "He's a videographer, sound engineer, editor, general all around techie; he does all the tech stuff I don't want to do."

"Or don't know how to do," Ben said smiling even brighter.

"Ben has inferiority issues," Bart confided.

Ben laughed and shook his head.

"Sides," Bart continued, "He's been doing all the hard work since film school so I put up with his peculiarities."

"Don't forget the Doctor, Bart," Ben said and nodded towards the elderly white man.

"Thank you, Ben," Doctor McClean said.

Bart gestured with his head towards the white man and said, "That's Doctor Kevin McClean, he's acting producer for us."

"Acting is right," Doctor McClean interjected.

"But," Bart continued, "When not on sabbatical he moonlights as a professor of archaeology at some Podunk school called Berkeley. Doubt you ever heard of it."

"Wow," Gardner said showing he was impressed. "How'd Bart talk you into spending your sabbatical at the redneck capital of the world? Particularly when you have to put up with Bart in the process?"

Doctor McClean laughed. It sounded genuine.

"Doctor McClean came to me," Bart said. "He's got a lot of personal interest in this project. Hoping to get an article or two out of it I assume. You know publish or perish."

"He'd have to have an interest, and a large one," Gardner stated truthfully.

"I've invested more than just interest," Doctor McClean answered ruefully.

"He's also paying for most of it," Bart chimed in.

"What's the interest?" Gardner asked. "That is if you don't mind my asking."

"I've been working on a book," McClean stated, "It's about the origin of the mound building cultures. Mostly I've focused my research on the Cahokia site in Illinois, but that caught a snag. So I'm trying to pick back up here. This film's my proverbial 'foot in the door'."

"Sounds like a long sabbatical," Gardner stated innocently.

"Tenure," Doctor McClean offered as both an explanation and excuse.

"So Doctor, any leads?" Gardner queried, "Any idea why these behemoths were built?"

Doctor McClean casually removed his sunglasses and focused his eyes directly on Gardner before saying, "Not yet. This is the place to look however."

"Any reason besides this is where the mounds are?" asked Gardner.

"Yes," Doctor McClean replied. "This is where the mounds are obviously, but there are many other mounds in the Southeast, the tallest mound, for instance, is located in Florence, Alabama, and there's actually another mound park, smaller than this of course, but still a mound park near Moulton."

"Didn't know that," Gardner said politely, "It's a pity really as I've lived in Alabama my whole life. Shows how insular we can be, I guess."

"I suppose," answered Doctor McClean then went on with what he thought was fascinating history, though Gardner wouldn't have concurred. "Most of those mounds have been explored and whatever was there has been either disturbed or removed. One really can't make valid judgments or theories when the items being theorized about have not been thoroughly documented, in situ, by an expert. But most of these mounds have never been touched; some were examined but only rudimentarily and over a half century ago. Who knows what's out there?"

"What about the digs in the Thirties?" asked Gardner, "I thought they were very large?"

"Well sure," admitted McClean. "But they hardly touched the mounds. Treasure hunters investigated a few mounds and didn't find anything worth the effort; else the mounds wouldn't be intact. The word got around that there was nothing there. For the most part, that was the assumption of the dig leaders in the Thirties. Of course, their classification of treasure and the classification of treasure by a modern scientist are far different."

"That didn't change until Grandpa," Bart interjected.

Gardner shot an evil look at Bart and grimaced. Then he returned his attention to Doctor McClean.

The Doctor continued his speech, ignoring Bart's comment, just as if he had been a lecturer in the saintly halls of Berkeley, speaking down to his subject, as is the way with most professors. "Well, it was inevitable really that man would do some searching here. Man has no limit or control of his curiosity. It's been that way since Adam if you believe such. It's as if man is destined to search for impossible questions. The endless quest for why we are here."

"In other words," Gardner said, "We're all looking for the 'truth'."

"Well, not necessarily," Doctor McClean replied. "Is there really just one 'truth'?"

"Look out, Gardner," Bart warned, "The good doctor is an atheist."

McClean held up his wrist and the copper bracelet he wore glistened in the sun. "Well look at this," he said, motioning with his head to the bracelet, "What faith I have is certainly unconventional. To be quite honest, I don't know what I really do believe. This bracelet? Does it really bring good health or is it mere placebo? Is that any different from the poor soul that makes the sign of the cross at every misfortune? I don't know. What about you Gardner? What do you believe?"

"Uh," Gardner acted as if he was being asked to hold a rattlesnake and pray for divine intervention.

Bart laughed, dispelling the tension. "That question makes us all uncomfortable Doc." Bart grabbed Gardner by the elbow to lead him away and said, "Come on kid, we've got five years to make up."

Doctor McClean said before they pulled away, "By the way Bart, we made the paper," he held up the paper he had been reading to make his point.

Gardner said back over his shoulder as they walked away, "Bart says to frame it."

Bart laughed and added, "You heard him."

The two cousins walked through the beauty of the park. Lush green grass, immaculately manicured, cut twice a week and fertilized, though it wasn't necessary, and watered daily, though that wasn't necessary either. It was a place of beauty and of serenity. The park had a fence that separated the park from the Black Warrior River and had contributed to keeping unruly school children inside the park and out of those dangerous currents. Bart was flipping through the manila folder that Gardner had given him, the one that contained his grandfather's journal.

"Small crew," Gardner said offhandedly.

"Small budget," Bart replied just as off handedly. "We're roughing it. No grants this time. No anything." Bart continued to look into the folder as he talked, then he stopped at the fence and looked out on the mighty river. "The Black Warrior," he said.

Gardner glanced at him and just nodded. They stopped at the fence and looked out at the peaceful river. It wasn't always peaceful but today it was and it rolled mightily to the sea, gently curving this way and that as rivers do. It seemed a bit high to Gardner, probably recent rainfall up stream. It had been the lifeblood of the people that had once lived near this location, here where once resided the largest city in North America. It had provided food and transportation to both them and their enemies. Gardner wondered if they had praised it or cursed it. Probably both. Now it was a place to fish on weekends for the locals, a creek banking destination for the college kids, a place to get drunk and hopefully get lucky for the high school kids. Probably not as lucky as they would have liked, regardless of the outcome- you can never get lucky enough in high school.

"My last year in scouts," Bart said, "We kayaked ten miles on that thing. As trite as it sounds, there's something real spiritual about just being on it, riding with the current or fighting against it, it resonates with the soul, as corny as that sounds. It's primeval."

"You sound like Doctor McClean," Gardner stated.

Bart laughed. "I still remember the blisters too. But I ain't like the Doc noways. He's clinging to a bourgeois fad that died a decade ago. Granted it ain't much worse than the legalistic crap people been buyin' into for centuries. Well there's nothing sincere in that kind of a belief, Gardner old pal. They're just trying to displace some innate fear."

"Or fill an innate need," Gardner suggested.

"Well," Bart agreed to some extent, "They think they need it. Folks always have. Reason most of us are crazy or going crazy, no doubt."

Gardner smiled at that remark, it was pure Bart Thompson logic, then he nodded his head towards the mounds and said, "That's what this dig's about. The people here were very cosmological, they thought their ancestors were the stars, and they were connected to them through the natural world. They thought they could communicate through signs. At least that's one theory."

"Not a bad thought," Bart replied.

"Maybe, but it was dangerous," Gardner continued. "They also thought only the chieftain could read those signs. It's what kept him in power, what kept the system working. Might've been what destroyed them in the end."

"Sounds familiar," Bart agreed. "Most systems work through inertia. When something finally happens that the system didn't expect or can't handle the inertia is finally overcome and crash goes the system, and usually the civilization that was held together by that system." Bart turned his gaze from the Black Warrior and looked at Gardner, "So you like this stuff?" he asked.

"Some parts," Gardner admitted. "Some parts are interesting. It's easier than most things, at least for me. Lot easier than differential equations for instance. Not as boring as English Lit. Course, like everything else it has its good and its bad."

"Never pegged you for a scientist," Bart stated truthfully. "Hell, last time I was home all you talked about was the new Star Wars movie. I figured you for a storyteller like me."

"I could never be like you," Gardner said ruefully. "But truthfully it is storytelling of a sort. That's what I like about it. You just have to prove what you make up- just like you, now that I think about it, except you don't bother to prove anything. Heaven help me, must be my bad karma coming home to roost."

Bart laughed and said, "Long as you ain't boring the rest don't matter in filmmaking, probably in life too. Average Joe couldn't find the truth with both hands and a flashlight."

Gardner laughed this time. "You're probably right," he said to Bart, "But archaeology is more Kels thing anyway. She doesn't see any of it as boring and in fact I find a lot of it so. I guess she got me into it more than any innate interest on my part. Maybe I should say I got nothing better to do and hanging around with Kelsey is better than not hanging around with her."

"I thought maybe it was grandpa," Bart said quietly.

Gardner glanced quizzically at Bart then turned his vision back to the gentle river. He had nothing to say on this particular subject.

"You'd make him proud," Bart continued ignoring the quizzical glance, trying to get Gardner to discuss what was obviously taboo for him. "You'd make him a lot prouder than I do." Bart continued, "I'm the scalawag that left the home place and moved to that heathen infested California. I also work at a questionable profession when I work at all. I think Gramps would have had his issues with me."

"Gramps had issues with a lot of things and a lot of those things were family," Gardner stated. "But you're right about one thing, I suppose. He'd be proud that his loins had sprung forth another archaeologist. Even if that archaeologist didn't exactly agree with his theories." Gardner turned back from the river and stared straight at Bart and asked, "What happened to you anyway? Most people that move away from here lose their accent, it doesn't get worse."

Bart shrugged with his eyebrows and said, "Just cause I'm not living here don't mean that I'm not proud of my heritage. We got our problems like any other part of the country but we got our good points too. Not that anyone outside the region would admit to it of course. They think we are all rednecks that marry our sisters; some find it hard to believe we wear shoes. But people are mostly people wherever you go. Some good, some bad, some smart, some stupid, all are ignorant about some things, even those with fancy degrees and lots of letters behind their names."

Gardner did not reply immediately, he motioned up the hill towards where the replica village sat and started to walk that way. Bart fell in lock step with him. "Let's check that out," Gardner said referring to the village, "Been a long while since I saw it last. Wonder if it's changed much, and wonder if I'll know even if it has changed."

As they walked up the hill, one tall and shaggy wearing a hunter's cap, the other small, but well groomed; had you asked who was the filmmaker most would have guessed wrong. Even more so if they heard them speak. They would have also guessed wrong as to which one was savvier to the ways of the world. Impressions (often wrong) guide our paths, which is very fortunate for those that recognize this flaw in the world, and not so fortunate for the world.

There are steps that lead up to the village and they were set at a time before the workman knew how hard it is on people to ascend rapidly, because the steps were very steep. The area was surrounded by immaculate grass. It looked more like a golf course than a park. Though there wasn't a sign that said stay off the grass, most people did either through courtesy or through habit; the grass did not look as if it had ever been trod upon.

Once at the village they stopped and in unison they looked at this recreation of a lifelong past. There may have been some truth to the village recreation, which was mostly just small replica wood buildings with statues of American Indians doing various and sundry things, such as scaling a fish, and watching a clay cooking pot, but Gardner wasn't advanced enough in his studies of archaeology to know if it was accurate or not. The village was at the highest point in Moundville and you could see all of the other mounds, the gorgeous forest and the lazy Black Warrior River from this summit. You could also see Bart's small crew, hard at work dozing in the afternoon sun. If this was work, Gardner would have hated to see a day off for them.

"You know," Bart said motioning towards the village, "Grandpa did a lot of good for this place. He don't get any credit but most people would have never heard of Moundville except for him."

"Is that what you call it?" asked Gardner with a smile.

"What do you know about it?" Bart queried. "All you know is what you've been told. And that ain't likely to have been a bit of the truth."

Bart walked into the village, opening and closing the gate and ignoring the sign that said, "Do Not Enter Except During Museum Hours." Gardner followed like a toddler after his mother. There were several replica huts, more like log cabins really, as they were made from wood and they were square and oblong shaped, not teepee shaped. Many people, from too many western TV shows and movies, think that all North American Indians lived in teepees and nothing could be further from the truth. People use what's in their environment to make their housing and most of America has plenty of trees. It was only the Plains peoples that used something other than wood.

"How's John the third doing?" Bart asked Gardner.

"Rather me be studying something else, and complains bitterly about paying for my useless education," Gardner replied, "Other than that, fine I guess."

"You know," Bart stated, "You're the last of the lot. Once Lucy gets married you'll be the last of us with the Patton name. And you the runt of the litter."

"Lucy married three years ago," Gardner laughed, "Earth to Bart Thompson read a newspaper every once in awhile."

"Well now," Bart said wistfully, "Looks like you are truly the last of the Pattons."

"Which means?" Gardner wanted to know.

"Nothing I guess," Bart replied, "You know better than me."

"My name isn't John the Fourth," Gardner said forcefully. "I'm my own person. You can't help what your name is, what your ancestors did or didn't do, or where you come from. You can only control where you're going."

"You could change your name," Bart reasoned.

Gardner cut his eyes at him and simply shrugged his shoulders, as if to say, "What's the use."

"You gonna see your mamma?" Gardner enquired. "Seeing as how you've been keeping up so much with the family doings, Lucy being a prime example, you might want to pass on some of the latest gossip. I hear that Aunt Ruth's heifer came down with the pinkeye. You can use that when you talk to her."

"She ain't talked to me since I made *Dogma*," Bart said. "Guess her religion outweighs any family connections."

"So?" asked Gardner.

"So, she can go to hell," Bart said, "I ain't here for that!"

"Then what the hell are you here for, Bart?" Gardner questioned. "Just for this infomercial?"

"It ain't an infomercial," Bart said defensively.

"Then what is it?" pressed Gardner.

"It's a wakeup call to this state," Bart said, prideful.

"You and your revolutions," Gardner said wearily and with a shake of his head.

"Come on kid, you know how important this place is," Bart stated forcefully, "There are answers here that affect everybody; just most of them don't know it, or even care." Bart forced a laugh and continued, "Folks jog here, they picnic here, they come out here on crisp fall afternoons with their portable TV sets and watch the games and drink beer. I mean jogging for Chrissakes! This is supposed to be a monument to a great civilization. It is one of the most sacred places on Earth and it ain't immune to the latest yuppie trends. You know, people rant and rave about racism down here, but they never mention a damn thing about what we owe those that came before us and why we must preserve something for those that will come after us."

"And you're going to call them out on it?" Gardner asked, "And that's the real reason you're here, to put the religion into the people of this state over an issue most could care less about."

"Hell no," Bart said, then he grinned that quick grin that he should patent, "I'm here because I'm broke. And because I was able to convince the good Doctor McClean to pony up the bucks for this expedition. Leastwise that's as good a reason as any. Sides, I was a bit homesick."

"That's less believable than your revolution," Gardner said. "I can see you going all guns and glory for some cause, I can sure see you wanting to make a buck; Lord knows I can believe that, but homesick? Not a bit of it. So what's the real truth?"

"Hell," Bart replied, "You think I'm any better than the average Joe at determining what the truth is? Maybe I'm here because of some quantum process. Maybe I'm here because God needs a laugh and thus inspired me to come. Maybe I'm here cause I'm as crazy as everyone else. Truth is, if there is a truth, because it annoys the hell out of my mother and your Kelsey! There could be worse reasons."

"Could be," Gardner admitted. "Speaking of Kelsey, I left her on her death bed, leastwise to hear her tell it, and I gotta get back. What was the present you had for us?"

"Oh yes," Bart grinned again, "The present." He reached into his back pocket and pulled out a beat up paperback book. He handed it to Gardner and said, "Ta da."

There was a lurid cover showing the mounds and an alien, you know the type- the classic gray, standing astride one. Beneath that was the Rattlesnake Disc in all its glory. The book was titled *Buried in the Mounds*. On the back cover was a photograph of a very familiar man, his grandfather, John Patton Junior, taken when he was in his late fifties or early sixties. Patton was wearing a gray outfit that probably resembled his CCC uniform. He was wearing his eye patch. The smile on his face would have given the Mona Lisa a run for her money.

"This is why I didn't grow up tilling the family farm," Bart stated, "And likely why you didn't either. Thought you might want to read it. Even if you think it's fiction and especially if you think it ruined your life."

"Of course," Gardner said, weighing the book in his hand, treating it with all the respect due a skunk. "Thanks."

"Do I detect disappointment?" Bart asked innocently.

"Not at all," Gardner replied. "I am greatly relieved actually, as I thought it was gonna be a DVD of your last movie."

"Naw," Bart replied, "That's too good for you. Sides the coppers confiscated the footage. Who woulda thunk the police would be movie buffs? Go figure."

Gardner gave Bart a penetrating stare, raising his eyebrows ever so slightly.

"There's a real truth for ya," Bart stated with a shrug of his shoulders, "It's why I'm broke; maybe why I'm here. Truth being as relative as any other word. Leastwise that's my story. While we're talking about truth, I got a piece of advice for you. When you're at the dig and we're filming you might not want to tell anybody we're related. In your class, I mean- business relationships are normally best for those sorts of things, besides that way you won't feel compelled to defend me should someone state some sorry lie about my carcass."

"Needn't worry on that score, regardless of what they know," Gardner grinned as he spoke, "But I'll keep it to myself." Gardner couldn't make heads or tails out of why it mattered but he would comply. Probably just Bart being Bart.

Gardner had enough of old times and paths not taken, so he nodded to Bart and stated succinctly, "Gotta go." He turned away to walk down the steps, returning to his car and hopefully Kelsey. As he hit the first step, Bart called out to him.

"Oh and Gardner," Bart said, "You really ought to read Grandpa's book. He's a hell of a storyteller even if he is lying, which I ain't saying he is. It's really all we have left of his, and it may not be much of a legacy, but it's how he wanted to be remembered. He's family Gardner, crazy or not."

Gardner didn't say anything about that particular pearl of wisdom; he just nodded acknowledging the sentence then continued his way down the steps, wondering if this was really a retreat more than anything else. Bart always had a way with words, even if he was lying half the time he was using them.

At the bottom of the steps, Gardner looked up and gave a quick glance at Bart. Bart was staring intensely at the village, doubtless forming some way to incorporate the village into shot 13, a dramatic, or maybe comedic effect. Gardner could see that Bart was staring at a recreation of an old man being buried by his fellow tribesmen, and yes, these particular Native Americans buried their dead and did not put them on long poles to be stripped by the birds and by the weather. Maybe there was some irony there, after all they were digging and hoping not to find the bones of those people that the recreation was showing. Maybe just another quantum fluctuation to use one of Bart's favorite phrases. Like Bart said, truth is hard to discern, even, or maybe especially when you find it.

A GENESIS FOUND

Just cause you talk stupid don't mean you are, but enough people confuse the two to give you a distinct advantage.

The Wisdom of Bart Thompson

There are better roads than the ones leading from Moundville to Tuscaloosa, and for sure there are less hectic roads. While the traffic might be a walk in the park for your average big city dweller it was definitely not for Gardner Patton. It was slow going, two lane most of the way, and this being harvest there were always various and sundry big tractors, combines and the like, making twenty five miles per on this majestic highway. A hassle it was, but it gave one time to think. There were some advantages, however small, to living in a state too cheap to build four lane highways.

As was often the case, when one is driving a familiar road, you can at least free part of your mind from the task of driving. It's almost a luxury in these days of instant access to information via the super highway and PDAs that allow you to schedule your day down to the last instant. Too often you have the facts to consider but not the time to think on the meaning of the facts, so Gardner was using this drive time to alternately curse the road and to ponder what he had learned this day, if he had in fact learned anything.

Gardner was reminded of a tale from his youth; he had been on a little league baseball team, possibly the worst little league team that had ever come together in a losing effort. They had no pitching, no hitting, and they looked like Methuselah on the base paths. They were always caught by the mercy rule, for those of you not conversant with that rule, it states that if a team is down by ten or more runs after a certain inning, the fourth as he recalled it,

38

the game would be called and there was no need to play the remaining innings. Their coach had been a likeable fellow who knew as much about baseball as the average Russian. He didn't give credence to the old saw that practice makes perfect; he preferred no practice and time to watch TV. Had there been a mediocrity hall of fame for little league coaches he would doubtless be a contender for induction.

After every walloping the coach would draw all the players together and have them sit still for a moment, which in itself was no mean feat considering the players he had. Without fail he would say, "I want you boys to go home and think on this loss." Gardner had done a lot of thinking that summer.

Now Gardner was doing a different kind of thinking. What, if anything, was Bart's game? Maybe Bart really was trying to revive some interest in the ancient ways of folks long shuffled from this mortal coil. Gardner doubted it, knowing Bart as well as he did. Any revolution that Bart may want to start would more than likely be focused on himself and would entail some flow of greenbacks from someone to him.

Still, people do change, or at least Gardner had heard it said so. Maybe Bart did believe that crud he was shoveling. His actions seemed to say he did. After all, it hardly seemed likely that a documentary on the dig at Moundville was going to pack them into the local movie house. Maybe it was a simple truth- maybe Bart had simply caught a sucker in the good Doctor McClean and he was using that to make a film. Any kind of a film. Bart was the type that was driven to do what he had to in order to do what he wanted. Maybe storytelling was all this was about. That and a few bucks from a guy that was book smart but people stupid.

Bart was a hypocrite in a lot of ways, but Gardner had known of his obsession to make movies for too long to doubt that there was enough reason in just that to bring Bart to Moundville. But a documentary? That was hardly going to have the kids standing in line at the local movieplex. Not even the Tuscaloosa movieplex. Besides, *Dogma* was some sort of documentary; at least Gardner thought it was, having never seen it, he wasn't exactly an authority on the subject. That had hardly made Bart into a household name. Still, bad work was better than no work, Gardner supposed, and even if you had to come to a Podunk town in Alabama to practice your trade, if you were a true artist you probably would. A true artist is just another name for crazy.

Gardner pulled into Tuscaloosa and hit, if possible, even heavier traffic. The largest city Gardner had ever driven in was Birmingham, and it was no fun, but still, he doubted there was a city anywhere in the U.S. that was harder to get around in than Tuscaloosa. It was a town made for maybe 50,000 people, that was its tax base, but during the school year there was another 35,000 students resident there. Mostly poor residents that didn't pay taxes, especially not city wage taxes, so a lot of the roads that should have been built weren't. Students are young as a rule and the young are poor drivers to start with and become progressively more so as they consume beer and what not. The result of all these factors was more wrecks, more congestion, and a lot more cursing. Finally, maybe through divine intervention, Gardner arrived at the parking lot for his and Kelsey's apartment (but shh, don't tell anyone, this is the South).

It was just another crappily built place for kids to stay while they drank beer, chased the opposite sex, and on occasion studied. Three stories of concrete and shag carpet, ants and cockroaches, and plenty of the other kind of roaches as well. Just another crappy apartment complex in a city filled with them, but it was home sweet home for Gardner, because it was familiar and more so because Kelsey was there. It was of great comfort to Gardner to come on most nights and discuss the trials and tribulations of the day. Tonight might be different however. Kelsey was definitely out of sorts.

A GENESIS FOUND

Twelve steps up, then twelve more steps up. You don't need a rowing machine or a treadmill when you live in a place like this; you get plenty of exercise climbing the stairs and walking hither and yon about the campus. No one, but no one, got to park close to anything resembling a lecture hall, either by chance or by design, if you wanted to make your classes on time, you walked, rain or shine, or even the occasional snow flake (Gardner had seen exactly two snowfalls of an inch or less in all his days in and around Tuscaloosa) you walked. There was something karmic there, Gardner was certain but it was too deep for him to figure it out.

There were all kinds of smoke odors that wafted out of the various apartments he passed as he made his way to his own sanctuary. Cigarettes of course and weed being predominate, but there was also pipe smoke and cigar smoke and maybe even some incense. To be honest, his olfactory sense was about overcome by now so it was hard to sort any odor from another. The only one he wanted to smell was the fruit flavor emanating from Kelsey's fresh washed hair. Just his luck that she wouldn't want to wash her hair tonight.

Gardner finally arrived at the faded blue door with an even more faded Roll Tide sticker on it. It seemed that the paint and the sticker had been put on the door about the same time. From the shape of both of them, it could have been in the 70s. They were testament to the faded glory of this apartment house and the faded glory of the football team. Not that it mattered how it looked, it fit Gardner's budget and even if he disliked it he would not have told anyone. What did it matter where you lived? It's how you lived that mattered, but Gardner knew that some students bragged about living in fancy apartment houses, or fancy fraternities. People could find the damndest things to be prideful over.

A GENESIS FOUND

The key had to fit into the lock just so or else you were left standing there pounding on the door and asking whoever was home to let you inside. Too high and the key wouldn't turn, too low and it would just keep turning and not engage the lock. Calls to the Super had yielded a big goose egg (Surprise!). Gardner had gone so far as to threaten to go buy a new lock and to take it off the rent, but he had never had the guts to do it and likely never would. Neither had any of the other tenants that had lived in this humble abode before him. He had learned how to turn the key just right instead, and now he always could get it to work. In the grand scheme of things a recalcitrant lock wasn't so bad. It even had the added benefit of ensuring no one could pick his lock. Course, what they would probably do is just break a window anyway.

The lock gave way, the door swung open and Gardner, as he always did, bellowed, "Kelsey, I'm home." He had hoped she was up and about and in her underwear, but she wasn't any of those things. Damn, Gardner thought, she must really be sick and in bed. That being the case she was unlikely to want to talk and even worse, unlikely to want to show him her underwear.

Gardner tossed the book that Bart had given him lightly onto the coffee table. The book landed backside up, showing the haggard, but still smiling, face of his grandfather. A black eye patch covered the right eye, the left was sparkling like a diamond in the snow and gazing intently at the camera, as if saying, "believe it or not it's true." Gardner was sure he had heard the story of how his grandfather had lost that eye but he couldn't bring it to mind. Maybe it was just an affectation, an old man thinking it gave him the mysterious look needed to sell an extra 100,000 copies of the book. Could be a con, Gardner barely remembered his grandfather and it was a touchy thing at best to discuss with his own father. There had been stranger tales told of his grandfather than just that he wore a fake eye patch, Gardner himself had told quite a few, particularly when the third beer kicked in.

Gardner walked into the not so spacious bathroom. It reeked of Pine Sol; mostly because Kelsey used at least a bottle a week fighting mold and mildew smells. The mold hadn't gone away but it at least didn't smell. Small victories are sometimes the most satisfying. Gardner turned the shower on to full blast which was just a shade above a dribble and put it on as hot as it would go which was still only warm at best. It did at least wash away the grime he had collected at Moundville, even if it did so grudgingly.

Grabbing a towel, Gardner began to wipe off the water and whatever grime was left. He went to the medicine cabinet, opened the mirror on front of it, catching a glimpse of a very tired man-boy in the process, and then removed his contacts. The contacts came out easily, as he had years of experience in their removal. Putting on his shorts and undershirt and grabbing his glasses from the bathroom counter where Kelsey always placed them after he left them lying around someplace, he proceeded to the bedroom to check on Kelsey, passing at least two more sets of eyeglasses that Kelsey left in strategic places about the apartment so he wouldn't scream "Where the hell are my glasses?"

Kelsey was quite asleep, her breathing as regular as a metronome. Gardner thought her a bit pale, but then she was quite possibly the whitest person in Tuscaloosa so it wasn't obvious. Her body was draped lengthwise across the bed, which meant that any effort on his part to enter same would disturb and likely wake her. Gardner reached out his hand and gently caressed her hair, ever so softy. Moonlight weighed more than his touch. Smiling he quietly walked away from her and out the door. Even more quietly he closed the door. It made less sound than a gnat's wing. The couch called and for once it wasn't because he had been kicked out of the bedroom.

A GENESIS FOUND

Gardner grabbed a couple of sheets from what served as a linen closet, it also served as a place to pile lots of junk that wouldn't fit elsewhere, so it was no mean feat to get the sheets and not create a noise. But love does give one perspective and Gardner would have rather slept undraped than to do something that would awaken Kelsey. Gardner lay one sheet on the couch, as much as to protect his body as to protect the couch, it was Naugahyde, which was a fancy word for plastic masquerading as leather. Without a protective cover, his body would sweat all night long, particularly since the air conditioning was none to effective in this apartment. As far as Gardner could ascertain, every apartment in the complex had a sofa like this one. Somebody had doubtless been in league with the Devil when they decided to purchase sofas for this complex.

With a stretch and a yawn and a scratch on his head, Gardner lay down. He was tired but not really sleepy. He grabbed the all in one remote and turned on the TV and the DVD at the same time. An old TV special narrated by Orson Welles called "Who's Out There?" came on. Gardner had spent a lot of time perusing Ebay before he found this little gem. Hamlet it wasn't but it was something that piqued his interest. He often wondered if Orson had just been hard up for money to have lent his name and his magnificent voice to this project

Welles stentorian voice boomed out, even though Gardner had the sound really low so that Kelsey wouldn't be disturbed. "Before the cylinder fell," said Welles, "There was a general persuasion that no life existed beyond our own minute sphere."

"Seen it and remember it," Gardner stated wearily to no one in particular. The remote proved its usefulness again and the TV went silent. Grudgingly, Gardner reached for the book on the table. He had never really wanted to read it, but maybe Kelsey was right- maybe he should out of respect for his grandfather if for no other reason. Besides, Bart seemed to think there was something

44

of importance there. Besides again, how many people have a grandfather that wrote a best seller? And sleep was nowhere on the horizon anyway.

The garish cover, still garish even though time had worked on the colors a good bit, proudly stated, "Over one million copies sold." Not a first edition then, Gardner thought wryly. The second headline on the cover proudly proclaimed, "The amazing truth behind the mysterious origin of America's first metropolis." Gardner flipped the book over and checked out the back cover again, this time he noticed more than just the photo of his granddad.

There was no getting around the photo, especially for Gardner. It showed an old man, with one eye patch, with an enigmatic, brilliant smile. At the top of the back cover, another headline only slightly smaller than the one on the cover, and likely due to having to compete with the photo for space, boldly informed the potential reader that this book was "Unlocking the secrets of Moundville, it will unlock some of your own. Read and Believe."

Could have been worse, Gardner supposed, it could have had flying saucers and not just an alien on the cover. It could have showed Sasquatch or Nessie, or even the Easter Bunny. Considering what it could have been, it was almost sedate. He opened the cover of the book and noticed the copyright date of 1973. Also, all rights reserved by John Patton Jr. Gardner wished idly, that old man had used a pseudonym.

Gardner opened the book, not really knowing what to expect, and started reading. The first line read, "Every summer is hot in Moundville, Alabama, and it was particularly so in June of 1938...."

Gardner was lost in another world.

A GENESIS FOUND

Some people believe in science, some in religion and some will believe anything at all. Thus do physicists, preachers and charlatans earn their keep.

The Wisdom of Bart Thompson

The journal of John Patton Junior was being read voraciously by Bart Thompson. It was filled with drawings and comments and scientific observations, that would have done a senior scientist proud and it was much more impressive when one remembers that Patton was barely twenty at the time he compiled it. Bart was particularly searching for one particular entry that was necessary for his designs. At last he found it, about two-thirds of the way through the journal, the page had the following phrase prominently displayed at the top "A Genesis Found." Bart's fingers skimmed the page like a rock skips across the water when thrown just right.

Bart nodded and said in a quiet voice, "Bout damn time."

McClean was looking over Bart's shoulder, scanning the page as Bart read. The other two crewmembers were waiting for some signal from Bart to vacate the trailer and do whatever needed to be done. "All right," Bart said and gave a meaningful glance to the good Doctor. McClean immediately turned on his heel and, opening the door, walked out into the muggy night. Like a shot Bart leapt from his chair and caught up with the Doctor in a heartbeat. The other two, not as eager perhaps, but still willing, stood and followed their erstwhile leader and financier.

They all gathered under the canopy they had erected to keep the sun off the trailer and make it a tad livable, anyway. Bart reached and grabbed his camera, he was smiling as usual, but none of the others were, they were just waiting, much as one waits for a bus, or a taxi, waiting for something, or in this case, someone to take them where they needed to go. McClean had a clipboard, Levi had a knapsack, Ben just had himself. As Bart walked, they all followed in lock step; no words were necessary. They rarely were between these men.

"All right," Bart said loudly as if bucking himself up as well as his cohorts, "Let's do this thing."

The quartet walked off into the pitch black with the sounds of frogs and crickets accompanying their every step. Bart was leading, maybe by accident, maybe on purpose, as they all knew where they were going. They turned on their flashlights as they got further away from the light of the trailer. Anyone waiting at the trailer would have seen the light from the flashes grow dimmer and dimmer until the darkness finally swallowed them. The forest, if it had an opinion about this, was silent except for the usual insects, amphibians, and birds. Thus this tale truly begins.

Talk loudly then get the hell out of town.

The Wisdom of Bart Thompson

Years before the eye patch and the need for eyeglasses, John Patton Junior was sitting in a 1938 Ford truck awaiting Doctor Jones. The night was crystal clear and you could almost reach out and touch the stars. In 1938, particularly in rural Alabama, there was no pollution, either by automobiles or by stray light sources. It was a beautiful night, quiet, warm, nice, just the kind of night that made life worth living even when you had worked all day and were particularly tired. Maybe even because you had worked all day and were particularly tired. There was something to the phrase that a hard working man rests best.

Patton gazed at the brilliant canopy of stars. He knew little of astronomy, but a night like this made him hunger for knowledge along those lines. Why were some stars red, others yellow, others pure white? Just how far away are they? Did they too have some planet where another young man or whatever the equivalent for man was on that planet, was staring at the sky and wondering why, and where and how? Patton didn't know it, but fifty years on a similar viewer of the stars would have fewer than half of the stars visible. But then again, half of infinity is still infinity.

Doctor Walter Jones came up from the mounds, whistling, carrying a shovel in his hands. The ever-present fedora lay upon his head and it was sweaty from this day's doing. The hat was neither the most pleasant thing to wear or to smell, but Doctor Jones would rather go shoeless than not wear it. Regardless of what shape it was in today, it would be right back on his head the next day, unwashed, but ready to see the next day through. Jones looked remarkably fresh for a man that had just worked in the dirt and grit and one hundred degree temperature for twelve hours, but then again, he loved it, so it wasn't so much work for him as one might expect.

"Got that last piece?" Jones asked Patton.

"Yes sir," Patton answered, polite as always to his elders.

"Thanks for the help," Jones said, meaning it. He heaved the shovel into the bed of the truck and continued saying, "Not many of the boys would have stuck around after their shift to help an old geezer, not with cards and a hot shower awaiting them."

"Cards anyway," Patton replied amiably, "You stay in a barracks like I do and you soon realize not everyone wants a shower after getting sweaty and dirty for twelve hours. Probably against their religion."

Jones answered with a smile, then opened the driver's side door and said before he got in, "You coming?"

"I'd rather ride in the back," Patton replied, "If you don't mind. The wind helps cool you."

Jones didn't respond but instead closed the door unentered and walked around to where Patton stood. Jones gestured with his finger to the sky and stated, "Up there, see it? That's Orion."

"Excuse me?" Patton responded and questioned at the same time.

"The constellation," Jones answered, "Orion the Hunter. See its belt?"

"Well, wha..." Patton struggled for words.

"It's right above us," Jones continued, "It's the easiest constellation to spot, I swear. See those three stars running diagonally there?" Again his finger pointed to the sky.

Patton tried to follow the finger, thought maybe he had and said "Uh-huh," although he wouldn't have wagered a thin dime that he did in fact see those three stars.

"Well, that's the belt," Jones remarked. "The rest of the body sprouts out from it. See it now?" Jones' voice was soft but insistent as if he was trying to convey something of importance.

"I reckon I do," Patton replied, and he was actually surer of his response. He did see three stars running in a diagonal and they seemed to be close to where Jones' finger was pointing. "I ain't too good at stargazing," Patton admitted and wanted to say what's the big deal but instead said, "That's the Hunter, huh. Why's that?"

"Yes," Jones responded, "The Hunter. The ancient Greeks named it, they thought they saw a hunter with a belt, though I'm damned if I see it. Still the name has stuck. Greeks saw lots of things in the sky. Maybe they took in more lotus leaves than history gives them credit for."

Patton smiled at that and said, "The Hunter, that's like us."

It was Jones' turn to smile. Patton might be little educated and what one might consider a country bumpkin because of that but he was plenty smart. "Just like us," Jones agreed. "How many of those artifacts with the eye in the palm have you seen?"

"Dozens," Patton replied, "Maybe hundreds."

"I think that's it," Jones said.

"What's it, Sir?" Patton asked.

"Orion," Jones replied. "I think that symbol is an interpretation of Orion. I believe that Orion was the final gate to the afterlife for the people that came to this site."

Patton was unsure just what Doctor Jones meant. Instead of saying so he just kept quiet, figuring the Doc would tell him. Doctor Jones was that kind of guy.

"Their souls," Doctor Jones broke the silence, "They pass through the eye to enter the afterlife. In their mythology, they would become one with the universe. It was their equivalent of heaven or nirvana."

Jones held out his arm, the palm stretched outward and motioned for Patton to look. Patton saw it fit neatly and precisely over the constellation. Jones then pointed upward and then to Patton saying, "They would pass through here," Jones indicating the precise middle of his palm, the location where the eye was located in the Rattlesnake Disc. "See it?"

Patton nodded, enthralled by the conversation.

Jones took two fingers on his left hand and slowly moved them to his eyeballs, almost but not quite touching them. "The eyes are the key," he said, "To their culture. To our understanding of it."

"So that's what it means?" Patton asked hesitantly.

"You think it means something else?" Doctor Jones matched Patton's question.

Patton shrugged his shoulders and reaffixed his gaze on Orion.

"Do you enjoy this John?" Doctor Jones asked looking intently at Patton.

"Stargazing?" Patton matched question for question as if it was payback.

"No," Jones answered finally ending the endless question loop, "archaeology."

"I reckon," Patton replied keeping his gaze on the starry sky. "I like it pretty good I guess. Beats farming and that's a fact."

"Have you thought about pursuing it after you're through here?" asked Jones.

"Well sir," Patton answered, "I can't afford to go to school. The only reason I was able to take your class is the Government is paying for it. I'd love to get an education, but I like to eat too, and I don't rightly see how I can do both."

"You don't have to go to school you know," Jones stated, his eyes flashing back up to Orion. "You just have to know the right people."

Patton didn't see the logic in that. What are a redneck's possibilities of knowing the right people? Everyone he knew put together and pulling at the same time couldn't have got him a job as dogcatcher much less as an Archeologist. Where he came from, education was for boys too sick to work the fields, the people he knew thought that PhD stood for Post Hole Diggers. But he didn't say any of this to Doctor Jones, after all the man was trying to be nice to him. But Patton had quit believing in the Easter Bunny a long time ago, and what Jones had said made even less sense than that. Maybe Doctor Jones was "the people?" Could be; still, Patton didn't believe he could be that lucky.

"Well enough talk for one night," Doctor Jones said and grasped Patton's shoulder. "You ready to go?"

Patton nodded but then said, "I changed my mind about the ride Doc. Think I'll walk back. Pretty night like this makes me want to enjoy it a mite more."

"Then, good night John," Jones said and put his fingers to his fedora, grasped the brim, and tugged ever so slightly, the standard way one guy said goodbye to another, back in the time when most wore hats. Jones walked around the truck and got in, cranked it and pulled away into the night. Patton watched the tail lights until they disappeared, swallowed by the velvet darkness that lay like a rug over the countryside. Finally Patton was alone, discounting the mosquitoes that seemed more than happy to keep him company. It seemed he spent much of his life alone and when not alone he was being pestered by something.

Unless you are a native to the country or else a city dweller that likes to hunt, you really don't know just how dark night can be. When there is no moon, and no lights, either car or home, it is really dark and sometimes that's the best time to see things, particularly in your mind. Patton, being a country boy, knew where the North Star was and from that he knew the direction to the barracks, so he began his journey, thinking on life and the future and on what Doctor Jones had planted in his mind.

Passing mounds and crickets and frogs and paying no mind to any of them, Patton strode purposefully back to the barracks. Maybe the Doctor was right, maybe there is hope for someone like him, someone that didn't speak the way an educated person speaks, or think the way an educated person thinks. After all, being smart and talking smart aren't the same thing, but most folks confused the two.

Patton cast off his mood. It was late, time to pack it in, sleep if possible. There would be time enough for thinking tomorrow, or maybe it was really praying.

The walk back to the barracks was accompanied by the pliant cry of a lonesome whippoorwill, calling to its mate, or just telling the world to go to hell, Patton was unsure which. Its screech could be heard for a mile, or at least that was common country logic. Other sounds competed with the bird's. Another bird, a hoot owl, found its voice, and let everyone know it too was alive and well in the forest primeval. A fish slapped on the Black Warrior, the crickets and the frogs, all forming a grand symphony, all making the sounds nature had provided them for nature's own purpose.

A GENESIS FOUND

To one not raised in the country it might have been spooky, but to Patton it was comforting, it was normal, and only on special nights like this did it even enter his conscious.

Patton topped the final ridge and finally saw the lights from the barracks. It was a beacon as it represented a quick meal and a good night's and well earned sleep. It was funny, but now that there was light he stumbled a couple of times; before he couldn't see the rocks but he somehow avoided them in pitch blackness, now there was light and he stumbled. There was probably a life parable there but Patton was too tired to think on it and he was too tired to curse the rocks when they twisted, which meant he was tired indeed.

Patton entered the barracks and hardly any of the boy-men gave him a glance, they were busy doing what the young do. A group was playing poker; another group was boasting of past exploits, real or imagined, with baseball and women being the subjects that gathered the most listeners. Young men who would have told you they had no future except for hard work and hard times. None knew that they would be fighting a war with countries most had never even heard of in a few years. None knew that they would be a part of building one of the greatest nations ever to exist in the annals of history. Even had they known, it would have likely not mattered; not much matters to you before you turn twenty-one.

With a wince, Patton weaved his way through the crowd, finally made it to his bed and plopped down, still fully clothed. He began to undress from his laying position, found it couldn't be done very effectively, then silently cursed as he sat up and removed his shirt, then stood and removed his pants. Modesty had been lost the first week he stayed in the barracks, and none gave a hoot what anyone else looked like in their underwear anyway, unless that person was a female.

A GENESIS FOUND

As he did every night, Patton pulled out his journal and began the day's entries. Some people passed the time playing, others, like Patton, working. It would matter over the course of a lifetime though it wasn't why Patton did it. He wrote in his journal because he wanted to capture that day, he wanted to be able to go back as an old man and remember what, if anything, he had accomplished. Patton opened his journal to the page that had his rendition of the Rattlesnake Disc. He carefully studied it making sure it matched what his mind's eye had seen. Maybe Doc was right, maybe the key to this civilization was the eye in the hand. Then maybe not, maybe it was just a neat drawing, the art deco of its day. These people were human, after all. What makes anyone think they were rational?

Suddenly Patton heard a voice say, "That's what Patton said." Instinctively he swung his head to determine who was talking about him and what they were saying. Might have known, it was Shaw holding court as usual. This night his entourage was less than most nights; only one tall, young, gaunt, pimply-faced individual that Patton hardly knew, but thought his name was Dobbs. Shaw saw Patton turn towards him and immediately lowered his voice. What he was telling the youth was either too hot or too secret for the ears of John Patton Junior. But Shaw kept on talking, and every now and then both he and Dobbs would cast a glance at Patton for some reason that was known only to themselves.

Everybody's least favorite fellow, the guy whose name was at the top of everyone's list as being the one they would want most to catch in a dark alley sometimes, in other words the commander's pet, came striding through the barracks, strutting as he always did, and shouted, "Come on guys, lights out," then more stridently, "We all gotta crawl out of here at six a.m."

As usual the cadets just ignored him. "Come on," he almost whined, "We gotta get to bed before the commander pulls a bed

54

check. You guys want to get grounded? Come on you poker players, if you're winning, thank God, if you're losing, tough. You can get it back tomorrow." There was a general grumbling but no movement and the lights stayed on. No one seemed to care if the Commander did a bed check. There wasn't a whole lot of difference in being grounded and having the privilege of seeing beautiful downtown Moundville on a Saturday pass.

Patton ignored the commander's pet and turned his attention on Tim Shaw saying to him, "What did you say Shaw?"

"What did I say about what?" Shaw asked innocently. Shaw was sharpening his knife on a whetstone; finishing, he handed the stone to Dobbs. Patton kept a fixed gaze on Shaw and said, "What did you tell Dobbs?" Patton motioned with his head to the gangly youth that was taking his turn sharpening his knife with Shaw's whetstone.

Shaw ignored Patton and carefully removed his shoes; he placed them very carefully at the top of the bed, in the space between the rail and the wall. He did the same thing every night, just like most guys brushed their teeth. Patton never understood why; most guys, himself included, just tossed them on the floor, but Shaw took better care of his shoes than most mothers did of their young.

"Why you care what I tole Dobbs?" Shaw asked when he had finished his nightly routine.

"I heard my name," Patton replied.

Shaw shrugged his shoulders as if that meant nothing to him. With one easy motion, developed from long practice, Shaw reached into his mouth, pulled out the gum that seemed to always be there and stuck it on the rail of his bed. The task was accomplished with ease.

"You said I said something," Patton insisted.

Shaw lay back in his bed and stretched. The cover was beneath him but he didn't care, it was too hot to sleep under a cover and it didn't itch him like it did others. "I was just sharpening my knife," Shaw replied defensively.

Shaw rolled to his side away from Patton. Like all conversations with Shaw, Patton could find no meaning in it and maybe that was the meaning itself. Patton frowned and lay down his journal. The lights went out suddenly leaving the commander's pet still in the middle of the barracks advising that the lights should be put out. Everyone but him found that funny.

Patton tried to sleep, but it didn't come easy.

Everybody's born ignorant. Most are happy to stay that way.

The Wisdom of Bart Thompson

Patton awoke with a start. Something was amiss in the night. The fog in his brain lifted slowly, like the morning dew reluctantly giving up to the sunrise. What was it? Finally his eyes focused and more importantly his brain focused, he didn't hear the steady breathing of Shaw. Glancing to Shaw's bed he confirmed it was empty.

"Damn," Patton said and meant it. If they catch Shaw in one more shenanigan his butt would be on the first bus back to Mississippi. Not that Patton cared a lot about what happened to Shaw, but Shaw's mama was a different matter altogether. She shouldn't be the one to be punished and God knows she would be. Not only would she lose thirty bucks a month, she would have Shaw back!

Fishing under his bunk in the dark, Patton finally found his flashlight. With more caution than a lamb sneaking by a sleeping wolf, Patton grabbed his clothes and shoes and made for the door. Just let some weasel see him and he would be on report (which he didn't mind) and out on his ear (which he did mind) so he was as silent as a whisper in a tornado.

Patton walked several feet out into the darkness before he stopped and put on his clothes. Then he went another twenty feet before turning on his flashlight, making sure it pointed away from the barracks. Still in tiptoe mode he made his way into the woods in search of a guy who really didn't deserve his consideration.

Sweeping his flashlight in front of him, Patton quietly called Shaw a lot of names you didn't hear in church. He even invented a few names that he was rather proud of. About thirty feet into the woods, Patton came upon a comic gum wrapper. Joe Blow was always a friend to Shaw so he had at least come this way. Patton looked in a straight line from the wrapper. There was a clearing ahead and of course that would be where Shaw was. With a disgusted "Umph," Patton headed that way. What was Shaw up to now?

Just before making the clearing, Patton heard a rustle in the trees next to him. There are very few things big enough to make a rustle in the forest and fewer still you want to meet on a dark night. Patton hoped it was Shaw.

A hand reached out and grabbed Patton from the trees. Patton didn't jump out of his skin but that was only because it wasn't physically possible to do so. Patton jumped and turned his flashlight towards the hand at the same time. A grinning Shaw was outlined by the light. Playing games as usual.

"Patton?" Shaw asked, with the ever-present grin on his face.

"Tim," Patton responded, "What the hell you doing out here?"

"Lookin' at the stars," Shaw said innocently.

Patton's stare would have taken the frost off a pumpkin.

"What the hell you think I'm doing out here?" Shaw said with a knowing look.

"We got a latrine for that," Patton countered.

"Yeah, well, Yarborough forgot to flush the valves again. I don't know why. Reckon somebody got sick in there. Why you care? You miss me so much?" Shaw asked.

"Listen Shaw," Patton said with a rush of breath, "I could care less about you, but I don't feel the same about your mama. I reckon she has enough trouble feeding the mouths left at home without adding you to the list."

"Well," Shaw said much louder than Patton would have preferred, "Patton the Preacher. Who'da thunk it."

"Look Tim," Patton said in a very quiet voice, "That story I told you about the treasure...."

Shaw's booming laugh interrupted Patton, "That's what you thought?" Shaw said through the laughter.

Patton felt Shaw's grin as much as he saw it. "Come on Patton," Shaw said still laughing, "Just cause I can barely read don't mean I'd believe someone like you. Hell, you're an inbred Central Alabama sharecropper, which makes you the least trustworthy person on this planet. You ain't said a word of truth since you popped out of your mama's womb."

"Beats bein' a low down Mississippi skunk by a long shot, I reckon," Patton answered.

Shaw laughed again, too loudly, as if it were forced, but if so, Shaw was a passable actor. Without another word, and more surprisingly, without another insult he turned away from Patton and walked towards the mounds. Patton almost said to hell with it and let him go, but reluctantly he too headed for the mounds whispering, "Damn redneck."

Shaw stopped suddenly at the base of a mound and Patton almost bumped into him in the dark. Shaw shot a look at Patton and jerked his head towards the mound saying "Now tell me that ain't creepy." Shaw said it as a statement of fact and not a question.

"Just don't go diggin' where you ain't supposed to," advised Patton. With that he had finally had his fill of Shaw. Shaw's mama was on her own now. Patton turned abruptly and walked towards the barracks.

With a flourish, Shaw grabbed some gum from behind his ear and popped it into his mouth. Patton was no longer visible and Shaw liked that. He returned his attention to the mound. "Damn creepy," he said softly, and then he walked up the mound. Once he got to the top, he stopped and stretched out his arms, embracing the night and the mood he was in. The night enveloped him, hiding him from all those that would stop him from doing what he wanted. "You're here," he said squatting down and patting the mound, "If not in this one, in another. I'll find you yet. And while Patton's a cross bred idiot, if he knows something, then by God I'll know it too!"

As the night drifted by, Shaw dreamed his dreams. But eventually dreams end and the world takes hold and so it was with Shaw. Laughing softly he came down from the mound and headed back to the barracks on tiptoe. He was too close to riches to be kicked out of here now, so he was very careful climbing back into his bed once he made the barracks. But he did sleep well, with visions of pieces of eight bouncing before his eyes.

Everything in life is a trade off and most of us trade for the worse.

The Wisdom of Bart Thompson

Go get an atlas. Go on. There is, if the atlas is worth a damn, a map of the goodly state of Alabama. Alabama is surrounded by Tennessee at the top, Florida at the bottom (and the Gulf of Mexico), Georgia to the east and Mississippi to the west. For many years the car tags in Alabama proclaimed it to be the "Heart of Dixie" which it surely was as it once contained the capital of the Confederacy in Montgomery. Sometime, somehow the word Dixie became a pejorative so now the tags said the "Stars Fell on Alabama" which is from an old song that no one remembers unless they are eighty years old, which few are, so most haven't a clue why the tags should say that. If you're really interested you can find it on the Internet and hear it. It's quite a lovely song.

Alabama though always changing, as every place changes, still is a creature of Dixie for many of its residents and they don't particularly care if the word is politically incorrect. Learned men have studied what exactly causes a region to develop from a larger culture. Why do people raised in the same country but hundreds of miles apart sound funny to each other when they talk? Why do Southerners sound funniest of all? What causes people to feel only they and their kind have the answers to everything? Why do people automatically think you are brighter or dumber just from whatever accent you happen to talk with? No one knows but it is a fact. Ask any Southerner that has watched TV. The dumb ones and the bad ones always speak with a fake drawl. And while there are both dumb ones and bad ones in the South, not all of them drop their G's.

All men are creatures of their region. Sometimes they can change, but not always and maybe not even often. Most don't want to and that's a fact. The average New Yorker or the average Californian can think that they are the epitome of this nation, and most probably do, but give me a farm boy if I want to chase cattle or a city boy if I want to find a subway. Neither is superior, they have just learned different things that they needed to survive. But there is probably no more fiercely proud man in this nation than a redneck, often proud of things that would shame others, but it is their way and they wouldn't have it any other way.

A GENESIS FOUND

Gardner didn't consider himself a redneck, nor a Southerner in particular. Generations are different and the culture wars of years gone by had changed the South probably more than any other region of the country. The days of Jim Crow were long gone, and Gardner was no more and no less prejudiced against another race than any other man in this country. He didn't really even think about it and never having left the South he didn't know that others did a lot; nor would he have cared.

But one can never get away from his culture entirely, and even though he didn't consider himself a redneck, it is doubtless that others would the moment he spoke. Why? It just was. Gardner often thought that one should do a book on rednecks and see what they are called in other parts of the country and of the world. Without doubt England, Ethiopia and China had their rednecks, as did New York and Los Angeles—they just didn't speak with a Southern drawl, but they still lived for car racing and beer drinking and they liked to hunt.

Gardner's eyes flickered open with that last thought. He smiled ruefully as he stretched his arms and got off the couch. "I ought to go into philosophy," he said to himself, "I'm forever arguing with myself and losing."

With his faculties awakening, the first thing Gardner noticed was that his grandfather's book was still spread-eagle, face down on his chest, doing wonders for its forty-year-old spine. The back cover drew his attention, with the old one-eyed man smiling. "Damn," Gardner thought, "I really do look like him. More's the pity."

Fully awake, Gardner put the book back on the kitchen table and swung off the couch. On his way to the bathroom, the photo he and Kelsey had sat for caught his attention. The photo was professionally done, no glare paper, showing two young and not unattractive young people that were either in love or good enough actors to fake the expression. Gardner remembered all the nagging it had taken to get him to finally find time for the shot. It had been worth it, though he would never admit it finding it a useful thing to have in his back pocket during heated arguments over his support or lack thereof, in this relationship, (didn't I take the time to have that crummy photo taken, well didn't I? I do too care about you and about us). It had proved a useful lie in the past and Gardner wasn't one to let go of any advantage in his relationship with Kelsey, because he truly had few.

Gardner picked up the picture and put it in his book to mark his place. With a grin he eagerly sprang towards the bedroom door where Kelsey lay. Time to see if Kelsey was well enough to make the morning worthwhile.

Entering the bedroom, Gardner immediately saw the bed was empty and was much rumpled. Since it wasn't made, he doubted that Kelsey was either really up or that she really felt much better. He knew her too well to think otherwise. He heard retching sounds from the bathroom. Gardner was both concerned and annoyed. He was even annoyed with himself for being annoyed. Kelsey couldn't help it. Still he was annoyed.

Rapping his knuckles quickly and sharply on the bathroom door Gardner asked, "Kelsey, you okay?"

A muffled "I'm fine," in a weak voice that Gardner still recognized as Kelsey's answered him.

"Yeah," Gardner said sarcastically but too softly for Kelsey to hear. He stared at the door for a moment, made his mind up about something, then abruptly turned on his heels and headed for the closet. Time to dress and face another less than lovely day at Moundville.

Nursing his cereal, like it was a five-dollar beer from the legendary *Chukker*, Gardner looked up as Kelsey walked into the kitchen. She was fully dressed, flawless in presentation down to the last hair strand as she always was, looking more like she was headed to an office job rather than to Moundville to dig and sweat and gather grime all day. Grabbing a bowl from the cupboard, she went through her daily routine of pouring cereal to the brim, topping it with skim milk and daintily eating it. Just another start of the day for two college kids that weren't talking about why one was sick.

Gardner started to ask Kelsey what was wrong, and then caught himself. It just had to be a nasty bug, cause if it was serious she would already have said something. To have something to say, Gardner talked shop instead.

"I think I'm gonna head out to Moundville," Gardner said through his cereal, breaking one of the favorite politeness rules of his mother. "Get there early; maybe help Bart prep for the shoot."

Kelsey gave him the look. It used to run chills down his spine but Gardner had become inured to it. "Don't you have Geography?" she asked but it was really a statement dressed as another, the statement was, "Are you ever going to grow up and attend your classes so you can graduate?"

"So I'll go later," Gardner responded. "It's kind of a frivolous thing to learn anyway."

"You say that about every class," she was obviously miffed.

"Well it's especially true about Geography," Gardner responded. "Sides, it's a big day. Wanna come with me?" he had to ask even though he already knew the answer.

"I'd rather pass this semester," she said testily with just a touch of emphasis on the word pass. "I'll take the carpool, so don't worry."

"You sure you don't wanna just stay in bed?" Gardner asked. It had no sexual connotation, which was highly unusual for him.

"Why?" she asked. "Do I look tired?"

"You look sick," Gardner said truthfully. A man never learns how to talk to a woman, so of course she took it wrong.

"Thanks," she said, without indicating any thanks at all.

"I mean it, you're still under the weather," Gardner said with a forced smile, trying to salvage himself. He really did mean well, if that ever matters in one of these conversations.

"I said I'm fine," Kelsey replied with a ring of finality.

Gardner would never, ever, understand women, or men either for that matter. Maybe not even himself. He continued to smile at her. Kelsey didn't smile back. They finished their meal, if it could be called such, in silence.

Leaving his bowl on the table for Kelsey to worry with, showing he was still without a clue on what it takes to show a woman you are concerned, and breaking his mother's rule about always putting your dirty dishes in the sink, Gardner got up from the table. Stretching his arms, he proceeded to the door. Surprisingly, at least for him, he found he was anxious to leave. Whether it was because he was getting away from Kelsey and her mood or because adventure beckoned for him at Moundville he couldn't really say. But it was a fact.

You can't fool all the people all the time but you can usually fool enough to make it a paying proposition.

The Wisdom of Bart Thompson

The crew was up and at 'em this day. Small budget, small crew meant long hours, many jobs and few hands to do those jobs. They all hoped it would mean more money to them than having a large crew. But it was still work and lots of it, even if you liked mostly what you were doing.

Gardner was trying to help by holding, with Levi and Ben, a small jib crane. There was a less than state of the art camera attached to the crane, which meant it was big, not small and heavy, not light. They moved the crane very slowly, trying to capture whatever the hell Bart wanted without jiggling the shot. Like it really mattered with the piece of crap camera they were using.

The camera was feeding a monitor that had seen better days too. Bart Thompson and Doctor McClean (McClean held his clipboard as he always did, Gardner thought it was an affectation rather than a tool as he had never seen McClean either write on it or even refer to it) were looking at the image coming over the monitor and making noises that may have meant something to them. It certainly didn't to Gardner as he couldn't hear them and if he could he doubted he would have understood them. Suddenly Bart shouted out, "Beautiful, keep it steady. Just a bit more and we'll have it."

Gardner was acting as a counterweight on the crane. Bart was either too broke or too cheap to buy weights. This was an adventure? Gardner wondered. With sweat rolling down his brow and into his eyes, eyes that he couldn't protect because of his damn position on the jib, Gardner was seriously missing Geography.

"Steady now," Bart commanded. Gardner thought Bart missed his calling. He should have gone into the military; there he could have bossed around soldiers to his heart content. Then again, you also have to take orders and that would not have suited Bart.

A small tingle on his arm caused Gardner to look down. Something small, brown and menacing was making his merry way through the forest of hairs on Gardner's arm. It was a tick, of course, and though it meant no malice in what it was about to do, it was going to do it anyway, unless something stopped it.

Gardner couldn't give up his purchase on the jib without ruining the shot, so he tried to blow the tick off his arm. The tick seemed to enjoy the cool breeze and continued on his meandering walk, looking for just the right place to sink his sucker. Gardner bent his head to blow harder, and his motion translated to the jib, which translated to the camera, which translated to the monitor and drew a "God sakes! Keep her steady kid," from Bart.

The tick stopped moving and Gardner let go of the crane with one hand and swiped the tick off him and onto some other poor unlucky creature of nature, he didn't care what or who, as long as it wasn't him. The movement did wonders for the picture on the monitor that Bart and the good doctor were watching and drew an explosion from Bart. "Damn it, cut!"

"Look," Gardner started to plead his case, "I'm sorry."

"You'd better be," Bart answered in no mood to accept an apology.

As the team tried to reestablish the shot, several cars drove up. Bart nodded with his head towards the lead vehicle and said, "I haven't seen her in a while, but I think that's Kelsey in the lead car."

Gardner turned his head and of course the crane again. Bart was right; there were a caravan of vehicles coming into the park and Kelsey was sitting on the passenger side of the lead one.

"Damn," Bart exploded again as Gardner's slight twist to the crane ruined yet another take. "Break it guys," he continued, "Besides those cars and trucks are cutting right through the shot anyway."

Gardner felt another tingle on his arm and damned if another tick hadn't taken up residence. This one wasn't so choosy as the last and it seemed to already be attached and enjoying its breakfast. Patton blood was most tasty to it. Gardner totally let go of the crane and grabbed the offending creature, dashing it to the ground. Having totally let go of the crane, the crane jumped up wildly and the camera was headed towards the ground and was saved from being dashed to the ground only because Ben reached in quickly and grabbed it.

"Whoa," Ben said as he leveled the crane and steadied it.

"Gardner," Bart instructed, "Watch what you're doing. The things a director without funds has to put up with!"

Gardner hardly heard the words; he was intent on finding the tick and putting it into tick heaven. With a savage "uh" he saw what looked like a brown speck on the ground and he stomped it as mightily as he could to make sure all God's creatures were safe from its design. Had a steamroller been available he would have commandeered it and used it to be totally sure of the homicide. There were just some things that God shouldn't have created.

"Damn Gardner," Bart said stridently, "You beat all. You about broke the camera, which ain't to say much, but it's all the camera I can afford." With a wave at the crew Bart said, "Come on, let's finish the break down, leave the jib here, we'll finish the shot after all those cars and trucks leave."

The team quickly began to disconnect the camera from the crane. Bart and Doctor McClean evidently didn't consider themselves a part of the crew as they were already walking away leaving the toil to Gardner, Ben and the ever talkative Levi. They were each grabbing part of the equipment to haul down to Mound F to film the days shooting. Gardner was messing with the monitor trying to get it unplugged from all of its equipment when he heard Bart say, "Gardner, leave around the back."

If Gardner really heard he didn't show it as he had quit messing with the monitor and gone back to the crane to help Ben complete the transfer of the camera. Clumsily he hit the crane as Levi detached it, the crane swung and caused both to curse.

"Sorry," Gardner called out and grabbed the crane to free Ben up to help Levi.

"Don't worry about it," Ben said. Levi and Ben finished removing the camera. Levi took off heading in the general direction of Bart and McClean leaving Ben the job of toting the camera.

"It was Bart's deal anyway," Ben said, "He earned a few bucks by selling the weights we needed. Sold about everything else too. Including some stuff that might not have actually belonged to him at the time of the selling."

"You know him well," Gardner said through a smile.

Bart and his entourage crossed the hill that separated them from Mound F and the parking lot. They headed towards a white truck. Kelsey was standing beside Doctor Sims. She punched him lightly in his side and gestured towards Bart.

"Doctor Kerry Sims?" Bart asked.

Sims smiled a smile that was polite but pointless and said nothing.

"Bart Thompson," Bart said smiling his best smile, "I'm the director of this documentary. This gentleman beside me is Doctor Kevin McClean. He is an archaeologist too, though we forgive him for that as he is also the producer of this epic."

"Yes," Sims replied, "We spoke on the phone, Doctor McClean and I. It's good to put a face with the voice."

The three men shook hands. Kelsey was eyeing Bart the whole time but she received not one glance from him. Finally she said "Hi Bart."

Bart nodded at Kelsey but still did not speak to her.

"We've got some waivers here we need the class to sign before the end of the day," Bart said.

Doctor McClean actually used his clipboard. He pushed the clasp down and extracted about twenty sheets of paper. Sims reached for them as they were offered. "No problem," he said after scanning one. "Now do you need anything special?" Sims asked.

"Just do what you're gonna do," Bart advised. "We'll get what we need."

A GENESIS FOUND

The students could be heard coming up the hill laughing and joking and laughing some more. Not having the status of Doctor Sims or the guts either, they couldn't drive up into the park but had to leave their cars in the visitor's lot. It didn't seem to bother them coming in, but after an eight-hour day, they would likely be less jovial as they carried out all the junk they carried in.

"Kelsey," Doctor Sims said as he turned and motioned with his heads towards the approaching students, "Why don't you go ahead with them and do your best to keep them out of mischief until I get there."

"Sure thing," she said, she took a final glance at Bart and then went down to join the other students.

Sims was looking over Bart's shoulder and said, "So, you've already met one of my students."

Gardner, more conspicuous than an elephant in a tutu, was coming down the hill carrying the monitor.

"Oh, yeah," Bart said evenly, "He showed up early and I put him to work. Independent film makers can't be choosy over whatever help they can finagle." Bart smiled and continued, "Ain't a problem is it? He was just being neighborly and I'd hate to see him get into any kind of trouble."

"None of my business," Sims said with a shake of his head. "I just..." the sentence faded to nothing.

"Yeah?" asked Bart.

"Well, it's damned unfair," Sims replied, "But his grandfather was John Patton Junior. I assume you've heard of him."

"I think so," Bart answered, "Name rings a bell. Probably ran over it in my research, at least such as it was."

Sims smiled. He knew research and yeah regardless of what you did such as it was sounded appropriate. One could spend their whole life in research and still never learn everything there was on a subject. If you doubt that try to get a PhD some day.

"Anyway," Sims continued, "This mound we are excavating, it was important to John Patton Junior. I Hope Gardner's involvement doesn't entail any ulterior motive. I surely hope he doesn't expect to find what his grandfather claimed to have found."

Bart took instant notice of the last sentence and Sims noticed Bart taking notice. "And what was that?" Bart questioned.

"You don't know?" Sims asked back.

"Not a clue sir," Bart lied.

Some research indeed, thought Sims, but said only, "Well I'm sure you'll stumble across it as you continue to research. It's caused some problems here in the past. Problems I'd truly love to avoid on my watch."

"So why dig here?" asked Bart. "Why not avoid it all together."

"We have been avoiding it," Sims replied. "We've been avoiding it for too long. It's time we put some things to rest. It's past time."

Bart gave a smile and nodded his head. This was a wise man. A very wise man indeed and one that could prove useful.

Gardner was sweating as he carried the monitor to the canopy. The monitor was damned heavy and this was Moundville the humidity capital of the world. Throw in a scorching day and anyone would sweat not perspire and Gardner was doing just that. Sweat flowed down his brow and into his eyes again. Wearing contacts was less fun when sweat got into your eyes than wearing glasses by a long shot and for the second time that day he couldn't wipe the sweat off his brow. Adventure my left foot!

Levi was standing under the canopy holding a boom mike. He put his fish eyes on Gardner and finally proved he could speak by saying, "Supposed to go around back," with all the subtlety of a ninth grader making a move on his first date.

Gardner didn't reply. He returned the evil eye of Levi's with one of his own. As he evil eyed Levi he noticed a red spot at the top of Levi's arm, to Gardner's admittedly untrained eye it looked like a rash. Levi followed the trail of Gardner's eye to his arm. Without a word or another look at Gardner he pulled his sleeve down.

Bart and Doctor McClean came walking up the hill talking quietly among themselves as they always did. Gardner wouldn't have been surprised if they couldn't even hear themselves. Bart certainly got a lot of practice at talking and at smiling.

"We got this covered, Gardner," Bart said as he grabbed the monitor from Gardner and moved it the last few feet to the table. "Thanks, but go help your class, or go home, but at least get out of our hair."

"You're quite welcome," Gardner replied with quite a bit of rancor. "Be sure to call me again if you need something. I ain't hung up the phone on anybody but bill collectors in a long time and I need the practice and the pleasure."

Gardner walked away from the group and headed towards the mound. Bart and Levi stood together watching as he walked away. Abruptly Bart turned to Levi and said, "Don't worry about it."

Levi, stone faced as ever grunted a reply. Bart crooked his head to one side as if trying to translate the grunt into English or redneck Southern but gave it up as hopeless. Bart walked past Levi and started grabbing some of his gear off the table. There was a movie to shoot and regardless of whatever else had to be done, the movie still had to be shot and Bart was the one to shoot it.

Gardner arrived at the infamous mound F still sweating but at least having the luxury of being able to keep the sweat out of his eyes. Several of the students were already attacking the mound with picks and shovels and rakes. Small piles of dirt were being made from the larger pile of dirt. They were no more immune to the humidity than Gardner was and sweat was pouring rapidly and voluminously from their pores. Was this what college meant?

A young man with matted black hair, wearing a t-shirt wet through and through with sweat shouted, "Eureka!" Everyone gathered around. Any excuse to stop digging. They were still more kids than adults in that respect, not yet understanding that work put off today usually just means more work tomorrow.

Doctor Sims came ambling over and parted the crowd as much by force of will as by his hands. Clearly visible peaking out of the mound was a white skeletal hand. Sims nodded his head in approval. This is what college meant!

"Remains," Sims stated the obvious. "You know the protocol unless you were asleep during that lecture. But then again, most of you seem to be asleep at a lot of my lectures. Why I can't imagine." Grinning good-naturedly Sims stated, "Cover it and flag it."

Behind the crowd of students, Bart's camera was taking in everything. A squinting Ben was at the camera with Bart standing beside him. They were trying to get the remains in shot. Sims took note and walked between the camera and the dig. Sims smiled straight into the camera and nodded. The smile was the very definition of tight. A film crew did not mix with archaeology. They were ignorant of what archaeology was and when you dug up something you couldn't explain at that moment they were too quick to jump to the most sensational interpretation.

Ben almost swore, he hated working with amateurs. Amateurs did not realize that a movie, documentary or not was most successful when it appeared natural on the film. Anyone acknowledging the camera immediately told the audience that this wasn't real. Being aware of the camera and not to show it that was how professionals did it. Amateurs. He would never know that he had totally misinterpreted the situation.

A GENESIS FOUND

The students had disbursed from the dig almost as quickly as they had assembled. Each went back to the business of making their own piles. The process was this: Enter shovel into the mound as gently as possible, gently remove the dirt and gently let it fall into the bucket. Each scoop was examined visually as it came out of the ground and as it was dumped, to see if any obvious relics showed. Once the bucket was half full or so, another unfortunate student would come by and swap the half full bucket for an empty one. Then that unfortunate student would carry the bucket to the most unfortunate students, those running the dirt screens. For you see, the students running the dirt screens had to dump dirt into the dirt screen all day long and gently agitate the screen, letting the dirt fall back to the ground and hopefully revealing any relics that had been dug from the ground. One could not imagine Indiana Jones doing this but it was the backbone of archaeology.

Doctor Sims approached another group of students, busily attacking their section of Mound F with possibly more enthusiasm than he would have liked. Sims called a halt and gave them an example to work from "Watch this as it is obvious to me that the class demonstration did not take," he said but without rancor or derision, just stating a fact. Besides the students knew him well enough to know good-humored ribbing when they heard it.

"Here's how it's done," he pronounced and proceeded to show how it truly was done. Slow, smooth, beyond gently, the shovel went into the ground. A small subtle shake loosened the earth; then a slow removal of the shovel; a scan of the shovel seeing if anything was showing; a slow dropping of the soil into the bucket, looking as it slid gently from one piece of steel to another. "That," Sims said with authority and not a little pride "Is how it's done."

The camera had caught every movement. The shot was perfect. Everyone had focused on Doctor Sims and Doctor Sims

73

had focused on his mission. Now that made a good shot and no crummy amateur mugged for the camera.

Gardner and Kelsey had obviously ticked off Doctor Sims at some point because they had the grand old job of sifting all the dirt. Dirt was everywhere, including in their hair and on their bodies, for no matter how gently you sifted, it still raised a cloud and that cloud had to settle somewhere. Gravity was their worst enemy. Gardner glanced at Kelsey as they worked and he knew there was something wrong with his vision for she still looked lovely to him, even covered in grime and sweat. Such was love he suspected.

The dirty young man that had found the first remains walked up with a bucket and put it down besides Gardner. Smiling he said, "Present for the love birds," and without another word picked up an empty bucket and headed back to the mound.

"Thanks Sean," Gardner answered without really meaning thanks to the back of the retreating figure. Gardner grabbed the bucket and slowly started pouring it into the sifter. Kelsey began the gentle rocking motion that separated the good stuff from the unneeded stuff and that also caused dirt to rise and settle on all of those about. Gardner helped her sift when he had finished the dumping. They didn't talk which was unusual but Gardner was determined not to say the first words.

Finally even Gardner, stubborn as the day is long, couldn't keep quiet and he said a bit softly, "You're being quiet."

"So are you," Kelsey countered which was hardly a reply at all.

Gardner smirked and half shrugged his shoulders. Oh well, he thought, whatever the hell was eating at her would come to light soon enough. Gardner glanced up and saw that Bart and crew had backed off a good ways from the dig. Gardner reasoned that they were filming a wide shot and was rather proud of himself for having picked up that piece of movie making lexicon. Course he wasn't totally sure of the term and it may actually have been a short shot they were shooting

Bart was behind the camera now and he was squinting and talking and squinting some more as he made the camera do what he needed it to do in order to accomplish what he wanted to accomplish. Levi was holding the boom and was as wooden faced as ever Buster Keaton had been. Gardner wondered what Levi had gotten for his personality when he had sold it.

Bart was making hand movements, which probably meant something to the crew, but Gardner couldn't tell what they indicated with his limited experience with filmmaking. Course it could be just Bart being Bart. Gardner thought he might be too critical of Bart given his recent less than fun experience with the man, but it was hard to forgive him. Bart had to be the only filmmaker that purposefully insulted his volunteers. Seemed to be a less than successful way of recruiting and holding on to free talent or any talent for that matter.

"You know, Mound F's grass looks deader than the others," Kelsey said apropos nothing.

Gardner had his mind on other things and did not reply but changed the subject, "Damn," Gardner grumbled.

"What?" asked Kelsey.

"I don't care for Bart in work mode," Gardner answered.

"I don't care for Bart ever," Kelsey replied.

"Am I ever like that?" Gardner asked.

With a shake of her head Kelsey replied, "I think he picked that up on his own. Not everything comes with being a Patton."

"Maybe," Gardner admitted, "Just bad eyesight and insanity. Of course there is also the plot at Tuscaloosa Memorial. So it ain't all bad. Goes without saying that if we get married I'll have to give that up to as it's only reserved for those that don't have mates."

A GENESIS FOUND

"Gardner," Kelsey said without looking at him, "If you're waiting until you can afford a ring, well you don't have to, that's all."

Gardner glanced at Kelsey but she still didn't turn to his eyes.

"I just wanted you to know. That's all." She kept on sifting as she talked. What that meant, if anything, Gardner wasn't sure.

"Okay," Gardner replied. There didn't seem to be anything else to say. Gardner resumed sifting with her. It gave him something to concentrate on that did seem to make sense. Pour in the dirt. Look for stuff, agitate, and look for some more stuff. Watch as the dirt trickled away. Do it again, and again. This he could handle, a live-in girlfriend in some mood that he had never seen, well he was unsure if he could handle that.

Every once in a while you find something. Pray you don't for whether you find it while digging or find it while sifting the end result was more paperwork than is required to apply for a house loan. Which mound, which hole, approximate depth, etc. Each bucket was labeled with the name of the digger and the mound and written in magic marker that wasn't so magic after a few trips so that it was rubbed off and God only knows where this stuff came from. Once something is found by the sifter, they had to identify the digger and ask lots of questions that went into a dirty paper log. Often it wasn't the truth that went into the log because the sifter was hot and dirty, the bucket was unreadable and who wanted to go ask of twenty students which one had found what and where. It was easier to lie and it was unlikely anyone was ever gonna read it anyway. Just make sure the story gets relayed to the higher ups in some shape form or fashion. They should just be happy to know which mound the relic was found in; else they could come out here and do it themselves.

Gardner was flicking some dirt out of a bucket with his hand and he hit on something hard. Gently he poured the bucket into the sifter. The dirt fell away as the sifter did its thing and there, in all its glory was a paperwork bonanza.

An eye, or at least most of an eye, in graven stone, still with some color left on it, gazed up at him. "Mmm..." Gardner said and Kelsey looked over and said magnanimously "Your piece not mine."

Gardner didn't even reply his attention was on identifying just who had brought the bucket and from where. Grabbing his gloves he slid them on his hand, following what may be the stupidest rule of the dig and that was to handle the artifacts only with gloves, Gardner was pretty sure that anything that could survive the elements for five hundred years could likely survive being handled by a human hand, but still he put the gloves on. Gardner picked up the eye and examined it from every direction and checked every dimension on it with a pair of calipers. He put the relic in a plastic bag and labeled it, Mound F, Sean Blankenship. Gardner was sure of the Mound as it was the only one being excavated and he was guessing at the digger because the bucket was not legible. He also put down it was found at a depth of three feet two inches, which was sheer fabrication, but he figured if he ever did identify who found it, the record could be set straight, otherwise, one depth was as good as another, besides it was really the responsibility of the digger anyway.

With the eye safely bagged and most likely erroneously tagged but still in hand, Gardner headed towards the mound. If he was right and it had come from Sean then all he could say was poor Sean, so little time, so much paperwork. Gardner came upon Sean still digging holes. Sean really didn't care for seeing Gardner but they both knew it wasn't anything personal.

"Sean," Gardner spoke holding up the object for Sean to see, "This yours? I'm pretty sure I saw it in your dirt." He wanted to add, you poor sod but thought it best not to.

"Don't know," Sean answered and only he knew the truth. "But if it was in my dirt then I got it from over there." He pointed to a sizeable hole to the left of where they were standing.

"Exactly there?" asked Gardner. "You know the protocol; we've got to document the exact location as accurately as we can. Including where on the mound and depth if possible."

"I know, I know," Sean replied irritably. The truth was he had tried not to find anything but you couldn't see everything in a shovel of dirt. "It was near that flag. We found remains and Sims made us stop diggin'. He didn't make us stop diggin' quick enough I reckon."

"You reckon right," Gardner said. Grabbing a shovel from the rack, and then commandeering a wheelbarrow Gardner walked over to the spot to see if there was anything else to find. His curiosity was up and besides, he was already gonna have to do paperwork anyway.

As Gardner was about to put the first shovel in he heard a loud "Gardner!" He turned and saw Doctor Sims looking at him with that look parents have for unruly children. "See the flag?" asked Sims, "Means we found remains there."

"Yeah," Gardner replied. He knew better but he was hoping to get away with it anyway. Gardner pulled away from the mound as if headed for the rack to replace the shovel, but then he saw Sims walk away and made a beeline back to the hole. He wasn't to be denied.

His first thrust into the ground uncovered the hand that had been found earlier. He gently moved it out of his way and prayed that God forgave him any sacrilege because he meant none. The next shovel hit something solid, so Gardner knelt and began to brush the dirt away. His reward was another piece of graven stone. Not taking the time to put on gloves, he pulled the clay out of the mound. It looked like another piece of the same disc. Holding the bag up, he put the other piece to the eye in the bag and it fit. A smile crossed his lips. This was archaeology.

Though Gardner didn't know, or probably care, the film crew had taken up position and was filming his efforts. Bart jerked his hand towards Gardner and Levi turned the lens control on the camera. They wanted a close up; for sure they wanted a very detailed close-up.

Gardner looked again at the skeleton hand he had uncovered. He dropped to one knee to look at it more closely. It was odd. There seemed to be a hole in the palm, the same place that the eye would be found on the Rattlesnake Disc. Not being worth a shuck at anatomy, Gardner wasn't sure if it was natural or not. Gardner had removed a toothbrush from his back pocket and was flicking the dirt off the bones when he heard from directly behind him, "Found somethin'?" It was Bart asking in a very eager tone.

Gardner dropped the bones and quickly kicked some dirt on them. He hoped it looked casual and it did look about as casual as a longshoreman heading for his paycheck.

"Just looking for the rest of this," Gardner said holding up the relic he had found.

"What you think it come off of?" Bart asked perhaps a little less eagerly.

"A burial disc," Gardner answered, "Probably but who knows. I would think it's something ceremonial. It's the kind of thing we are supposed to be looking for. You wouldn't know it though the way Sims got us dodging remains. When we dodge them, we're probably dodging a lot of other stuff too."

Gardner stood up and stretched and walked to another part of the mound. Whatever he had found, he sure as hell didn't want Bart to get his camera on it. Sims was likely to be mad enough as it was, even when Gardner told whatever lie he had yet to make up.

Bart wasn't to be left out so easily; he continued to film and continued to focus the camera on Gardner. Gardner didn't particularly like having a second shadow and felt it was odd that he was the focus of whatever it was Bart was trying to do, but then again, who could fathom the mind of Bart Thompson.

Suddenly a loud voice stopped all work and sent a chill down Gardner's spine. "Gardner!" Sims had shouted.

Gardner immediately went into fight or flight mode, trouble was if he fought he got an F and if he ran he got an F. That mode was quickly replaced by the "aw-shucks-I-didn't-mean-any-harm" mode.

Sims came striding up, oblivious to the camera and said or rather shouted, "Didn't you hear a word I said?" Not giving Gardner a chance to speak Sims continued, "I said it today and yesterday and the day before and every damn day we've had class. We do not disturb remains. If we do it by accident we stop. If we do it on purpose we repeat next semester!"

"I found part of an artifact," Gardner said defensively.

"I don't care if you found the Holy Grail," Sims boomed, "We stay away from remains."

"How are we gonna find anything, sir," Gardner stated rather than questioned. "If we recover every piece of bone we find. For a complete excavation...."

"This isn't a complete excavation," Sims thundered, "It's an exercise, and a student exercise at that. Unless you have a piece of paper showing that the tribes have given you special permission to dig up their ancestors, we're staying away from remains. That goes for all of you. Understood?"

"Yes sir," Gardner said in a quiet voice.

"All right," Sims said, his voice dropping at least ten decibels, "Recover this, now."

Gardner took his shovel and went back to the hole that he had casually tried to recover with dirt, a casual attempt that had failed miserably. Blast Bart anyway, trying to keep Sims off your back and that fool is filming for the whole damn world to see. As Gardner put a full shovel of dirt on the still visible hand, Sims watched and seemingly satisfied turned abruptly on his heels and in doing so almost stepped right into the camera crew.

Sims glared at the camera but said, "Excuse me." His voice did not indicate that he truly wanted to be excused at all. Sims stepped around the camera and walked away.

Bart called out to Gardener stopping him in mid-shovel, "Why are y'all avoiding remains?"

"You heard him," Gardner replied, "This is an exercise," then just a tad bitterly he added "A student exercise."

"Sure that's the only reason?" Bart pressed Gardner.

"Why?" Gardner asked back, "You know of another one?"

Bart made a slicing gesture with his hand just below his neck. You didn't have to be a film student to know that meant cut the camera off. Bart stepped towards Gardner and did not stop until he was close enough to whisper conspiratorially, "What are you doing tonight?" his voice though quiet was strident and Bart's eyes never left Gardner's as he asked the question.

Gardner gazed back uneasily. He shrugged his shoulders indicating not a whole lot.

"I think you ought to stay out her with us," Bart said insistently.

"Why?" Gardner asked.

"Cause I think you might have found something," Bart replied. To emphasize his point he stooped to the ground and picked up the bag, which contained the relic that Gardner had found. He flipped it to Gardner and Gardner caught it in midair.

"Found what exactly?" Gardner queried.

"You'll see," Bart relied. "Or not. Hell might be nothing. Might be something. Come around, Gardner and we will all see together."

A GENESIS FOUND

Often even when we get where we're going we are still lost.

The Wisdom of Bart Thompson

Archaeology 357 "Mississippian Cultures 800-1500" was over for the day and the students were heading to the parking lot en masse. Gardner and Kelsey were walking with the group, not leading, not following, just part of the herd heading in the same direction. If here had been a dirtiest contest, they would have been the winners hand down. The same went for tired. Gardner figured he deserved it as he was always atop Sims get that bastard list, but Kelsey was just guilty by association and that hardly seemed fair. But fair or not that was how life worked.

"You'll be okay?" Gardner asked as they approached the parking lot. Gardner had planned on driving her back home until he had received that mystery invitation from Bart. Now wild horses couldn't drag him away.

"Sure," Kelsey replied as she wearily leaned against a car. "There's nothing wrong that a shower won't cure," she said, "I'll come back in the morning though, I don't want to give you an excuse for skipping any more classes, not that you aren't fully capable of making up some doozies on your own. It would be refreshing if you actually went to a class for a change."

"It's okay," Gardner answered with a smile, "Missing another one won't hurt, besides if the teacher never sees me he might not ever know I skipped in the first place." Gardner laughed but Kelsey didn't. "Well," he continued, "I'll see you back at the dig regardless."

Kelsey smiled wearily and sniffed. She said "I'll bring you back a change of clothes, regardless."

Gardner laughed and said, "Don't worry about it. Let Bart worry about it. He's the one that will smell my sweet bouquet tonight."

"What about your contacts Four Eyes?" Kelsey questioned.

"I'll be fine," Gardner answered, "I can rough it for one night. Besides," Gardner pulled out the toothbrush he had been using at the dig from his back pocket and held it up and said, "They say all you need is a toothbrush."

Kelsey smirked at Gardner and said. "Okay. You got your cell phone?"

"Of course," Gardner said as he reached out and grabbed her and hugged her, which was a lot of emotion for Gardner as he didn't even like to hold hands in public. The sound of a laboring truck headed their way ended even that brief public display.

Levi was driving the truck, Bart was hanging out the rider's side window mugging at all of the students they were passing. Ben and Doctor McClean were in the back of the truck both sitting on and steadying the fragile equipment.

"Come on kid," Bart yelled.

Gardner motioned with his hand as the truck pulled to a stop next to him. "Hold your horses," he said loudly so that he could be heard over the rumble of the truck engine. Bart smiled at the couple and made a kissy face and for about the millionth time Gardner wondered if they were truly related.

"You're sure you'll be okay?" Gardner asked Kelsey, "I mean are you really feeling all right?"

"I'm not gonna be your excuse out of this," Kelsey replied then after a short pause, "Kid."

Gardner forced a laugh, but it was an obvious force.

"Besides," Kelsey continued, "You need to spend some time with him. God knows why you do, but it's the truth."

Gardner tilted his head to one side as if questioning her last statement, but he didn't say anything. There was both something for what she said and an opening for a comeback. He let the comeback go with the breeze, simply smiled at her, hugged her quickly then ran over and jumped in the back of the truck, just missing the blasted monitor.

The truck, loaded with the small crew and one naïve lad pulled away. Bart smiled broadly at Kelsey as they passed, their eyes locking for a second upon the other's. Kelsey did not smile back. Neither waved. Then Gardner came into view and they both locked eyes and the smile that passed between them was one of those genuine smiles that artists always try to capture but somehow never can. Kelsey waved and Gardner waved and they continued waving until the truck rolled around the bend and out of sight.

A worried Kelsey frowned as she made her way back to Gardner's truck. She knew she was worried over nothing in particular; she just had a deep and abiding dislike for Bart. It was not rational, perhaps as they hardly knew each other and her impression was likely greatly colored by Gardner's tales of his youth with Bart, which she had no doubt were highly exaggerated. Still she was worried even if Bart was family.

The crew bounced and jiggled as the truck slowly made its way to the campsite at the top of the hill. Gardner wondered if Bart had sold the springs on this damn truck. The only one talking was Bart and Gardner was spared his voice due to the roar of the engine.

Upon reaching the campsite five weary individuals began the task of securing the equipment. It had to be put away in apple pie order to make sure they could get to it again in just the manner that was needed. That was the first thing you learned as a filmmaker, plan tomorrow today. Well, maybe the second, the first was probably how to survive without a steady paycheck.

Darkness had settled by the time they had finished. Gardner was no longer worried that his own smell might be offensive after mixing with the rest of the crew. He might be the least smelly of the lot.

"Damn," Bart complained, "That always takes too long," then he smiled and said the welcomest words of the day, "Beer awaits folks."

No air conditioning was right and obvious as you walked into the camper. It had been locked (as if someone would steal any of the crap in that camper) and had the sun shining on it all day. It was hotter than the hottest of hot houses. It was too damn hot and too damn humid but the magic word Beer might just turn it into a Nirvana. But it wasn't to be.

Once everyone was in the camper, Bart announced, "All right, everybody grab a seat." They scattered to couches and beds and chairs while Bart remained standing in the center of the camper and as always in the center of attention. Theatrical as always.

"Gardner?" Bart asked, "You got that relic on you?"

Gardner nodded.

"You know it's a federal crime to steal from a dig?" Bart asked seriously.

Gardner just stared at Bart. He had no intention of stealing the piece; he just had conveniently forgotten to log it into Doctor Sims before he left. It happened all the time. Gardner had just wanted to look it over for a while before Doctor Sims took his play pretty away.

"Well let's see it," Bart said with a laugh.

Gardner pulled the relic from his pocket and handed it to Bart. Bart glanced at it then passed it to Doctor McClean for a closer inspection.

Doctor McClean held it up to the light, viewing it through the plastic bag, nodding his head as he turned it this way and that; he seemed impressed. "Wow," McClean muttered, "This... you might be right Bart."

Gardner doubted it was ever possible for Bart to be right but he said nothing.

Doctor McClean went over to the kitchen table and picked up their copy of John Patton Junior's journal. Quickly he flipped through the pages then stopped. There it was, a drawing of a Rattlesnake Disc with the eye in the hand. It looked exactly like the partial artifact that he was holding very gingerly in his hands.

"This certainly looks like a match," Doctor McClean stated still eyeing alternately the drawing and the piece in his hands. "Almost sure of it," he added.

Gardner watched all of this with increasing awareness that something most definitely was up.

"Remember where you found it Gardner?" asked Doctor McClean.

Gardner did not reply. He turned to Bart and stated, even though it was in the form of a question, "This ain't about a movie Bart, is it? Not by a long shot."

Bart for once was silent. He met Gardner's gaze with a stone face that Levi would have envied.

"What are you looking for?" Gardner asked.

Answering a question with a question Bart asked, "You got the book I gave ya?"

"What?" questioned Gardner neither comprehending nor understanding what one had to do with the other.

"You got the book?" Bart insisted.

"Yeah," Gardner said. "I got the book." He walked over to where he had dropped his backpack and moved things around until he found it. He pulled it out to show everyone then handed it out towards Bart.

"No, you keep it," Bart said, "And turn to page 49 and start reading." Bart's eyes were most intent.

"Why?" asked Gardner.

"For heavens sakes just do it Gardner," Bart said testily, "I'm tired of playing twenty questions."

"Where do I stop?" Gardner asked the twenty-first question.

"You'll know," Bart said wearily. "You will damn well know. Now read, there'll be time for talking when you are done."

With a doubtful glance at Bart, Gardner retired to his sitting place on the bed. Wriggling. He tried to get comfortable. That brought another dagger glance from Bart. Gardner half smiled because even if it wasn't strictly a Christian tenant, he did so love to irritate Bart. But the time had come to read, so he turned to page forty-nine and began.

Never look backwards. There's plenty enough trouble in front of you.

The Wisdom of Bart Thompson

Reveille was shrill as always, and as always drew a curse from most of the lads, Christians included, to their discredit. Patton heard and cursed like the next guy, and just like the next guy he yawned and stretched and hopped out of bed to make a beeline to the latrine. As he always did he also shouted at Shaw to get up and make his mama some money, but this time there was no one in Shaw's bed to hear the rejoinder.

Patton looked at the bed, as his words had not drawn an insult in reply. The bed wasn't made however and Shaw was not residing therein. Shaw up early? Casting his eyes to the far end of the barracks, he saw that Patrick Dobbs bed was also unmade but that Patrick was nowhere to be seen. Patton hoped he was guessing wrong but with those two both missing at the same time, well, Shaw's mama wasn't likely to be happy at the outcome.

A GENESIS FOUND

DeJarnette walked in bigger than hell and all of the cadets scrambled to attention, even those halfway through with pulling their pants up. They stood in their shorts with their pants bunched at their feet but it was still better than being put on report and although it has been said before it can't be repeated enough, thirty bucks was thirty bucks and was something to hold on to in this depression, even if you looked rather foolish in the process of holding on.

DeJarnette strode through the barracks as if he was a general and not a commander in the CCC, which was actually kind of an insult in the Army, but insult or no, he took it seriously. He stopped before each bed and made sure there was an occupant that could lay claim to that bed. All could except Shaw and Dobbs. After this impromptu inspection, the commandant turned and gazed directly into Patton's eyes, causing Patton to almost lose his not yet eaten breakfast.

"Patton," DeJarnete commanded, "I need to see you in my office right away."

"Yes sir," Patton responded. DeJarnette turned on his heels in correct military bearing and chest out thrust and back straighter than an ironing board he walked out, a military man to the core, even if he only commanded half educated rednecks. Patton quickly dressed and didn't walk but ran to the commandant's office.

Arriving at the door, Patton almost just blundered in, but catching himself, he drew a quick breath and said, "Hell man, he can't have me shot," to himself though he was quite unsure if it was a true statement. He rapped on the door and received a muffled "Come in," for his efforts and he quickly did so.

Doctor Jones was sitting behind DeJarnette's desk. DeJarnette was standing in the corner next to a window with the morning sun to his back. Jones was smiling; Patton didn't think DeJarnette was. Actually it was hard to see him the way he was positioned, but knowing DeJarnette that was probably planned. Besides, Patton had never seen DeJarnette smile, and even as little as he knew of this situation, he doubted it would turn out to be funny.

"Sit down," Doctor Jones said friendly but a bit soberly

Patton saluted even though he knew he wasn't supposed to salute a civilian then he sat down and was thankful to do so. Jones had a photograph in his hand; he passed it over to Patton. It was one of those pictures that they were all the time taking around the camp, you know, squad picture, division picture, a whole camp picture, that sort of a thing, this happened to be as picture of Patton's barracks. It was also the barracks of Shaw and Dobbs. If you are a stickler for details it was Barracks A. The picture had two large red circles on it. One was circled around Shaw the other around Dobbs. Funny that.

"Do you know either of these cadets, John?" Jones questioned obviously knowing the answer before he asked. Doctor Jones eyes had latched onto Patton's eyes much to Patton's discomfort.

"Tim I do," Patton replied.

"What about Dobbs?" Jones pressed.

"Not so much sir," Patton stated. "I recognize him of course, he's in my barracks and we all know each other by sight and usually at least by the last name. But I don't rightly know him."

"Did you see either one of them leave the barracks last night?" Jones asked.

"No Sir," Patton answered truthfully.

"You sure?" DeJarnette asked causing Patton to flick his eyes towards him and to be blinded for his trouble as DeJarnette had stepped away from the window and the sun was shining directly into the room. As quickly as Patton had flicked his eyes towards the commander he flicked them back towards Jones, if he had to talk with someone let it be anyone but DeJarnette. "Am I in trouble sir?" Patton asked of Jones.

Jones shook his head. "Not you John. The jury is still out on Shaw and Dobbs. Last night the museum repository was broken into. Several choice artifacts were stolen. Tim Shaw and Patrick Dobbs are missing; well you can imagine who we think is responsible. We're just not sure if there were other cadets involved, nor can we really be sure of anything until we can find Shaw and Dobbs. It may be they simply took French leave for a day or two."

Suddenly the harsh voice of DeJarnette stated, "You were with them last night weren't you. Come clean boy, it will be better for you in the end."

The jarring voice of DeJarnette made Patton physically jerk. Considering Patton was bigger, stronger and younger, it made little sense that DeJarnette frightened him, but he did. Shaking his head in response to the outburst, Patton focused his attention back on Jones. "I've not seen them since last night," Patton said in a voice that he hoped did not tremble.

Jones smiled at that and said, "We just have to question everyone who might know something." Patton wondered why he was so lucky as to be at the top of the list of those that might know something for it was one honor he truly did not relish. "Now did you see Shaw or Dobbs act strange in any way last night or before last night?"

Patton knew he could keep them there all day and into the night with stories of just how odd Shaw was, but he had been around long enough to know that the quickest way to prolong this was to start jabbering. Besides, DeJarnette would chew him out but good if he admitted that he had suspicions about Shaw but kept them to himself, so discretion was the better part of valor and Patton just shook his head. Let them find some other jackass to worry, he had enough problems.

"Did you see then interact with anyone else regularly?" Doctor Jones pressed. "It could be important."

"Shaw had the bed next to mine," Patton answered telling them what they already knew. "He bothered me the most. Felt at times like I was the only one he did talk to, but Shaw was friendly, in his way, with most everyone. It's a barracks Sir, we all yak to each other."

Jones nodded and again smiled at Patton. The constant smiling bothered Patton, mostly because he didn't see anything to smile about, but he took it to mean that Jones did not suspect him of anything. Which might be wrong but at least it was a pleasant thought for a change.

"Thank you," Doctor Jones said simply.

From the corner came a loud "Dismissed!" the word that Patton was most happy hearing. Patton stood and saluted, turned on his heels and left the room as quickly as he could without actually running. Patton knew that wasn't wise, that it probably made them think he had something to hide, but they could think what they damned well wanted to as long as he wasn't in the room while they cogitated. Once the door was closed and he had walked five feet from it, he could finally breathe again. He used his first good breath to say, "Damn Shaw."

Having an audience with the commandant at least ensured you would miss breakfast. Not having to stare soggy eggs and fatty bacon in the face wasn't all that bad on a day when you were queasy from the getgo. Unfortunately it did not mean you would miss work. Patton joined his mates as they formed up to head to the mounds. After all, there were still Injun things to find.

This day, like all the others was full of dirt and sweat, but unlike most days there wasn't much laughter. Word had gotten around about Shaw and Dobbs, and as Patton had said, it was a barracks and Shaw being Shaw, everyone knew him. Most liked him. The quiet gave the mind a chance to talk to itself and Patton's mind did just that. He had remembered a fire and brimstone sermon where the pastor had railed about how man was meant to earn his bread by the sweat of his brow. The preacher worked himself to a fever pitch, which wasn't all that difficult as he was a hiccup preacher anyway and he had said, "Sweat, work, this God demands. It is the path to Heaven." Patton would like to believe that for barring a major backslide on his part he was sure he had his ticket punched.

For the umpteenth time that day he stopped and wiped the sweat from his face. As his eyes flickered about the site he noticed a comic gum wrapper boldly trying to push its way through the grass with what little power the slight breeze was imparting to it. His eyes drew a direct line from the wrapper to the top of a mound that to his knowledge had not yet been disturbed. He thought he saw some broken earth there, and perhaps the grass was muddy from boot prints, but it was a far distance so he wasn't certain.

"This ain't a picnic, Patton," a voice to the rear of him said loudly, "Use the shovel for diggin' not leanin'."

"Sure Chuck," Patton replied. As he applied himself once again to the task at hand he asked the straw boss Chuck, "Say, what mound is that Chuck?" he used his shovel to point to where he thought he saw the broken earth.

"Damned if I know," Chuck replied honestly, "They all look the same to me." Chuck took a quick look at his clipboard and said "Mound F it says here. You found something?"

"Naw," said Patton, "Just curious."

"You ain't paid to be curious Patton," Chuck stated, "You're paid to use that shovel."

"Got it," Patton replied and he began to apply the shovel.

A GENESIS FOUND

When I was a child I thought as a child, I spake as a child and I acted as a child, but when I became a man I mostly just drank beer and chased women.

The Wisdom of Bart Thompson

Patton was trying to read as he did most nights, always to varying degrees of success. Most of the other guys around him weren't trying to do much of anything except raise enough hell to have fun but not enough to draw the ire of a supervisor. Another lovely night in the barracks.

Some books are page-turners, this one, not so much so. It was titled *Certain Aboriginal Finds on the Black Warrior River Basin*. And if you thought the title was a yawner you should have cracked the cover and tried to read it. It did however have a chapter on Moundville and even a page or two about mound F, though after reading it, Patton couldn't truly say he had learned anything he didn't already know and it was deadly dull. He looked around for something else to read and he spied the *Scientific American* he had lent to Shaw. It was at the head of Shaw's bed between the mattress and the wall.

Patton jumped out of bed and grabbed the *Scientific American*. As he pulled it away from the wall he felt something behind it. He pulled the "it" out, as he was curious, and even if Shaw ever showed up he was unlikely to report a theft.

What "it" was was a folded piece of paper. The front of the paper had the word "Secret" written in a child like scrawl. Shaw's handwriting, Patton guessed, although it was surprising he had spelled it correctly.

Patton unfolded the paper and turned it over. It contained a crudely drawn map of Moundville Park. The Black Warrior was represented by two squiggly lines, the mounds by inverted U's. There was an X in the corner. At the bottom was a legend that showed the wiggly lines were the river, the U's were the mounds and that the X stood for a cave. Leave it to Shaw to have to have a legend for a map that only had three symbols.

All around Patton, men or old boys, depending upon the preferred definition, were lost in their own world, oblivious to all that Patton may have discovered. In one corner of the room some young man had just won a poker pot. "Come to Daddy," he said loudly and raked in his fortune of 47 cents. One of his fellow players asked, "How do you do it?" "Hard work and clean living," came the reply. The other fellow who knew him quiet well questioned, "And you know this how?" This was followed by much laughter, even though the same riposte had been used innumerable times in innumerable card games.

Patton did not hear the joke. Patton did not hear anything. His mind was only focused on the map. DAMN SHAW!

Never be ashamed of talking to yourself, it's probably the only intelligent conversation you will have all day.

The Wisdom of Bart Thompson

There would be little sleep for the CCC boys that night. They had been summoned by the commandant to search the entire park for the missing boys. The cadets had plenty of company, as there were state troopers and sheriffs and deputies already busy scouring the nooks and crannies but more manpower or boy power was needed and the call had gone out. There were even some of the local people there. This was bigger than the Fourth of July parade and in the days before television, any excitement was much sought after.

Patton had marched out with his barracks and they had begun to separate into groups of twos and threes. He found it easy to disengage from all of them and did it by simply hanging back until they left him. They were all off on a lark and were laughing and cursing and being kids. They wouldn't have missed the departure of an elephant.

The map, if one could be so kind as to call it so, was hidden away inside of Patton's shirt pocket and it stayed there until he had put some distance and night between himself and his pals. After the laughter had died and the cursing was barely audible, he pulled it out and focused his flashlight on it. Crude as it was, it made sense to Patton and he began to follow it as best he could, given that it was night and that Shaw had never heard of putting North on a map to show some sort of direction.

The woods were mostly silent, the crickets and frogs having been put off their game by the loudness of the other boys. The creatures had the sensible notion that noise meant danger and not particularly wanting to be eaten, they had simply shut up. Let the predator find them some other way! Until the noise was found to be nonbelligerent they would keep their position to themselves, thank you kindly. They might just be the most intelligent creatures in the forest this night.

Patton stumbled in the dark, said words his mama would not have approved of, then stumbled some more. The flashlight did as much harm as good, it kept him from hitting a tree, but it wasn't much good at discriminating rocks from the rest of the muck on the forest floor and the rocks hurt. He stopped and looked at the map yet again, shone his flashlight first on the map, then on the forest floor then straight ahead. There was a mound. Maybe the mound he was searching for, hard to tell, but give it a try until further sleuthing proved it wrong. Following the general direction away from the mound indicated by the map he found a trail of sorts.

Following the trail, his flashlight would occasionally show a glitter. Stopping, he reached down and felt to see what it was. Whatever it was, it was gunky and yucky, a dark brown that would have been hidden save for the way it reflected light. Patton did not know what it was, but he did know one thing it wasn't and that was blood. Being a person very familiar with the woods he knew it wasn't something you see every day. It made a path of its own, a drop or two every few feet. It lay along the trail he was following, so whatever it was, it maybe part of this puzzle and he kept following it but he sure as hell didn't step on it or stop to feel it again.

Patton lost the trail, backtracked, found it, lost it again, cursed, found it, and cursed some more. He was more lost than he would have ever thought possible. Still he kept on, hoping to find Shaw and Dobbs, hoping for some answer to questions he hadn't even thought of yet. Finally he came to the end of the trail and there, beneath a bluff was a big dark empty place. His flashlight could not yet show if it was a cave but he went there to find out.

A passing boat on the Black Warrior assisted his own flashlight and he saw a crate at the base of the cliff. As he came closer he saw that the crate was intact and stenciled on it were the words "Property of Alabama Museum of Natural History." There was dark stuff all over the crate. He expected it to be the goo he had been following but even with the bad light he could tell it was blood. Some still wet, some dried, but it was blood. "Damnation," he said and started to back away from the crate as if it were a plague carrier. Patton's feet stumbled on something in the darkness, but this time it wasn't a branch nor a rock but a shovel. Picking it up, he ran his light along the length of it. It too had a dark stain and without further investigation, Patton knew what it was: more blood.

A GENESIS FOUND

Casting his flash like swinging a scythe, Patton saw an area just to the left of him where there had been recent digging. Something had been put into the ground there and the shape and size of the area sent a shiver through him. It was absolutely against his better judgment, and he called himself fifteen kinds of stupid as he did it, but something drove him to push that shovel deep into that mass of dirt. The shove resulted in a sickening crunch and a sound that would haunt Patton in his sleep for the rest of his life. Shuddering, Patton went to his knees and began to carefully move the dirt away from the object he sought. The third handful of dirt removed revealed a bloody hand, covered with ticks, half curled as if on its way to a fist that it would never attain.

Cursing Shaw and Dobbs and mankind in general Patton stepped away quickly and then tossed his lunch and supper. Again he was thankful that he had missed breakfast as that would have just been projected from his mouth too and this was one time when more was definitely not better. After a moment, his stomach settled and he was as normal as he was going to be, he returned to the grave. It had to be either Shaw or Dobbs and he needed to know. His money was on Dobbs and after a minute or so of digging he confirmed his bet.

Patrick Dobbs, never handsome, was far from it now. His face was bloody and blue, with a generous portion of dried blood giving it a patina that would remain in Patton's memories forever. A large red, angry gash was just above the temple, the nose was crooked and slightly flattened, and blood was oozing from both the nose and the gash. The right eye had gone amiss and Patton would have lost future meals when he saw that if it had been physically possible.

After seeing the missing eye, Patton lost what little strength remained in his body. He crumbled as much as he lay down. Had anyone observed him they would have seen a very frightened boy and not a young man. A boy not used to violence. A boy that had been raised in a small Southern Baptist church, his father a lay preacher when not fruitlessly pursuing his fortunes as a sharecropper, his mother the piano player. They both taught and practiced nonviolence. Patton had never had a hand laid on him as a child and had never even gotten into a fist fight as a kid, which said a lot considering the part of the country he hailed from. Knowing that violence existed in this world was one thing, and he wasn't stupid, he knew it did exist, it was just that it had never existed before in his world and it was taking a whole damn lot out of him to adjust his world view.

A man adjusts to his world and that was what Patton became in the five minutes he lay on the ground. Not only was he recuperating, he was changing, maybe not for the better. Now a man stood and stared down at the body of Patrick Dobbs, a man that had to find a boy. A boy named Timothy Shaw. Find Shaw and perhaps an explanation, but find Shaw regardless.

Turning towards the bluff, Patton's sweeping flashlight showed an area darker than its surroundings. He bet it was the X marked cave. The map was no longer necessary. What was necessary were legs that obeyed the mind and courage, Patton forced the legs, where the courage had come from he did not know but come it did. First he walked in small steps, then he strode. The cave entrance was there and he walked right into it as if entering his own home.

The cave wasn't large. It was a typical limestone cave that was familiar to any farm boy from the South, a small semi-circle with a few boulders strewn about, some quite large. On one of the large boulders sat Tim Shaw. Patton needn't have worried about the encounter; Shaw was no danger to him. Shaw was shirtless, covered with blood, his head sunk into his chest, looking more dead than alive.

"Jesus Tim," Patton said as he surveyed the scene. "What the hell? What did you do dammit?"

Shaw did not respond; if he even knew that Patton was there it didn't show in his face or body. Patton walked over towards Shaw flashing his light all over Shaw's body. The wrists were awash in blood and had obviously been cut. Patton trod on something that felt hard and menacing. He looked down and saw Shaw's knife, a knife he had seen more times than he could remember being cast to the ground in a game of mumbly peg, covered in blood, glistening, and evil.

"Jesus," Patton said and it was as much a prayer as an exclamation.

Coming even closer to Shaw, his flash showed a body covered in angry red whelps and where there weren't whelps there was just angry red. Shaw was covered in ticks and Patton gave up counting after twenty, but he would have wagered at least fifty. And that was just on the visible part of the body, heaven knows what was covered by the few clothes that did remain on Shaw's frozen form.

Patton's legs began to tremble again and he quickly sat down on a boulder next to Shaw. As he sat down, something bumped his elbow. It was a tarpaulin. Lifting it he saw a lot of Indian artifacts. Many of them were labeled already which meant Shaw and Dobbs had stolen them from storage and not found them in the mounds.

"What in the hell did you do Shaw?" Patton asked knowing he would not get a response. "Kill Dobbs for the booty? If so, why kill yourself? You just crazy Shaw? Where in hell you planning on selling this crap? Where's the damn market for a bunch of old artifacts? You plan on opening up a damn stand in downtown Tuscaloosa?"

Patton's breath was returning, the shock or the horror or both, was beginning to recede. It would be awhile before he would be able to eat rare meat but other than that he was functional. Time to get the police and let them unravel this mess. If they could!

A GENESIS FOUND

Swinging his flash once more about the cave prior to departure, Patton saw a shovel standing straight up, the bottom part sunk enough into the dirt to allow it to stand on its own. It had the same brown yucky goo on it that Patton had noticed as he had followed the trail to the cave. Curious, he went over for a closer examination. The ground below the shovel was covered with the gunk.

Patton started to dig. The first shovelful uncovered a ceremonial disc. While it was similar to a lot of the discs he had seen at the site, even a quick glance told him this was different. There was an oblong face on the disc, and the face had very large oval eyes. Carefully he put it on top of a boulder next to him and then he resumed digging.

The next shovel uncovered bones that were covered with the goo that Patton was seriously starting to hate. Going down to his knees he carefully examined them. They were very white, much whiter than the bones he had uncovered on the site. One of them looked like a hand, but a very odd hand indeed, as the palm seemed to have a hole clear through it. The hole resembled an eye socket. Patton shuttered and had he been a Catholic he would have crossed himself but he was a Southern Baptist so he cursed silently. He knew little enough about bones but he had seen too many skeletal hands to think this was even close to normal.

Carefully picking the bones out of the hole, he laid them on the boulder next to the ceremonial disc. While gently removing them from their grave he noticed even whiter beneath them. Moving dirt about and doing nothing particularly earth shattering he picked up the item that would change his life forever.

It was a small oblong skull. There seemed to be no mouth. There were elongated eye sockets that were much shallower than one would find in a human skull. "Damn," he said, then "Jesus," possibly to make up for the curse. Patton knew it wasn't aborigine and it wasn't white man or black. He knew what it wasn't but he had not a clue as to what it was.

Carefully, even more than carefully he put the skull with the rest of the bones. All of them were covered with that damnable gunk. Patton did not know what to do with them, but letting them be found by that popinjay DeJarnette was out of the question. This was something that might change the world, it might be the single most important archaeological find of all time and DeJarnette was as likely to just burn it to keep from having to do the paperwork as he was to giving it to the academic community for study.

"Why did you bury these things, Shaw?" Patton asked of the dead man, who unsurprisingly did not reply. Patton swung his flashlight to Shaw as if to catch some movement but none was caught. Shaw was far past movement. But the light showed something written on the wall behind Shaw. Patton shined his light on the writing. Someone had scratched the words "I Found the Genesis", into the cave wall. Patton shook his head and said aloud "You found hell."

Patton returned to the pile of bones and the ceremonial disc. His flashlight shined on the skull and the eye sockets glistened with the goo looking as if there were real eyes staring back at him. What should he do with this stuff, if anything? Heaving a sigh, he sat down to think over a decision that he knew, even before he made it and regardless what it was, would haunt him forever.

A GENESIS FOUND

The only thing you need to know about the logical capabilities of most men is that those that are opposed to capital punishment are for abortion and those that are against abortion are for capital punishment.

The Wisdom of Bart Thompson

Patton had always thought he knew right from wrong. There was seldom any gray in the life of a poor young person, of any color, in the Depression era United States. You worked hard, you went to Church, you didn't steal, you treated everyone with respect, even those that had not earned it. Having lived his life according to the Good Book, it was hard to contemplate doing something against authority, but he was contemplating it any way.

Being a good Christian, Patton knew that there was not any possibility that there could be a creature that his very eyes told him had existed. Being a scared boy, he knew that being found with this stuff would complicate his life, and probably not for the better. Being a thoughtful young man, he questioned whether he should even let it be found by the authorities. DeJarnette might relish the find, but he was just as likely to ignore it, burn it, rebury it, or even toss it into the Black Warrior. DeJarnette was a soldier and soldiers took orders. Doctor Jones would likely try to protect this, as it would be the find of the century. But he was one man, and a pretty powerless man at that.

Patton had used his shirt to make a crude but effective carrying bag. In it he had placed the bones and the disc and most importantly of all, the skull. He wished he could have placed all the sins of Shaw and Dobbs into that bag to spare their kinfolk from the shame that would attach to their thievery and ultimately their death. His heart might have been big, but his shirt was not. Shaw and Dobbs were dead and were thieves and their parents would know of it and there wasn't a thing in the world Patton could do to prevent it.

Patton was resolved to hide the lot he had wrapped in his shirt. Let some other poor sod find them. Let him be famous, or cursed, whichever would ultimately happen. Patton had enough troubles for the time being. There was a place he knew, a place that he could find blindfolded if he knew where the hell he was starting from, which he didn't, but he would find it anyway. Slinging his burden over his shoulder, he and his trusty flashlight and the shovel he had swiped from Shaw's cave went out to find that place.

Struggling with his load and struggling even more to be quiet, it surely wouldn't do to have someone find him carrying this stuff. There would be no explanation good enough for the Army. They would have his hide and his parents would too know shame. But being a woodsman, he hid when he needed to and walked when he could. Eventually he found familiar ground and shortly after that he found the place.

Patton passed by several mounds on the way to where he wanted to bury this treasure. It had to be a special place. A very special place.

Patton dug a deep hole, much deeper than was necessary and he put the shirt in the hole. Meticulously he covered the bones and the disc and the skull, then he packed the dirt down, then he stepped on the dirt and jumped on it and packed it some more. Then he grabbed branches and leaves and covered the dirt. Maybe an Injun would know something was buried there, but no white man he had ever met would know. The place would stay in Patton's memory. He knew he could find it again if he wanted to, but he doubted he ever would.

A GENESIS FOUND

Shirtless he stumbled away from the place, tired and sleepy and maybe just a bit in shock. Somewhere in the gloom he tossed the shovel. Let them find it, it would be meaningless to them. His flashlight had finally died and he was accompanied only by the darkness, and the sounds. The crickets and frogs had evidently found no danger from the strange noises they had heard, so they were chirping and croaking once again. It was actually comforting to Patton to hear them. His eyes picked up lights in the distance and his ears heard the language of men. There was even laughter, oh if they only knew. Patton paused to grab some leaves off a tree and to wipe his hands carefully of any of that goo that might be remaining. Then he walked towards the lights. Then he rushed towards the lights. Then he was in the lights and among humanity once more.

Daylight that glorious proof of God's love was piercing the night. It was still more dusk than dawn and as a result Patton was stumbling and falling and trying to catch himself. His hands were bleeding; maybe from the falls to the ground, maybe it was Shaw's blood, he didn't know. He couldn't rightly say that he could feel his hands, or his legs for that matter, but he walked, stumbled, maybe even crawled, towards other humans. There they were, his brain told him and he went that way, stumbled fell, looked for them and didn't see them. Over there then. He walked over there or crawled, he really didn't know which, and no, they weren't there. There? No that's not it. Say this is kinda funny; he had invented a game that only he knew how to play. Let's play hide and let them find me instead. He stopped at the edge of the woods; it was still too dark to see him. He smiled and almost laughed but caught himself, he didn't want to ruin the game and make it easy for them.

In the clearing stood Doctor Jones and that old bastard DeJarnette. They were studying a map, so clearly they were have trouble finding him. Damn he was good at this game. "I know what you want," Patton said mischievously and was about to lay down where they surely couldn't see him. Then in a flash, sanity returned, and Patton struggled into the clearing, walking and crawling alternately. The dawn was breaking behind him; it was a beacon showing the world that one of its own was returning.

For some reason, Patton never thought to shout or to make any noise. The part of his brain that made those decisions just wasn't functioning. Had he, he would have been found instantly, because Doctor Jones, Commandant DeJarnette and a lot of state troopers were no more than fifteen feet from him. It seemed to take forever as he made his way through the tall wet grass but finally he drew the attention of Doctor Jones.

Jones looked up at the nightmare that was John Patton Junior. At first he saw only a bloody apparition. The sun was directly behind Patton and his face was obscured, and Jones was really expecting either Shaw or Dobbs so recognition came slowly, but it did finally come. "John?" he asked as much as stated. Patton took another step towards that friendly voice and then collapsed.

Quicker than a shot Patton was surrounded by men. Still punchy, Patton almost fought against them as they lifted him up from the cold wet ground, but then he saw Doctor Jones through the mists that were setting up shop in his mind.

Patton looked straight at Jones and said. "I know where they are."

A GENESIS FOUND

One interpretation of Quantum Physics is that we make our own reality, this may be so, but how does it explain Tiny Tim? The musician, not the cripple, Levi.

The Wisdom of Bart Thompson

Gardner was staring at his grandfather's novel. Gradually he lowered it and looked at Bart. Bart was right, he knew exactly when to stop reading.

"Finished?" Bart asked.

Gardner ignored this, and only read the last the last paragraph aloud, "I could only ask why God had cursed me and I really prayed for the first time. God, oh God, what does finding this thing here in the womb of a first civilization imply? Ironic, I found God when I found proof that he could not exist." Gardner closed the book and laid it gently on the table. He considered his words carefully then asked, "Why did you want me to read that Bart?"

"Ain't it obvious?" Bart pulled his favorite trick of answering a question with a question.

"Yeah, maybe it is," Gardner replied. "You believe this tripe don't you? You wanna find the skull, that's why you came back."

"It's the first time you've read that, huh?" Bart continued with his questions, "Still sound crazy?"

"You sound crazy," Gardner said in a tired, listless voice, "You sound loonier than Gramps ever did and let me tell you that's some more looney. How can any of you, but especially you Bart, think any of this actually happened? It's the ramblings of a crazy and bitter old man, trying to puff himself into something more than he was for posterity."

Bart smiled that superior smile of his. Gardner knew that one day Bart would smile that smile at the wrong person on the wrong day and he would be forced to eat it along with a few teeth. "It ain't just the book," Bart said, "There's corroborating evidence as the prosecution likes to say. I've got a folder somewheres that have photostats of news clippings from June of 1938, there was a Shaw and Dobbs and they were found dead and were suspected of robbery. The bodies were found just like Grandpa described.

Bart walked over to his desk and amidst the chaos he quickly laid his hands on a folder. He reached into the folder and pulled out a photostat of a newspaper clipping from 1938. He held it up for Gardner to see and said, "See." The headline read "Moundville State Monument: Thieves Found Dead."

Holding the newspaper clipping in his hand Bart said "I almost know this article by heart. It even mentions the mysterious gunk that Grandpa's journal talks about. Shaw and Dobbs had train tickets on them. What the article doesn't explain, what no one can explain, is what made somebody who planned something this precise, go crazy on the day of the big payoff. The article said that an examination of Shaw's body showed he had a rash. That explains everything."

"Could've been murdered by whoever they were gonna sell to," Gardner ventured

"Yeah," Bart replied without conviction, "Cepting none can say why the buyer would leave all that booty. Shaw and Dobbs had swiped 55 pieces and whatever was in the crate. All of it was recovered. What kinda genius kills the thieves then leaves the loot? Don't make sense."

"Still doesn't prove Grandpa's writings are true," argued Gardner, "He was at Moundville in the CCC at the same time this happened. He woulda had to have been deaf dumb and blind not to have known about this ruckus. Maybe he just kinda put it in his book. Sales increase based on body count I've heard. Add in a fake alien and you have a million seller, which is what he wanted and what he got."

"Maybe," Bart said, "But Grandpa is mentioned in the article."

"Show me," Gardner challenged.

Bart pointed to a sentence in the article. Gardner read it and said caustically, "Undisclosed cadet?"

"Then explain this," Bart held up the artifact that Gardner had found, "You're the one that found it. And it was right where Grandpa said it would be."

"Proves nothing," Gardner replied with a rising voice, "It was a popular motif. Could have been left by anyone at anytime. Could be a different artifact all together."

Bart cut in saying "Oh yeah, and Sims won't let you touch remains because he's ethically opposed."

"Why would he carry it back to the mound?" Gardner exploded, "Why not leave it in the cave? It makes no sense unless he made this up. It's ridiculous."

"No way kid," Bart exploded right back, "Grandpa couldn't trust the world to understand the find. He was protecting it for future, more enlightened times. Course those times will never arrive, but it does make sense and you know it kid."

"Do I?" Gardner asked.

"Look," Bart the explainer began, "You've been scared of him your whole life. And not cause of what John the Third told ya, cause he probably told ya a lot of crap. You're scared because you want to believe and sometimes you do, even though you won't admit it to yourself."

"Bart!" Gardner threatened with a hand held high as if to ward of a blow.

"Guys," Bart said and jerked his head towards the door. The silent crew, Ben, Levi and Doctor McClean left without a word or a single glance towards Gardner. Gardner had been so caught up in the moment and the argument with Bart that he had forgotten they were even there. He barely noticed them leaving.

A GENESIS FOUND

"Don't act like you know me Bart," Gardner testily stated, "You haven't been around for a long time, I'm not a kid any longer. I have a brain. I almost have a degree. I can think and it may surprise you, but I actually do."

Bart smiled and said, "You ain't hard to figure Gardner. You may think you're grown but you're just like you were when we were kids playing spaceman. You've got an imagination and you think that if you don't kill it you're gonna wind up like Grandpa. Don't let it blind you to the truth. Use that brain you're so proud of."

"Oh I'm blind-" Gardner said with disgust.

"That's right," Gardner continued, "You think I'd be wasting my time here if I didn't think this was a sure thing. You think we don't have a lead?"

Gardner just glared and kept his words to himself.

"You're supposedly a Christian," Bart continued, "You know about creation. There was water, God made dirt, then made Adam out of the dirt. Same goes for the Jewish creation story and the Muslim. Most of the major religions have some variation on this. Course that's not surprising as most of them came from the same place, but the folks in the Americas had their creation stories too. You've heard of the Creek Indian story? It's the same except there was a mound first. Same goes for the Seminole, the Chickasaw, all the major tribes they think they came from this place. Most have a story about a flood; the Choctaw even have one about a mound of Babel."

"So?" challenged Gardner.

"History becomes myth," Bart said. "Shared myths are evidence of a common heritage. An unconscious memory of the past." Bart reached into his folder and moved things about until he found what he wanted. Gardner wouldn't have been surprised if Bart pulled a rabbit out of that particular folder. But it was a magazine article that Bart came out with and handed it over.

A photo in the article showed a fossilized hand with an indentation in the palm. The caption below the photo asked, "Has the Hand of God been found?"

"That fossil was found in Mesopotamia," Bart stated. "I think your archaeology textbooks call that the cradle of civilization or some such."

Gardner looked at the article and then looked at the magazine name at the top of the page. The article had been published in *Celestial Connections*. Gardner looked up at Bart and asked, "Couldn't afford a *Weekly World News*?"

Bart ignored the jibe. "Check the date," Bart said.

Gardner did. May 2001.

"You think Grandpa used that to make up his story?" Bart asked his voice dripping with sarcasm. "What if he was right? What if this thing he found is some sorta missing link between the world's cultures. A metaphorical Adam."

Gardner shook his head. "He said we came from aliens; DNA and evolution say otherwise."

"Just cause it's alien don't mean it's from another planet," Bart defended his grandfather. "All civilizations began with a leap-usually a spiritual one. What if this was the messenger? One the rest of us forgot a long time ago."

"Doesn't track," Gardner said with a shaking head that was also spinning just a little. "Religious iconography didn't appear here until a century after the mounds were built. We have no proof that they were built because of their religious beliefs."

"And no proof they weren't," Bart responded. "Religion replaces the soul. Did they not think they had one? Isn't there as much likelihood that they came here for a spiritual revitalization? A revitalization that may have been brought about by this messenger? The spiritual convictions of the past may have become the soulless dogma of the future."

110

"If that's true," Gardner responded, "Finding one relic, even one that might be an alien, wouldn't prove it or disprove it. So what good would finding it do?"

"I don't know," Bart said truthfully or at least as close to the truth as anything he would ever say. "But I want to, and so do you. What if Grandpa was wrong, what if this is proof God does exist? It would make us rethink everything they shoved down our throats at Sunday school wouldn't it?"

"Is that what you really want?" demanded Gardner. "Is that what this is about? Your vendetta against the closed minds that ain't gonna open regardless of what you do or show or prove?"

"What this is about is proving Grandpa wasn't a liar," Bart responded.

"Then what the hell you want me for?" Gardner demanded.

Bart ignored the question and instead asked one of his own "Help us look for it?"

"When?" responded Gardner, "Tomorrow?"

"Now," Bart replied, "Why else you think we wanted you out here tonight? It sure as hell wasn't your sunny disposition."

"No way," Gardner nearly shouted, "Besides, what do I know? I can't help you anyway."

"You know where you found this," Bart said holding up the relic Gardner had found.

"No!" Gardner said, "It's a crime, it's wrong, it's pointless."

"You really believe it's pointless Gardner?" Bart questioned, "I mean what you really believe?"

Gardner couldn't face Bart. There wasn't a good answer to that question. What did he believe? He really did not know what he believed. He hadn't since he had read that damned book.

"We gotta go Gardner," Bart insisted, "Trooper makes his rounds at two and seven. If you don't come now, come out to the mounds sometimes between then. We'll be out there proving the impossible."

111

Bart stood up, put his precious folder back on his desk; perhaps in the same spot he had pulled it from, the desk was too cluttered to be sure. Without a word, he headed towards the door of the camper. Just as he arrived at the door and opened it, he turned to face Gardner and locked his eyes onto Gardner's eyes, "Gardner," Bart said, "Regardless of what you do, this stays here."

Gardner nodded.

Bart nodded back, gave a quick smile, then proceeded out of the door, closing it more gently than usual. Gardner watched the door close. It drifted back and softly clicked. The fact that he didn't slam the door was some credit to Bart given the heated conversation the two had either just finished or given up on. Gardner wasn't sure which was true.

There it was then. Bart was looking for the skull and perhaps for his grandfather's good name. Bart, of all people, wanted to disprove six thousand years of science. Bart the storyteller wanted to do that. Quite a leap for Bart's personality Gardner thought.

Go or stay? You're a Patton; defend your grandfather's honor. You're a Patton; let it lay. Gramps was crazy, try to disprove that, and even if you find something you'll be labeled the same as he. Want to be crazy? Go or stay?

There are times when a man needs a good stiff drink. This was one of those times, so Gardner was chugging a glass of water. He wasn't a teetotaler; it was just all he could find.

The irritating whine of his cell phone announced a new voice mail. With a shrug he played it. It was barely audible and not much more intelligible. "Gardner, I need to tell- if you could- I can't really- message so-" then it petered out altogether. Gardner recognized Kelsey's voice of course but did not have a clue as to her meaning.

Pressing the call back button did no good as the phone merely beeped indignantly and let him know right away that there was "No Service" available. Gardner ever the optimist went to two different locations in the trailer with the same results for his efforts. There would be no discussion with Kelsey this night and Gardner wasn't really disappointed. There was enough turmoil in his life with Bart this night and Kelsey's problem, whatever it was, could wait its own good time.

Gardner's eyes lighted on the magic folder that Bart had been burrowing through all night. A bold red label proclaimed it to be "Grandpa Research", Gardner wondered how long it had taken Bart to come up with that title. Well, truth be told, Bart wasn't the most eloquent man the South had bred.

Picking the precious folder up, Gardner sat down and began to peruse the contents. There was some truth in what Bart said about him not being that hard to read. Heaven help him, he was curious. Bart had probably left the folder just so that Gardner would find it and read it. And he did.

There were innumerable photostats of newspaper clippings. Most of them were about his grandpa; a few were about the "Moundville Incident", as it was known in the Thirties. The old man might have been crazy but he must have made for good copy in his day. Maybe he made for good copy because he was crazy.

There was an article from the Huntsville Times that was really a wire service story courtesy of the Associated Press. That made sense. Huntsville was way up in North Alabama and Gardner doubted anyone much cared or for that matter even knew about Moundville at the time the article was published (May 1953). The headline boldly proclaimed "Archaeologist's Work Breathes New Life into Search for Mounds Origin." There was a photo of John Patton Junior, now going on mid-thirties, stocky (read chubby) with two good eyes (though his right eye was showing a bit of the problem that would result in his eventually covering it with an eye patch- another casualty of the war) and a smile that was more posed than genuine.

A GENESIS FOUND

Gardner scanned the article and learned exactly zero over what he already knew. The next article was from 1965 and stated "New University Requirements Costs Jobs For Uncredentialed Professors." Grandpa had of course been one of those. He had always been too busy searching and teaching to finish his PhD. Since he could no longer be a professor without it, he had either quit or been asked to resign, truth depending upon who you happened to ask on a given day.

An article from 1973 proclaimed "Patton's Claims Dismissed By Experts-Book Still Tops Bestseller List." Had it ever. That damn book had made Gardner's life miserable from the time he could first remember. Everyone was always confusing Patton's book with that other book by Von Däniken. How in the hell they could was beyond Gardner. One was an Alabama redneck, but at least with a modicum of archaeology training and experience. The other was a former hotel manager from Switzerland that had never taken the first archaeology course. Besides there were no ancient astronauts in Patton's book. Just a story about an incident that may or may not have happened. Patton had never claimed the skull was from Mars, just that it wasn't of American Indian origin.

The last article that Gardner read proclaimed, "Hearing to Determine if Patton's Research was Falsified." Some hearing. A bunch of jealous archaeologists that couldn't get anyone to read their papers had held court and decided there was no truth in Patton's works. They had let it be known that they did not take kindly to some bumpkin achieving fame that was rightfully theirs. Things are always the same. Maybe the media changes, but not human emotions. Those that had a vested interest in the status quo never took kindly to anyone upsetting their apple cart and less kindly still if the person doing so was now considered an outsider.

There were a lot of photos in the folder. Some professionally done but most just snapshots. Heaven knows where Bart picked those up. It was a progression of John Patton Junior's life, from child in Sunday "Go to Meeting" clothes up to an old man smiling at the camera, with one good eye and a patch over the other holding a grandchild on his knee. The grandchild was shy and had hid his face into his grandfather's shoulder to prevent the camera from catching his face. The grandchild was holding an ET doll. Gardner didn't need to read the handwritten notice below the Polaroid that stated his grandfather was holding him.

Time stopped, the way it does when something unseen and unthought about comes barging back into your life. Gardner stared at the photo, his mind a blank. There it was then. He was a Patton. Didn't matter in the least if he didn't want to be. Didn't matter if he found it unbearable at best. It defined him. No matter what a man wants to be, he is what he is.

Gardner carefully laid the folder back on the mess that was Bart's table. He hoped he had put it back where it belonged. He sure as hell didn't want to give Bart the satisfaction of knowing he had read it. Then he sighed and walked back to the bed and sat down. Knowing better but hoping he could get through to Kelsey anyway, he pressed the recall button on his phone. "No Service." It was his mantra for this day.

Gardner pulled out his copy of the *War of the Worlds* from his back pocket and looked at the cover. He was more than a little surprised that Levi, too, had been reading the book. They may be distantly related, or at least distantly related in law, but Gardner knew he would never claim any kinship. It was bad enough to have to own up about Bart.

A GENESIS FOUND

The thesis of many poets is that life is beautiful. I don't know what evidence they could possibly be basing that on.

The Wisdom of Bart Thompson

An irritating whine awoke Gardner from an awful sleep. He had been chasing aliens and had been chased in turn by same. It was a lot more fun when it was a video game and not quite as real as a dream can be. What was that whine? An alarm? He half opened his eyes and half opened his mind. For a moment, he did not know where he was or even why he was. But the moment slipped away. Then he knew he was in an awful sweatbox and that he was too damn close to Bart for comfort.

The whine again. This time he easily identified it as his damn phone. No service Hell! No service when you need it was more like it. Just like a damn electron, never could find it when you were looking for it, only when you weren't.

Somehow a message from Kelsey had flown through the air, bounced off God knows what things and wound up hitting his phone at the worst possible time. Silently cursing but considering making it official by actually speaking the curse words out loud, he rubbed his red, puffy sleep deprived eyes. "Ouch," he said aloud and it was to his credit that he hadn't screamed for he had torn a contact in his right eye, and not only could he not see in that eye, the damn thing was lodged in it like a damn boulder.

Gardner jumped off the bed sending the phone and his book in opposite directions. He let them fly; he had other problems. Walking swiftly to the mirror over the kitchen stove he looked into his eye to see what damage the blasted contact had cause. It was significant.

"Great," he said almost inaudibly. Carefully he removed the torn contact. His eye was scratched and irritated and he was officially blind in one eye. Just give him a patch and he would be Grandpa. With disgust he cast the torn contact into the trashcan. Covering his one good eye he looked at himself in the mirror, all that he could see was a blur, which was really an improvement over the way he really looked. Well, Kelsey would bring his glasses or a new set of contacts tomorrow and he would endure until then. He had endured much worse, including Bart's company of late.

Moving away from the mirror to return to the bed, he saw that damn *Celestial Connections* article with his good eye. Looking down on it the indentation in the hand was alternately blurring and crystal clear depending upon whichever eye he happened to be using. Beside that article was a photo from the Thirties that was part of a news clipping Bart had picked up somewhere. The photo showed the cave where the body of Shaw had been found. Bringing the photo up to his good eye as closely as possible Gardner looked at the cave and more importantly something that was written on the cave. There it was the words that had been written by his grandfather in both his journal and his book "I Found the Genesis."

Gardner stared at the picture. Things were shaping in his mind. Things he did not want to shape, but shaping still. He looked at the photo of himself with his ET toy sitting with his grandfather. He was a Patton, the same as the old man, and the old man deserved to have his name cleared, if what he had said was true. In a flash, Gardner had made up his mind.

Gardner walked out of the camper. The small crew was looking up at him from the comfort, if that word really applied, of their rickety lawn chairs. All eyes were on him. Was he in?

"I think I know where it is," Gardner announced.

117

Bart smiled and nodded his head. The small crew left with Gardner in tow, heading for where it was or at least where it was thought to be.

Is global warming real? If it wasn't before it is now considering all of the hot air that's being spouted on the subject.

The Wisdom of Bart Thompson

Their flash lights danced like fireflies drifting slowly and lightly on the ground, illuminating little but enough to avoid the large trees. Bart, as always, was in the lead. Gardner was walking almost beside him but just a little to the rear, which was odd to his mind, because he thought he was the one that knew where to look. They didn't speak, maybe the sound of a voice would have broken the spell or maybe they were just all talked out. Regardless, it was a silent five that approached Mound F.

Each of them carried a shovel, except for Ben. Ben had shouldered the camera and it was already going. What he hoped to gather in this Stygian darkness only he knew but it was going, as if recording something of significance, even if recording poorly.

Just before they arrived at Mound F, Bart checked the clock on his phone. Evidently they were between the rounds of the state troopers because Bart said, "All right, we should be all alone."

They marched up to the mound and played their flashlight on it to give them a sight of what could be the most momentous discovery in the world of archaeology, and possibly the world as we know it. The grass was mostly dead, brown, which was odd, as the first frost had not yet hit. "Mound seems to be sucked dry," Bart said to Gardner, "The only one too."

A GENESIS FOUND

"Then let's do it," Gardner replied with more determination than he had ever felt before. Gardner walked to the backside of the mound, reached down and grabbed the tarp covering the mound and with zeal tossed it off. There was a red flag stuck in the soil, and with more satisfaction than he would have admitted to he said "Here!" The thrill of finding the skull was unlikely to be any more satisfying than the thrill of digging in the precise location Sims had forbade.

The others watched as Gardner attacked the mound with a vengeance. His first shovel full came up with bones, he ran his flash over them, they were standard American Indian, or at least non-alien bones, so he set them aside and went for another shovel full. Three more shovel full of dirt revealed nothing but the red soil of Moundville. Undeterred he shoveled some more. The next time he put the shovel to its task there was a dull thud. Gardner carefully worked his shovel underneath the object. Gently, ever so gently he raised it.

Levi came over with a brush and began to clear away the dirt from the shovel. Not a word was spoken. Gardner heard the whirr of the camera. Nothing like having a federal crime filmed for posterity. Gardner's eyes flicked from person to person. Doctor McClean relaxed, almost smiling. Ben worked the camera; it was impossible to see his face. Bart watched Levi intensely. Bart not talking. It must be important.

Gardner heard a tearing sound and his eyes automatically went back to Levi. Levi was cutting and tearing something. It sounded like canvas. Gardner did not try to reason as to what it was. This moment was not for wondering, this was action time.

Levi gasped and stumbled stepping away from the mound. Ben came in tight with the camera, the camera light focused directly on the shovel. Gardner saw it for the first time. His eyes grew wide. "Jesus Christ!" Doctor McClean exclaimed and it took Gardner a moment to understand what he had said because

119

Gardner wasn't concentrating on McClean and McClean was speaking northern and Gardner was listening Southern.

There it was, whatever it was. It sure looked like a skull. A skull covered in gunk, wrapped in a dirty fabric that might have been the remnants of a shirt. It had large shallow eye sockets. It was elongated. The parts not covered by goo were extremely white. It was damn spooky. Surrounding it was what looked like the pieces from a ceremonial rattle snake disc. A Genesis Found?

"Jesus Christ!" McClean said again, just a bit louder and this time Gardner understood him perfectly, his ear having adjusted to the northern tongue.

"Whaddya think Doc?" Bart asked.

Sliding on vinyl gloves, Doctor McClean did not speak at first. Cautiously he bent down and picked up the skull. He put his flashlight on it and he turned it from side to side, rotating it and looking at every crevice. What wasn't covered by the gunk was porcelain white and the light reflected off it as if it were glass. Excitement practically screamed in his motions but the Doctor said in a very calm voice "I think we have something of importance. Perhaps something of paramount importance."

Glancing sideways at McClean Gardner thought this is a very eager Doctor indeed. Most scientists would be more circumspect, more considered in their response. Hell, Gardner was only a junior and he had doubts. "I'm not so sure," Gardner said. Everyone turned to him including the camera. The look they gave him was akin to a spider's to a fly.

"It might be deformed," Gardner continued, "There's nothing that proves this is anything but an American Indian skull. An odd one for sure, but it'll take a DNA test to prove one way or another."

Bart laughed as he often did before he was condescending, "They got you good didn't they," he stated. "You can't even see it when it's in front of your eyes."

To show his lack of concern for Bart's comment, Gardner used those eyes to shrug.

"Now that's strange," McClean said aloud and Bart immediately transferred his attention to him, as did the all-important camera.

"What's strange?" Bart asked.

"There looks like a discrepancy in the ages of different areas of the skull," McClean replied. "Areas covered by this brown gel seem younger. It must be some kind of a preserving agent."

"Huh," Bart said, "Any idea what it is?"

McClean turned his head in an "I don't know" gesture and stated, "It's not a natural substance, at least I don't think it is. I've never seen anything like it in my field studies. What if this gel was applied on purpose to preserve the skull?"

"Maybe," Bart reasoned, nodding his head, and yes the camera caught every statement and every movement. "Can you make a guess at its age?" Bart asked McClean.

Doctor McClean stood up and looked right into the camera and said, "It's certainly ancient. The discrepancy in the different areas makes it hard to determine age with any great accuracy but from the exposed areas, I would guess it was much older than 800 years."

Gardner couldn't contain himself and blurted out, "You mean it was here before the mounds. That it preceded the Native Americans?"

Doctor McClean nodded.

"But how can you tell-?"

"Just look at the condition of the exposed areas," McClean replied. "From experience I can roughly estimate the age based on the coloration of the object. We will have to do tests to show its true age, of course. But still, Bart, this is phenomenal. This is really phenomenal."

A GENESIS FOUND

Gardner tried to imagine himself as a learned expert in a field of study. Was this how he would act if he thought he had found something earth shattering? Would he call on field experience and professional standing to answer what should be a simple question? How could you tell if this was really a phenomenon? The truth is you can't not without the proper tests. Even with his own limited experience in the field Gardner knew you couldn't make any pronouncements about age due to the coloration of an object. There were just too many variables that affected color. The right professional answer was, "Don't know yet, let's wait for the tests." This was bunk.

Gardner glanced around at the rest of the crew. Levi was staring off into space, making no attempt to follow this conversation. Ben had the camera going but Gardner noticed he was yawning. Ben noticed Gardner looking and quickly put a hand to his mouth to cover the yawn. McClean was as cool as an iceberg resting in the Arctic Ocean. Only Bart seemed excited.

"One thing that is troubling me," Doctor McClean said, voice as calm as a Methodist preacher's, "If this was buried that long ago, how could Shaw and Dobbs have stumbled onto it while looting? Could they?"

"Just cause it died a long time ago," Bart replied, "Don't mean it was buried a long time ago."

Gardner didn't say anything. His eyes were busy roaming and looking at all the incongruities that were evident even to a guy blind in one eye like himself. For instance, there was a bottle of weed killer poking its head up from the bag Bart had carried to the site. What the hell was that for? Poisoning the grass to cover their tracks? That's why the damn grass is dead on this mound and none of the others. But it was an excavation? Why would they need to cover their tracks? Trial holes were everywhere. Seemed like a wasteful luxury, if they were just digging to find something. It'd only be necessary—if they wanted to plant something.

"Better git," came the excited voice of Levi and it seemed to bring everyone out of the past and into the present. "I see lights coming and coming fast."

"That's not the state troopers," Bart complained, "Too early. Probably the university police. Gardner do you know anything about this? Do they patrol at random?"

Gardner answered a different question. A question that only he had posed. "It's a hoax," he said flatly and none to brightly.

"What?" demanded Bart.

"Everything's too easy," Gardner continued. "This is all staged and rehearsed. Hell, just how dumb do you think I am?"

Bart's eyes blazed for just a second, and then he smiled. He glanced at the approaching lights.

"Damn it, Gardner," Bart went back to the subject of the approaching lights, "Did you know about this? Do the cops know what we're doing?"

"Dammit yourself, Bart," Gardner answered. "It's all a hoax." Gardner's tone had gone from flat to strident. His face was turning red, though none could see it in the dark.

"Damn it," Bart said taking a step towards Gardner, "Answer me. Did you tell the cops anything?"

"No, dammit Bart, I want an answer-"

At the next moment Gardner felt a sharp object in his side. The ever stoic Levi was standing beside him in a none to friendly manner. Levi had a hawk bill knife opened and the blade was just barely pushing against Gardner.

"What about the cop?" Levi asked. Now he starts talking!

Gardner flicked his eyes to Bart and said, "I didn't tell anyone. It's probably a random patrol. There is a dig going on. Cops probably don't won't any kids loitering and getting into mischief."

"Then let's get outta sight," Bart commanded and proceeded to lead the way out of sight.

Hurriedly Bart threw the tarp back in place, leaving the one of a kind skull where it was. Ben killed the light on the camera and cut it off. They all hurried back up the hill, trusting to the dark and chance, as none would dare turn on a flashlight. Levi kept the knife to close to Gardner for Gardner's liking but then, even if it had been in Birmingham it would still be too close for Gardner's liking.

The police car rolled to a stop, spotlight flashing hither and yon like they were trying to snag a deer. Unsurprisingly he did not find anything amiss. The only crooks they were going to catch with their engine roaring and their spotlight glaring were those both deaf and blind and while some crooks may be one or the other, not many were both. After a few moments, the car pulled away and the cops continued to do cop things in cop ways, and people wonder why criminals are so rarely caught.

The group had made the trees and had all flopped down on the cold, dewy grass. All were panting, some from exertion but more from fear. As the car pulled away, Bart relaxed visibly, as did Gardner. Gardner was less concerned that he would be harmed from menace than from accident.

As they all began to stand up from their belly flops, Ben began to fiddle with the camera once more but Bart stopped him by saying, "Leave the camera off for a spell, Ben." Turing to McClean, Bart stated, "All right, Doc, you and me are on clean up duty. We wait half an hour then go down and place the skull further along on the excavation. They're finding it tomorrow." Bart smiled yet again.

McClean nodded, he knew his part.

Bart turned to Ben and Levi and spoke "You guys are going camping, like we talked about. Ben you get the files and the gear, but stay clear of that cop car. And remember, as soon as you hear it on the news; we gotta have a camera outside after the lock down."

Ben shouldered the camera and then left at a trot for the camper. The camera didn't seem to slow him down much.

"Levi," Bart commanded, "Get Gardner's cell."

Levi gave Gardner a slight nudge with his knife. Gardner needed no more encouragement and gladly handed over his phone. Levi could have had his pants if he wanted them. Levi passed the phone to Bart. At least he didn't grin as he did so.

"Sorry kid," Bart apologized to Gardner "But you've got to hang tight for a few days."

"Why do it Bart?" Gardner asked genuinely curious. "Why go to all this trouble to convince me? Why bother with all the crap about Grandpa and his legacy?"

"You still got the Patton name kid," Bart replied. "That would have made even bigger headlines." With a nod to Levi, Bart walked away. After a few feet Bart stopped and said "Oh and Gardner, thanks for the advice. The next time I try to take someone down a primrose path I'll make it harder."

Levi pushed Gardner before he could make a reply. Looked like they were going campin'.

Bart was shaking his head as he walked up to McClean and he said "You were right Doc. Didn't fool him for a second."

"I've done this before," McClean replied. "Too easy and they don't buy it. Gotta make them work for it."

"Well," Bart considered, "At least he's out of the way."

Bart examined the phone he had taken from Gardner. There was an unanswered message. It was none of his business so naturally he checked it. He popped the message onto the screen; it stated "I'm Pregnant." Needless to say it was from Kelsey. Bart considered things for a moment then pressed reply.

Don't be afraid to contradict yourself. It keeps the other guy guessing.

The Wisdom of Bart Thompson

Kelsey was tossing, then turning, then tossing some more. She knew she should sleep and not just for herself. But knowing and doing are not always, and maybe not even often, the same. A buzz, her phone, she leaped from her sleepless bed and grabbed the phone off the dresser.

Her phone said she had a "New Text Message from Gardner." Praying, she opened the message. It was very short and not at all sweet. "Need time. I'm sorry."

Kelsey looked up from the phone and happened to see her reflection in the mirror. Thank God it was dim in the bedroom; otherwise she would have liked what she saw even less. What she saw was a tired, scared young woman, with red eyes that had tears welling in them.

She went back to bed. Sleep did not come.

I believe in the theory of relativity. If you've got enough relatives to sponge off of you don't have to work for a living.

The Wisdom of Bart Thompson

Being shoved left, then right, then left, then straight, then... ad infinitum, Gardner made his way through the woods with Levi and his knife ever too close for comfort. Levi seemed to detest the spoken work and instead of saying "Go right," he just shoved. Gardner took it for way too long and finally said "You don't have to shove, Levi, I ain't deaf, just stupid. Say left or right, I'll catch on to what you want."

Levi shoved him even harder. Gardner kept his mouth shut after that. He wasn't that stupid. Nobody was.

Gardner caught sight of Ben coming through the woods, intersecting them at an angle. Levi put his flashlight into the general area where they heard Ben and it provided enough light for Gardner to see that Ben was carrying two backpacks with two sleeping bags draped over his shoulder. Gardner would have given pretty good odds for anyone willing to bet who was going to be sleeping on the ground this night.

They met, either by design or by chance, at the Black Warrior River. The river seemed to be running fast, but it was hard to tell in the dark, and maybe it was just Gardner imagining the worst. Gardner hoped they were going with the current. Again he guessed who would have to do the paddling if they were headed upstream and he didn't like the answer.

Ben got to the river first and was looking up stream and then down to make sure they had no company. There were often barges on the river, and any time of the day seemed okay for them to do whatever it was they did. But luck was with them and against Gardner as there wasn't anything in sight. "Looks clear," Ben stated, "We'd better get going. We want to be in the cave by dawn."

"You got the gun?" Levi asked and the question made Gardner's blood run cold.

Ben gave Gardner a quick look then replied, "We're not gonna need it, dude."

Levi grabbed a backpack from Ben. Ben started to hand the other backpack to Gardner saying, "I think I got everything," but Levi reached out and snatched the backpack before the transfer. He put the flashlight in his mouth and shined it into the bag and reached in with his free hand and moved things about. Eventually satisfied he handed it to Gardner.

For the hell of it, Gardner imitated Levi and rummaged through the bag. Levi, if he had a sense of humor, which is very much in doubt, did not laugh. Ben smiled though then tossed Gardner the sleeping bag. "Make yourself useful if possible and carry my bag."

Walking swiftly over to a bunch of bushes, Ben grabbed an inflatable raft and brought it out to the river. "Least nobody swiped it," he said philosophically. Ben put the raft into the river and steadied it with his strong hands. "Get in," he said and nodded towards Gardner. Before Gardner could move, Levi jumped in front of him and made his way to the front of the raft. Turning, Levi stared at Gardner and Gardner caught the drift, he started to step into the raft. Gardner stumbled as he put his foot up on the raft, hitting the ground he was out of sight of both Ben and Levi for a moment and his hand came in contact with a rock. He took advantage of the incident by palming the rock and wrapping it tight in his hand so it couldn't be seen. Gardner didn't know, even in that instant, whether it was an accident or planned. He would always tell it as planned of course, especially as he aged. Memory, like a wine, often finds full fruit in age.

Gardner straightened out and stepped slowly into the raft. Levi eyed him coolly, Ben eyed him with a smile but they both eyed him and they wanted him to know they were going to keep an eye on him as much as possible. To hell with them, Gardner wanted to say but didn't. As he settled into the raft, he glanced over at the river. Staring back at him was a haggard, drawn face. Too tired to care, he lay back in the raft and looked at the clear bright night above him. Millions of stars, with trillions of life forms and none more alone than he. The thought was stupid, and maudlin, even if true, and he knew he would one day look back and wonder how he could have been so dopey. But he was, and a man felt what he felt even if it was trite.

Levi sat behind Gardner, paddle at the ready. Gardner had guessed wrong about the paddle. A little logic would have told him they wouldn't let him have a paddle, it being the proverbial blunt instrument, but logic was hard to come tonight. Ben pushed off with his paddle then walked gingerly by Gardner to the front of the raft. They were off to wherever and Gardner could only think of the stars, stop it stupid, keep alert, look for an opening, he kept telling himself, over and over and he kept forgetting what he had just said. But the internal badgering seemed to be having an effect as he was finally getting the fog out of his mind, for what good it would do him

They reached mid river in a few minutes, they seemed to be going upstream but not cross stream as they were staying within twenty feet or so of the near bank. Gardner casually let his hand over the side of the boat to feel the current. It didn't seem too fast, although not being an expert it was damnably hard to say for sure. Casually he looked ahead then back over his shoulder. Both of his captors were intent on their task and weren't paying the least attention to him, and that suited Gardner fine.

In one sudden movement, Gardner leaped towards Levi and brought the rock in his hand crashing down on Levi's head. The movement rocked the raft and the lunge resulted in both of the boys tumbling into the river. The very small Gardner landed first and was hit by the very large Levi as he tumbled.

"Whoa!" shouted Ben, "What's going on?"

Gardner and Levi were grappling in the water. Gardner desperately wanted Levi to go away and as he came to the surface he shouted, "Let go. Dammit!" at least he tried to say that, but the amount of water in his mouth lent a lot of doubt to the actual words that came out of his mouth. Levi seemed to hold more tightly rather than less so Gardner grabbed the sleeping bag strap that was wrapped about Levi's shoulder and started to dive using it to pull Levi further under. The strap broke and Gardner found himself, either through luck or determination, free and he made the most of the freedom by immediately swimming away from Levi and towards the nearest bank.

Ben's flashlight was dancing across the water and found Gardner. Ben shouted, "This doesn't have to get violent." Gardner kept on swimming wishing he was the grandson of Mark Spitz rather than John Patton Junior. But swimming wasn't a strong suit for Gardner and even though he was swimming for his life he was giving up a foot of reach on Levi and Levi knew how to swim too. He caught Gardner within ten feet of the bank.

Levi seemed angry for some reason and the first thing he did when he caught Gardner was dunk him. Then he dunked Gardner again just as Gardner's head cleared the water and he was trying to grab a breath. Not more than a gallon of water went down Gardner's gullet. As he arose again he shouted at the top of his lungs "Okay!" but it must not have been because Levi dunked him again. As he arose once more, Levi punched Gardner hard across the left eye. Satisfied, or tired of the fun, Levi pulled Gardner through the water and back to the boat.

Somehow, the two of them managed to crawl back on the raft. Levi's face had more expression on it than Gardner had ever seen or ever cared to see. Gardner only had to endure the expression for a moment, as Levi was too tired to do anything but flop in the boat. Gardner did the same, they both stretched out as best they could and breathed that most wonderful of God's creation, pure country air.

It took Gardner a few moments to even recognize his surroundings much less to think on them. But finally his breath evened and his pulse quieted and as he looked around he could see even less than before. It took his dulled brain a minute to figure out the problem; then it hit him. His remaining contact had joined the dead at the bottom of the Black Warrior River. Totally fuzzy sights presented themselves to his so called vision and he said "Wonderful," but it wasn't really wonderful at all.

"Through?" asked Ben.

"Fraid so," Gardner replied. The raft resumed its journey and Gardner was more than content to let it take him to whatever undiscovered country awaited. The rest of the ride was filled with both grumblings and a total concentration of attention on Gardner from Levi. Gardner would have gladly told Levi not to bother watching as he barely had the strength to breathe much less to fight King Kong again. But he kept his silence, as he needed the breath for other purposes.

The journey continued in silence with nothing but the slight sound of the paddles dipping into the mighty Black Warrior making any noise. After about another fifteen minutes Ben announced, "That's the spot." The raft came up next to a slight incline on the bank and Ben jumped out and pulled the raft up out of the water. Ben and Levi both kept their eyes on Gardner as he shakily exited the raft. Ben steadied the raft as Levi exited, then he easily picked up the raft and took it to a clump of bushes and pushed it behind them. The paddles were placed on the raft and a few loose bushes that had evidently been secured earlier were used to cover both raft and paddles. It wasn't much of a hiding place but then there weren't likely to be a whole lotta people it had to be hid from.

As they turned to leave Levi said, "Wait a damn minute." He pulled a first aid kit from his backpack and proceeded to doctor himself. A loud "Ouch," followed the application of the alcohol, and then he put a bandage on his head. Levi gave Gardner the evil eye several times during his ministrations and Gardner, being too tired to care, evil eyed him back.

"Let's fix this bird," Levi said to Ben and motioned towards Gardner.

A GENESIS FOUND

Ben nodded and reached into the other backpack and pulled out a rope about three feet long. Gardner smiled and held out his hands. In a moment they were tied.

"Feel better?" Ben asked Levi.

Levi didn't answer; he just shoved Gardner ahead of him. Ben pulled out his Blackberry and turned on the GPS app, and after a moment of studying it stated "Straight on." The trio began their quest.

Gardner walked and caught up with Ben and walked beside him. Gardner found it safer, for at least, Ben didn't push him when he wanted to change directions but just called out. Ben kept his eyes on the GPS. It beeped. They changed directions based on the beep. The dawn was just breaking and yet it was already a hot and muggy day in Southwest Alabama. Gardner's luck was holding true.

At seemingly random intervals the GPS beeped and they all changed directions with Ben leading. The damned unit seemed to beep too often for Gardner's liking. He wasn't familiar with that GPS unit or any other but it seemed to him that whatever criteria it was using to determine when to turn was inefficient at best. A straight path would have been much preferred by this tired young man-boy. His body ached in ways he hadn't known was even possible. He had a monster headache. He couldn't see. Wherever they were going he wanted to get there as fast as possible and at least sit down. Beep.

Fifteen more minutes of either walking or meandering was followed by very welcome words from Ben: "There it is," and they had finally reached their destination. There it was, a cave, and Gardner was pretty sure it was the cave his grandfather had visited in 1938. Gardner's brain was too tired to see the irony, if it was ironic.

Entering the cave was equivalent to entering a garbage dump. There was just enough light from Ben's flashlight and the slowly

A GENESIS FOUND

rising sun to show beer cans, food wrappers, plastic bags and other items that are rarely discussed in polite company. The cave walls had a lot of lewd phrases and even lewder comments about some of the local talent. There were an inordinate number of lewd comments referred to Sally and some of the things she liked to do. Gardner, tired as he was, still knew he really should look her up when he got out of this mess.

One wall still had the phrase "I Found the Genesis," scratched into it. How it had survived all of the local scribes over the years was an open question. It may have been luck but Gardner suspected it was more likely due to the fact it had a biblical term and even a drunk redneck was still unlikely to want to test fate by being sacrilegious. The phrase had acted like a loadstone and was now surrounded by other phrases of like ilk including "I Believe" and "The Truth is in Moundville."

Regardless of the mess and the new age sayings it was still a place where a man could find a place to sit and rest his over weary bones. Gardner did just that, finding what looked like a comfortable boulder; he went to it and sat down, nearly sighing as he did.

Levi took the opportunity to be kind to Gardner in his own way, "There's ya a bed," he said, punching Gardner on the shoulder and pointing to a much abused, dirty, and stained with who knows what sleeping bag in the far recess of the cave. The sleeping bag was likely a Noah's ark for the insect community of the Black Warrior River as it looked like it contained two of each kind of insect in existence and not just one. Still Gardner almost took Levi up on his invitation as the more tired he became the less ugly the bag looked. But there was his pride (or stubbornness if Kelsey was right about him) and he did not want to give Levi any satisfaction, especially any satisfaction that came at the expense of his dignity so Gardner instead went to the opposite wall, kicked out some McDonald's bags and sat down.

Levi smiled one of his rare but irritating smiles, then sat down himself, carefully placing his backpack on the floor. In a second he had the backpack open and had pulled out a rope that looked to be about ten feet long. Quickly Levi tied the rope about his waist then he looped the other end of the rope around the rope on Gardner's wrist. "When you move," Levi told Gardner, "I'll know it. Meaning don't."

Gardner was too tired for any discussion or to even glare at Levi, instead he just lay his back against the cave wall, closed his eyes, and thought of Kelsey.

Even as tired as he was, fate would not yet allow him to sleep, for there was a sharp "BRRR" that indicated some jackass's phone was notifying someone of a text message. For a second, Gardner thought it to be his, then smiled at his own lack of lucidity. Half opening one eye, he saw that Ben was the jackass. Ben was looking down at his phone, "It's from Bart," Ben told Levi. "Everything's set, all we gotta do is wait."

Levi nodded, and half looked up from his cave setting up duties. Levi had hauled out a small portable television that had obviously been hidden somewhere in the cave, these guys might be low life criminals but they did seem to be able to plan effectively. Pulling the antenna out, Levi turned the TV on and began to look for reception. After having turned the dial a couple of times he announced with some disappointment, "All I get is public."

"Need anything for your head?" Ben asked Levi.

"I'm fine," Levi replied.

"Might have something in my backpack," Ben insisted.

"I'm fine," Levi said again stressing the word fine to let Ben know the subject was closed.

"You the man," Ben replied. Ben took his sleeping bag off his shoulder and began to search for the least dirty spot in the cave and the truth is there weren't a lot of choice spots. Eventually he selected a spot that met some criteria that wasn't obvious to any outsider and began to kick out trash and pick up small stones and fling them about. Eventually the area was clean or at least clean enough for Ben and he lay his sleeping bag down. With a groan, Ben lay down and turned his face to the wall and away from Levi and Gardner.

Levi was still testing the television to no great satisfaction. Finally he left it on a channel that at least had a picture. "Damn public TV," Levi growled. Some sort of documentary was being shown that told the much-told tale of the panic caused by the *War of the Worlds* radio broadcast of the Thirties. Orson Welles authoritative voice was booming loudly from the TV and bouncing off the cave walls, making him even more eerie than he had been during his heyday on radio. "I am extremely surprised," Welles said, "That a story which has become familiar to children should have had such an immediate and profound impact."

Gardner laughed.

It's more easy to trust a guy if you've got something on him than to trust him if you don't.

The Wisdom of Bart Thompson

Eight a.m. resulted in a caravan of students streaming to Moundville. Students that had slept the night before and that were young and reasonably happy and that laughed and cajoled and kidded and were students making discrete glances at other students. If you have ever been to college, or even high school, you get the picture. A bunch of rowdy kids facing another dig day at Moundville, with one old professor, trying to maintain some semblance of sanity and attempting to put rigor into the chaos about him, and as usual, having imperfect success. Doctor

Sims was that old professor and this day would age him much more than most.

Bart and Doctor McClean, not at all rowdy, stood at the top of the hill, underneath the canopy of the tent and looked out upon the arrival with some degree of anticipation. They began to ready their equipment and their talk was low and could only be heard by themselves

Kelsey was walking with the students towards the dig site when she spied Bart. Immediately, she left her own group and made a beeline for him.

Kelsey got within five feet of Bart with a look of determination on her face and she demanded, "Where's Gardner?"

"I don't know," Bart said which may have been factual but not necessarily truthful. "He sent me a message," Bart continued, "Tellin' me he was leaving for a few days," a statement that was neither factual nor truthful. Bart looked directly into Kelsey's blue eyes, smirked and asked, "Didn't he tell you?"

"Leaving?" Kelsey demanded, "Where did he go?"

"No idea," Bart answered. "I reckon he got a ride to somewhere. I figured he knew what he was doing and I also figured it wasn't none of my business."

"You seem real concerned," Kelsey stated.

"Am I my cousin's keeper?" Bart questioned with a misquote from the Bible. "If he wanted me to know he would have told me. See how that works? Hell, I figured he would tell you more than he would tell me."

"Well, he didn't," Kelsey responded, her blue eyes resting uneasily on Bart. "And I don't know why."

"Well are y'all having problems?" Bart asked innocently.

Kelsey's eyes shot daggers at Bart. Without another word, she turned and walked quickly down the hill and away from her less than favorite soon to be cousin in law. Her hand had unconsciously gone to her stomach and she was holding it on her way down the hill. Bart just smiled.

Doctor Sims was standing on the mound lecturing the students in the loud voice that he had perfected from many a long and strident discussion; Kelsey heard Doctor Sims giving his daily lecture on digging etiquette even when she was ten feet away. Always one to repeat himself, the Doctor was telling the students the umpteenth time about the law and about showing respect to any bones found. After attempting to put the fear of God into them, Doctor Sims began to discuss the salient features of this day's excavation. "Truthfully," Sims said, "From this point on, the digging goes from boring to really boring, but it will be rewarding too."

Holding a clear plastic bag containing arrowheads, Sims continued his professorial pitch to a bunch of polite but disinterested students, "Nothing beats the thrill of finding something," Sims said with a smile as broad as the adjoining river, "Particularly when the things you've found have been lost for hundreds of years. Finding things like artifacts are great but we also find other things like how these people thought and how they lived. Out here we're connected to them, to the people that lived here, through the things they left us."

Taking a dramatic pause, Sims looked out over the students hoping to see rapt attention, instead he saw mostly students checking their cell phones, never mind, he had something to say and he would say it. "We're connected not just through things, like the artifacts, but through the dust they trod on as we trod on it, through their sweat and labor as we sweat and labor, through the research we do. It's important not to forget that. You are part of the search. The search that has been with humanity as long as there has been a humanity. Be proud of yourself, I know I'm proud of you."

Sims smiled broadly once more and stepped down from the mound to let the children have at it. Sims walked over to where Bart and McClean were standing and nodded to them and to the camera, hoping that they had filmed his inspirational speech and hoping more it would be featured in the documentary. At the mound, the day's work had begun and shovels were busy doing their excavating and students were busy discussing just about everything except Doctor Sims inspirational speech. As the buckets filled they were being transferred to the sifter and the sifter was doing its best to make sure no one left the site with even an inch of clean skin.

"Hell of a speech, Doc," Bart said to Sims and might have meant it but with Bart it was impossible to tell truth from lie.

Sims nodded his thanks to Bart and replied, "Sorry if this gets a bit monotonous. I don't know how you are going to make an exciting movie out of a bunch of kids getting dirty. But I guess we can't always be looking for the Ark of the Covenant or the Holy Grail."

Bart just smiled at that remark. Reaching down he grabbed the camera from the ground where he had placed it earlier and shouldered it. With a click it was running and he approached the mound and started to film what was going to be anything but boring. Kelsey was shaking the dirt as usual, looking as fresh as could be expected and not yet, covered totally in dirt. She and Bart saw each other at the same time. Bart turned his camera to film her and she immediately turned away. That gave Bart something else to smile about.

Turning back to the mound, Bart noticed that one of the students was just about in the right spot to make this day memorable. Quickly he walked towards the area, positioning himself so that the camera would film the actual discovery. This was the money shot and sales were just about to double.

A GENESIS FOUND

Sean was the lucky student, if this was truly luck, which was destined to have his fifteen minutes of fame. His shovel had hit something hard, and he had abruptly stopped digging. As he was leaning down to see what he had discovered, he almost drew back, "Damn," he said softly. As if by telepathy the other students stopped their digging and looked over to Sean, seeing him standing there looking down with maybe awe but certainly surprise, they all scrambled over to see for themselves what had been discovered. Bart was filming and jostling the students to ensure he was filming what he wanted to film, and Doctor Sims, seeing the crowd, sighed and walked over to get the kids back to work. He knew that there was trouble when Bart said to him as he passed, "And you said this was going to be boring."

Sims passed a glance at Bart and raised a quizzical eyebrow but he continued to walk through the students and asked as he walked "What's going on?"

Sean just pointed at the skull and the skeleton he had uncovered with his shovel. His face was proof enough as to what was going on. Everyone at the site was eyeing the skull and it was eyeing them all back, as if imparting to them the secrets of a long lost civilization. The skull sent more than one shiver down a spine.

"It's just remains," Sims tried to say calmly and curtly but it came out at a higher pitch than he would have liked. "Sean please just cover it with dirt and flag it, then work around it please."

Sims turned to leave, hoping to see Sean begin to cover the skull and skeleton, but he was disappointed, though not surprised. No one else was leaving; all eyes were focused on the skull.

"Did you hear me Sean?" Sims demanded.

"I heard you," Sean replied. His shovel still did not move, nor did the rest of the class budge from their spot. Doctor Sims may have authority over them in many ways, but none of them really believed that they had just uncovered human remains. They had seen too many bones in the past few days to not recognize something truly out of the ordinary.

"Come on," Sims said forcefully trying to regain control, without luck, "What are you all gawking at? You've seen remains before."

"They may be remains," Sean replied, "But I've not seen their like before. If they are remains, what are they the remains of?"

The other students began to talk in hushed, almost reverent tones. Kelsey came walking up, drawn by the odd actions of the group. Seeing what the others saw, her eyes widened and she almost took a step back.

"Ridiculous," Sims argued, "They're obviously human, a bit misshapen perhaps but human." The last part of his sentence had trailed off and was forced from his lungs without any conviction. Sims was truly looking at the remains and he knew better than the rest that they weren't human, not misshapen, not the result of an injury, not human.

Taking a second to study the bones, Sims made up his mind to try a different tack with the students, "Before this gets out of hand, I think it's best if we keep this quiet. You all know the legends told of this place, we don't want people thinking-" Sims stopped in mid-speech. All around the mound cell phones were taking pictures and mini-movies. Texting had already begun and photos were being sent out to parts unknown. Sims sighed heavily; he knew this was going to be one lousy and long day.

Several students were engaged in telephone conversations with obvious excitement in their voice. Kelsey pulled out her phone and was about to call Gardner when she saw Bart staring at her. He smiled and shrugged his shoulders, which meant not a whole lot to Kelsey at the time. Kelsey stared back for a moment then closed her phone. If she spoke to Gardner, she did not want Bart to be eavesdropping. There was something amiss here and Kelsey needed to know that Gardner was not a part of it. She didn't want to give Bart any ammunition to pin something on Gardner; besides, there were other things to discuss and that was definitely not for Bart's ears.

Bart sidled up to Doctor Sims and asked, "Still want to bury them Doc?"

"I don't know," Sims replied distractedly.

Doctor McClean walked up to the duo and said, "I may have a suggestion," and he had a beneficent smile that was even bigger than the adjoining river.

You can't excommunicate a guy that ain't been communicated to start with.

The Wisdom of Bart Thompson

Levi didn't have much of a picture on his portable TV but it was picking up sound and the particular sound being made was music to his ears and hopefully money in his pocket. Levi was sweating heavily and the red spots that had just covered a small portion of his body a couple of hours earlier had now spread to ever spot available both visible and not visible. Never one for correct posture, Levi was slouching even worse than usual and staring at the screen as if entranced by the non-existent picture. Ben was busy ignoring Levi and gathering his stuff. There were things to do and he was just the guy to do them. Ben was smiling as he listened to the TV. Gardner was damned well listening and every word made him that much sicker, fearing for his ultimate fate at having been caught in this mad scheme.

"The lock down occurred just after one p.m.," a female voice was saying amidst scrambled frequency noise. "At that time the field class was moved to the site's David L. DeJarnette Research Facility, where they are reportedly still being held." After a very long and what the anchor surely hoped was a dramatic pause she continued, "The remains are also being held there. Though there are concerns as to why such extreme measures are being taken, representatives for both the Alabama Museum of Natural History and the University of Alabama stated that these precautions are largely due to the concern that the quote 'irregular remains might be widely misidentified' unquote. Officials have assured the media and the public that every effort will be taken to ensure the remains are both properly identified and treated with respect."

Ben glanced to the TV and said, "Hey Gardner, there it is. How do you think it looks on camera?"

Gardner looked at the fuzzy screen. Even if the picture had been perfect he wouldn't have been able to see it without contacts or glasses. "Real as life I'm sure," Gardner answered, "Least as real as you guys could make it."

"Pretty good considering the quality of the broadcast," Ben said with a note of satisfaction. "And would you look at that."

Gardner didn't bother to look as his eyes were still hurting from the abuse they had suffered of late and because he did not have contacts and because not looking would irritate his captors and that was a good enough reason in itself. But he did listen. A large crowd had gathered at the Moundville research center. There were signs saying "Long Live John Patton" and "Tell the Truth" and the lunatic fringe was already claiming there was a cover up.

The female newscaster was very good at stating what was obviously on the camera, which was good for Gardner considering his plight, but he did wonder just how many other blind people were trying to watch this particular broadcast. "Now with this activity at the center," the newscaster stated in that flat tone that was so prevalent and so irritating, "the concern of the University seems well founded. As you can see a large crowd has formed." Gardner couldn't see but he took her at her word.

142

Ben glanced at Levi and said, "I think it's gonna be even bigger than any of us thought in our wildest dreams." Ben grabbed his backpack from the floor and looked over at Levi before departing. Levi was hitting the canteen pretty hard, chugging it like it was the first beer he had right after hauling hay all day.

"You guys are gonna be out of water soon," Ben noted, "There's a spring just behind this cave. Might want to go fill up. And here's my Blackberry— it'll help you find one, or this place, you get lost. We'll be in touch when we can."

If Levi heard he made no response to show it. He started to investigate the Blackberry and was engrossed in some fascinating electronic function. "Where are those games you always play?" he asked of Ben.

"I wouldn't be playing with that thing Levi," Ben advised and admonished, "It's already pretty drained. It won't do you any good even if a signal can reach it in here if it ain't got any power."

Ben opened his backpack and as he did his shirt rode up above higher than usual on his arm. There was an angry red spot that he noticed and he smiled when he saw it. It looked a lot like the rash that was covering Levi. Gardner noticed the spot at about the same time that Ben noticed. For a heartbeat, Gardner's eyes and Ben's eyes locked on each other's, both knowing the other had seen the spot, but Ben just looked away from Gardner without acknowledging the incident. Ben ignored the rash too and simply pulled his shirt back down to cover it.

Ben removed some folders from his backpack and tossed them to Levi. A picture of a young John Patton Junior fell from one of the folders in flight and landed on the cave floor. "Better leave these with you," Ben said then he turned and walked to the cave entrance. Just before exiting he said, "Look for me on the news. Don't like to brag, but I've been told I photograph well."

Ben's departure was ignored by Levi and even before the other's shadow had cleared the entrance of the cave Levi had found the games and was making the Blackberry beep to high heaven. Levi had also turned off the TV set, much to the chagrin of Gardner.

"Didn't you hear him?" Gardner asked.

Levi glanced over to Gardner, gave him his patented stone face, then returned to his games.

"Look," Gardner said, "You're sick and I'm blind. We're gonna need that thing."

Levi grudgingly turned off the Blackberry. "I ain't sick," he announced, then put the canteen to his lips and began to chug again. Gardner thought he could see Levi's eyes becoming red but he knew that it could just have easily been his imagination, as he couldn't see for spit.

"Can't you turn the TV back on?" questioned Gardner, "Or at least a radio if you've got one."

Levi shook his head. "The noise bothers me," he stated. "I'll give you something to pass the time," Levi said generously, and he opened his backpack and rummaged around for a second. His hand brought out a magazine and he tossed it to Gardner. "Great," thought Gardner, "give a blind man a magazine to read." Only Levi could think that was being kind.

"I can't see," Gardner reminded Levi.

"Tough," Levi responded as he leaned down to pick up the picture of John Patton Junior from the cave floor.

"Did he really think he found something?" Levi asked Gardner.

"I don't know," Gardner replied truthfully. "I think he was just nuttier than a fruitcake."

Levi glanced from the picture to Gardner and said, without irony, "You kinda look like him."

"Nobody ever noticed before," Gardner's reply came back resplendent in sarcasm.

Levi, not the most observant of fellows even when well, did not seem to take issue with Gardner's reply, his stoic face remained so and he just began to leaf through the folder, looking for something or just looking only he knew.

"Can I ask you something," Gardner asked and before Levi could give or deny permission he asked, "What the hell are we doing here? I mean y'all already pulled it off. I can't stop it. You're committing a felony for no good reason."

Levi didn't look up from the folder and continued to leaf through it, looking doubtless for the hidden secrets of the universe.

Gardner was not one to be put off easily and even without a response from Levi he continued to press for information, "Y'all can't get away with it. I don't care how good you made it, that thing won't pass any real tests by real scientists. Even if you guys manage to forge some tests, it still won't be taken seriously without independent verification. I mean, hell, some people ain't gonna believe even if you had found the real thing."

Levi continued his non-response but he evidently wanted to change the subject as he tossed the folder to the cave floor and asked, "You got anything I can look at in your backpack? I'm about tired of aliens."

"I'll see," Gardner replied. He opened his back and foraged. It resulted in his discovery of his copy of *Buried in the Mounds.* Well, it wasn't strictly about aliens. He removed the photograph of Kelsey that he had used as a bookmark and tossed it to Levi. Levi caught it and without thanks, and a little bit of a glare, began to look through it.

Gardner held up the photograph of Kelsey, getting it as close to his blind eyes as he could. Her delicate features were there, either visible or from memory and they brought a wistful smile to Gardner's face and another moment he would remember as being totally maudlin. Carefully, treating it as if it were fine china, he lay it down on the magazine that Levi had tossed him. The magazine was a *Scientific American,* and that was a surprise considering Levi had been the one carrying it. The cover had a drawing of a fetus, and the article was about abortion. But Gardner would only remember that drawing in years to come and would not know what article it referred to, nor would he care.

Like a bolt of lightning, he suddenly knew with certainty why Kelsey had been sick and moody, why she threw up, why she cried at the drop of a hat, why she would scream about small things that had never bothered her before. Gardner also knew he was fourteen kinds of stupid at not figuring it out before, but then he was a young man and young men do not often think on these things. But he was now and he knew he was going to be a father. "Oh God," he said in a quiet voice. That's why Kelsey had wanted to get in touch with him.

I don't mind somebody thinking that I'm going to hell; I do mind them trying to help me get there.

The Wisdom of Bart Thompson

Things were happening inside the research center. There were cops of every flavor available in Alabama inside doing whatever cops do in an emergency. There were several administrators holding emergency meetings and several doctors holding emergency meetings. There was also a lot of inactivity in the center as a bunch of tired students sat in a waiting room that was too small by half waiting for someone to tell them what to do and while waiting discussing just how famous they might become from this incident.

Bart was there also and his camera was rolling to beat all hollow. There were lots of great shots and each of them was sending dollar signs through his brain. Just as Bart caught a shot of the pretty blonde closing her tired eyes, someone pulled on his shirt. Looking quickly at the puller, it turned out to be Doctor McClean. They smiled at each other but said nothing. Bart followed McClean into a room that contained Doctor Sims and a very unique skeleton.

McClean walked over to stand beside the table with Doctor Sims and Bart filmed it all, particularly the skeleton. It looked real spooky laying there all by its lonesome on the metallic table. Another money shot.

Given that this might be the only table in the world, in the only room in the world that might contain an alien skeleton, you might have thought it would be a special room. Well, it wasn't. It was an old and slightly barren research room, with not enough equipment and a wobbly table that had one leg too short. Everything in the room was well beyond its useful life, economic or otherwise. Thus are world-class discoveries stored by our great learning institutions.

Doctor McClean was carefully examining the remains with white latex gloves. The camera was filming the good doctor as he performed his magic. Doctor McClean would look at the skeleton, and then talk straight into the camera as he told some mumbo-jumbo about some trait or feature that showed this skeleton could not be human. He was smiling of course and he was the picture of the scholarly, kindly, doctor of archaeology that he actually was. The camera couldn't show the deviousness in his heart, but other than that, it did a remarkable job.

Doctor Sims was talking on the phone to someone much higher on the food chain than he was, if all the sirs that were flying out of his mouth meant anything besides good manners. "Yes sir," Sims said yet again, "Getting them home okay is my top priority. But until we get an escort here I am obviously hesitant to let them go. There's not only the press to consider, sir, there's a bunch of crazies out there." A pause, he listened, then again the sirs. "But the staff will be ambushed by the press as well as the students. While the remaining staff might keep their opinions to themselves, who knows what the kids will say." Another pause, "I understand but we've already kept them so long that it's gonna raise questions anyway and I am worried about that crowd."

Sims grimaced and shook his head at something that was evidently disquieting. "All right, yes sir," he said and to his credit he did not scowl when he said the word sir, "We'll keep working. I'll be ready to make a statement in a few hours."

Sims replaced the phone on its hook and took a moment to compose himself, and then he began to complain as most humans do when under stress "Jesus Christ! It's just getting worse. We have to get some kind of proof that this thing is human. And we gotta get it fast."

"What if you can't?" Bart asked from behind his camera.

Sims ignored the question and turned to Doctor McClean. "What do you have Doctor?" Sims asked.

Doctor McClean replied in his most stentorious and professorial voice, "It's so unique. I don't really want to make a guess without radio carbon dating, but several centuries old at least. Its disfigurement, if that's what it is, looks natural wouldn't you say."

"Sure," Sims concurred, "But that doesn't mean it's from outer space."

"I agree," McClean said, "I can't see anything that would classify this as solely extraterrestrial, not that I would know something that was solely extraterrestrial if I did see it of course. But the gelatin, the small bone length and irregular density, the dolichocephaly, the shallow obits, the abnormalities, those things do not discredit that possibility either."

"Well," said an exasperated Sims, "How do we discredit it? What do we need to prove that, beyond a doubt this is human and not a spaceman?"

"Honestly," McClean answered closing his trap, "Forensics. DNA analysis. Genetic fingerprinting. Those are the only tools we have that can remove all doubt."

Sims smiled grimly and stated the obvious, "Well we can't do that here."

"I know," McClean replied.

"Damn," Sims said. "This has already gotten out of hand. If we can't prove it to be human in 48 hours, 72 tops, it'll be John Patton Junior all over again. This place will be swarming with crazies. They'll do more harm in a day than we can fix in ten years."

"Then we're going to have to move to another facility," Doctor McClean stated. He was smiling knowingly.

"You have one in mind?" questioned Doctor Sims.

"I have everything I need, and more, at my lab in Berkeley," Doctor McClean assured Sims.

"Berkeley," Sims responded, "That's too far."

McClean replied in a soothing voice, "If I make arrangements immediately, I can get to work as soon as tomorrow morning. There aren't a lot of places with the kind of facilities and the kind of equipment we need. It would take us longer than a day just to arrange for one closer, not to mention getting access to whatever special equipment we might need that they do not have."

Sims brain mulled that over for a moment, then he said, "Tomorrow morning. You sure?"

McClean nodded and stared straight into Sims eyes

Just then Bart's phone rang. Bart pulled it out and looked at the message screen, "Ben Calling."

"Excuse me," Bart said, "I have to take this." He lay down his camera and walked outside to chat up his fellow conspirator.

A GENESIS FOUND

Life ain't particularly cruel, just indifferent.

The Wisdom of Bart Thompson

Look up the definition of controlled chaos, if there is such a dictionary, and you would find a description of what was going on at the research center. Some students, sleepier than hell, were trying to doze amidst the constant jabbering of other students, and the blare of the TV and the cops and administrators and who knows what else, roaming the hallways. The local TV station was going 24-7 with the news of the reported finding. And the news changed very little during the whole time the crisis was on, as is true of most news on most 24-7 news channels. About every ten minutes a picture of an alien, the gray kind with big dark oval eyes, was shown and there were even some mounds drawn about the alien. What the artist had lacked in ability, he had more than made up for in speed.

Kelsey was not one of the sleepy students, her mood was more anxious than relaxed. She shook her head tiredly and her brownish blonde long hair went to and fro and would have excited Gardner no end had he been there. Picking up her phone, she looked at it for a second, staring down at Gardner's name, evidently making a decision which she made by closing the phone and not pushing the speed dial for Gardner.

Bart came out of the laboratory with a phone up to his ear. He did not seem to notice Kelsey but she noticed him alright. Kelsey watched him as he walked down the hallway.

Bart entered an empty room and figured he was far enough away from prying ears to speak freely and he did, "You back?" he asked. "All right, yeah, get everything you can outside. Interview the hell out of the ones willing to talk. The more the better. I want everybody's opinion on this thing. The nuttier the better goes without saying. Yeah, don't stay at a motel under your own name tonight, pay cash, yeah, the cops may be on the lookout. I may be

150

on my way to Berkeley. Yeah I know, like falling off a log. Let's hope it stays that way. Make sure you make duplicates of everything. Don't want to lose any of this."

Bart hanged up the phone and put a self-satisfied grin on his face. As he started to leave the room he glanced out of the window in the door and saw Kelsey staring at him. He nodded and turned his grin into a smile and opened the door slowly and walked out.

"Was that Gardner?" Kelsey asked.

"I don't think it's any of your business who that was," Bart replied coolly.

"Just tell me Bart," insisted Kelsey.

"No!" Bart answered which was no answer at all because Kelsey didn't know if he meant it wasn't Gardner or he meant he wasn't going to tell her.

"Is this some kind of a prank?" Kelsey asked, "Is Gardner involved?"

"What?" Bart almost screamed.

"You're not being totally honest with me," said Kelsey, "And this is too big a coincidence."

"Hold on," Bart said, "What are you talking about?"

"I have to know why he's not here, Bart," Kelsey said.

"Okay," Bart replied, "you're right Kels. I ain't been fully honest with you. Gardner did tell me why he left. He told me you were expecting and that he was scared. That he felt guilty but needed time." Bart was intensely studying Kelsey's face as he spoke as if looking for some signal that told him she believed or did not believe his story.

"Gardner said he kind of expected it," Bart continued, "That's why he wanted to come out to the park to spend some time with us in the first place. Now I'm sorry if that hurts you, I didn't want to have to tell you. But you don't need to be thinking I had anything to do with Gardner taking off, it was just between you and him."

"He told you." Kelsey stated the sentence and it was not a question. Her face was frozen solid; she did well to even talk.

Bart nodded.

"How could he?" Kelsey asked no one really but herself, "How could he leave me when I need him the most?"

Bart turned his face from Kelsey. She had been staring a bit too intensely at him and he surely hoped she could not see his soul for it was blacker than the blackest lungs of a smoker. Bart felt badly about lying to Kelsey, not for the lie itself, for he was rather proud that he could spin a yarn so quickly, but he was sad that it had done some damage to Kelsey herself. But he had a job to do and do it he would, regardless of the cost in either money or hardships to himself and others. He just hoped the yarn was good enough to fool Kelsey and to make her leave him the hell alone.

"Well," Bart said with his back to Kelsey, "Don't get too mad at him. He is just a kid."

If our ultimate fate is to be dust in the wind at least we can hope to irritate some jerk's eyes.

The Wisdom of Bart Thompson

Gardner was trying to read without much success. Blind in one eye, couldn't see out of the other and still trying to read. Boredom does that to a person and it may be a bit surprising, but it is true, there is more boredom than any other emotion, including fear, when one is being held captive. But even boredom can't be overcome when you really can't see a dang thing and Gardner gave it up as a lost cause, tossing the magazine to the cave floor.

A GENESIS FOUND

The other occupant of the cave and Gardner's captor was snoring and snoring loudly. Gardner wouldn't have minded except his life may well depend on Levi and Levi was not one to engender confidence. Levi had seen better days. Whatever the rash was, there was a ton of it, getting redder and angrier by the minute. Sweat was dripping from him as if he were running a marathon instead of sleeping. Every few seconds his body jerked as if someone was pushing him as he had pushed Gardner. Maybe Levi was railing against windmills in his dreams. At any rate, like a good Christian, Gardner was worried about Levi, but not in a Christian way. Levi was dangerous enough when he had whatever sense God had bestowed on him and Gardner really didn't want to face him sick and half out of his mind.

As Levi's body jerked for the umpteenth time the Blackberry slipped from his grasp and it dropped noisily to the cave floor. Gardner eyed it greedily and began to slowly ease towards it, hoping to get a hold of it without Levi awakening. Gardner's legs trembled as he came up out of his prone position. He had been sitting quite a spell and his body was rebelling against him. At about the third step his legs gave way for a second and Gardner stumbled, pulling the hell out of the rope attached to Levi. The rope jerked, but Levi's body had jerked so much that it did not register to his brain that anything was amiss. He kept on snoring and Gardner kept on praying.

Gardner forced himself to stand steady for a second to let his legs grow accustomed to standing once more. His eyes flicked around the room during that instance and he saw the photograph of Kelsey. That brought a tight smile to his lips and more grit to accomplish the task at hand. Just before he made the next step his eyes went to the wall that still had the childish scrawl announcing "I Found the Genesis." He hoped it was appropriate for the situation, for if Genesis meant hope then that was exactly what the

Blackberry represented. Of course it had meant madness in the Thirties but Gardner didn't dwell on that.

Taking a deep breath, Gardner continued his seemingly endless journey to the Blackberry. Still praying as he went, though Gardner would be the first to admit he wasn't particularly religious, he approached ever closer to his goal and possible salvation. Just as Gardner was about to swoop down and claim his prize the damn Blackberry buzzed louder than Gabriel's horn. Levi's body jerked even worse than it had been jerking and he opened both eyes and stared, perhaps a little dumb founded at Gardner.

Slowly Gardner could see the wheels turning in Levi's mind and then Levi went into action. Levi stooped down and picked up the Blackberry and looked at the screen, which told him, "Low Battery." Levi was either a slow reader or his brain had quit functioning properly as he stared at that message for at least five seconds before he turned his gaze to Gardner. Gardner wouldn't have minded if Levi had never turned his attention to him.

Gardner considered saying nothing but felt that even in a stupor Levi was better placated than not so he lied, "I was just getting the folder." Gardner smiled for all he was worth and continued, "I can't read the small words in that blasted magazine without my contacts. I was hoping I could at least look at some of the drawings my Grandpa made. It would help to pass the time."

With a snarl, Levi picked up the folder and tossed it to Gardner. Then he pulled out his knife and said menacingly, "I told you not to move."

Gardner broadened his smile and nodded. "Won't again," he assured Levi with another lie. Gardner went back to his cleared space and sat down and made a big production out of going through the folder. Well, at least he did have something to look at for a change. His grandpa may have been crazy but at least he wrote in large legible letters and he made pretty drawings.

A GENESIS FOUND

Refusing all eye contact, Gardner leafed through the journal. Levi wanted eye contact, he was staring intently at Gardner, and you could almost see his mind working its way up to some sort of a decision. Levi said something but Gardner did not hear what it was nor did he want to hear, he had no desire for any conversation so he ignored Levi and tried to lose himself in the journal. It wasn't hard, his grandfather could tell a story, and Gardner could follow it even with no contacts.

On the third page of the journal, Gardner found the phrase, "I Found the Genesis," It was written in a bold handwriting style and not the childish scrawl that was written on the wall. His grandfather had written, "This is the truth I've ran from most of my life," in the following passage. A chill went down Gardner's spine. He believed that statement. He thought his grandfather was crazy but he was still an obsessed man. Gardner didn't know if the craziness was the cause or the effect of the obsession. But his grandfather had truly believed the nonsense he spewed. It wasn't much of an excuse, even a common excuse for a crazy person. That's how they become crazy after all, believing in something with all their heart and soul regardless of evidence, but it was so.

There was a sequence of numbers at the top of the page. The sequence was 133036^-8737453. What in hell did that mean? Maybe Gardner was the one that was crazy for looking for some meaning in the meaningless meanderings of a crazy man. But then, when John Patton Junior had written this he hadn't necessarily been crazy.

As he went through the journal Gardner found several more entries with numbers at the top of the page. On one particular page John Patton Junior had drawn the Rattlesnake Disc and on the top of that page he had put the sequence -8747457. Odd. It was part of the same sequence. Gardner looked at the hand drawn map of Moundville at the front of the journal, the ^ symbol had

155

characterized north on that page; maybe this was some sort of a code.

The Blackberry buzzed again, but even though it was the very same sound, the difference to Gardner's ears was the difference between thunder overhead and thunder in Birmingham. Still the sound brought him from the depths of the journal to his immediate surroundings.

Gardner saw that Levi was sleeping the sleep of the wicked again, his body sweating and sometimes shaking. Levi was clutching the knife in his right hand tightly as if it was the last dollar he would see until payday. Temptation crept into Gardner yet again, or stupidity, and it was waging a war against safety. The Blackberry meant communication with the outside world; it meant Kelsey. Gardner tried not to think what the knife meant.

Half rising, staying in a squat, Gardner began to creep towards the Blackberry and heaven help him towards Levi and that blasted knife. Finally, after a few thousand years, he reached his destination. Gardner picked up the Blackberry very gently from off the cave floor where Levi had once again dropped it and slowly backed away from Levi. Gardner spent a couple of life times backing away, slow, gentle, letting no motion translate from him to Levi through the rope that connected the two like some diabolical umbilical cord. Any movement was slight and the rope did not jerk. In Levi's condition probably only a jerk or a stick of dynamite going off would awake him.

Finally making his way to the cleared of section of his corner, Gardner sat down, put the Blackberry in the folder to hide it and breathed his first good breath in what seemed an eternity. Now he began to make hay with his prize. The first thing he did was try to text message Kelsey. He was not surprised but he was disappointed that it returned the infamous "No Signal" message. Talk about your dead zones, Gardner decided if he ever had money to invest he would build a blasted telephone tower in Moundville regardless of the payback.

Just as Gardner was about to turn the Blackberry off and on hoping to stir up some unknown connection to work, he saw the menu selection "GPS Navigator." Could the numbers be latitude and longitude? Gardner entered the coordinates from the third page of his grandfather's journal and until he ran out of room on the screen and pressed "map it." The navigator retuned a location, "Eocene, El Salvador." Well it had been a stupid idea anyway.

Still it was odd that the numbers roughly coordinated to a latitude and longitude. Gardner rechecked the numbers. Yeah he had entered them in correctly. Pulling an ink pen from his backpack, Gardner began to see if he could break the code, if there was one. Under what he took to be the latitude he put a 7, under what he took to be the longitude a 6. He then marked the one out and the eight out. He was left with a new number, 330026 – 837453 both six digits. Gardner entered this as the new latitude and longitude and pressed map it. The gizmo returned, "You are Here." So not much of a code his grandfather had used. A completely useless first number and then, latitude and longitude.

Hastily Gardner went through the entire copied journal and removed the first digit from all of the number sequences. Carefully he took the list of numbers and entered them into the GPS. Each coordinate mapped another location close to Moundville. This would definitely lead Gardner somewhere but the question was where?

A trail? Maybe where one was supposed to go but what made one location more important than another? What was the key? Any dot could be the "it." What made one dot special?

Then a sudden insight. What if the cave marked the start of the trail? Gardner looked at the map. Carefully he marked an x lightly below the dot representing the cave. The map made a rough sort of sense. It was a snake like trail, but it did have a beginning and an end. Perhaps, just perhaps, Gardner had found the Genesis.

Treat the other man like you would expect him to treat you. Then run like hell.

The Wisdom of Bart Thompson

Doctor Sims was on the phone again and he was not a happy camper. His ear actually hurt from having a receiver pressed against it all day, his insides were still in knots, and if he said, "yes sir" just once more, he knew he would lose his nonexistent lunch. This day had been nothing but talking with people that had power but no knowledge. All of them wanted to direct Doctor Sims, most in 180-degree directions. "Yes sir," Sims said once more and didn't vomit though he would have liked to, "I'll tell him."

Doctor McClean and Bart Thompson were sitting on tall kitchen style stools, watching Doctor Sims work feverishly. They, on the other hand, were very calm and very collected and they were very proud that they were.

Sims hanged up the phone and gave a sigh, which may have been for show. He turned and smiled a non-smile, the fake ones that we save for people we haven't seen in ten years and can neither place their face, nor remember their names, and told Doctor McClean, "Okay. You can take them to Berkeley." Sims face did not register joy or satisfaction with the statement, but he said it anyway. "I'd advise you to hurry however," Sims continued, "As the next call might just reverse that decision."

"If I may use your phone," McClean replied, "I'll start making the arrangements right away."

A GENESIS FOUND

Sims returned a curt nod and said, "I'll release the class." As he started towards the door he said, "I'll even give them extra credit." Though neither Bart nor Doctor McClean saw it, Sims smiled at the last statement and it felt good, he hadn't smiled in quite a while.

As the door closed and Doctor Sims exited, the other Doctor looked over to Bart Thompson and they exchanged a grin.

Kelsey was sitting in the lobby, bored, listless, worried, disgusted, and scared but still beautiful. Her mind had been turning somersaults over what she should do and then it crystallized. She quickly picked up her phone from the table and pressed the speed dial for Gardner. She did this as fast as humanly possible as if afraid her nerve would fail.

The phone buzzed in her ear and she heard a phone ringing at the same time. That was odd. Casting her eyes about looking for the location of the ringing she saw Bart through the window in the lab. Bart lifted up a phone that looked a lot like Gardner's. Bart seemed to press a button. The phone stopped ringing in ear and her phone call ended at the exact same point. Gardner's phone! How long had that SOB Bart had it? She knew the answer to that was just on the other side of the glass window, she also knew it might as well be in Mexico for Bart would surely deny all.

Doctor Sims had taken up a position in the middle of the room and he stood up on a plastic chair to be both visible and heard easily. He waved his hand to draw the attention of the students and stated in his back of the room voice "Listen up. Good news. Everyone gets five points added to their final for all this nonsense. Bad news, reporters are waiting outside and will undoubtedly jump you as you leave. Tell them it's a false alarm and that the remains are human." It wasn't the first lie he had told in his life and maybe not even the worst. "Tell any reporter that happens to get a hold of you that the remains are human even if you believe the opposite or else you will be on every television station in America tonight and will find it quite difficult to get a job when you graduate, at least a job at a respectable university. Digging tomorrow is cancelled, but we will meet in the classroom. Drive safely and as I said, watch what you say or you will regret it."

The students began to grab their stuff and make that God awful clamor that only the young can generate. Sims still had something to say and he had to shout to be heard. "Listen there are a few crazies out there so we've arranged for several University Police to be available to escort you. It's best if you stay together and really best if you don't talk to the media."

Kelsey was the only student not moving. She sat perfectly still, almost rigid, staring at Bart through the lab window. Doctor Sims noticed her and came over to speak for a second. "I don't see Gardner. Is he not here?" Sims asked.

Kelsey didn't speak but just shook her head. Doctor Sims arched his eyebrows and looked at Kelsey for a second, doubtless there was a tale that went with whatever was bothering Kelsey but Sims had learned long ago not to get involved with the love life of his students. Hormones and scholarship didn't mix. Scholarly advice was seldom wanted in affairs of the heart and it seemed to always come back and bite you when offered. Besides, the less he thought about Gardner Patton now the better. Just what was that lad up to?

Without another word, Sims stood and walked back to what he knew best, archaeology. Any advice that Kelsey needed could come from Dear Abby.

Kelsey continued to stare at Bart for another few seconds, then wordlessly she stood up and joined the exiting class. They walked out of the center en masse, surrounded by police and as far from the crazies and the reporters as was feasibly possible. The police had put up barricades to keep both the throng of people and perhaps more importantly the microphones out of the way of the students, and it worked. The students were able to get by without one of them being stopped and interviewed. The fact that steely eyed policeman surrounded them and almost growled when a microphone was placed in the way, might have helped.

For what it was worth, it was a beautiful day, though muggy of course. The sun was shining brightly and off in the distance, birds were singing their tune just as they did on days when strange alien skeletons were not found. The walk to the cars was up hill and it was a tired group and a breathless group that finally arrived. Much to their delight, police cars were lined up to give them an escort at least out of the park, and possibly all the way to T-Town.

Kelsey lost herself in the crowd initially then she worked her way over to the far left. They had made it by the crowd so the policemen were only in front of them and behind them. And the cops were not looking at the students, for they didn't think they had too. They were worried about outsiders, so their eyes were peeled either to the front or to the back and not to the side.

As they approached the nearest point to the woods, Kelsey quickly darted into them. No one called out, and if anyone had seen her they must have figured it was her business.

Having traversed these woods many times, Kelsey had no trouble getting to the trailer. There it was sitting in the clearing, the hot sun beating down on it, as seemingly empty as Bart's conscious. Cautiously and slowly she walked the final few feet to the trailer, what she hoped to find there, only she knew, but it was a place to start the search for Gardner.

Kelsey did not knock but rather tried the doorknob very gently. It opened easily, if a bit creakily and she pushed it inward very slowly. No one was visible at least so she entered and began her search looking for something but not knowing what that something was.

The camper was sweltering and it wasn't likely to get cooler anytime soon as the sun was beating down to beat the band. Kelsey knew that Bart had to be fourteen kinds of stupid not to have found a shady spot for this damned contraption, for given this heat, even at night it would not cool down completely. Kelsey looked through every room in the camper and found no one. She could at least search in peace.

Switching on the overhead light, Kelsey began to look in earnest. The first thing she saw was Gardner's beat up old copy of the *War of the Worlds* on the kitchen table and lying beside it was a photo that looked to be of Gardner's grandpa holding a small child. Picking the photo up, she noted on the bottom that it was a picture of Gardner with John Patton Junior. Despite herself, she smiled. People pick the damndest time to get sentimental she thought, but she slipped the photo safely back into the book all the same and did not feel overly ashamed at being sentimental. But then she was a woman.

A green duffle bag with a broken zipper lay on the floor, showing someone's underwear sticking up above who knew what else. Kneeling she began to go through the contents, feeling a bit disgusted at having to shift the underwear around, but then she had been handling bones of late so her squeamish meter had reset at a fairly high value. About halfway down to the bottom she came onto a mound of folded paper. Pulling it out of the bag she placed it on the kitchen table and began to unfold the mound. Kelsey knew nothing of blueprints and part drawings and the like, but you would have to be an imbecile not to recognize this drawing of an alien with dimensions shown and instructions provided on how to cut the skull of a great ape and morph it into an alien. Proof! Let that SOB Bart Thompson try to wiggle out of this.

Carefully refolding the blueprint, Kelsey was able to make the mound into a skinny, long piece of paper that could be carried in her hip pocket. After placing the blueprint in her pocket, she attacked the rest of the duffle bag with glee, not even dirty underwear would stop her enjoyment of this search. After tossing just about everything out of the duffle bag, she found the pistol.

Having never seen one before, much less used one, she picked it up with must trepidation. It fit her hand very well and she held it.

Git gone before it's time to git.

The Wisdom of Bart Thompson

Sims was still on the phone, but for this conversation, he was seated with his feet propped up and relaxed for possibly the only time that day. "Nothing to worry about honey," he said in that voice we reserve for the one person in the world that uses the same voice on us. "I'll be home for dinner," he stated, possibly optimistically but he really meant it at the time. He hanged up the phone and for the one and only time that day, he really smiled a true heart felt smile.

McClean too was on the phone, talking in muted tones, eyeing Bart every few seconds, resisting the urge to wink. Bart seemed to take no note of the glances. Suddenly Gardner's phone buzzed that it had a new message. Bart opened the screen and read "Found plans for the remains. Meet at camper. Kelsey." Bart, without allowing a single muscle in his face to move, digested the message, then duly erased it.

Doctor McClean hanged up his phone and smiled profusely, as if a weight had been lifted from his shoulders. "It's all arranged," McClean announced, "I'll be flying out in a few hours with the remains. Doctor Sims, your worries are over."

"Excuse me," Bart interrupted. He walked over and opened the lab door and then went out without a glance backward or another word.

"Damn," Sims said, eyeing Bart suspiciously, "That guy gets more phone calls than my teenage daughter."

"That's Hollywood for you," McClean replied with a laugh.

"Well he can have it," Sims stated. He stopped a moment, eyeing the skull. It hadn't hit him before, but Bart got calls like he had something cooking; McClean wanted that skull a little too completely. Maybe he oughtta eye their previous track records before he gave that skull completely away. He nodded to McClean, adding, "I'll go get everything ready for you." Sims lied. He hoped he was a good enough actor not to give away his real intention.

Doctor Sims exited the lab leaving a very satisfied Doctor McClean. McClean would have been less happy had he known Sims intent.

Education can be great preparation for life. Usually though it's a waste of your time and a waste of your daddy's money.

The Wisdom of Bart Thompson

Gardner was still contemplating the map. The far point, the point he had known just five minutes ago, had to be the location of the remains, turned out to be far outside the park boundary. It had been easily seen when he laid his grandfather's map over the GPS. They happened to be roughly the same scale and his bubble had burst just a tad when he realized his solution was no solution at all.

What was he missing? He began to put the points in numerical order; based on the numbers that he had so callously ignored thinking they were some code to throw off the trail. Using a spare piece of paper and a leaking pen he began trying to solve one of the most important archaeological problems in history. Surprisingly (at least to himself it was a surprise) he was able to do just that. Using the numbers and the dots and then connecting the dots sequentially, it just reached out and slapped him. It was a representation of the constellation Orion. Even crudely drawn, Gardner recognized it from the representations in his grandfather's journal.

Now Gardner looked for the eye. It was just where it should be; a tiny blip that was no different from any of the surrounding blips, but it was exactly where the eye should be. That had to be it. Gardner put in that point into the GPS as his destination and circled it on the map he drew. He managed to put the map in his pants pocket, which was no mean feat considering his hands were tied and he did not want to make any movement that would awaken Levi. Then he leaned back and smiled. Regardless of the outcome, he had discovered that his grandfather had indeed left behind a legacy.

Even in the South you sometimes dislike a person because of what he is and not for the color of his skin.

The Wisdom of Bart Thompson

Morning. It wasn't exactly cool, but at least it wasn't hot. It was about the only time someone could bear the heat in midsummer in Moundville Alabama. Particularly in 1938, a date long before air conditioning had come prevalent. On the other hand, you don't miss what you've never had so the people in Moundville this day was just thankful for what cooling the morning did bring. And doubtless they were tougher in those days.

A GENESIS FOUND

John Patton Junior was lying in his bed working on his journal writing and drawing as usual. He finished his drawing of Mound F and with a self-satisfied flourish he made a very big circle around the mound. He circled it not because it contained the buried remains of an alien but because he had found some interesting things there, more so than at the other mounds he had investigated, and therefore he wanted to be able to find it from all its brethren in the future. It was no more sinister than that. Had he known it would sidetrack an investigation 60 years in the future and assist in the setup of one of the great hoaxes of history, he may not have circled it. Then again, he might have anyway. Patton did have a passable sense of humor.

The commandant walked by the front of the barracks and looked in. His eyes went right to Patton, and he saw Patton drawing and writing and it did nothing but increase his distrust of that cadet. DeJarnette was still half convinced that Patton was somehow involved in the theft of the relics, but he had no proof and even in the Army or a subset of the Army, which the CCC was, one had to have some proof if there was to be any hope of a conviction.

DeJarnette started to walk in and make Patton jump to attention, just because he could and he was feeling a bit mean. But he didn't. There was no doubt that he could be petty, he even sometimes prided himself on this ability, but he would not be petty without a purpose. Patton, guilty or innocent, was clear of all charges unless something new presented itself to DeJarnette. But DeJarnette was considering a few choice assignments for Mr. Patton.

Patton, totally ignorant of DeJarnette's schemes, was trying to draw a map. It was a very special map; it was a map that had to be hidden in plain sight. Something that would allow him to go back and find his special cache whenever he felt the world was ready for the knowledge. Being a man well versed in the pulps of his day, not all of his reading was for his betterment; he had stumbled on a code in one otherwise forgettable story. It was neat; it combined the latitude and longitude with a keyed numbering system. He had forgotten how the hero had made out in that particular epic, but he had remembered the coding.

Patton drew the map himself that his code represented. It too was neat. He had fashioned it after the constellation Orion, with the eye representing the repository of his world-shattering discovery. His was the deep satisfaction of the young man that had accomplished great things; things that the world would one day understand and doubtless appreciate. But he was looking at it through the eyes of youth. As he matured he would know better.

Patton never tried to find the bones again, even after he had written about them and got wealthy and gotten called looney. He never had a rational explanation for why he had not dug them up to world renown, not even to himself. Sometimes he even thought he was crazy, but he still remembered what he remembered and he still never, ever thought the world was ready for the real truth. Sometimes, on particularly dark days when the world seemed much more enemy than friend, he even doubted he had buried them. But doubt does not make a best seller, and this was 1938 not 1973 and he was a happy soul, with a secret. That was more than enough for the present.

Two wrongs don't make a right, but it generally provides some satisfaction to the second wrong doer.

The Wisdom of Bart Thompson

There was a loud noise in an otherwise very quiet cave. The noise had come from Gardner's captor and it wasn't a pleasant noise, but it was loud enough to draw Gardner's attention back to his situation and away from his conquest of his grandfather's journal. Levi wheezed, then coughed, then opened wild eyes to look at a world his brain was not ready to comprehend. Gardner thought Levi was worse than before, if that were possible, with angry red whelps and angry red skin and possibly an angry mind.

To say sweat dripped from Levi's body would have not done justice to the word dripped. It gushed. Eyes red and swollen looked straight at Gardner. Not saying a word, Levi yanked violently on the rope that connected them. Gardner jerked forward and almost fell. Levi seemed to enjoy that as he smiled. Never, ever did Levi have a pleasant smile, and this one was the worst Gardner had ever seen. With a growl, Levi took the canteen from his lap and drained it. If it quenched his thirst, there was no evidence shown on his face.

Demonstrating just how empty the canteen was, Levi turned it upside down to see if any water came out. Sticking his tongue out he put it into the mouth of the canteen and Gardner decided right then that he would go thirsty before he would drink out of that container. Wearily, Levi let the canteen slip from his fingers and it fell to the floor of the cave. The canteen made a dull sound that echoed through the cave. "We gotta get water," Levi said in a very calm voice, much like a teacher explaining the particular logic that had to be employed to prove a geometric theorem. "So hot," Levi complained, "Can't keep the damn stuff inside me."

Standing, Levi grunted and pulled his shirt off, letting it fall to the floor. It was so filled with sweat that it fell like a rock and not like a piece of fabric. Gardner, for the first time could see all of Levi's upper body and it wasn't a pleasant sight. Levi's upper torso was blanketed in red. The whelps were even larger on his torso and Gardner, for the first time, really began to worry for Levi's life. Gardner didn't know what Levi had, but he was fervently hoping it wasn't contagious.

"Oh my God," Gardner said when he saw Levi's upper body and immediately regretted it.

Levi's eyes focused, or at least tried to focus, on Gardner. A strange look came on Levi's face, like he was remembering something of great importance. Holding up the knife that had always remained clinched in his hands, even when asleep, if it had been sleep, he carefully examined it, as if to see that it was in working order for some very important task. Something clicked in his mind; you could actually see his eyes register some new thought, probably sinister. Looking around carefully he asked the question that Gardner feared the most, "Where is that damn thing?"

Gardner didn't have to be told what that damn thing was; quickly he shifted the Blackberry under his leg. He kept his face as blank, looking like he looked when trying to sleep through a lecture and not get caught. Noting Levi's penetrating stare, Gardner responded with his best nonchalant face. I'm clueless Levi, his face said, "I don't even know what damn thing you were talking about."

Just as suddenly as he had looked at Gardner, Levi seemed to lose interest in him. Cursing, his hand flew to the back of his neck and he pulled off a tick that had evidently disturbed a hair or two. It was a big tick, gray and full with blood, not brown and empty.

With more satisfaction than Gardner thought was deserved, Levi squished the tick between his fingers. Blood flew everywhere, including onto Levi. If it bothered him, it didn't show. Levi laughed a short laugh at his accomplishment. Gardner had not found it particularly amusing.

"Lousy parasites," Levi complained. "They'll suck you dry if you let em. Make ya sick. They take all the water. Don't they?"

Gardner thought silence was the better part of valor and did not respond to the question.

"I betcha they're sucking on you too," Levi said. Levi's face showed a lot of satisfaction with that surmise. Then another thought came into his addled mind. "Maybe it's you that's sucking my blood." Levi raised the knife menacingly. He tugged the rope to get Gardner's attention. He got it.

Levi twirled the knife as best he could, making threatening gestures and grinning mirthlessly. All things considered, Gardner thought it best if Levi just passed out, but Levi wasn't that accommodating. Had he not been sick and dehydrated and totally incoherent Levi might have done something that he would have regretted later and that Gardner would regret now. But he was sick and dehydrated and ever so tired. The fury left him faster than it came. Giving Gardner one last evil eye, he collapsed to the cave floor in a heap of red whelps and red skin. Gardner was somewhat sorry for Levi but truth be told he was happy about it.

I've been good and I've been bad. Bad pays better.

The Wisdom of Bart Thompson

Even though the camper belonged to Bart, he still knocked on the door. While he knew Levi was supposed to be with

Gardner in the cave, he was still Levi and about as predictable as a random number generator. Levi could get spooked and Levi had that damned pistol. So Bart knocked and wasn't embarrassed about it in the least.

From inside the camper came a feminine voice that was a bit put out. "I'm tired of asking," Kelsey said. "Tell me where Gardner is."

Bart was about to tell Kelsey where she herself could go but she opened the door before he came out with his riposte. When he saw the pistol he had feared would be in Levi's hand, instead in Kelsey's prim hand all he could say was, "Jesus, Kelsey."

Looking mostly at the gun, but also eyeing Kelsey, Bart tried to read the situation. What he saw wasn't encouraging. He saw a determined young woman that was, worried, angry and tired. He also saw that the safety was off. For once in a very long time, Bart was speechless.

Never hire an attorney that's spent more time in the joint than you have.

The Wisdom of Bart Thompson

Doctor Sims was an archaeologist, which made him a scientist, and which also made him a natural born skeptic. It is no accident that science is based on cold hard facts, the reason is only the skeptical and the "show-it-to-me-and-maybe-I'll-believe-it" types go into science. As a scientist, Sims had studied enough math to know that the probability of his finding an alien skeleton that had been hidden for hundreds of years was exceedingly small. Besides, as a man that had been passed over for the head of the archaeology department, he knew he couldn't be that lucky.

A GENESIS FOUND

Just because he had permission to release the skeleton to Doctor McClean did not mean he would come out of this blameless if something happened. He had to perform due diligence, and a wonderful way of doing due diligence was the Internet. You can find lots of dirt on lots of people and find it in a hurry on the Internet. Providing it wasn't bogged down with porno being downloaded at the time you needed it.

Doctor Sims searched first on the name of Bart Thompson. What he found mostly were reviews, few of them flattering, on the various film projects Bart had been associated with in the past. Bart seemed mostly a two-bit player in a two-dollar industry. Probably the only reason he was allowed to film at Moundville was that he was an Alabama native. Not too many of those, and fewer still that desired to work in the state itself. Oh well, on to Doctor McClean.

McClean had been a busy man. Before coming to Moundville he had been at a related site in Cahokia. There he had found remains that he claimed were the Cahokia giant. There was a legend of a race of Native Americans that lived in the Southeast before the coming of the white men that had been exceedingly tall. Their civilization was supposed to be associated with a mound culture that was centered where Cahokia is currently located. There had been journals of settlers and frontiersmen that spoke of them. There had been newspaper reports, particularly during the yellow press era, on the tribe. Trouble was, the remains had never been found, until Doctor McClean found them.

How did Doctor Sims know that Doctor McClean had found them? Well it hadn't been written up in any professional journals, which might be considered odd, as this was a sensational find if ever there was one. But there was a well-reasoned article in the *World News Daily*. There was also a picture showing a smiling Doctor McClean standing besides the Cahokia skeleton. On the opposite page was a photograph of Sasquatch that was currently

172

living in a suburb around Pittsburgh. The Sasquatch interview was most enlightening. Seems he was deeply concerned about heath care.

There is nothing so sad as a sucker wising up.

The Wisdom of Bart Thompson

Gardner gave Levi a full five minutes before doing anything. That almost included breathing. At the end of the five minutes, Gardner cautiously began to get on with his life. First he brought out the Blackberry and typed, "Kels it's a hoax. Trapped in cave. Bart knows where. Send help." Just as he was about to send the message, the map that his grandfather had drawn fell out of his pocket and on to the cave floor. Gardner looked at it, shook his head at his own gullibility and stupidity, but pressed cancel on the Blackberry any way. He would find it, if it was there to be found.

Just to be sure Levi was truly out of it, Gardner jerked hard on the rope and yelled, "Hey wake up! We need more water." Another jerk. "Hey!"

Levi didn't move at first, then he jumped up and came at Gardner wild eyed, the knife waving dangerously.

Gardner pulled on the rope with all of his might. That brought Levi back to his knees almost as if he was praying. For a second he swayed back and forth, his eyes looking but not seeing, then he collapsed for the second and final time. A fighter taking a strong right cross never folded so completely. Levi's body jerked once, then again, then he just lay there, breathing as if every breath would be the last.

Faster than he had moved since he was six years old and being chased by that damn bully, Boyd Floyd, Gardner closed in on Levi and jerked the knife out of his hand. Backing away slowly, keeping the knife ready just in case, Gardner put a good five feet between himself and Levi. When he finally got as far away from Levi as the rope would allow, he went to work on the ropes with the knife. It took only a second to release himself and for the first time in hours, Gardner was no longer at the mercy of Levi and for the first time in hours, Gardner smiled.

As the ropes slipped to the cave floor, Gardner slipped towards the cave exit. Even as he made the mouth, he knew he couldn't just leave Levi passed out and helpless on the cave floor. Gardner had once saved the life of a mangy hound when he was a child and Levi was human, probably. Sighing, he went back into the cave, walked over to Levi and put that smelly, almost obscenely dirty, sleeping bag on top of him— the one Levi had joked about earlier. Just deserts.

The bag smelled of old socks and was probably infested with all types of vermin. So there was some justice in the act. Levi was burning with fever and Gardner did not know if covering him with a sleeping bag would help or hurt, but Gardner knew it would help his own conscious and that was sufficient. Half rolling Levi up in the bag, and partially zipping it, Gardner gave him a final pat, more for luck than out of concern. "Sorry if this smells bad kid," Gardner said in his best Han Solo voice.

Gardner began a running trot out of the cave and down the trail, following the map on the Blackberry as well as he could. At about the third step, the device went deader than a mackerel. Gardner put it in his front pants pocket and pulled the map he had made of his grandfather's numbering scheme from the journal from his hip pocket. Thus he began his quest: tired beyond belief, sleepy, blind, with a brain functioning at fifty percent at best. He went out to flail against his grandfather's windmills.

The trail down from the cave to the woods was steep and rocky, and either would have caused a fatigued Gardner to stumble, acting together they caused Gardner to stumble a lot. His journey was not made any easier by the fact that he could barely see, and what sight he did have was focused halfway on the map and halfway on the ground, giving neither the attention that was demanded by the situation. Still onward he went, hoping he would reach the destination he had crudely marked on the map.

Assuming he had drawn the map correctly, big assumption in itself, he should be able to find the hidden cache by following a line from the X (the cave) to the eye of Orion. Simple, except it was hard to scale up precisely in his mind, what he had drawn on the page. But he would try. As he reached the woods, he took a few moments to study the map as well as his eyesight would allow, and that was none too good. He marched off at about a forty-five degree angle and started dodging trees. He hoped he would find the remains. He hoped even more that his eyesight wouldn't fail completely.

Too often Religion is just another excuse for a man to not have to think.

The Wisdom of Bart Thompson

Doctor McClean was reading a newspaper and trying with some success to hide all of his anxieties. For the tenth time in five minutes, he looked at his watch. What was keeping that idiot Sims? How hard was it to make a couple of phone calls and to set up an escort to the airport? Damn bumpkin.

Doctor Sims opened the lab door and entered. In his hand was a piece of paper that Doctor Sims wanted to ask Doctor McClean about. Just as the lab door was about to close, a very large policeman pushed it open and walked inside. The door then swung close with a slight rattle. McClean smiled at Doctor Sims, but did not receive a return smile. McClean sighed, he had hoped this would work, but he and Bart were pretty sure it would not. They were prepared for either eventuality.

"Doctor McClean," Doctor Sims said in a grave voice and holding out the piece of paper to McClean that had the Cahokia article on it, "We need for you to clear up a few things for us. And we need you to do it now."

McClean just stared at Sims. Sims stared back. Then he smiled.

When the unexplainable is explained, the universe loses a bit of its luster.

The Wisdom of Bart Thompson

Staring at the pistol in Kelsey's hand wasn't helping Bart's disposition. He wasn't afraid of Kelsey shooting him on purpose but Lord how she waved that gun about. Things were too close to panning out to be shot because Kelsey wasn't sure just how to handle a pistol. At least she could put the safety on.

Motioning with the pistol, Kelsey indicated that Bart should lead the way to Gardner. After he had advanced about five feet in front of her, she fell in behind him. Bart had gotten over his fright enough to start talking again or at least complaining, "Jesus Kelsey, I get the point. You can put the gun away. I don't need Gardner anymore and I'll be happy to be shed of him."

Kelsey didn't speak, but just continued to trail Bart.

A loud buzzing announced that Bart's phone had received a text message. Bart reached for it but Kelsey stopped him by saying "I want to see."

Bart flipped the phone open and showed the message to Kelsey at the same time he read it. "Here it is," he announced, "Make what you can from it."

The screen showed 10301938.

"It's just a bunch of numbers," Kelsey said "What does it mean? Does it have anything to do with Gardner?"

"It's the day Mars invaded Earth," Bart answered.

"What?" asked a dumb founded Kelsey.

"It's code," Bart explained, "McClean sent this to let me know he had been caught. It's the same day that Orson Welles hoaxed and panicked America."

"Then it's over," Kelsey said with a sigh of relief.

"Not yet," Bart replied, "Not if they don't find me. If they find me too soon then it is over for all of us, including Gardner."

"Is that a threat?" Kelsey demanded.

"Not at all," Bart replied smoothly, "I'm making a deal." Bart held up his phone and said "One call gets the cops out here. Now I don't think you believe Gardner is not involved here. Even if he isn't I can make it look like he is."

"Say your piece," Kelsey replied.

"I'm the only one that can guarantee Gardner gets out of this clean," Bart said, "I think that's worth something." Bart had spoken very carefully. Somehow he had lost some of his Southern drawl when he spoke those words, and his eyes never left Kelsey's face.

"I don't see it," Kelsey replied, "If I let you get away, how does that help Gardner? It just makes him look more complicit."

Bart laughed, "This ain't ever been about getting away. You think I'm stupid just cause I drop my G's when I speak? We knew going in we would get caught and revealed. We counted on it. But in order to make this thing profitable I need a few days- big dealings and such. Then I clear this thing up and clean up Gardner's name in the process."

"Why?" Kelsey asked, "What does a few days buy you?"

Bart pulled a small videotape from his shirt pocket. His movement caused Kelsey to stop mid-step and to level the pistol at him. Bart either didn't notice or didn't want Kelsey to notice that he had noticed, as he just smiled at her.

"I've got to get this to somebody," Bart said. "I gotta get a signed contract. Gotta be there in person. I'm dealing with Hollywood scum, can't trust them. They might try to take advantage of a good natured cuss such as myself."

"Oh I can trust you..." Kelsey said as if she didn't trust him at all.

"I might be a liar," Bart admitted, "And a scallywag and a no good SOB. But I'm still family," he nodded at Kelsey's stomach.

Kelsey's mind was working hard and she just stared at Bart.

Never quit. Just take up other interests.

The Wisdom of Bart Thompson

"This way," Gardner muttered and ran right into a low hanging branch that was still high enough not to be seen. Cursing for the umpteenth time, he walked around the branch and wiped the tree bark off his forehead. Then he squinted at the map and tried to draw a conclusion as to where to step next. Damn his eyes.

"Further down," he again was talking to himself and further down he went. Finally he reached the river. The squiggly lines he had drawn represented the river, great, he was almost there, or else he was totally lost. Stopping for a second, Gardner dropped down and sat on the riverbank. The Black Warrior was winding its way to whatever its destination was. It did not seem to be too concerned with Gardner's plight. It just kept on moving.

Gardner looked into the river and saw his own reflection. Not only could he see his reflection he could see a lone star in the sky, barely visible in the daylight but there nonetheless. Gardner knew he was stupid squared to be following some half-baked map trying to find what his grandfather had probably never buried in the first place. Don't really know how this happened, he thought, except that I'm an idiot. He answered his own question.

Putting the map flat on the riverbank, Gardner got as close to it as was humanly possible. Studying it more intensely than he had ever studied for any test, Gardner finally was able to see that he just might be able to find it by taking a direct line from this riverbank. But where could he start? Map seems to show south. Was that a squiggly line? Damn faint, but maybe. Gardner's mind, or what was left of Gardner's mind at least, headed his feet south.

There was a branch or a creek if you wanted to speak in true redneck Southern. Nothing peculiar in that, lots of branches feed the mighty Black Warrior. The map seemed to show that there was a dot just opposite a branch. This branch? Gardner walked over. Then he sat down on the cool grass and carefully laid out the map. Yes, it almost screamed at him. This way! "Hang on Gramps, I'm coming," he thought. Gardner started walking towards his destiny.

I always get maudlin when the deed is done. Particularly if I left any money on the table.

The Wisdom of Bart Thompson

The fading sun bounced its rays off the mouth of the cave making it look even eerier than was normal, which was saying something. The mouth of the cave resembled a long and somewhat sinister tunnel. Bart and Kelsey walked in anyway. Neither found what they expected.

"Christ," Bart exclaimed on seeing Levi. He quickly ran to his cousin and put his hand on Levi's forehead. The fever was breaking. Levi was hot but not burning.

"Where's Gardner?" demanded Kelsey not showing much concern for Levi.

Bart pulled out his canteen and was giving Levi what was a much-appreciated drink. He answered in his most sarcastic voice, which was sarcastic indeed, "He ain't here. Reckon he's gone somewhere else."

Kelsey saw Gardner's backpack. On the floor just beside it was the photo of herself and Gardner. She walked over to it, stooped and picked it up. "Why did he leave all of his stuff here?" she asked.

"I reckon," Bart responded still in sarcastic mode, "He was in a hurry. Escapees usually are."

Kelsey gathered the strewn papers from the cave floor and thrust them into the backpack. Then she put the remnants of the folder into the backpack. The last thing she found was a picture of John Patton Junior. She picked it up and studied for a moment, and then she thrust it into the backpack. Kelsey glanced over to Bart and saw that he was still fussing with Levi. Levi was still dead to the world.

"Looks okay," Kelsey said in her best imitation of Bart's sarcastic voice, "Reckon he'll be up and about in no time." She nodded at Levi but for Bart's benefit. Not waiting for a reply, Kelsey shouldered the backpack and walked out of the cave. She saw the etching "I Found the Genesis" as she passed out of the cave. It meant nothing to her.

Kelsey was no more than five feet out of the cave when Bart caught up with her. Bart was talking a mile a minute. "I'm telling you Kels, he's probably already back in Tuscaloosa. Better get a move on. We gotta get Levi some help."

"Don't worry Bart," Kelsey said with a toss of her head, "You'll get your head start. I'll call the cops when I find Gardner. I'll let them worry about Levi."

Women are like wine. They gotta age some to be worth a damn.

The Wisdom of Bart Thompson

"It's gotta be here," Gardner exclaimed as he came across the branch. He knew that there was no one there to hear him but he was talking anyway. He began to walk and he began to look and he began to pray and all of this was going on in a brain that was firing synapses faster than the speed of light.

Gardner stumbled-scrambled around a tree trunk. His eyes went up the tree trunk, there, high, was a faded X marking on the bark of the tree. X had to mark the spot, at least he hoped. He went to his knees and began to dig with the only tools available to him, his hands.

"Come on! Come on!" he shouted. Gardner lost his footing and almost slipped into the small creek behind him. He grabbed a large root and steadied himself. Carelessly he ran his fingers through his hair. Glad I can't see my reflection now, he thought, he was covered with dirt and green leaves and probably a stick or two. He stood up and straightened his aching back for a moment and then immediately went to his knees and attacked the dirt with a vengeance.

Gardner felt something crawling up his neck. He grabbed it and looked at it before tossing it into the creek behind him. It was a tick, what else. Wasn't there any other insect that infested these damn woods? He fixed his eyes on that faint X. It was twenty feet up, maybe higher, and faded. How fast do trees grow anyhow? Could that X have been left by his grandfather?

John Patton Junior was hot. Sweat was pouring from every pore in his body and he was sure he was covered in enough dirt to start his own corn crop, but the deed was done. He took his shovel and smashed it into the tree trunk, first to the left, then crossing it to the right. He repeated this movement several times. Then he was satisfied. That X would last for a long time.

Gardner's eyes rested on the X. Had to mean something. Had to. Kneeling again he ripped at the dirt, his hands bleeding.

John Patton Junior shoved his shovel into the dirt.

Gardener dug deeper. Deeper yet.

John Patton Junior covered his work. His shirt had gone for a good cause; it contained the remains. He leaned back. It was a job well done. He smiled.

Gardner ripped at the dirt. Again. He pulled out a root. Find it. Find it!

The land was typical of West Alabama. Pine trees everywhere. A slow grade, due to eons of rain run off. Flat otherwise. Kelsey walked and looked and listened and walked some more. Her thoughts were on Gardner, not on the topography of the land, not on the cruelty of life (particularly a life that contained Bart Thompson), not the brush underfoot that made walking a pain, and not even on the rattlesnakes that had been known to lay in that same brush. Strictly on Gardner.

Then she heard something to her right, running water and what sounded like a grunt. Quickly she twisted her legs and walked faster, almost running. There was something there, something that made sounds. Then she heard a loud curse. That was the voice. "Gardner," she shouted as she broke into a run.

Gardner was digging. His hands were bleeding; his elbows were raw from ricocheting off the hole he was making. There was hardly any feeling left in his hands. Still he dug and dug some more. He didn't hear the crickets start their serenade as they did everyday at dusk. He was oblivious to the mating cry of the bullfrogs. He hadn't even heard Kelsey shout his name. There was nothing in the world, no, nothing in the Universe, except the hole in front of him and the remains that were to be found. This was his quest. This was his vindication.

John Patton Junior stood stock-still. His shovel was filled with the last pile of dirt. He slowly let it drop on the grave he had dug out and then filled up. Then he patted the dirt down smooth. He grabbed some brush and pulled it over the grave. Grass and leaves would cover the spot soon enough. He was tired, very tired. But he was ecstatic!

There it was! Even Gardner's weak vision couldn't miss it. His efforts had yielded a protruding bone. He reached to grab it and was stopped by a shrill "Gardner!"

With his hand an inch from the bone, Gardner turned to the voice. It was Kelsey. That's all. He turned back to the hole, at that moment nothing in the world mattered to him except this. Not even Kelsey.

"I see it Kels," Gardner said, "There."

"What?" she asked.

They both looked in the hole. Kelsey also looked at Gardner. His elbows and hands were bloodied, mincemeat. Dirt covered every inch of his body except those inches covered by mud. His hair was wet with sweat and matted. He smelled. None of this mattered. It was Gardner. At least it looked like Gardner. Hardly acted like him.

"Gardner," Kelsey said softly and put a hand softly on his forearm, very softly. Gardner reached out with his own hand and grabbed hers. "You see it?" he asked excitedly, "It's there, by damn, it's there."

Kelsey looked more closely into the hole. Sadly, she shook her head. Quickly she reached into her pocket and pulled out Gardner's spare set of eyeglasses.

"Quit squinting," she said handing the glasses to Gardner, "You'll ruin what few looks you have."

Gardner didn't respond to the slight verbal jab, as he would have normally. He hurriedly put the eyeglasses on and peered down into the hole. The bones, the sacred relics were nothing but a mass of white roots.

Gardner collapsed to the ground. Men don't cry, particularly Southern men and so he didn't though the truth be told he would have if Kelsey hadn't been there. Stupid ignoramus. Dumb stupid ignoramus.

"I fell for it again," Gardner complained through pants of breath. "Like a six year old. Just say it, Gardner will believe it. Stupid."

"What were you looking for?" asked Kelsey.

Gardner gave her the look, the one that says, "Where have you been?" He didn't reply, just shook his head and panted like a hound dog.

"The skeleton?" Kelsey asked, still surprised that Gardner believed that fairy tale.

Gardner laughed. It wasn't maniacal but it was close.

"Bart, that SOB," Gardner said, "Was so wrong. I wasn't afraid it was out here. Damned if I wasn't afraid if it wasn't." He grinned as if there was some joke that he and only he knew and understood.

"Why?" Kelsey asked.

"Because it would prove there's something else, you know," Gardner said shaking his head at his own cupidity. "That life's not just facts and fiction. That we're more than just dirt." He shrugged his shoulders and gave it up. He didn't know if he could explain it even to himself, much less to Kelsey.

Suddenly Gardner forgot all about grandfathers and aliens, he remembered the magazine cover and he remembered that he was going to be a father and Kelsey a mother. He reached over and touched Kelsey's stomach. They both smiled. Not ironic smiles. Not sardonic smiles. They smiled real smiles. The smiles of those in love that knew they had a lifetime together.

Kelsey hugged him, dirt, stink and blood ignored. Gardner hugged her back. There was more to life than the facts of science; and more than the idea that everything science could not prove is simply "fiction." Lots more. Gardner had just been looking in the wrong place for answers.

Kelsey disengaged from the hug and to her credit she did not make a face at the stink as it wafted its ways to her nostrils. She pulled out the photo of John Patton Junior from her pocket and handed it to Gardner saying, "You dropped this."

Gardener reached out and took it gently from her. Looking at the photo, he felt like he was seeing it for the first time.

"You look like him," Kelsey said quietly.

"Yeah I do," Gardner replied, "You can stop reminding me. I've enough crosses to bear."

Kelsey really smiled now. Gardner was back.

Gardner matched Kelsey's smile with one of his own. For the first time he noticed the pistol in her hip pocket.

"How did you find me anyway?" Gardner questioned; his eyes added, "and why in the hell did you need a gun?"

A GENESIS FOUND

Before Kelsey could answer there was a rustle of bushes and a crack of a branch from behind them. The voice of Bart Thompson rang out, "Cuz."

Bart walked out of the underbrush and stood directly opposite Gardner. "If Kelsey ain't told you," Bart said matter of factly, "It's over. I'm going, just thought you might want this back," he tossed Gardner the cell phone he had taken from Gardner the day before. Gardner caught it in mid air without taking his eyes off of Bart.

"Look," Bart continued, "for what it's worth, I didn't think it would come to this. Didn't count on you being so smart."

"You don't gotta apologize, Bart," Gardner said, "I ain't- I'm not pressing charges. Just get the hell out of here."

Bart took one last look at Gardner, he didn't look at Kelsey, this was family doings and she wasn't family, at least not yet. Bart nodded slightly then turned to leave. Before he had taken the first step, Gardner spoke.

"Was it worth it Bart? Your revolution?" Gardener said it flatly, without accenting any word.

Bart stopped and looked directly at Gardner. He started to speak, stop, smiled, then did speak. "The money maybe; I'll find out soon enough. But it wasn't just the money. Sorry I had to lie to you kid, but there are some things more important than you and me. Even more important than money, though it pains me to say so. People have got to see how they manipulate themselves looking for answers. Everything's just perception, all stories...there's nothing beyond that. We're just desperate, our culture, desperate for justification even if it's only a myth."

Gardner did not respond to Bart's philosophy, if in fact that's what it was. More likely it was just an excuse for Bart to do what he wanted to do, which was make money. Whatever it was, Gardner did not respond to it, he just said, between clinched teeth, "That's the last time you call me kid."

A GENESIS FOUND

Kelsey made a production out of pulling her phone out and beginning to dial, "You're losing your head start," she said ominously.

Bart glanced at her, smiled a fake smile, almost an evil grin. Glancing one last time at Gardner, he raised his eyebrows, meaning God only knew what, and walked off and Gardner hoped, out of their lives forever.

Gardner kept his eyes on Bart until he was out of sight. Honestly he didn't know if he watched because he was afraid that Bart would return or was hoping he would. Bart would have an exit speech, of course, a last goodbye, one to remember him by. Gardner knew this moment would last him until his dying day. Not Bart's speech, but the end of the madness, or the end of the adventure, whichever it had been. Whether it had made a man of him, or had simply made him crazy was debatable, but it was without doubt memorable.

After Bart had disappeared into the bushes and was out of earshot, Gardner turned to Kelsey and said, "You know, Bart is one more SOB, but he is a hell of a storyteller."

Kelsey replied, "Well you got the SOB part right. Gardner, we need to get some help out here. That other SOB Levi needs medical attention."

Gardner acknowledged with a lift of his eyebrows. He opened his phone and saw there had been a previous call to 911. "How about that," he said, "I think that's already been taken care of."

Gardner handed his phone to Kelsey. She saw it and smiled ruefully.

"He probably thinks this makes up for everything," she said just a bit sadly.

"Let it," Gardner replied. "We oughtta wait with Levi." Immediately Gardner started up the gentle slope to the cave. Kelsey started behind him, and then noticed something on the ground; she picked it up and slipped it into the front pocket of the backpack, in doing so she fell several feet behind Gardner.

"You coming?" Gardner asked.

She nodded, then held out her hand. Gardner took it. They walked slowly towards the cave.

When building a mathematical model that predicts anything, it will be wrong, and the more it predicts the wronger it will be.

The Wisdom of Bart Thompson

Bart Thompson had cleared the woods and was heading towards his car. The camper would have to be sacrificed. He scratched his arm absentmindedly. Then it dawned on him. Yes, a rash. Bart laughed. Get the damn film to the producers. Get the damned contract signed. Then get to a hospital. He was pretty sure that even without insurance he would soon be able to afford the stay. Visions of dollars were dancing in his head as he removed the syringe from his front pants pocket and tossed it into a trashcan. It had served its purpose.

Life is what you make of it. That's why most lives are screwed up.

The Wisdom of Bart Thompson

Gardner was reading his grandfather's journal, as he had been doing a lot of lately, as if the madness was just in remission and not over. There was an entry entitled "The

A GENESIS FOUND

Endless Search- Unlocking the Mounds' Origin." His grandfather may have eventually been crazy but he wasn't crazy when he wrote his journal. It was both scholarly and readable, which made it a rarity.

Gardner reached into the backpack to find an ink pen so he could underline a few cogent passages. He found one; he also found a patch that had "CCC" on it. It looked to be off a uniform. Curious that it was in his backpack, but then both Levi and Bart had been in the pack and they may have put it there. Whether they had found it and slipped it there for keeping and forgot it, or more likely they had a more nefarious purpose for it that they had not found the opportunity for, was an open question and one that Gardner could care less about.

The door lock jiggled. It still wasn't fixed and Gardner doubted it ever would be. Kelsey came striding into the apartment, fresh as a daisy, and made up to a T as always. She had a newspaper in her hands.

"Hey," Kelsey said.

Gardner nodded in greeting, "Hey yourself," he answered. "How was Sims?"

"The usual," Kelsey stated, "He said if you missed another class don't worry about failing, worry about being arrested."

"Sounds like him," Gardner agreed.

"I think," Kelsey said with that teasing voice that was so damned irritating, "He's still convinced you masterminded the whole thing and did it just to make him look bad."

"Well I failed miserably then," Gardner said, "It didn't make him look bad, it made him look good. He caught the bad guys. Maybe he'll give me a few bonus points for all the help I've given his career."

"Not just his," Kelsey responded. She handed Gardner the newspaper. Distaste showed in her face.

189

Giant headlines read "Halloween Hoaxers Face Law Suit. Could See Jail Time."

"Now that's Bart's kind of headline," Kelsey said.

"Yeah," Gardner agreed, shaking his head. "Well, I'll believe it when I see it. They'll get out of it someway. You know Bart."

"He already has," Kelsey replied.

"How's that?" Gardner asked.

"He's in the hospital. They all are," she stated.

"For?" asked Gardner.

"Rocky Mountain Spotted Fever. Levi was just the first to show symptoms. You're lucky you weren't infected," Kelsey said.

"Maybe," Gardner agreed, "But they may be lucky they are."

Kelsey nodded her head at that statement. "People are saying it's punishment enough," she agreed.

"Ain't nothing punishment enough," Gardner growled and meant it. "Odd though, some of the newspapers from the Thirties conjectured that Shaw might have had it. It would have explained how he looked and maybe how he acted. That was a long time before they had forensics that could have told them conclusively of course. Plus no one really cared. Still it is damned odd."

"I suppose," Kelsey said, "Everything about this affair has been odd."

Gardner's phone buzzed. He glanced at the display screen and said "Great." It was a new text message from Bart. He showed it to Kelsey and rolled his eyes.

"Probably wants help stealing the crown jewels," Kelsey said.

Gardner opened the message, it said, "Celestialconnections.com." Kelsey was leaning over Gardner's shoulder and she read it at the same time. Their eyes locked. "Damn," they exclaimed in unison.

Quickly Gardner scrambled from his chair and made a beeline to the computer in the corner of the apartment. It seemed to take an hour for the computer to come on and connect on line.

Eventually it did come up, though, and Gardner entered the link. He had to enter it twice as he mistyped it the first time, which brought a Bronx cheer from Kelsey.

Celestialconnections.com was just what the link name suggested. The front page was a garish page with lots of weird colors, and lots of different types of aliens shown on the front page. Skeletons of a particular alien ran as a border around the front page. Gardner knew where that idea had come from. One of the links connected to the front page showed in large letters:

Moundville "Hoax" a Cover-Up! Video leaked to Youtube reveals the truth!

Gardner clicked on that link. It had a youtube video embedded in the linked page. Knowing he was stupid for doing it, but doing it anyway, Gardner clicked on the video.

There was Bart, bigger than hell, standing next to Doctor McClean. The grand opening of the finding of the alien remains had been captured for all posterity to see and for Gardner to live down. It was silent, maybe by accident, but most likely because they didn't want Gardner's questioning of the find in the video. Below the video ran a caption, "Was a real alien skeleton found before the authorities produced a fake?"

"Over 16,000 views already," Gardner told Kelsey pointing at the counter. "It'll be a million before it's over, I betcha."

Gardner read a few of the comments attached to the video, they were all excited statements about the truth being in Moundville, or else diatribes against the "authorities" for hiding yet one more truth from the public.

"Another Roswell!" Mulder106 proclaimed.

"Can't wait to see the movie," said Kolchak12.

"The truth is truly in Moundville," stated Skully153.

"They had the same fever!" by seefartherthinkclearer.

191

"A culture of myths, Gar" was the comment by unnamed.

"Wonder who that's from?" Gardner asked with a laugh. "Well, at least he didn't call me a kid."

"Gardner," Kelsey asked, "How many of those comments did Bart or his posse write?"

"It wouldn't surprise me if they didn't write any of them," Gardner said while looking at the screen. "Bart was right about one thing. Some people want their myths to be real. Truth is in the eye of the beholder."

"I'm surprised there's not a link to the video shop selling his documentary already," Kelsey said in a disgusted tone.

"Bart's too smart for that," Gardner said, smiling, "I hate to admit it but he's scoped this out pretty well. Let the net spread the rumor. Let the true believers take the lead. He could come out right now and say it was a hoax, and he likely will to avoid jail time, but it won't die. Soon it will be the must see documentary. Bart'll clean up."

"No justice in this world," Kelsey replied. She walked away towards the kitchen, as she passed the table she grabbed a plush ET toy from a box marked storage. "Little early," she said, but smiled. She would definitely keep it for the baby.

Gardner just shrugged.

"Gardner," Kelsey said to get his attention.

"Yeah," Gardner replied to show she had his attention.

"Do you believe?" she asked.

"Believe what?" he answered a question with a question as he did often and usually just to irritate.

"Like all those other people," Kelsey continued, "Do you believe that something could really be out there?"

"Even if it is," Gardner replied, "It doesn't have all the answers. My guess is it'll be just as lost as we are."

Kelsey nodded her head then started back towards the kitchen.

A GENESIS FOUND

Gardner suddenly remembered the patch and picked it up showing it to Kelsey. "Kels, did you find this in the cave?"

"No," Kelsey replied, "In the woods. I thought you had dropped it."

"Near the creek?" Gardner asked.

She nodded then the conversation over for her, she exited to the back.

"Huh," Gardner said aloud. He examined the patch closely. There was a brown-black tarry substance on the back and some on the front of the patch. He rubbed it and then put his finger to his nose and smelled. He looked into his backpack and found a busted ink pen. Ink? He laughed. So much for a preserving agent.

There was something beneath the ink on the pen. With his fingernail, he scraped the ink away and found a tick. Well no surprise there. Still the patch had been found close to the creek. Maybe it came from an old shirt, maybe his grandfather's. Maybe, just maybe, he should take the right tools and go back out there. Hell he was just wasting a few hours of time, in a life, what did a few hours matter?

Gardner put the patch back on the coffee table and picked up his grandfather's journal. The photograph of his grandfather as a young man slipped out and fell to the table. It seemed to be staring at him. A life full of purpose, full of hope, a dedicated life. Now remembered as a nutjob. Was that the legacy his grandfather had wanted? Was that the life he wanted for himself? For Kelsey?

Gardner lay the journal down beside the patch on the coffee table. He picked up the patch and as he did he saw his own reflection in the clear cover of the coffee table. He didn't much like what he saw.

The "Endless Search" be damned. He stood up, stretched, then walked over to the trashcan. He tossed the patch in and slammed it shut.

Life's a big snipe hunt. There's us who know better, and us runnin' round the dark wasting our time.

Legends & Tell-Tales

Variations and unseen moments from the story told

Every variable is possible. For instance- in a parallel universe, Gar, maybe you ain't so dumb.

The Wisdom of Bart Thompson

Gardner almost shouted with joy. His obsession was over. Time to do anything but think of John Patton Junior and alien bones. He walked to the door, about to go out for a bit of air. Just as his hand touched the doorknob he said very softly, "Damn." He turned and headed towards the trashcan.

Too often enlightenment just means you've changed your prejudices.

The Wisdom of Bart Thompson

They had no need for the year. If they counted time, it wasn't the way we count time. They knew that time passed, they knew of seasons. But it wasn't AD 800 to them, it was just another day.

It was the first mound ever to be built. The mound signified something to them, what we do not know today, but it meant something. It had to. They labored too long to ensure it was just the right height, just the right width, it was perfect to them.

They had a ceremony of sorts as they buried it. Some thought the ceremony over long; some thought it was too short. The Shaman, or Priest or Preacher, call him what you will, made sacred movements with his hands and said sacred words, as is expected of a shaman, or a priest, or a preacher.

Had they known they were laying the seeds for deception in the future would they have cared? Do we care today when we knowingly go to a church and sing praises and hymns that we

197

don't believe? They were as we are. Maybe the skin color is different but mankind is the same. More's the pity.

Then it was over. They went away. There was no need to guard it. Only they knew it existed in this world and they would not disturb the holy ground. But one turned as he walked away and wondered just what it was they had buried.

When you are up to your neck it helps to remember the first rule of holes. Stop diggin'!

The Wisdom of Bart Thompson

Was it worth it? They stared at each other, these four, and though none voiced a concern, it was uppermost in their mind. Was it worth it?

"We come out of this the way I want, we're rich, we're famous, maybe infamous, but we are rich all the same. I say go for it." He was a tall man; he spoke with a deep Southern accent. Most thought him stupid because of that accent. They were wrong, but he didn't bother to correct them.

"I don't know," the older man with the bracelet said. "You guys are young enough to fight it off. I may not be."

"We all gotta go sometimes, Doc," the Southerner replied.

The Doctor glanced sharply at the Southerner, then shrugged his shoulders and smiled. "Okay, we're all fools that will probably die, but I hope we at least die rich."

The Black Man didn't say anything at first, then, "You think it's the only way?"

"Don't know," the Southerner replied. "I do think it's the safest way. People pity those that land in a hospital. We can use that to advantage, if need be. Maybe, hopefully, it won't need be."

A GENESIS FOUND

The Fourth Man had long black hair and was silent as was his proclivity. He just nodded.

"Times a wasting," said the Southerner. "Average time for infection is 7 days. Varies per person of course."

He reached out and removed one of the syringes from the table in front of them. He injected himself in the arm. Then he nodded and said, "I could really use the company guys."

Each in turn injected himself. They each tossed their syringes away, except the Southerner; he kept his for purposes of his own.

"We've got a week to pull it off," the Southerner said. "Let's go. Time to get rich or die trying."

The end of one thing is usually the beginning of another.

The Wisdom of Bart Thompson

In the midst of the depression you got by as best you could. This was particularly true of rural Southern people, black or white. The War Between the States was long over but not the effect of losing that war. Added to that was a general lack of education. Together they formed a recipe for poverty such as the world had rarely seen.

John Patton Junior was carrying a shotgun almost as large as himself, which wasn't saying much. He was all of twelve years old and he was hunting for Hoover Hedgehogs to add to the family's dining table. It was either one of those or hunger this night.

Unless you're over fifty you probably don't know what a Hoover Hedgehog is. They are rabbits. See there was a president named Hoover and he believed in free markets, or he didn't believe in free markets, it depends on who you asked. Now this Hoover fellow might have been able to do something about the

Depression, or he might not have. Again it depends on who you ask. But the general feeling in this part of America was that Mr. Hoover had caused this here depression. So speaking despairingly of him was generally appreciated and the fact that people hunt rabbits or starve had given the lowly animal their nickname. Besides, it didn't make them any less tasty.

Patton was cold, his coat, if you could call it that was full of holes. He was very small, very thin. He would be handsome one day, but you sure could not have predicted it by the way he looked now.

His hunting led him through these strange mounds. Injuns had built them, or maybe the Vikings, or giants, he never knew which story to believe. He stopped for a moment to look at them. They didn't look scary, though he had heard tales of course. Once there had been a lot more but the farmers had knocked them down to get good fertile soil. He heard they had found neat things, but then again, you hear all sorts of stuff.

The wind blew and he pulled his jacket tight as he could about his thin frame. Maybe, just maybe one day, he would know why they were built and who built them. But that was another day. Today he needed a Hoover Hedgehog and he walked off from his destiny without a backwards glance.

A Genesis Found

Now on DVD & Video on Demand

www.agenesisfound.com

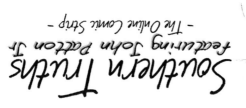

Southern Truths
featuring John Patton Jr
- The Online Comic Strip -

Discover More Adventure with John Patton Jr...

The world of *A Genesis Found* is growing this Fall with the launch of *Southern Truths featuring John Patton Jr*, a bi-weekly online comic strip that begins where the film left off.

Years have past, but John Patton Jr. still hasn't shaken the burden he unearthed in Moundville. Through War, Love and Loss, John's successes are overmatched by the discovery—the secret—the fears he can never explain. War Hero, Archaeologist, and Husband & Father—the best years of John's life are put at peril by mounting obsession and his search to get back what was took.

John's search for God carries him through ball turret service in the Pacific War, and continues with his rise to prominence as one of the most important archaeologists of his day. But in science he can find no answers—until he's willing to put it all on the line for the search of a mythical ancestor, "The Itinerant Man"—John's last chance to explain away what he found, and reclaim what he lost.

Scripted by *A Genesis Found* scribe Lee Fanning, and drawn by newcomer Kevin Maggard, follow the bi-weekly serial free online at **agenesisfound.com!**

There's more behind this mystery...

Look closer behind the mystery with **Buried in the Mounds,** the literary counterpart of *A Genesis Found,* the independent feature from Wonder Mill Films. The title's special features include:

- ✄ The first chapter from John Patton Jr.'s **Buried in the Mounds,** the book that started it all.
- ✄ An anecdotal essay by Assistant Director Markus Matei about the making of the film.
- ✄ An in-depth interview with Writer/Director Lee Fanning and Producer Benjamin Stark.
- ✄ The original shooting screenplay in its entirety, illustrated throughout with stills from the film.
- ✄ A bonus pilot comic from *Southern Truths* featuring *John Patton Jr,* a web serial that picks up where the film leaves off.

Experience more from the world of *A Genesis Found* with **Buried in the Mounds!**

Flip *Buried in the Mounds* Over for Another Book!

A Genesis Found: The Film Companion is really two books in one— **Buried in the Mounds** & **A Genesis Found: The Novelization.**

A Genesis Found: The Novelization is an exclusive, brand new interpretation of the story by mystery author Wilson Toney. *The Novelization* goes into depth where the film can't, with exciting new details, extended scenes, and brand new sequences you won't find in the film!

Buried in the Mounds

Buried in the Mounds

John Patton Jr.

Adjunct Press
New York, NY

Buried in the Mounds

Contents

Chapter One

Every summer is hot in Moundville, Alabama, and it was particularly so in June of 1938. I sweat my share that summer, and toiled my share in those fields, sowing nothing and reaping nothing if not a cartful or two of long-dead bones, and maybe as much in broken bits of ceramics. Others were building the Jones Museum that summer, or laying down roads through the site. As luck would have it, I was assigned to excavation under the direction of Walt Jones himself and another man named DeJarnette.

It wasn't my first summer in Moundville. I grew up just outside Tuscaloosa, born to honest God-fearing parents who were poorer than dirt even before the Depression. I do believe, as bad as things got, there were a number of folks like ourselves whose lot improved, if only a little bit, when the Depression hit and the rulers of this land finally began to take notice of her poor. Anyhow the Park was as good as my backyard, though it was a miles-long hike away. I never went there in particular; there was nothing special about the mounds to me—I knew, or at least had heard, that they weren't natural, that giants or Vikings or Indians had built them—but to me they were hills, all the same, and nothing very impressive about them. I ended up there, often enough, because I liked to follow the meanderings of the Black Warrior, either hunting rabbits (or anything else I thought my small rifle could kill), fishing, or hiding from my elders. I never got lost as such, for I knew the country too well, and yet I did lose myself willingly in that wilderness, where every gnarled tree and every jutting rock called to me. There's not much as can weigh your spirit down when you're all of maybe ten years old. Times were hard and hungry, but with a homemade fishing rod, a rifle,

1

or my father's shotgun if I were lucky, I did not feel that life was other than it should be.

Twenty years of my life passed before I ever went further from home than Moundville, the occasional trips into Birmingham aside. When I was first assigned to Moundville with the Corps, although that was good fortune for my family and me—at least it beat sharecropping—still I thought little of the place, at least not all at once. Then in 1942 I went to the Pacific Theatre of Operations, where I served as a ball turret gunner in the 63[d] Bombardment Squadron. By the time I came back home, the Corps was gone, but I knew that my place was in Moundville. I don't rightly remember now, what it was that first caught my imagination and life-long curiosity—whether it was the slow realization of the powerful yet subdued presence of the womb-like mounds; or if maybe it was the first time I saw the mysterious, ancient images left behind by the Mississippian culture; or maybe it was the first time I uncovered a skeleton, the meager remains of a once-living human being.

Man has a certain amount of grace while he's living and can bring himself to think fondly on most anything he's done—and myself, I do tend to romanticize those days. From the dead, particularly the long dead, that grace is surely gone—gone out from the body at least. A skeleton, whether or not time has spared it some remnant of cloth, is naked, in every conceivable way, hiding nothing but also revealing nothing. The eye sockets of a human skull, though empty, still hold the most intense stare a living man can meet. It's a stare you can't quite look away from, and it's a stare that means something or wants something, like Death lives in that stare. I am no mystic, but I can believe that God in His wisdom deemed that certain things ought not be seen, and so compelled men to bury their dead. Perhaps then I have sinned in digging up what was rightfully buried, and in studying what was

2

rightfully hidden. And perhaps for this I have also been punished. However, desecration of graves was not my intention.

Somehow the same thought always occurred to me when I gazed on these ancient dead. These men, I thought, and women and children, did not know Christ; and they had no Bible. I still don't know why precisely this thought should have occurred to me. I considered myself a Christian, as did every decent person I knew, but I never was a church-going man, although my father was a Lay Preacher, and my mother gave me hell for it (fearing for my sake the one with the capital H). I liked to listen to the stories, and even tried to read many of them for myself; but truly spiritual feelings were not in me, at least not as far as I could tell. All the same it troubled me, that a whole race could be damned at its birth.

The more I learned about the Mississippian people, however, from Dr. Jones as well as through my own careful studies and observations, the less troubled I was by this thought. Instead I sometimes had an eerie, indescribable feeling, like I was walking in the footsteps of ancient men; in some sense breathing their air, and at times I even felt as though I could see a thing through their eyes. Without even meaning to do so. Of course, I *did* mean to; it was an all but stated intention of my job—but that's science. I imagine a physicist or an astronomer, looking at the ways of the world and the universe, sometimes is surprised to find himself filled with an awesome, sub- or super-rational sense of the totalities of existence. Even if it's the very reason he chooses his discipline, the calling of his life, he's still surprised each time to hear the call with the same force and luring appeal, a siren's call for the man of learning. Yet the call often goes unanswered; and in the name of objectivity a scientist will always deny the validity of any such experience. But I believe that every living soul—scientist or not, Christian or heathen, everybody—we are all after that same thing, in one form or another.

BURIED IN THE MOUNDS

Hoping for greater insights, I have tried to answer such calls. And indeed I have learned much about the Mississippian peoples in this way. Still, for all my efforts, and for those of other dedicated scientists alongside of whom I have worked, the Mississippian culture is still and always will be mysterious. They had no writing system to speak of; and it seems they were already in decline before Columbus arrived, so there is not even any significant European record relevant to their culture. The interpretation of prehistoric evidence is not an exact science and is particularly problematic in this case. The Mississippian religious and/or cultural iconography, while consisting mostly of easily identifiable motifs, is esoteric with respect to its symbolic and ideological meaning. One of the most common of these, the Eye in the Hand, is said to represent a Deity, or else a portal into the afterlife (as Walt Jones thought). But this and other such theories are essentially educated guesses—and with the amount and nature of evidence available on the subject, 'educated' in this instance is a rather meaningless, euphemistic epithet.

People once believed that the mounds could not have been built by the American Indians or their ancestors—that these people were too primitive to have done so. It was even suggested that the Indians destroyed an earlier civilization which had built them all over the continent. But who actually made the mounds? The scholars of the last century plucked their answer straight out of the sea, saying it was the Atlanteans, after leaving their sinking continent, some of whom migrated eastward and constructed the pyramids of Egypt, others of which went westward and built all the pyramids and mounds of the Americas. Still other learned men would say that it was the Lost Tribes of Israel. The archaeological evidence, of course, makes it absurd to think that anyone but the Indians could have built the mounds. Nonetheless, the greater part of the mystery has remained.

BURIED IN THE MOUNDS

I became convinced early on, while just a cadet in the Corps, that Moundville held secrets unlike anything heretofore seen in the anthropological world. It was a gut feeling, but that gut feeling would be proved right much sooner than I could ever have imagined—and when it happened, I was not ready for it. I have spent the greater part of my career looking for an easy explanation, or any kind of explanation, anything with which to diminish the fearfulness I inherited along with the grasping of Moundville's greatest secret. But all the explanation I have ever found is the one I wanted so dearly to avoid. And so for thirty-five years I have kept the secret, half hoping that somebody else would discover it and relieve me of my burden, or else that God would strike me down and the secret with me.

This has not happened. The secrets have been kept too well. For centuries they had lain buried in the mounds; they are buried there still, awaiting the right time to be born out again. Through all my years of research at the Moundville site, I have been concerned with the beginnings of the Mississippian culture and with its ultimate end. In so doing I have studied the fragments of ancient mysteries that were left behind, which when pieced together begin to tell stories of genesis, exodus, and revelation. The last revelation, which destiny or chance alone could have given to me, I now pass on for the sake of my children and my grandchildren that they may confront and overcome what I have always feared.

JOHN PATTON JR.

1973

The War on Weekends

The Production of *A Genesis Found*
By Markus Matei

My guess would be that most people who hear the title "assistant director" think one of two things: it's the director's personal assistant or it's a creative collaborator. Neither is correct. The AD is who keeps things organized on the set. "Keeps what organized?" you may ask. The answer is: everything. At any given moment, I had to know the answer to any logistical or practical question (very much the same way Lee had to know the answer to every creative question. And he did.)

The opportunity to work on *A Genesis Found* came to me in November of 2007. I knew Lee Fanning from taking some film classes with him at the University of Alabama. I'd helped him the year before on *The Metal Wings*, his senior-year short film.

The Metal Wings was shot over several weekends in early 2007. Lee, Stephen Lucas, and I were all in the same film class in which we had an entire semester to work on one short narrative project. Stephen was the director of photography on that project as well while I divided my time recording sound and doing grip work (read: carrying stuff). That was the time when I really got to know Lee and Stephen. I was intrigued by their enthusiasm and open-minded approach. Lee and I helped Stephen on his experimental short *Hallways*, and Lee played a small part in my ill-fated crime drama *Rotten Apples*.

Lee sent me an email asking me to work on *Genesis* as the assistant director. It was all very official, and he had attached a

letter outlining their needs and expectations, the requirements of the job, and why he thought I would be a good candidate. In some ways, it seemed ludicrous to see such an official request coming from a friend. A regular email with some quick info and the script would have sufficed. But I don't think Lee was just trying to get someone to fill the position. We were mostly working with friends and others who very quickly became our friends, and while that allowed for a great set atmosphere to develop, it's very dangerous for people to become too comfortable in that kind of situation. As a result, bad habits develop; creative people get lazy, and stop challenging each other. Everybody has a great time, but the work suffers. I don't want to overstate things, but in a way, Lee's initial email set a tone of professionalism that was necessary for the production to be successful.

At this point, I still had two semesters of school ahead of me. I'd pretty much completed all my film classes for my major, so going out and doing it for real was an intriguing prospect. The commitment was considerable. Looking at the production schedule, I could tell it would take over a large part of my summer. Back then, I still knew nothing of the incredible physical and mental challenges that awaited.

Our first production meeting was sometime in December of 2007. It obviously wasn't my first taste of driving the two hours and ten minutes from Tuscaloosa to Huntsville, but it didn't prepare me for my future familiarity with the drive. I've done that drive around thirty times by now, 150 miles there and 150 miles back. This includes two weddings in late summer of 2008. That's a lot of mileage, but I don't know where I would be without it now. I don't know whether I really would have chosen to try and pursue this career. It was a challenge. I had to put a lot of time and energy into it, but the process and the result were both extremely rewarding. It would be a shock to me if I ever worked on a movie as physically challenging as *A Genesis Found*.

BURIED IN THE MOUNDS

I think if I ever do manage to break into the business, it'll be more hard work and long hours, but I can't imagine it being more physically taxing than the *Genesis* shoot. We shot in the woods near Decatur, Alabama where we had to descent a half mile into a valley carrying all the equipment, tents, chairs, food, coolers, and everything else. We shot inside a beat-up 1970s camper, having to cram up to eight or ten people into it at the same time. We shot inside a damp cave we could only access by navigating a series of strategically placed rocks in a brook that lead into the cave. The camera and the lights had to go in the same way. We occasionally had a herd of cows watch us do this. All that on top of the heat, the humidity, and the ticks. It was incredibly exhausting. And at the end of every two-day shoot awaited the two-hour drive home.

We had auditions in January and February. We wanted to reach a lot of people, so we had auditions in Tuscaloosa, Birmingham, Huntsville, and Nashville. After that, we had callbacks in Huntsville. My job was to greet the actors, have them fill out a sign-in sheet, and direct them to the script pages (called "sides") for the different characters. I think in all, I signed in around one hundred actors. They're an interesting breed, to say the least. In Tuscaloosa, I had a group of college girls who were wearing short skirts and low-cut tops. Remember, this was in January, and it was the one day when it snowed in Tuscaloosa. This is an event that only occurs once every couple of years. They asked me if I was the guy who could get them the part. I gave them an ambiguous answer. Next thing I knew, they started adjusting themselves in front of me. The bathroom was right down the hall.

But on the weirdness scale, nothing tops one actor in Birmingham. This guy must have been around forty-five. That didn't stop him from reading for the role of Bart Thompson (a role eventually filled by Luke Weaver). He was one of the last ones to show up, and waited well over an hour. He told me that

he worked with horses and some other things I can't remember. He practiced his lines continuously, reading them out aloud. At one point, he practiced in the glass-enclosed passage between the entrance and the interior of the building. He chose me as his point of reference and proceeded to deliver his lines at me. I could hear him even though I was still sitting behind my desk. Lee and Ben were similarly horrified by his audition but were somehow able to keep it together. The video of the audition has gained a legendary reputation in Wonder Mill circles.

We had our table read on March 29. When it got time for everyone to introduce him or herself and talk about his or her job, I took the opportunity to establish the way things would work on the set. I said that in the universe of the project, Lee was God. This was obvious overkill, but I was only half-joking. I wanted to set the tone, let people know that there wouldn't be any screwing around, and most of all, make sure that everyone would respect the hierarchy of the set. I have no recollection of how my statement was received, but I knew I had to say it, and I would do it again.

I had been familiarizing myself with my job in theory during preproduction. Initially, I didn't know anything about it. Any production on which I had worked previously was lucky to have more than two people behind the camera. An assistant director was an unthinkable luxury. During the first couple of weekends, it became very obvious that a great part of my job would be to be the asshole on the set. I couldn't let people get too comfortable, joke around too much, lose focus, drop the ball, sit around too much, eat too many peanut butter crackers. All this wasn't actually a completely conscious decision of mine, despite the way it sounds. I can look back on it now, and it's pretty clear why things worked out the way they did. Basically what I did was make sure that people moved fast, often reprimanding them in a half-joking way. It was always a challenge to get people to hustle, but preserve

a good working environment. The fact that I never had to chew out anybody (although I would have if necessary) shows that we had a group of serious individuals who knew what to do and who worked well together.

What they tell you is that as the AD, the set is yours. You run the set. So it was my responsibility to ensure that everyone adhered to the proper workings of the set, the hierarchy, and the professional attitude. To be perfectly honest, a lot of the time this just boiled down to pure nitpicking, but someone had to do it. We couldn't drop our standards, because that's just the first step of several that lead to creative compromise, disagreements, misunderstandings, and ultimately, chaos.

As I keep mentioning, there is a very clear hierarchy on a film set. And even though our budget was practically nothing on any professional scale, it was still a real movie. The process of making it had to reflect that. To this day, that's what impresses me the most about Wonder Mill Films. We probably could have made this film in the familiar chaotic student-film manner, where friends help each other out without much dedication and motivation, but *Genesis* would have been a grueling experience, and I'm convinced no one would have come back for *The Nocturnal Third*.

Because we had such a small crew, everybody had to do their part carrying equipment and setting up camp. From time to time, one of the departments needed additional help. I was right in the middle of that. As AD, I was constantly worrying about the status of every department either on set or at camp. My job was equally rewarding and nerve wrecking. It was a great thrill to be effectively in charge of the set. It was every department's duty to come to me with any questions, updates, and concerns, because the director can never be approached directly, most of all when he's dealing with the actors. I was the direct line to Lee Fanning, and I tried my best to keep reminding people of that fact (Ben Stark will tell

you that my tenure as AD was a nonstop ego trip, and there's a little truth in that).

At the same time, I was under constant pressure. I was the go to guy for any questions about anything regarding the schedule, any requests to speak to the director, the time to the next shot, the time allotted for each shot, information on setup changes, and more. Also, I was in charge of keeping the time code log where I recorded good and bad takes. Whenever the P2 Card hard drive in the camera got filled up, I had to give the time code sheets to our workflow engineer Hope Lavelle, who would immediately start transferring the clips to two backup hard drives. We had two P2 Cards, so by the time the second one became full, the first one would be ready to go. It was a good system, and it actually made things a lot easier for Lee once he got ready to edit the film. Every clip would already be named and marked as either a good or bad take, and everything would be organized by scene and date.

When I say the system worked well, I mean that it's an efficient way to shoot while minimizing the chance of losing footage. Mind you, minimizing does not mean eliminating, and we were painfully reminded of the fleeting nature of the ones and zeros of digital files on July 19, 2008 in Decatur, Alabama.

The land in Decatur belonged to a really great guy by the name of Danny Hyatt. He was happy to let us use his property and also let us use the power box he had set up at the top of the hill. We were able to use Danny's backyard as a parking lot and our base for all the equipment we could do without. Still, most of it had to go with us, which meant that most of us ended up making numerous trips down and back up. Apple boxes, C-stands (heavy), coolers full of bottled water and soda cans (heavy!), the light kit (HEAVY) – you name it, I carried it down the hill. We all did. And then back up twelve hours later. The path down was littered with rocks of different sizes. I was taking a coaching soccer class during that time. Our professor insisted on us actually doing the

training exercises ourselves, so my legs were already sore by the time the weekends came around. That hill made me feel like my legs were going to come off.

While racing against the disappearing sunlight in the heavily wooded valley in Decatur, producer Ben was the bearer of horrific news. He had sprinted down the hill at suicidal pace and informed us that the clips of some of the last takes we had done were corrupted. We had been forced to use a different laptop to try to get the clips off the card because our P2 Card reader had stopped working. In that process, the files had been damaged. We were still half a dozen shots away from making our day, and had already moved on to a different part of the woods.

In our circumstances, not making our day was not an option, especially at such a difficult location. Lee and Ben decided that we would just have to finish the scene we were working on and then go back and reshoot the three shots we lost. "Hustle!" was our motto as it has been on so many occasions before and after.

We already moved quickly pretty much all the time. We just had to. There were a certain number of shots we had to get each day. There was occasionally a little bit of room for dropping a couple of shots and picking them up on another day, but certainly not as a rule. We had a very tight schedule, and were usually looking at over twenty shots a day, which, from what I've heard, is about twice as many as you would do on a normal Hollywood production. I got into the habit of announcing the time we had for each shot. Whenever we fell behind schedule, I would announce that too. Five behind. Ten behind. Forty-five behind. We're three hours behind. It happened. More often than we would have liked, but we always made up for it somehow. It wasn't any different this time. We had been dealt a cruel blow, but we had to keep going. In the end, Lee didn't feel he compromised despite the staggering pace at which we moved.

BURIED IN THE MOUNDS

But it wasn't all woods and caves. As anybody who is reading this knows, the story revolves around two excavations at the Moundville Archaeological Park. We got to film in the actual park for several days, but conducting a real excavation was out of the question. On the other hand, without those scenes, there wouldn't have been a movie. So what we came up with was to build our own mound. Lee and Ben managed to find someone who owned some undeveloped land in south Huntsville. The surrounding area could be passed off as Moundville. A few months prior to shooting, the construction of the fake Mound F began. I wasn't able to be part of it, but the result was impressive, as anyone can see in the film. We ended up shooting parts of the same scenes 160 miles apart, and it worked very well. Since we were shooting near a road and right next to a subdivision, we always had to make sure not to get any cars or houses in the shot. But the most memorable of the shoots at Mound F occurred the day after some heavy rain. The dirt road leading to the site had turned into a muddy nightmare, and only the bravest of us even tried to make it there by car. The rest of us had to park at the side of the road and walk. Alabama's red dirt has the consistency of clay and our shoes immediately became caked with it. Walking this way was interesting, to say the least.

When making call sheets, I always included the weather forecast in one corner. There were a number of predictions for scattered showers for the entirety of the shoot, but it never rained. The exception was the one day at fake Mound F. It cost us a few hours, but overall, we were very lucky. Considering that almost all of the film was shot outdoors, we encountered very few weather related problems.

I suppose in my own limited way I can make this analogy and say that making *A Genesis Found* (and later, *The Nocturnal Third*) was like going to war every weekend and coming back home Sunday night. It's two different lifestyles with two different

13

groups of people, but you alternate every week for three months. Monday through Friday, you work and spend time with your friends and family. Saturday morning, you go back into the Alabama wilderness and shoot an adventure movie. Sunday night, you come back home to all the familiar things and faces, but something's different. Maybe you have changed. Maybe you need to readapt to things at home. You need to take into account people's feelings and expectations. In the jungle, the only person you can trust is yourself and the crewmember next to you. You can only hope they know what they're doing. Once you're there, there are no more guarantees. But somehow, among all the chaos, everything makes sense. There is a hierarchy, and you just go with whatever events unfold. There is a game plan, but it always changes, and sometimes you just have to make the choice and ball it up and throw it into the Black Warrior. You just do what you have to do. People at home wouldn't understand.

We were very fortunate to have a cast and crew comprised of very talented and dedicated individuals. For example, I would never have expected a small production such as ours to have such a talented makeup artist as we had in Jackie Hadwin. The same goes for our costume designer Peyton Fanning. But I really wouldn't know what I'm talking about if I didn't single out Stephen Lucas, our director of photography. His experience, enthusiasm, and professionalism make him the poster child of our group. I think everybody found it helpful how he introduced authentic production conventions and lingo into our independent production. It definitely allowed me to take the project very seriously. For example, in the movie business, clothespins are called "C47s." We use them to clip colored gels, diffusion, and other things to the lights. They're practical and can withstand the heat of these powerful lights. Extension cords are called "stingers." One day, Stephen went into a gas station to buy some gum. Noticing his California driver's license and a bunch of C47s

clipped to his shirt, the clerk asked him: "Is that some kind of California thing?" I guess you could say it is.

The morale on set was almost always excellent. I can't really imagine a better working environment. Everyone was always prepared and ready and willing to work. Whenever we needed to solve a problem, we put our heads together and came up with something. We worked with what we had. We improvised. This was crucial since it was such a difficult film to make. An outsider would never have guessed that we were not getting paid for this. This was by no means a normal experience for me. I've worked on projects where egos clashed, artists compromised and went home at the end of the day disappointed and bitter. Sometimes I worked with people who clearly didn't want to be there. To a certain extent, you can't blame them. Making a film is hard. It's not glamorous. It certainly isn't when you're working a sixteen-hour day in the middle of the summer in a tick-infested part of the woods in Nowhere, Alabama. For some people, it takes this kind of tough experience to figure out whether this is the right job. I could only hope the people around me on *Genesis* shared my work ethic. Fortunately, they did. We were spoiled to have a group of people who didn't mind the difficulty, but faced it head-on. The mood on the set was always focused and often whimsical. I always loved giving Elliot a hard time and (jokingly) crushing his ego. Jokes helped everybody bond and deal with the stress. *That's what she said* jokes were especially popular. The best one I got was when Peyton, who was working on a costume, said: "Push it in gently, dear."

Looking back on the making of *A Genesis Found*, I'm amazed by the physical and mental effort all of us put into it. Not only that, but the fact of how willingly all of us accepted the situation and did whatever was necessary to get the job done was amazing. You either had to be crazy or really love the process. It might surprise some that I hold Lee in such high regard despite

the number of things I have complained about concerning the physical strain. I was happy to do it. How could I not have been with Lee always keeping his good attitude? It was both infectious and reassuring.

Lee and Peyton were married on August 23, 2008. Ben and Danielle (who did prop and décor work on *Genesis* and went on to produce *The Nocturnal Third*) followed less than a month later. I was happy to make the drive up to northern Alabama on both occasions. It was a truly satisfying ending to the summer. I was a bit out of the loop after that since my job was done, but the anticipation to see the finished film kept on growing. On April 27, 2009, we finally had the premiere at the Bama Theatre in Tuscaloosa. It was the culmination of a great experience and a great satisfaction after all of our hard work.

A Genesis Found played at several film festivals in the months afterward, and a good number of the cast and crew returned for *The Nocturnal Third*, Ben's directorial debut, later in 2009. As of this writing, *The Nocturnal Third* is in post-production, and we're all looking forward to its release, along with the DVD release of *A Genesis Found*. The film itself was the genesis for lifelong friendships and hopefully long and successful careers for all the involved. The film was a terrific experience, and for me personally, it made the difference that made me decide to try and follow this career path. On the way, I met a lot of great people that I'm happy to know.

Tuscaloosa, Alabama
February 2010

Making Movies in Moundville

An Interview with
Producers Lee Fanning and Benjamin Stark

Interview by Benjamin Flanagan/Story Published April 24, 2009

Benjamin Flanagan: Both of you are outspoken fans of the fourth Indiana Jones movie, and <u>*A Genesis Found*</u> *focuses heavily on archaeology mixed with mystery and adventure. Did that film or just the Indy films in general have a loose or direct influence on the conception and follow-through with this story?*

Lee Fanning: Actually, very much so. The film is, I think, conceptually a way to deconstruct the expectations of the supernatural adventure that, essentially, *Raiders of the Lost Ark* is the pinnacle of. So we kind of took that genre, and actually, you'll see in the film that a lot of it kind of deals with this character using the awe of this supernatural mystery to lure this other character, who is very much skeptical at first and against it – he kind of lures him into this world, and he uses storytelling to do that. So I guess that's one of the sub-themes of the film: story as manipulation, and this idea that we are a culture that is so obsessed with these supernatural myths, that I think Indiana Jones is a perfect example of, and a lot of Spielberg's work. There's a lot of Spielbergian references in that way that we point to how story can manipulate truth, and that's the main antagonist's role throughout. He's a storyteller, a documentary filmmaker, and he uses story as a means of getting people to believe something a bit more extreme,

17

but also as a tool to show how manipulative it can be and how our culture is based on this heavy dependence on storytelling. His objective is to show that that can be dangerous.

Benjamin Stark: There are several sequences in the film that take place in the 30s, and it was a conscious decision to, because that was a bit of a more exploratory time and a mysterious time, stylistically, that there is a disparity there between the 30s and the modern day sequences, because it seems almost that power of storytelling may have been a little more effective as a tool back then because of the way communication was, the way media was. So on that surface level, obviously there's a little bit of a nod to Indiana Jones there taking place in the 30s. But from a publicity standpoint, from a superficial level, I don't think there was anything taken from the fourth Indiana Jones movie because I don't think we knew anything about the plot of it when Lee started writing. Did we?

LF: No, we didn't know anything about it. Actually, it scared the hell out of me.

BS: Yeah, last summer and even leading up to shooting, we had several conversations where Lee was very nervous about the new Indy film and what the twist or what the story element might be that we all came to figure out what it was and how it would affect the film, but we think that it's been long enough, and, thankfully, that film hasn't been received too well, so I don't think anybody's even going to remember it by the time they see our film.

BF: Yeah, but it was received well by you guys.

BS: Yeah, but I'm not going to call us rip-offs.

LF: It's not a cultural event like *The Dark Knight* was.

BS: Right, my mom isn't talking about *Indiana Jones 4.*

BF: Ben, describe Lee's directing style in terms of how he manages a set but interacts with his cast and crew.

BS: It's very specific. He does his homework more than anybody on the set, at least as much as the hardest worker on the set. As far as commanding the set, there's that old cliché of directors as the general of the army, and with our setup it wasn't necessarily that way because the least of his concerns should have been what the mood or what the day looked like because he needed to focus on spending time with actors and kind of perfecting the shot list and things like that. But he did set a hardworking pattern and openness and honesty and just kind of a friendliness that was almost always there on set for everybody. But pretty much just specificity and very hard work. He demanded time with the actors every single day, which I think is important and I think is pretty rare in filmmaking on our level. A lot of the times, young directors often kind of go for shots and that kind of stuff before acting and performance, but he made that his number one goal.

BF: Lee, was Ben able to keep you on your toes throughout the production? At times producers and directors fail to see eye to eye on scheduling and budget, but you two have worked together for years.

LF: Yeah, actually Ben and I had a really good working relationship. I think the only time there was a little bit of heightened tension was like the last shoot day because we had so much to get done. I was co-producer, so we had to both address

those kinds of issues going in, those practical issues. Now there was a lot of me saying, "Hey, don't worry, we have to get these shots," and Markus Matei was our assistant director, and he was probably the more vocal kind of "Hey get your tail moving," which is what his job was. But there were times when Ben was just honest and said, "We need to do this, if you can do this better, let's do it." It was always like that. It was never a, "Look, you've got three hours to get this, and if you don't get it, you don't get it." Of course, he's a director, so he has an understanding of what I'm doing, and he wants to make a good film. And because we were not working on something where another day is going to cost us another $5 million because it's such a small scale – granted, we don't want to waste people's time, and he wasn't by any means going to let me be, uh, what's the word I'm looking for?

BS: Self-serving?

LF: Yeah, self-serving, and just kind of waste people's time, but he understood what I needed as a storyteller and what we needed to get the film done, and we were honest with each other. He would tell me if we can do it better, let's do it, and I would think about it. And that's the good thing about working with Ben and Markus because both of them are directors, too, and so I was able to kind of take practical problems and address them from a story standpoint and kind of make them work for us because, granted, things happen and things don't turn out exactly as you originally planned on the day of the shoot. So there's two ways of doing it. Either you can just kind of compromise and say we'll work with what we've got, or you can say okay well let's use this the best we can, and allow it [even] if it changes something in the story as long as it still works. And looking at the cut now, I don't really see anywhere that we compromised, and that's kind of a testament to

Ben. Granted, things change, but there was nothing where we were like, "I don't know how we can do this without it, but we'll just do it anyway and hope it works." Every time we had an issue, we addressed it, and we tackled it, and we said, with the specific mindset of, "Let's make it work for the story, let's use it, let's address it to some kind of major theme." That was very unique.

BF: During their time at film school, students have trouble checking their egos and accepting someone else's creative vision instead of embracing collaboration. Ben is also a director who has ambitions on making his own feature films. Were you able to find an early comfort and accept your role as producer during the shoot while Lee directed? Were you both happy with the working relationship you developed on set, in the vein of a Ron Howard/Brian Grazer or Kevin Smith/Scott Mosier team?

BS: There were definitely moments of weakness where I did feel like directing, but it wasn't ever like, (forcefully) "I want to direct this movie. Give it to me." But for the most part, I think that I learned more about directing doing this film as a producer than I have at any other time when I was directing anything else just because we were working very closely, and I was learning a lot about Lee's process and kind of what we thought to be the best process. And I was learning a lot from Markus and also Stephen Lucas, our director of photography who's also done a lot of directing, so it was a lot of that open filmmaker mindset that I was able to draw from, so it was satisfying on that level anyway. We have worked in kind of a leapfrog kind of fashion where one of us produces while the other directs, which has made us both learn exponentially faster than we would if we were kind of directing

every single time. I wouldn't call us a producing/directing pair forever necessarily in that way, but I do think that it's a pretty good system that we've figured out.

BF: Are you essentially taking turns? Lee, will you produce the next film Ben directs? Do you have plans for that kind of thing down the line?

LF: Oh yeah, Ben's got a final draft done on the next thing we're doing. It's called *The Nocturnal Third*. I'm producing it, and we're trying to shoot that again in about late summer-early fall. Our idea is, we're going to keep doing this until we don't need each other or until we both have money where we can direct our own things...but right now because we're essentially working in a place where there's not a whole lot of industry and there's not a whole lot of hired director opportunities, you have to generate your own opportunities here if you want to direct. I know some people who do that and who only direct, and you kind of get your own projects going, and it's a turnaround time of like three to four years. They do everything in post on the first project, that's been two years there, and then you have to go and write your next film and that's another year. Then you've got to get the money for it, and that's probably another year. So, about three years later, you're ready for another one. But by then, you know, your 20s are over. So our idea right now is to kind of expediate that a little bit, and therefore we constantly have something at least in development, in the pipeline, that's not killing us. I don't want to be writing five scripts at the same time because none of them will be worth anything. I was just a bit more drenched because I was doing some editing during shooting, so I was probably a bit more preoccupied with *Genesis* throughout that whole process. I'm not saying Ben wasn't extremely busy, but he did have a bit more free

time to kind of focus on the idea that he'd been working on, and he developed that, and all throughout post-production he's had a lot more free time than I have just in terms of what projects we're doing, so he was able to kind of knock out the script for that film, and we've already got kind of the basic layout and we're starting to get the production team for that together. And if it was just me directing and him producing, Ben would be waiting on me to get started on my next project, so it is an advantage in that way.

BF: What about the Moundville locale was appealing to this story? Did the script specifically name Moundville as its setting?

LF: Oh yeah, it's exhaustive in its detail dealing with Moundville. Actually, going in, the initial idea was going to be a story set in the 30s Civilian Conservation Corps excavations that were there. That kind of came because I was interested in that kind of entity. The New Deal was a very interesting era. My grandfathers worked in the corps, and it had a certain kind of spirit of adventure quality to that, yet still in a domestic kind of American setting. I was just going to make something up dealing with Moundville, and I found out there actually were excavations at Moundville in the 30s, so I just kind of did a lot of research into the site, and I found a lot of things to root to. So actually not only does it name Moundville, it shows some period digs that are as accurate as we could make them. They're pretty small scale, but all the [real] digs were pretty small scale. There's a lot that deals with the history of the site. A lot deals with the theories and the imagery and motifs of the site and of the Mississippian culture. All of that's in the script, and all of that is accurate. The modern day story deals with a field school excavation at the University of Alabama actually. So I got to go see a couple of field school excavations, and I had a couple of

anthropology guys take a look at the script and kind of get some technical advice. It's very much an attempt to use something very real. It's not just "this is mountain place." It is the real history of the site.

BF: These days, it's pretty rare for independent or studio productions to shoot all principal photography in the state of Alabama. Do you both feel another sense of accomplishment in that you were able to start and finish a film like this in your home state?

BS: Yeah, absolutely. It's very satisfying because it's something you, especially when you're a younger filmmaker, feel that you're just going to have to blindly go to L.A. to do what you like, but it seems like so far that we've been pretty blessed in being able to do it here.

LF: Yeah, it's satisfying. Well, the story was so specifically designed for Alabama and this area, so of course that's rewarding in that we were able to take the resources around us, so it's not like a crutch. That was one of the big things we talked about, too. We don't want to tell a story that's supposed to be set in Colorado and shoot it here, and everyone's like, "Well that doesn't look anything like Colorado," you know what I mean? Use what you have, and so that was kind of rewarding in that we were able to make something that I think works pretty well as a narrative, and it does all take place in the state and is all shot in the state, and it makes sense that it would be that. Not just, "Oh, well they're from there. Of course, it's just a crutch," you know? I think the story, it works, and the Moundville site was kind of key to that because it is a pretty important archaeological site. But also from a production standpoint, it was very satisfying because I've talked to

some people – Stephen has talked to some people and I've met some people recently and just kind of talking to people about who have done and do films in L.A. and other places – and they just tell me that the worst part about doing it there is that everyone's a jerk about locations, and they want money, you know, because it happens there all of the time. But here, the only location we had to pay for was Moundville, and for that we paid like 500 bucks for like free reign of the site for five days. Everything else, like the school and the University of Alabama, we got for free just because people were excited about the production...oh, well Ben has something to say.

BS: Except for one location. We had everything coordinated with some landowners when we were shooting. I won't say what location it was, but we were shooting on one location, and it was kind of in the middle of nowhere. We had all of the location coordinated with the landowners, and everything was fine and we were shooting when all of the sudden one day this angry man showed up near the location right at our crew base. I was on set and somebody walkie-talkied me, and they were like, "Ben, you've got to come to camp right now." So I walked out there, and there was this angry man cursing, I think, and asking what was going on, and I explained to him, you know, we talked to these landowners that were fine to shoot here. Apparently, we were caught in the middle of some sort of family dispute that had like three players in it, and we didn't know what was going on, so we had to coordinate something with him, but we ended up working out a little deal. But that was the only real location problem I think we had.

BURIED IN THE MOUNDS

BF: Was your experience with shooting in Alabama generally positive? Were the local governments and citizens supportive?

LF: Oh yeah, extremely. We never had any issues with anything. We were shooting out in the middle of nowhere lots of times, so that's good because you're not running into people going, "Hey, what are you guys doing?" you know. We didn't have any of that. There's actually no city scenes.

BS: Yeah, I don't think anybody really knew what we were doing anyway because we were so detached from everything.

LF: When I was in Moundville - that was probably where we had the most people seeing us shoot, and there still wasn't that many people there - but there was actually a photographer there who was also a filmmaker from, I think he was from Texas or something. And he came up to us and was talking to us and was like, "Hey, cool. I'll check for it in festivals," and so that was kind of interesting, just kind of a weird coincidence just that some guy who was just traveling through and decided to take some pictures of Moundville and was a filmmaker. But no, it was all very positive. Actually I was very surprised - because we had to shoot some at the University of Alabama - and I was afraid there was going to be just some red tape to kind of deal with and that kind of crap. They were very helpful and were very nice, and they actually busted their butt to get us this location because we had a location kind of fall out on us and we had to get another one. It happened the week before we were scheduled to shoot there, and it was actually downstairs at Rowand Johnson, and they were very cool about that and busted their butts to get all of that legality

straight so that we could do it. So yeah, we didn't have any issues with government or anything.

BF: *Neither of you seem eager to ditch Alabama and pursue potential careers in Hollywood. Is the idea to stay where you are, develop as filmmakers with the resources you have and let whatever is next just come to you?*

BS: Yeah, right now I think we're just kind of whatever we've got to do, we'll do that. So far, moving hasn't really been a logical option. Kind of displacing yourself takes at least six months to a year away from you. Logistically and emotionally you've got to get settled back in. Right now, the call to do it differently hasn't come up yet. If it will come up, we'll answer that as it comes.

LF: Right, yeah. The main thing is that, you've got to start at the bottom, particularly in the film industry and particularly when you're from Alabama. So our kind of reasoning is, at least as of right now, you're going to start at the bottom wherever you are, so you might as well be making your own stuff. That's why we decided to go more for ultra-low budget stuff right now. Granted, I don't want to be making 15k features my whole life, but as of right now, it's a lot better than being a P.A. (production assistant) for a hundred dollars a day or whatever.

BS: I do kind of think it's the wave of the future anyway because the medium has gotten so cheap. It's kind of like the printing press has been invented and everybody's literate now, and now making a movie is no longer like a divine thing. It's becoming more and more the storytelling medium of the masses, which a lot of people thought would be impossible. So I think we're only one

in a million people our age that are doing the exact same thing. I think in ten or fifteen years, it's all going to be decentralized anyway.

LF: Yeah, and another thing just to add on that. I guess that the business, too, they're actually seeing a rise in films like ours being made because they give you such a...you have a lot more freedom in the sense that if you have fifteen grand, you probably don't have a very aggressive investor in the first place; and second off, you don't have to make a whole lot of money when you sell the film in order to pay back your investor and to actually make any profit. That's a big advantage if you're trying to sell it because we've known people who have had to make a lot of compromises with their distribution deals or whatever because they had such a big budget, and because we have such a little budget, we can keep ownership of the film, we can keep everything essentially. It's just that we don't have to sell that much, and we don't have to sell it *for* that much. It gives us a big advantage artistically as well as monetarily because if you can just make a profit on that – you could probably do it for a couple of years.

BF: Lee, this is the first feature film you've directed. Other than length, how does that transition from short to feature take its toll on a young filmmaker?

LF: Actually, I loved it so much better than short films. The main reason is, with short films, you do this yourself and it's just kind of a little thing. You kind of rush yourself a little bit, and you kind of aren't as prepared as you probably should be going in – at least this is my experience with them. You do them quicker than you probably should. Ultimately, just from a storytelling standpoint, you just don't have the amount of time with your script and with

your characters to kind of get something out of it that I think is really worth your time. I think they're great learning tools, don't get me wrong. I'm not dissing the short film medium. I'm just saying I much prefer the feature medium now that I've made a feature from a directorial standpoint. It's harder in some senses, particularly when you're doing so much. We were having to do so much more work than typically a director would do during a feature and typically a producer would do during a feature. So that takes its toll from a stamina standpoint. We were working five days a week, and then we were shooting on weekends. Sometimes we were working five days a week, shooting Friday nights, Saturdays, you know. So there was really no rest, which was very rough when you're shooting for three months. But the real challenge for me has actually been in post just because it's been a year since we started shooting, essentially. Granted, that's because I'm having to do all of the sound editing and all of the mixing and all of that kind of crap – and that really sucks that I'm having to do all of that by myself. I'm not going to do that again. That's the toll of being able to stick to the same thing for two years because I started writing the script in May of '07. So it will be about two years total whenever the film is starting to play festivals. So that's tough just from a storytelling standpoint, I guess. Just being able to get a story that you care enough about to stick with for two years. I was actually looking at some of my shorts just as an exercise, looking at things that took us maybe four months to make total. I was like, man, I could not have spent like two years on that story, I mean even if I did it as a feature. So I guess that's what the challenge is going in and getting a story like that, and yeah, production is just exponentially harder. Aaron Greer actually told us going in, "It's not like a short film times five. It's like a short film times 500." Everything is just exponentially harder because there are no breaks. It's every weekend. And every week we had sort of a mini-disaster. I swear, every week. So yeah, take care of

that through the week and get everything prepped. Like I said, Ben and I had a lot more to do than usual because, essentially, everyone was volunteering. Sometimes people couldn't do something, and some people could be a bit unreliable. We didn't really have an issue with that too much, but it did happen, and we had to kind of compensate for that to get it done. Eventually, though, it kind of drags you along with it. For some reason, the shoot, it was tough, but it never felt like, "Oh God, what did I get myself into?" because you just kind of say okay screw it, we're doing it, and you kind of go with it, and you drag with it, and it becomes this monster, and you've just got to keep the monster going until it's over. So it's probably been harder for me personally in post because that's all on me. It's like no one's forcing me to edit. I just have to do it. That and just the commitment, I guess. But it seemed very natural. Nothing has seemed like, "God, I want to get this over with, and then I'm going to make short films for the next ten years." Everything was very natural, and I'm very much ready to do it again.

BS: No, just the commitment thing. It didn't hit me until a little bit later and even now, as I'm writing my own feature-length script that it's amazing how long you can go as a creative person and just be cool with whatever you're doing before you realize you've got to stop and ask yourself the important question of, "Is this worth my time?" Because in college, and pretty much in the way the mindset of parents and teachers when you're young is as long as you're doing something creative, it's cute and it's fun, and you're doing real good. But as you get to be an adult, you have to really weigh whether or not what you're doing is worth the time. So that kind of hit me early on in the production, as to "Wow, this is going to be really hard," and you have to ask yourself the hard question, which is, "If I'm going to do this, I've got to believe in it." So pretty much the same thing. It's just severe commitment.

BF: How many UA alums or current students or faculty were involved with this production?

BS: Hold on, let me think. I'll just roundabout say fifteen. Just about, maybe fifteen more.

LF: Maybe more than that. Some cast were from UA, too.

BS: So, uh, like I would say 80 percent of the cast and crew.

LF: Not cast. It was probably 80 percent of the crew and like 40 to 50 percent of the cast.

BS: You were wrong in thinking we could answer that question.

LF: It was a lot. I think essentially all the crew except for maybe two or three people because that's where our crew base came from. And then the cast we had casting in various places, but actually most of our main characters came from UA. I think it's because we were a bit more saturated there, so we knew what better places to advertise for actors, so we had a little bit better pull I think there than other places. But we had some pretty good people up in Nashville and...

BS: Birmingham and Huntsville.

LF: Huntsville surprisingly, yeah. We had a couple of leads from there.

BS: We had four auditions in Huntsville, Nashville, Birmingham and Tuscaloosa.

BURIED IN THE MOUNDS

BF: Did your experience at UA have any direct influence on your styles and approaches to filmmaking, particularly with this movie?

LF: I definitely think so. I think from just a practical standpoint. At UA, the program there is not out to make you...your thesis isn't shot on 35 millimeter, you know what I mean? Even the projects you do in class, because we did so much stuff outside of school, it seems like you just kind of have to earn a bit more there because you don't have the kind of opportunities you would if you went to a bigger film school. I actually have a couple of friends at FSU (Florida State University) right now, and they were telling me that it's great because they have so many resources and stuff they have to do, but at the same time, they have to do the scripts they're given and that kind of stuff. So at UA, you could just not like do much, and that's what people did, like sift through and get your degree. And maybe shoot car commercials and get another job doing something else, whatever. Particularly Aaron (Greer) more than anyone else was just kind of this ethos of you've got to do it, and you've got to earn it, and I'm not going to make it easy for you. And that was consistent, and it's great because Aaron has still kept a dialogue up with us even throughout this whole project. He's in Illinois, and he doesn't have any reason to keep any attachment to us. He's just really cool about that. So I think that was a huge part of, going in, our mantra was to kind of, "No one's going to do it for you *and* no one's going to make concessions for small budget." No one's going to make concessions because you're young. People are going to watch your film the same way they're going to watch *The Dark Knight,* and if it can't hold its own to a certain degree.... I mean I guess audiences will make some concessions, but they're not going to say, "Oh, well you know they couldn't help the fact that the movie sucks because they didn't have much money." What they'll say is, "They didn't have

32

much money, but the movie still sucks." And at the very best, they'll say, "Well they don't have a lot of money, but it's pretty good." And I guess that's about the best we can hope for. That was one thing where we were like we have to make it work with what we have and make it legitimately work and not just, "Well it works for a fifteen grand budget," and I'm not sure how successful we were with this, but at least going in we were like, "It has to look like, even if we had $200 million, this is what we would make." Granted, that's a bit of wishful thinking on our part going in, but that was our ethos.

BS: I think the biggest thing that helped us at UA was Aaron Greer because he always forced us to ask ourselves the hard questions. He never gushed over anything ever. He was just a very, very hard critic, and that's exactly the kind of teacher that you need. But also the atmosphere there – while everything was all so friendly and supportive, I was working for the Center for Public Television at the time, and everything kind of taught us how to hustle and figure out how to get equipment and editing space by whatever means necessary. And we can say this probably now because there's no repercussions really I hope, I hope to God there's not. But we kind of twisted the system a couple of times to just get things done, and that definitely helped us figure out how to overcome little annoyances while we were making a feature.

LF: And you do have to overcome a lot of – when you do a feature, particularly because we had so many locations – the fear of a) rejection and b) the fear of asking, in general, favors of people, and sometimes, "I don't know why you would say yes to them" kind of favors. Not like they're illegal or anything, it's just they do require a lot of people we don't even know to do things,

and usually very though things, for free. I was amazed at how helpful people wanted to be and at how excited people were.

BS: We actually had a land developer and owner in Huntsville that let us use part of his subdivision that wasn't developed yet to build our fake mound F.

LF: And he built a road for us, like a dirt road, and a mound and did it for cost.

BS: Yeah, and all we paid for was overhead. And he was just very interested and excited and just friendly about everything. And it's amazing because that's one big thing that we've learned, that you cut off that part of you that has all of those social graces and kind of just a fear of rejection – you just kill that part of yourself because you realize that's what you're going to have to do is ask people things that they don't hear ever, if ever or at all. Most of the time it helps, and even if you get turned down, you at least sacrificed a part of yourself that you didn't need to begin with.

LF: There's been very few dead-ends. Even things that didn't turn out to be like the ultimate lead, it led to something else. So there's only a couple of times when I could say, "Yeah, that's pretty much a closed door that probably didn't need to be opened to begin with."

BS: Yeah, there was never any really stupid ideas. Every idea led to something.

BURIED IN THE MOUNDS

BF: Talk about Stephen Lucas as a director of photography. How has he grown since your collaborations at UA?

LF: Stephen and Joey Brown were essentially our camera team. A couple of days, I think they had Greg Taylor, who is another UA alum now, and he helped them out, and then we had like a camera P.A. one day, Andrew Richardson. But aside from that, it was Stephen and Joey, and they were doing everything. So one thing is that Stephen is extremely professional. He is an extremely hard worker. If you kept him fed, he'll freaking do everything you need. He'll be honest with you. And the great thing about Stephen is that he understands photography as a storytelling device, which you wouldn't think that would be hard for DPs (directors of photography), but in my experience it's really how graceful and smart he is about it. It's really not common that you're going to find someone who's really smart about that aspect of Videography. I think a lot of it has to do with the fact that Stephen is such a director and storyteller himself. But I would tell Stephen like, "Okay, here's the shots I need," I'd tell him the scene, and then I would tell him exactly what they're supposed to function as, from a story functionality standpoint, this has to get across that "Oh, Gardner is alone." I don't know, something that would be obvious, but it also needs to kind of suggest this. I'd tell him that, and he'd be like "Oh, okay, I got you." And that's all he needed. That was very rewarding. He wasn't like, "Well, I don't care," you know what I mean? I was able to kind of give him a feel and a functionality standpoint from not just a storytelling but from also a thematic standpoint, I guess. The functionality of a shot or a scene, and he completely understood it and completely knew how to achieve it. And another thing about Stephen is he had a very consistent design palette in his head going in, and a lot of that was kind of his prep. He wasn't the kind of guy where he would give

you a color plate and say, "These are the kind of colors I'm gonna..." you know. He was just really smart, and he had his kind of ethos going in about what his lighting style approach would be. For modern day, he was like, "We're going to crunch the blacks, color-wise. It's going to be very realistic. The light's going to be very motivated." That's how the world of the modern day story is. It's much more realistic. It's much more domestic. It's much less kind of mysterious and hyperbolic, but in the 30s, we did a lot of day for night and a lot of lighting that's just kind of ambient kind of stuff, atmospheric, magical...What did he call it? Universal?

BS: Cosmic. He would do a setup, and he would be like, (dramatically) "It's cosmic."

LF: That was a direct decision he had going in. That shows a lot of maturity that he's not just trying to overlight every scene. He was very practical about his lighting styles. He used as few lights as he could. A couple of interiors with windows he was able to do with no artificial lighting aside from maybe a bounce board. So that was really fantastic because he didn't have much to work with to begin with. So that was good that he went in with that kind of idea. I think one thing that I've seen that he has improved since we were students would probably be delegation and trusting Joey particularly. Joey was his right-hand man to get what he needs because we used a lot of steadicam for the film, and Stephen, when he got in that thing, he couldn't do anything. So it was up to Joey to essentially adjust all of the lights and to make the tweaks he needed and that kind of stuff. So he became very trustful of that. I think he became more confident in his decision-making. I think also he became, again, more able to underlight. I mean, he's a perfectionist, don't get me wrong. But he was able to do a lot with less while in school we would always use every light we had

and kind of spend forever lighting a scene. He would do everything himself. He went out to L.A. for a little while and came back in, and I think that's one good thing that really rubbed off on him was that professional kind of delegation and having a more practical approach. Just do what you need. Don't be excessive. But, again, he's not just someone that would just do what you need to make it look cinematic and to make it to where you can see everything. And he had a distinct plan to how he lit and the setups he used, and he was consistent in every location. He saw the structure of the film visually, and that's something that we should be paying for. It's not something that you should find with a volunteer DP or a deferred DP. But we got really lucky with that.

BS: The biggest thing I could say that helped me and that I was very happy with was that Stephen's kind of like a sponge. His understanding of the process of moviemaking was a huge help not just from a directing standpoint and storytelling standpoint, but he helped us a ton. I mean I would say 75 percent of the good habits that we developed about running the set came from what Stephen taught us, maybe more than that. And we had a meeting before shooting ever started of how things needed to go, how things needed to flow, and Stephen was really instrumental in kind of showing us and telling us how the big league does it but also why. We weren't doing things in kind of a ritualistic kind of way when running the set where, "Well this is how they do it in Hollywood, so this is how we have to do it." It was all practical, and he helped us figure out kind of a perfect work flow. That paid off big time because we had a very efficient set. A lot of that came from Stephen. It was very professional. I don't know how many compliments we've gotten from the actors and from the other crew people that have worked in other areas of the industry, telling us that our set was the most professional set they've ever

been on, and they've worked on bigger independent films and maybe even some studio films, I'm not sure. But that can all almost be attributed to the discussions that came out of what we talked about with Stephen and Markus and us, too.

LF: And he did have a lot of energy kind of spilling over and kind of his work ethic, I know it inspired me. And I wasn't out there to be lazy, but even I felt guilty, sometimes, seeing someone else who was working so hard. When you show up on set, you're like, oh Stephen is here, and he's going to work extremely hard, and he can't be working harder than me. And I think that was for a lot of people. People were like he's got such a focus and he is such a hard worker that it inspires you to kind of do the same and kind of get on the same pace with him.

BS: Yeah, you feel guilty when you're on a film set eating a banana, and you see people running around with conviction in their eyes. It kind of makes you stand up and do the exact same thing. Not that I was ever sitting down.

BF: When going exclusively local and independent, filmmakers will find it difficult to find actors whose on-screen presence doesn't feel amateur or awkward nearly every second of a film (especially on a college campus). Describe your search for your principal cast and your assessment of their overall performances.

LF: Going in, I knew that, just from experience from working with a lot of collegiate actors and older actors who are around who I knew would be the actors we would have to get, that on average you're probably going to find better younger actors in Alabama than older. The reason being, the younger actors are still here,

though they're going to move off to L.A. or New York and have successful careers while the older actors who are here, for a lot of them it's just kind of a hobby they decided to get into when they got older, or maybe if you're lucky they used to do professional theatre or professional work and now they're just kind of teaching and what not and doing something else. Going in, when I was actually writing the script, I'm not saying that's the reason I wrote it young, but that was kind of a happy accident that we used. All of the cast were pretty young. All of the principals were young, like in their early 20s. Because, again, I knew that I could find stronger younger actors here probably on average, at least more stronger actors that are willing to work for no money. But going in, it was a real test to us being able to trust ourselves and our assessment of actors and of potential in people. One thing that I found that helped the most in casting, and Ben and I have talked a lot about this, but the best thing to look for—well yes, it is look and it is how they handle the material with the sides and auditions. But primarily, just their intelligence and if they seem smart, that really goes a long way. Most everyone we cast, we cast because in the audition they were just smart, and you could tell that there was never a moment where they were a deer in headlights when you were talking to them. They were vocal, they were willing to talk to you about what they were doing. People were nervous. I'm not saying just the people who were very cool and casual, we cast, because that's not true. But you can tell, I think, when something's going on up there that's not just, "Oh, I've had audition classes. How do I react to this?" And I'm not trying to be condescending at all. People have their own ways of doing things. But the one thing we were looking for was a kind of honesty just in that person, just an honesty and an intelligence. We were very lucky with the older actors we got for that reason I said. And all of the older actors we have were very, very good. Dr. Steve Burch actually was in the film, who is a UA professor. All of the older

actors who were in bigger supporting roles were former professional actors that are now teaching and are still really good, and they just do independent films now whenever they can get them just for fun – just to stay in practice. They liked the script enough to do a really good job. I think with the younger cast, they were very hungry. It was everyone's first feature. They were all extremely excited about that, which is good. You want people to be very excited about the film. I've worked on independent films with even bigger budgets than this where everyone was doing it as a day job, and they hate it, and it's a stupid movie. It sucks out the energy of everything on every level. And here we are, this is everyone's free time for the whole summer working on this. What drove them to do such a good job is the excitement of the project and liking the project and not getting the opportunity anywhere else. They were craftsman. I'd say all of the performances were really good. We had one actor, Luke Weaver, who played Bart Thompson, the red-headed guy in the trailer. He was amazing because that character, I knew, was going to be very hard to cast because he was very specific. He was kind of this guy who went out to L.A., he was this really smart filmmaker, he was from Alabama; and he kind of does the Billy Bob Thornton thing, he kind of overdoes the southern thing a little bit to kind of serve him well out there and make it kind of his persona. He kind of has this sort of vendetta thing for his home going on. I knew that was going to be hard to cast because a lot of the people who read for it...it's kind of a hard thing to understand. He overdoes the southern thing a little bit, but it's got to come off like he's not trying to do a bad southern accent. And Luke was a guy who's from Guntersville, Alabama, and he was trained professionally in New York, lived in L.A. for a while, so he understood the character perfectly a) from a personal standpoint, but b) he's just a really, really strong actor, and he's very, very smart, and he was very, very professional. All the actors were great, but Luke was probably the

most professional in terms of just he knew everything and was there to work, and he was a UA guy. Elliot Moon (Gardner Patton), he was our lead, and Elliot was great. Again, he was really smart. He listened to me, and was very good at taking direction. That was another big thing we kind of looked for. And he was willing to talk to me about it. And he was a kind of guy where it seemed from his performances that...he and Luke were both this way, where kind of the first couple of takes they worked the materials and had new ideas, and they were dynamite, and they were kind of feeling everything out. And after that, their performances got a bit more set. I wouldn't say they were stale because they weren't bad. But there was a little less exploration, so it was good with them because I always got stuff in the first couple of takes. We didn't have to do that many takes with him. That was very different from some of the older actors. But that's a different process, which is something you learn about distinguishing when you're directing. And then Elise Zieman played Kelsey West, who was another lead, and I thought she was great. And she was like very book-focused, very organized. And, again, she was really smart and just understood the process of acting well and understood her character well. And the only sort of amateurish or untrained actor we had was the other lead, Bennett Parker, who played John Patton Jr., who was actually a friend of mine from high school. I hadn't worked with him in a long time. We had made stuff when we were in high school together. I was just talking to him about the film, and he said he wanted to come out to audition. And so I wasn't going to give him, by any means, any special treatment because I knew him. But he did extremely well. He was probably the best natural talent that I've seen in a long time because he has no training. Also, I know him well, so that was an advantage of me casting him because he understood me as a director and just understood me as a person. But, again, he was really smart and everyone brought their A-game, I thought, so I'm

very happy with the performances. I don't see anything that I felt was off. Even the supporting characters were freaking on, so everyone worked really hard, and I think we were pretty right in casting for intelligence and for that honesty.

BS: Yeah, I think one additional gauge we used was a sense of humor because that's a pretty good gauge for intelligence in acting and that kind of way. People that you could be honest with. A big, useful thing that we went to time and time again on this thing was being able to call shenanigans on each other and being able to be honest enough with each other and say, "I don't buy that" and "I'm not sure if you're giving this all of your attention." Lee and I were able to do that with each other, and he was able to do that with his actors. I was never in any of the private conversations, but I'm sure they were able to do that with him, too, where if something wasn't specific enough they could ask a question, and Lee wouldn't be like, (forcefully) "Because I'm the director, and I said so!"

LF: Elise actually called me out on that one time, and I'm glad she did because I had to kind of reevaluate it, and I gave her a reason, and it wasn't something I just pulled out of thin air. They cared enough about it. They weren't just like, "Okay, I'll do it this way." They were interested in every aspect of the scene and what leads point A to point B, and they were very thorough about it and they were as hard on me as I was on them. There were times when we saw it different ways. There was never any time when I was like, (forcefully) "We'll do it my way, and we'll do it your way!" We came to an understanding and got the best thing out of it. I'm not saying that there weren't times when we didn't agree, but generally it never brought up gunslinger moments. It was always very vocal, and we understood, and we talked.

BURIED IN THE MOUNDS

*BF: I'm aware of most of Ben's major influences –
Eastwood, the Coens, Sturges, Spielberg for starters.
Lee, whose work would you say you mostly draw from?
What films were you watching before and during your
writing the script and making the film?*

LF: The director that I most admire and probably want to draw
from the most would be Orson Welles. I was watching a lot of his
work going in, and we did do a lot of deep focus in this film. That
was more just because we used a lot of steadicam, but at the same
time that was kind of a conscious decision. A lot of the shots did
call for that kind of thing, which of course Welles was a great
master of. I'll probably say that I'm most influenced by Spielberg.
Particularly for this film because, in a lot of ways, it is kind a
reaction to a lot of his adventure work. I'm not saying that it's a
conscious kind of – that it's a way for me to get away with ripping
him off, there's not that – it's just there are certain elements that I
could certainly say probably have a Spielbergian influence on
them, and it's good because the film is a deconstruction of the
modern mythmakers, which he's probably the most influential of.
And then actually going into this, I had like a list of reference
films, but I won't bore you with all of that. But going in, I was
watching a lot of *X-Files* which I don't know if I want to say that or
not, and it doesn't much bleed into the script, but I did watch a lot
of *X-Files* going in, which I really, really like. And *Star Wars* of
course, is probably the one that, mixed with like *Batman: The
Animated Series*, probably led me to storytelling to begin with.
And I wish I could tell you things that sound a lot cooler, man.
(Laughs) But honestly, I'd say the two directors I think I drew
from the most, at least for this film particularly, would be Welles
and Spielberg.

BURIED IN THE MOUNDS

BF: Ben, who do you see in Lee's work? You're pretty good at assessing styles. Is there anything you've noticed any differently than what Lee has said?

BS: A lot of the kind of moving in – the pushing in and observing things and kind of investigating things – that happens a lot in the movie just from a perspective standpoint, and a lot of that reminds me of [David] Lynch a little bit. Specifically just that one part in *Blue Velvet* where it goes underground, and it's just kind of like a thematic way of saying, "This is what I'm doing right now is I'm investigating this specific thing." So I think Lynch is there probably a little bit, but other than that, I'm not sure because it's such a subconscious thing. I'd have to carve his brain open and look at the gooey insides to figure out exactly what. But we never had any discussions or conversations of, "And now this is going to be the part where we do it like Ridley Scott did it" or anything like that. But yeah, the only thing he really didn't mention and that I can kind of see is David Lynch.

BF: Why might you recommend staying in-state (or away from Hollywood) to graduating or budding filmmakers who hope to make feature films? Does it always depend on what kind of story you want to tell?

LF: I think so, a lot. I think a lot of people, though, who want to get into filmmaking tend to do it for different reasons that aren't to tell stories; and that's not necessarily a bad thing. That's just what they want to do. For that reason, I don't see much reason to stick in the state if you're not going to create your own opportunities, at least as of right now because there are so few opportunities for you, unless you're willing to make your own. So that's why a lot of actors that I know go out there for a little while, or at least go

44

other places like Austin or Florida, or some places that aren't New York and L.A. but do have a little bit better of a scene. I can't begrudge them of that because if you're not directing or writing your own crap where all you need essentially is investors, then you really have to go where there are jobs. And I'm working a day-job now, and I know what it's like to work a day-job that's not really what you love to do all the time, and not get what you really love to do because there's not enough opportunities here, which sucks. But I think if your goal is to make your own film, make your films the way you want to make them – and be that telling stories or be that, some people believe that movies aren't a primary form of storytelling, and that's fine if that's what you want to do – but if you want to make films your way and you're from here, I guess it does depend primarily on what you're doing, but I just don't see much reason to go somewhere that's a lot bigger because all you're going to do is have a lot harder of a time because you won't be able to make things your way. The good thing about being in an area where there's not a whole lot of industry is if you can get some money, then you're going to have a lot of free reign. I guess it all depends on your investors. If you can get some pretty good kind of passive investors, and you're willing to work a little harder for a little less money and get people on board who might be working for deferred salaries, then wherever you're at is the best place to do it. Because it's like Ben said, you don't have to transition. You don't have to transition into a move. You don't have to meet a whole new set of people. One of the big things that helped us make *Genesis* when we made it was a lot of the crew base was either in school or out of school and were in transitional areas themselves, and we knew them from school, and we were able to say, "Hey, well do this for this last summer where you're at home with your parents." (Laughs) I hate to kind of give that away, but that really was an advantage that people were that free yet still really mature enough to do a professional job on the film. It

wasn't like I was in high school. I do think, though if you're telling a story, it does depend on your story. I don't really see the point of making a film set in Manhattan if you're going to shoot it in downtown Birmingham. But it's not like it can't be done, and I'm sure that people do it a lot. I personally think if you're going to tell stories in a place, it's a much bigger advantage to tell them about that place than to try to make it set it on Middle-Earth or something.

BS: Which is where our next project is set. Yeah, I would say that it all just determines on what you want and what you need. I think that filmmaking is a collaborative art form, which is great because that means you don't have to be one thing. If you're not a good screenwriter, that's okay. That doesn't make you a bad director and vice-versa. So I think if you're just honest with yourself and ask yourself the hard questions, you'll figure out exactly what you want to do, and that will determine the best places for you to do it. Right now, if you want to be a production designer, apparently here is not the best place to be. But I think if you want to be a production designer, your best bet is to probably go somewhere else. But you have to be specific about that, or you're going to get there and realize, "No, I want to be a screenwriter," which actually that might be a better place to be, too, than here. But what I'm saying is once you're honest with yourself and determine what you want to do through experimenting, you need to focus on that; and if you want to be a filmmaker, you have to determine what kind of filmmaker you want to be. You could be a narrative feature filmmaker or a documentary filmmaker. There's a huge difference, I'd say. They're two completely different art forms. You could be a music video filmmaker. There's nothing wrong with that. For some reason, people are kind of demonized with that. There's nothing wrong with that, but that doesn't inherently make you a feature film director because they're two completely

different art forms. I think if you want to be a music video director, going somewhere else will probably work better than here because you're going to be focused on market demands a little bit more than narrative feature filmmakers are going to be. So there's kind of like a false nobleness in wanting to be a director and going to L.A. and doing it. But it's so much more complex and specific than that.

LF: But there is a certain amount of draw. To me, it makes sense now that the film industry as it's getting, or at least certain aspects of it, are getting more inexpensive, there will be more of a push for regionalism in film. The main reason being, though it's always been an industry because it's so expensive, but as costs go down, filmmaking is innately an art form, which makes it different from any other industry out there. So it's almost like with novels. Southern gothic was such a huge movement in the 20th century, and it's so important where you're from if you're a writer or if you're a painter because it affects your work and how you approach your work and what decisions you make. And that's true with film, too. So I think we're starting to see that already with the rise of digital technology. We've seen elements of it since film's been in existence. But I think now particularly it's becoming more prominent. And people are more willing to watch independent films and are more willing to watch digital films, and there's the internet where you can download full feature films, hopefully not illegally, that are by independent filmmakers. There's more of a draw to and a more development of a kind of decentralization. The film as an art form, particularly the American film, which has always been one thing, is starting to break out a little more into different styles and into different kinds of things. And I know that a little bit of that's kind of wishful thinking of me right now, but I think definitely in the next ten to fifteen years, we're going to see more of a push for that, more young filmmakers interested in

telling stories that are more closely associated with the areas that they're in and colorized by the areas that they're at, as opposed to them going out to L.A. and just kind of shooting something that's neutered and standard and kind of pale and boring and well that's just kind of the standard thing. The standardization is going to kind of change more hopefully, and we're already seeing that.

BS: Yeah, I think it's just kind of common sense if you look at the patterns of decentralization. In the 70s, Lucas was audacious enough to move his whole operation out of L.A. completely, although it's not very far away in San Francisco. But that was the first step, and then you see Rodriguez in the 90s set up an entire movie studio in Austin, and that place is growing exponentially and has its own little mini-industry now. I mean, I won't comment on the output, but he did it. Now, even if you look at Indian film and *Slumdog Millionaire*, the popularity of that, even though that's kind of a fake Bollywood movie because it has direct Hollywood roots, it's still a testament to the fact that people will embrace and watch a movie that has no superficial links to Hollywood, and it's kind of a good thing for independent film but for also decentralized film. And I think combined with globalization and the fact that the art form is getting cheaper – in metaphorical terms, that the paper and the pens are getting cheaper – you're going to see authors come from all over the place. And it will be marketable, which is all that matters at the end of the day as far as a future is concerned. As much as creating art is important, having a place in the marketplace is still important, and the idea that it needs to be an investment and a building upon itself.

LF: And to get philosophical for second, tying on to Ben's globalization thing, I think the world's getting smaller it seems like

in terms of mass communication, and this has been happening since television, but I'm just saying, particularly with the internet, the world seems to be getting smaller and seems to be one thing. And you're starting to see a bit of a reaction against that. A lot of it with right-wing conspiracy theorists, which I'm not agreeing with, but I'm just saying that I think you're going to see more of a reaction against this kind of theory of an autonomous, one world, because it's not. We have different experiences, and different towns have different experiences. So I think you're going to see the same kind of a reactionary movement in popular art, and you'll see more of a specificity in the world, kind of a need for that, a need for different perception, different stories, different types of things. Because we're not getting it, we're starting to lose that awe of how wide the world is.

BS: Yeah, everybody's interested in other cultures and able to learn about other cultures, but everybody's okay with that fact, and nobody's threatened by it. We can all watch *Slumdog Millionaire* and not feel like, "Oh God, they're going to make us believe the way they do." And I think that that reaction to globalization is going to be reflected in movies the same way that we can read the Harlem Renaissance stuff and just understand that that's how it works in a different part of the nation. I think the way America works is the same way the world's going to go, and I think that filmmaking being the populist medium of our time is only going to go the exact same way. Transcribe that!

BF: What are your distribution plans with this movie?

BS: You want to buy it?

BURIED IN THE MOUNDS

LF: As of right now, that's unfortunately been the one thing that's probably a tad vague and that we're probably going to look back on and say, "Man, I don't know why we were so idealistic about that." But right now the game plan has been festivals first. We've talked to a couple of people. We know a producer who has expressed interest in helping us sell it and that kind of thing, and that's great, but we really want to get a bit of that festival experience first, see what happens. We're not really expecting anything huge, but as of right now nothing's locked down, but the plan is to kind of play some festivals, get a feeling for crowd reactions, get a feeling for general interest in the piece, particularly since a lot of the festivals we're hoping to play first are nowhere near here. Right now we've been kind of nurturing a very small regional following of people who know about the film. Not too many people know about it, but there's enough where people have asked me about it that I don't even know, so that's kind of cool. We kind of want to see the reaction there, and see what happens. There may be that wonderful luck where we get an offer at an early festival, but we're not banking on that. Our plan is to see what happens with the first couple of months at festivals, and if things seem to not be going anywhere, then we'll try some other avenues that come open to us, such as a DIY tour and a DIY release. And worst case, we're just interested in getting it out there, so we're not above sending it directly to distributors, saying "Hey, take our film," or just trying to get them to buy it just from solicitation. There's a lot of really good outlets now that are DIY. It's like self-publishing for film. There's like IndieFlix and stuff like that, which is definitely not going to be where we first go, but it will kind of be our last resort to do it all ourselves just because we're not distribution guys. So I don't really want to get into that because in order to be successful as a DIY distributor, you've got to be smart and innovative, and I don't know that that's where our talent lies. So we'll see, but that's one of the things I was talking

about earlier about the advantage of a small film is we have an advantage because we have a very, very passive investment and everyone's on deferred. So essentially we could do a very, very, very, very, very inexpensive deal, and we're not going to make much money, but we could get pretty nice distribution or at least some kind of distribution that's in our favor. So that's an advantage we have and we are going to kind of nurture it, since we don't have investors calling Ben every three weeks saying, "If you don't sell the film within the next three months, then we'll execute powers and take over the film." So we don't have that pressure, and we're taking advantage of that, and that's the only reason we're able to have a bit more of an unplanned distribution approach. It's not unplanned entirely.

BS: Yeah, whenever we first mapped everything out as far as our five-year business plan goes, we're not banking on this being *Blair Witch* or *Primer* or one of those really low budget things that explodes. We're not banking on that, and we understand that the likelihood of that is very small. So we went in with a small enough investment and small enough hopes to just kind of use it as a learning tool. We believe in this film the same way we would if it was our last film, so it's not like, "Let's just throw something out there to get started." But we do understand that it all works in steps, and we're trying to be pretty humble with it in that way. But one of our direct plans is to kind of focus on sci-fi conventions and sci-fi festivals because deconstructionist movies are so popular right now, especially with genre markets. *Watchmen* didn't make a lot of money globally and nationally, but on a comic book genre perspective, it's a step in the direction of that deconstructionist movement that everybody knows is coming. So we're looking at that kind of direction as far as marketing the film to those kinds of festivals.

BURIED IN THE MOUNDS

BF: You've described this experience as a "résumé-building thing" or a reason to get something "of note" under your belts. Does it only go that far, or was it more personal than that?

LF: It's a lot more personal. From a professional standpoint in terms of me being blatantly cold and honest with myself, ultimately I knew the film might not mean more than that to anyone else, and especially if enough people don't really like the film and there's no response to it, then at least I have something on the resume. So that's sort of where that statement came from. But it's a lot more personal. Like I said, the CCC is something that I've been personally interested in for a long time, and my grandfathers were in it. A lot of the subtext is kind of spiritual subtext, and in a lot of ways, it's a character's search for God. And in a lot of ways, that's certainly a personal thing that everyone can kind of attest to within themselves. The continuity I'm really happy with. It's a pretty thick kind of history in the world, and I really like the characters. It's not something I'm planning on making into a franchise or anything, but it's something that I would kind of like to revisit and use characters to revisit later. And because there's kind of a longevity to everything. Actually there are some guys making a promo mockumentary just kind of adding on to the continuity right now. We have some friends who are making that, which is cool. So that means a lot, and it's your first feature. It's like your first baby. I think I really do like the story, and I think it has everything that I like in films. I think it's introspective, and its structure at least means something more than what you see at face level. But at its core, it is an adventure film that moves pretty well, and it kind of has just a basic conflict between these two cousins, and a character and ideas that may or may not be true. So all of that kind of makes it sellable, but it is very personal.

BS: Yeah, and I think from a production standpoint it would have been impossible to just look at this as kind of an arbitrary process of just going through the motions of getting something out there and getting something made. Because if it was that, I would have quit several months into it because it was very hard. It was very personal, it was very emotional but in a satisfying way. Like I said earlier, I think we've all kind of come as far in one sitting as filmmakers with this one experience than with any other. So I think that even if I had been detached at the beginning, it wouldn't have stayed like that, or else it wouldn't have continued happening.

BF: Do you both still want to be filmmakers?

BS: No. (Laughs) I'm just kidding.

LF: Completely, yeah. There was never any point in it, and I think Ben probably agrees, where I was ever like, "This is the wrong choice." It's hard, but it's amazing because it's amazing how much you like it. I think back, even now, and I'm working on it constantly, I come home and I edit. That's all I do. Peyton keeps complaining. When I'm not working, I'm working on the film. The physical exhaustion it was didn't even phase me. It was just, "Okay, this is what you've got to do." And thinking back, I'm like, "Man, that was crazy," because seriously it was. Whenever we were on lunch breaks, we were working at the same time. We were talking about it, and throughout the day we were talking about it. And when I got home that night, we prepped for the shoot that weekend. Like I said, every Monday, there was a catastrophe of some kind, of some magnitude. Sometimes, it was like Wednesday, and that was the worst because we had to shoot Friday or Saturday. But, no, despite all of that, I want to do it

again as much as I did going in. It's kind of unreal to me right now because it's actually finally going to be tangible, and people are going to be looking at it. And it's kind of scary because, again, it's your baby, it's your first thing kind of getting out there. But in terms of do I want to stop while I'm ahead? No.

BS: From my perspective, it was a little bit hard for me doing the producing thing because I will say I don't want to do that forever. But it was extremely satisfying. It's the kind of freakish hard work that you can't believe you're doing and you can't believe you're going through. But at the end of the day, it's very satisfying. And I remember on the last shoot day, when we said, "It's a wrap," that was a ridiculous feeling. If anything, it's just calcified me. It's like a no-turning-back thing. You've put so much of your emotional part of you into it that you can't turn back now because it'd be just a big waste of time. Not only that, it's just you've done something and you've come to a realization with it, and it's the kind of satisfaction you just can't turn away. So no, there's no way that I'd ever do anything else.

LF: And also from an artistic standpoint, there's things that I'm even noticing now – and granted, I'm seeing the film every day, so I'm too close to it, and that's the danger of editing your own work, which I hate that I had to do that – but you see things that you would do differently. And there's moments, where seriously, you're like, "I don't even know if this works anymore. I can't get my head around it." So there's a certain amount of liberation, going on to another film, and well I've learned so much from this one I want to apply it to the next one because there's only so far you can take this one. I'm not saying I'm just throwing it to the wayside or anything, I'm just saying that, at this point, there's not too many more artistic decisions I could make on the film. It's

what it is, and if I made the wrong ones, then tough. That's the way it is. So you look forward to the opportunity to get to do that again. But that's one of the things I have a hard time understanding about the special editions of *Star Wars* as much as I love them. Going back to your work 30 years before and enhancing it seems like, to me as a storyteller, it'd kill you because, like I said, a) there's nothing I could change that much anyway, but b) I wouldn't want to. It's a testament to what it was, and what I was then, what I am now, and that's it. Then I can go on, so at the beginning of the next film, you start from scratch. So there is a certain amount of desire, just strictly from that sense, just wanting to apply what I've learned. I don't want to just sit on my butt and forget about it.

BS: Although, we are planning in 20 years to digitally replace Elliot Moon.

LF: That's right.

BS: With a giraffe.

Via Skype
April 2009

55

Lee Fanning & Benjamin Stark, April 2009.
Photograph by Andrea Fanning.

A Genesis Found

The Shooting Script
By Lee Fanning

EXT MOUNDVILLE - NEAR MOUND F - 1938 – DAY

JOHN PATTON JR.– a dirty yet bright-eyed young man- digs in mud, revealing bone. He peels back more and reveals an eye socket. He turns.

JOHN

Found another one!

EXT MOUNDVILLE - CCC EXCAVATION - 1938 – CONT

Moundville Archaeological Park is ROARING with working young men from the Civilian Conservation Corps. Archeological excavation units are plotted at the base of several of the site's monolithic, man-made mounds. Large excavation crews work in these areas. The SCRATCH of screens sifting dried mud can be heard, as can the THUMP of shoveling, and the GRUMBLE of passing work trucks.

One winds through the site towards Mound F.

BURIED IN THE MOUNDS

EXT MOUNDVILLE - NEAR MOUND F - 1938 - CONT

John digs, now aided by TIM SHAW-- a dirty yet well-groomed young man. Tim pops bubble gum in his mouth and tosses away the comic wrapper.

> TIM
> How big you reckon he'll be, Patton?

> JOHN
> What?

John sees the work truck pull up. A man in a fedora steps out.

> TIM
> I heard they found some out here, nine
> feet tall. Giants, you know-- s'posed to
> done the grunt work on these things.
> Say they're in the Bible.

                    JOHN
          I doubt he's nine feet tall.

John watches the man in the fedora. This is DR. JONES-- the
site's chief supervisor. Beside him is DEJARNETTE-- the army
officer in charge of the cadets.

                    DEJARNETTE
          All right boys, let's pack it up.

John approaches Dr. Jones.

                    JOHN
          Seen anythin' like this before, doctor?

Dr. Jones sees John. He smiles and nods.

                    DR. JONES
          Oh yeah. We've been finding these all
          over the site. You're in the archaeology
          class, aren't you?

                    JOHN
          Yessir. John Patton Jr., sir.

They shake hands.

                    DR. JONES
          There's not many of you.

                    JOHN
          No sir. I was wonderin', sir... you talked
          about, how the site was probably

                      59

JOHN (CONT'D)
abandoned by 1400... um, I was wonderin' when you thought these were buried, they seem—

DR. JONES
Shallow?

JOHN
Yessir. I know erosion's a factor, but they just don't seem as deep as some artifacts from then.

DR. JONES
I agree with you. These were buried well after 1400 A.D.

JOHN
What does that mean? Folks were here longer?

DR. JONES
There's no indication anyone lived here. Just that they were buried here.

JOHN
It turned into a graveyard?

Dr. Jones nods.

> DR. JONES
> I think this place was a spiritual
> sanctuary to the people who lived here--
> a pathway to God-- even after it was
> abandoned.

> JOHN
> What makes you say that?

Dr. Jones smiles.

> DR. JONES
> Let's just say it looks that way.

He nods to the excavation. John sees, for the first time, all that has been unearthed-- over half a dozen skeletons, arranged in a circular pattern, with a few sprouting out from the edges. It looks like a large hand, with an eye in its palm.

> DEJARNETTE
> Let's get a move on, Patton.

Dr. Jones tips his hat and walks back to the truck.

INT BARRACKS - 1938 - NIGHT

John is in bed. He reads *Certain Aboriginal Finds on the Black Warrior River*. In the bed beside him is Tim, who chews gum and reads a pulp magazine. On its cover is a skeleton rising from the grave.

TIM
All right. Ain't stomachin' this again.
What you readin' Patton?

JOHN
You wouldn't like this, Shaw.

Tim reads the cover. He laughs.

TIM
That some kinda school book?

JOHN
Somethin' like that.

Tim takes out a pocketknife and plays with the blade.

TIM

Sure do care about this stuff, don't ya Patton?

JOHN

What's wrong with that?

TIM

Nothin', I reckon. Just creepy to me, diggin' up corpses all day long.

JOHN

It ain't creepy. It's science.

TIM

Science, huh? So's Frankenstein. I just think some things oughtta stay in the ground.

JOHN

I thought ya wanted to find you a giant, Shaw.

TIM

Shoot– I don't wanna find nothin'. Next thing ya know we'll be stumblin' onto some kinda cursed tomb, mummy chasin' us around. (laughs) Backwards place like this, I wonder if even God knows what's out there.

> JOHN

Well he don't have to. It's our job, be it giants, cursed tombs or buried treasure--

> TIM

Treasure? Out there?

John looks to Tim. He grins.

> JOHN

It's a local secret. North Mississippi yokel like yourself, don't think I should tell you about it.

> TIM

Aw, you're pullin' my leg--

John shrugs. Tim stares at him.

> JOHN

I heard, we might be lookin' for it, just--

He puts a finger to his lips. Tim smiles.

> TIM

Aw, now that'd be nice-- wouldn't mind stumblin' onto that. As much of my pay they send to the folks, it's like I'm workin' for that goddam bank-- can't even spare a dime for no new readin' material. You sure you ain't got nothin' else?

                    JOHN
          You ain't got a Bible, Shaw?

                    TIM
          Come on, I can't read that good. What
          else a preacher for?

John sighs. He reaches under his mattress. Tim watches; a smile creeps to his face.

John removes a magazine and tosses it to Tim. It's a *Scientific American.*

Tim just looks at it.

                    JOHN
              That's all I got.

Tim shrugs. He takes gum out of his mouth and slaps it on the bed rail.

John resumes reading. He flips to a photo of the "rattlesnake disc." He stares at the center illustration, of a hand with an eye in its palm.

He grabs his journal, a pencil inside. He flips to an illustration of the burial site configuration. He compares the two.

He copies the "eye in the hand" from the disc. Tim notices.

                    TIM
          Whatcha got there?

JOHN
You don't wanna read this, Shaw. It's just a buncha notes.

TIM
As much as you study Patton, you shoulda stayed in school. How's that gonna do ya any good in the corp?

JOHN
I reckon it'll do me good someday. When I'm in the ground they won't have to dig me up just to know somethin' about me.

TIM
Hell, ain't nobody gonna read it then neither, Patton-- not even your grandchildren.

INT HOOLE LIBRARY - MODERN DAY - DAY

GARDNER PATTON-- a modern, affable young man, and also John's grandson- stares at his grandfather's journal, which is thicker and more worn than in the 1930's. This is the first time he's seen it.

He closes it and examines the cover.

INT HOOLE LIBRARY - COPY CENTER - DAY

Gardner sits near a copy machine and reads H.G. Wells' *War of the Worlds*.

BURIED IN THE MOUNDS

An ATTENDANT makes a copy of the journal.

The first page copied reads: "Journal of John Patton Jr., Property of the University of Alabama Libraries-- Special Collections-- Restricted use Only-- Do Not Circulate." The next is a two-page map of Moundville Archaeological Park and surrounding Black Warrior River Valley as it was in the 1930's. Gardner doesn't notice either.

His cell phone BUZZES. The screen reads: "Kelsey calling." He answers, still reading.

> GARDNER
> (near whisper)
> Hey... nah, I'm at Hoole actually--

Gardner follows as he reads with his finger. He fumbles the book and drops it SMACK on the table.

The attendant glares at him. He forces a smile.

> GARDNER (CONT'D)
> I'm doing Bart a favor. Yeah, he got in a few days ago-- just now called me though. He's campin' at Moundville with his crew. Yeah. Listen, I gotta head over there after class if you wanna go, I gotta give him these copies... just, some stuff that was my grandpa's... Bart tracked it down, I don't know-- can you come? He said he got us a present. (laughs) Nah, it's cool, I understand. Oh, I finished our badges, by the way.

> GARDNER (CONT'D)
> For Halloween-- we're still Mulder and
> Scully, right? People'll know who we
> are, it ain't-- it's not that old.

Gardner notices a small photo on the floor. He picks it up.

> GARDNER (CONT'D)
> Yeah, I'll be here a while-- just meet me
> at class. Love you too.

Gardner hangs up. He flips the photo over. It's of his grandfather, when he was in the CCC in the 1930's.

Gardner considers it.

INT TEN HOOR ARCHAEOLOGY LAB - DAY

Gardner sits at a desk beside KELSEY WEST-- an attractive yet modest young woman, and Gardner's girlfriend- in a filling classroom. Kelsey reads a newspaper while Gardner reads *War of the Worlds.*

Kelsey feels her forehead.

> GARDNER
> You okay?

> KELSEY
> Hm? Yeah, just a bug.

She eyes something in the paper.

KELSEY (CONT'D)
Gardner look at this.

Kelsey points to an article: "DOCUMENTARY FILMING AT MOUNDVILLE: Tuscaloosa Native At Helm." By the headline is a photograph of BART THOMPSON-- a rugged yet modern young man, who wears a "trademark" hunter's camo ball cap.

The caption reads: "Bart Thompson, whose 2004 *The Dogma War* was the controversial favorite of the Sundance Film Festival...."

GARDNER
He'll love that.

KELSEY
You sure? You can barely read it.

                    GARDNER
Well they ain't-- haven't-- mentioned
him in here for years, it's worth
something.

                    KELSEY
Not as much as a bigger headline.

                    GARDNER
Give him a break Kels. He's still a
Patton, it comes with the name.

                    KELSEY
Is that a threat?

Kelsey smiles. Gardner nods. He forces a smile.

Kelsey grabs a manila folder from Gardner's desk. Inside is the
copy of John Patton Jr.'s journal.

                KELSEY (CONT'D)
This what you're taking him?

Gardner nods.

                KELSEY (CONT'D)
You read it?

Gardner shakes his head.

                    GARDNER
Why would I wanna do that?

                    KELSEY
        It was your grandfather's.

Gardner just shrugs.

                 KELSEY (CONT'D)
        I'm just, surprised you're not curious.

                    GARDNER
        Look, all I need to know is that if I'm
        serious about this anthropology thing--
        if we're serious-- we wanna stay away
        from him.

                    KELSEY
        Well that seems unfair. He wasn't
        always crazy, was he--?

                    GARDNER
        Kels--?

Kelsey nods. She flips through the journal. She turns to the photo
of John Patton Jr. from the 1930's.

                    KELSEY
        Is this him?

Gardner nods.

                 KELSEY (CONT'D)
        You look like him.

Gardner shrugs.

                              GARDNER
          I can't help that.

INT TEN HOOR ARCHAEOLOGY LAB - LATER

DR. KERRY SIMS-- a respected and affable professor- lectures
the class. On a projector screen is a diagram of a mound, labeled
"Mound F-- Moundville Archaeological Park."

                              SIMS
              We'll be excavating Mound F, in the
              southeastern part of the site. According
              to modern theories, this mound may
              have been used exclusively for
              ceremonial and burial purposes by one
              of the higher clans. Now, our primary
              objective here is to learn more about
              religion as a social system-- not grave
              robbing-- I don't care what time of year
              it is. We'll leave that to the medical
              school.

The class laughs. Sims holds up a plastic flag.

                        SIMS (CONT'D)
              Any remains found in trial holes will be
              re-covered and flagged. All right? Now,
              what do I mean by religion as a social
              system? Let's talk about that-- this is
              very important, so please, every one
              wants to pass, chin up, ears out....

Gardner ignores this. He draws a "tripod death machine" from *War of the Worlds* in his notes.

Kelsey notices this. She glares at him.

> GARDNER
> (whispering)
> It ain't like I can't hear-- I mean--

Kelsey doesn't let up. Gardner sighs and scratches it out.

> SIMS
> ...Moundville is important because it was one of the earliest significant communities established in prehistoric America-- a "recent" example of how mankind progressed to civilization. What we don't know is why it was built in the first place. I think we'll find that answer when we can better understand their religion. This is difficult; we're dealing with essentially a lost civilization. All we have is the dirt they lived on, and the clues they left behind.

Sims changes slides to a photo of the "Rattlesnake Disc." Gardner draws the symbol.

> SIMS (CONT'D)
> This is the "Rattlesnake Disc", a prime example. Now take a look at this symbol here-- the "eye in the hand." This is not exclusive to Moundville-- in

SIMS (CONT'D)

other cultures, it's often defined as the "hand of the creator" or the "eye of God." It's not necessarily perceived to mean that here, however. We have our own theories-- the most prevalent that the symbol was a configuration based on the constellation we call Orion. There are other interpretations, some less cosmic--

Sims sees Gardner.

SIMS (CONT'D)

Some more.

Gardner looks away. Kelsey looks to him.

SIMS (CONT'D)

Essentially guys, what we're looking for is the answer we've been after for over a century-- the key to the origin of the mounds. Good luck getting an "A"....

The class laughs.

Gardner scratches out his drawing of the "eye in the hand." Kelsey notices-- then leans forward. She touches her forehead.

GARDNER
(whispering)

Kels?

Kelsey exits, knocking the folder from her desk.

Gardner watches her leave. He picks up the folder. He eyes the map of Moundville inside. On it he notices Mound F is circled.

He flips past it to the "eye in the hand" drawings from the 1930's. He eyes the burial configuration.

Something catches his eye at the top of the page-- a number sequence: "-873743>."

Gardner's phone BUZZES: "New Message from: Kelsey." The message reads: "Can U take me home?"

> SIMS
> ...Now please listen up guys, this information is essential-- passing essential....

Gardner just smirks. He gathers his things.

EXT MOUNDVILLE ARCHAEOLOGICAL PARK - DAY

Gardner's car enters. He turns toward the camping area, passing joggers. He looks wide-eyed to the mounds before him.

EXT MOUNDVILLE - CAMP GROUNDS - CONT

Gardner's car pulls up to a beat up camper, a canopy tent set outside it. He steps out, folder in hand.

EXT CAMPER - CONT

Gardner knocks on the door. LEVI ALLEN-- a quiet yet harsh looking young man- opens it.

> GARDNER
> Um... is, Bart Thompson--

> BART
> (OS)
> There he is!

Gardner turns to see Bart, who approaches, drying his hair. He puts on his camo ball cap.

> BART (CONT'D)
> I apologize, just woke up.

Gardner glances to his cell phone's clock.

> GARDNER
>
> Same old Bart.

> BART
>
> Come here!

Bart and Gardner hug.

> BART (CONT'D)
>
> Where's your ring kid? Been gone five years, ain't get hitched yet?

> GARDNER
>
> Nuh-uh. Not for a while.

> BART
>
> Where is Kelsey anyway?

> GARDNER
>
> She's got some, bug thing--

> BART
>
> Oh yeah, sure-- I know she ain't much for me kid, don't worry about it-- just make sure I get an invitation, all right?

> GARDNER
>
> Why, expect us to wait another five years?

Bart laughs.

BURIED IN THE MOUNDS

                    BART
          Smart ass. Levi, sorry. This is my
          cousin, Gardner Patton. He's part of
          the dig we're shootin'.

Gardner holds out his hand. Levi hesitates, then shakes it.

                    LEVI
          We got somethin' in common.

                    GARDNER
          Oh yeah?

Bart nods.

                    BART
          He's my cousin too. My dad's nephew.

                    GARDNER
          Oh, okay. Are you from here--?

                    BART
          You know it. Me and Levi grew up
          together, when I wasn't babysittin' you--
          Sunday school, cub scouts, baseball...
          we quit just about everything.

Gardner notices Levi holds a book about Orson Welles' *War of
the Worlds* broadcast, titled: *Panic! Sensation! Invaders from
Mars!*

                    GARDNER
          Cool book.

Levi just nods.

> BART
> Levi, throw this in there will ya?

Bart hands Levi the towel. Levi exits inside.

> GARDNER
> He dumb?

Bart laughs.

> BART
> That whole side, kid--

> GARDNER
> I mean--

> BART
> Ah, I think he's sick-- but he usually
> ain't much better. Come on, rest of the
> crew ain't so quiet.

Bart and Gardner exit.

EXT CAMPSITE - BEHIND CAMPER - CONT

Bart and Gardner approach a tent. Beside it, in chairs, sit BEN
WATSON-- a longhaired, polite young man- and DR. KEVIN
MCCLEAN-- a shaggy yet educated man, in his late fifties, who
wears a magnetic bracelet. Ben plays a video game on his
blackberry; Dr. McClean reads a newspaper. Both stop.

> BART

Ben, Doc, this is my cousin I told ya about.

Ben smiles and waves. Dr. McClean smiles and nods.

> BART (CONT'D)

These are the two who won the coin toss.

> BEN

The camper doesn't have AC.

> BART

That's Ben Watson, videographer, sound engineer, editor-- does all the tech stuff I don't wanna do--

> BEN

Or don't know how to do.

> BART

Ben has, inferiority issues--

Ben laughs.

> BART (CONT'D)

And he's been doin' all the hard work since film school.

> BEN

Don't forget the doctor, Bart--

MCCLEAN
Thank you, Ben.

BART
And this is Dr. Kevin McClean. He's
acting producer for us--

MCCLEAN
"Acting" is right--

BART
--but when not on sabbatical,
moonlights as a professor of
anthropology at Berkeley.

GARDNER
Wow. You get talked into spendin'
your sabbatical down here?

McClean laughs.

BART
Doc McClean came to me, actually.
He's got a lot of personal interest
invested in the project--

MCCLEAN
I've invested more than just interest.

BART
He's also payin' for most of it.

GARDNER
What's the interest-- if you don't mind
me askin'?

MCCLEAN
I've been working on a book actually,
about the origin of the mound building
cultures. Mostly, I've focused my
research on the Cahokia site-- but, that
caught a snag, so I'm trying to pick back
up here. This film's my proverbial
"foot in the door."

GARDNER
That's a pretty long sabbatical.

BART
You know what they say about tenure.

> GARDNER
> So, Doctor... any leads? Do you know why they built them?

McClean takes off his glasses.

> MCCLEAN
> Not yet. But they say this is the best place to look.

> GARDNER
> Why's that?

> MCCLEAN
> Because most of these mounds haven't been searched in over a century. Who knows what's out there.

> GARDNER
> What about the digs in the 30's? I thought those were the largest.

> MCCLEAN
> Well sure, but they didn't touch the mounds. Then it was assumed they had nothing left to offer.

> BART
> That didn't change 'til Grandpa.

Gardner looks to Bart.

MCCLEAN
Well, it was inevitable really. Man has
no limit to, or control of, his curiosity.
It's been that way since Adam, if you
believe such-- as if we're destined to
search for answers to impossible
questions.

GARDNER
In other words, we're all looking for the
"Truth."

MCCLEAN
Well, not necessarily. That's if you
believe there is only one "Truth."

BART
Look out, Gardner, he's an atheist--

MCCLEAN
Well... (looks to bracelet) What faith I
have is certainly unconventional-- but to
be quite honest, I don't know what all I
believe in. What about you, Gardner?

GARDNER
Uh--

Bart laughs.

> **BART**
> That question makes us all uncomfortable, Doc. Come on kid-- we gotta make up five years.

Bart leads Gardner off, who waves to Ben and McClean.

> **MCCLEAN**
> By the way, Bart. We made the paper.

> **GARDNER**
> He says frame it!

Bart laughs.

> **BART**
> You heard him.

EXT MOUNDVILLE - NEAR BLACK WARRIOR RIVER - DAY

Gardner and Bart walk along a fence over looking the Black Warrior River. Bart flips through the folder.

> **GARDNER**
> Small crew.

> **BART**
> Small budget. We're roughin' it this time-- no grants or, senators. That the Black Warrior?

Gardner nods. They stop.

BART (CONT'D)
My last year in scouts, we kayaked 'bout ten miles of that thing. As trite as it sounds, there's somethin' real spiritual in bein' out on the water like that-- like it's got some kinda, primeval resonance.

GARDNER
You sound like the doctor.

Bart laughs.

BART
Doc's clingin' to a bourgeois-fad that died a decade ago. Granted it ain't much worse than the legalistic bullshit folks've been buyin' into for centuries, but-- well, there's nothin' sincere in that

> BART (CONT'D)
> kinda belief, Gardner. They're just tryin' to displace some innate fear.

> GARDNER
> Or fill an innate need.

> BART
> Well, they think they need it. Folks always have.

Bart nods to the mounds. He resumes walking, as does Gardner.

> GARDNER
> That's what our dig's about, actually. The people here were real cosmological; they thought their ancestors were the stars, and were connected to them through the natural world. They thought they could communicate through signs.

> BART
> Not a bad thought.

> GARDNER
> But dangerous. They also thought only the chieftain could read them. It's what kept him in power, what kept the system working.

> BART

Sounds familiar. So you like this stuff, huh?

> GARDNER

The interesting parts. It's easier than most things-- it's just facts.

> BART

Never pegged you for a scientist. Hell, last time I was home all ya talked about was the new *Star Wars*. I figured you for a storyteller like me.

> GARDNER

It is storytelling, really-- that's what I like about it. You just gotta prove what you make up-- kinda like what you do.

Bart laughs.

> GARDNER (CONT'D)

It's really more of Kelsey's thing, though. She don't mind the boring stuff. I guess she got me into it.

> BART

I figured you'd say grandpa.

Gardner doesn't respond.

> BART (CONT'D)
> You'd make him proud. More than me,
> anyway. I'm the scalawag that moved to
> California.

Gardner laughs.

> GARDNER
> What happened to you, Bart? Most
> folks leave here, they lose the accent.

Bart smiles.

> BART
> Just 'cause I'm not around don't mean I
> ain't proud of our heritage here. He
> don't get the credit, but he did a lotta
> good for this place.

> GARDNER
> Is that what you call it?

> BART
> What do you know about it kid? All
> you know's what you've been told.

Bart glances to Gardner, walks off. Gardner follows.

EXT/INT MOUNDVILLE - DIORAMA HUTS - CONT

Bart and Gardner walk up to and through the huts as they talk.

>   BART
> How's John the third doin', by the way?

>   GARDNER
> Rather me be studying something else,
> but, aside from that, all right I guess.

>   BART
> You know, once Lucy gets married
> you'll be the last one of us with the
> Patton name.

Gardner laughs.

>   BART (CONT'D)
> What?

>   GARDNER
> She got married three years ago.

>   BART
> Oh. Well looks like you are then.

>   GARDNER
> What're you trying to say?

Bart shrugs.

>   GARDNER (CONT'D)
> My name ain't John the fourth.

>   BART
> Don't change it.

GARDNER

You gonna see your mom? Sounds like y'all've been keepin' up pretty well.

BART

She ain't talked to me since I made *Dogma*.

GARDNER

So.

BART

So, she can go to Hell. I ain't here for that.

GARDNER

Then what are you here for, Bart? This infomercial?

BART

It ain't an "infomercial."

GARDNER

Then what is it?

BART

It's a wake up call to this state.

GARDNER

You and your revolutions.

BART

Come on, kid, you know how important this place is. There're answers here that affect everybody. Folks here, though... (laughs) I mean people come here to jog! Monument to a great civilization and even it ain't immune to the trends of the bourgeoisie. They rant and rave about racism down here but they never mention that.

GARDNER

And you're gonna call 'em out on it. So that's why you're here.

Bart shakes his head.

                    BART
      I'm here 'cause I'm broke.

Gardner smirks. Bart laughs.

                   GARDNER
      I should probably get back. Kelsey's, on
      her deathbed.

Bart nods.

                    BART
      Oh hey, that present.

Bart hands Gardner a book from out of his back pocket. It's titled:
Buried in the Mounds-- By John Patton Jr.

                 BART (CONT'D)
      It's why we didn't grow up tillin' the
      family farm. Thought you'd appreciate
      it.

                   GARDNER
      Thanks.

                    BART
      Disappointed?

                   GARDNER
      Not really. I thought it was gonna be
      your last movie.

Bart laughs.

                    BART
    Nah-- the, uh, footage got confiscated.

Gardner just looks at him.

                BART (CONT'D)
    Why I'm broke.

Gardner nods.

                BART (CONT'D)
    By the way, Gardner. For the dig, you
    might not wanna tell anybody we're
    related-- in your class, I mean. Business
    relationships are usually best for these
    sort of things.

                GARDNER
    Sure.

He starts walking off.

                    BART
    Oh, and Gardner.

Gardner stops.

                BART (CONT'D)
    You oughtta read it. He's a hell of a
    storyteller-- and it's really all he's got
    left.

Gardner nods. He considers the diorama, then exits.

94

Bart looks to the diorama: A Moundville family buries an old man.

INT GARDNER & KELSEY'S APT - LIVING ROOM - NIGHT

Gardner enters, book in hand. He tosses it on the coffee table. He exits through the hallway.

INT GARDNER & KELSEY'S APT - BATHROOM - CONT

Gardner, now in an undershirt and shorts, washes his hands. He removes his contacts and places them in their case.

INT GARDNER & KELSEY'S APT - BEDROOM - CONT

Gardner enters, now wearing glasses. He walks to the bed.

Under the covers he sees Kelsey, asleep, spread out over the length of the mattress. He smiles. He rubs his hand through her hair.

INT GARDNER & KELSEY'S APT - LIVING ROOM - CONT

Gardner spreads sheets on the couch. He lays down.

He grabs the remote and turns on the TV. Playing is the Orson Welles narrated special, *Who's Out There?*

                    WELLES
          (on TV; quoting from "WOW")
      Before the cylinder fell, there was a
      general persuasion... that no life existed
      beyond our own minute sphere....

Gardner eyes *Buried in the Mounds* on the coffee table. He picks it up.

The book's cover reads: "Over 1 Million Copies Sold! The Amazing Truth Behind the Mysterious Origin of America's First Metropolis!"

Gardner flips the book over. He sees a photo of his grandfather, from 1973, now an old man with glasses and an eye patch. The top reads: "Unlocking its Secrets will Unlock Our Own! Read, and Believe!"

Gardner opens the book and reads.

INT CAMPER - NIGHT

Bart flips through his grandfather's journal.

He stops at another entry titled "A Genesis Found." He skims it with his finger.

McClean opens the door.

                    MCCLEAN
          We're ready.

Bart nods.

BURIED IN THE MOUNDS

EXT CAMPER - CONT

Bart exits the camper. McClean, Ben and Levi wait under the canopy. McClean carries a clipboard; Ben carries his camera; Levi carries a large bag. All have flashlights.

> ### BART
> All right.

Bart exits, followed by the others.

EXT MOUNDVILLE - OUTSIDE BURIAL MUSEUM – 1938 - NIGHT

John Patton Jr. sits in a truck bed. He looks at the stars. Dr. Jones approaches.

> ### DR. JONES
> That the last pieces?

> ### JOHN
> Yes sir.

> ### DR. JONES
> Well, thank ya for the help.

Dr. Jones opens the driver's door. He looks to John, who hasn't moved.

> ### DR. JONES (CONT'D)
> You coming?

JOHN

I'm gonna ride back here, if you don't mind.

Dr. Jones walks to John. He points to the sky.

DR. JONES

You see Orion?

JOHN

Excuse me?

DR. JONES

The constellation.

JOHN

Oh. Uh...

DR. JONES

It's right above us-- it's the easiest one to spot, I swear. See those three stars running diagonally there?

JOHN

Unh-huh.

DR. JONES

That's the belt. The rest of the body sprouts off from it. See it now?

JOHN

I, reckon. I ain't-- I'm, not too good at stargazing. He's the hunter, right?

Dr. Jones nods.

> ### JOHN (CONT'D)
> Like us.

Dr. Jones smiles.

> ### DR. JONES
> Have you seen any artifacts with the symbol of the eye in the hand?

> ### JOHN
> Yes sir, a few.

> ### DR. JONES
> I think that's it.

> ### JOHN
> What's it?

> ### DR. JONES
> Orion. I think that symbol is a different interpretation of it. I believe that to the people who lived here, Orion was the final gate.

John just looks at him.

> ### DR. JONES (CONT'D)
> Their souls. They would pass through the eye to enter the afterlife, and become one with the universe.

BURIED IN THE MOUNDS

Dr. Jones holds his hand to approximate the points of the constellation and points to the palm.

> DR. JONES (CONT'D)
> They would pass through here. See?

John nods. Dr. Jones points to his eye.

> DR. JONES (CONT'D)
> The eye was the key. To their culture,
> and to our understanding of it.

> JOHN
> So that's what it means?

> DR. JONES
> You think it means something else?

John just shrugs.

                    DR. JONES (CONT'D)
Do you enjoy this, John?

                         JOHN
Stargazing?
                    DR. JONES
No. Anthropology.

                         JOHN
I reckon I like it pretty good.

                    DR. JONES
Have you thought about pursuing it
after you're through here?

                         JOHN
Well sir, honestly-- I can't afford to go
to school for nothin'.

                    DR. JONES
Well. You don't have to go to school,
you know. You just have to know the
right people.

John looks at him.

INT BARRACKS - 1938 - NIGHT

John sits in bed. He looks over his notes on the "eye in the hand."

                         TIM
                        (OS)
...that's what Patton said....

                         101

BURIED IN THE MOUNDS

John looks to Tim, who sits across the barracks on another bed. He sharpens his knife and talks with another young man, PATRICK DOBBS.

The rest of the conversation is inaudible.

> SUPERVISOR 1
> (OS)
> Last call here! Lights Out! Last call!

Tim hands Patrick the sharpening stone and returns to his bed. He sees John, who watches him. He ignores him.

> JOHN
> What was that about, Tim?

> TIM
> What's what about?

> JOHN
> What were y'all talkin' 'bout?

Tim shrugs. He takes off his shoes and pins them between the bed rail and wall.

> TIM
> Why you care?

> JOHN
> I heard my name.

Tim slaps his gum on the bed rail.

JOHN (CONT'D)
You said I said somethin'?

Tim lays in bed.

TIM
Just sharpenin' my blade.

He turns his back to John. The lights turn out.

INT BARRACKS - 1938 - LATER

The barracks are quiet. John is in bed, asleep. A door SHUTS, waking him.

He notices Tim's bed is empty. He examines the bunk. He sees the wad of gum is still on the rail-- and Tim's shoes are missing.

EXT BARRACKS - CCC CAMP - 1938 - CONT

John is outside the camp, near the woods, flashlight in hand.

He looks out to the mounds. He notices something on the ground.

It's a comic gum wrapper.

JOHN
(whispering)
Damn it.

He glances back to the barracks and turns off his flashlight. He walks towards the mounds.

BURIED IN THE MOUNDS

The trees SHAKE. John looks at them. He smirks, continues quicker, amid eerie sounds.

Suddenly an arm grabs him. John turns his flashlight back on.

It's Tim.

> TIM
> Patton?

> JOHN
> Tim? Jesus, what the hell ya doin' out here--?

> TIM
> Lookin' at the stars.

John glares at him.

> TIM (CONT'D)
> Pissin'. Yarbrough forgot to flush the valves again-- I don't know, I reckon somebody's sick. Ya miss me?

> JOHN
> Listen, Tim-- that, story 'bout treasure--

Tim laughs.

> TIM
> That's what ya thought? Come on, Patton, just cause I can barely read don't mean I believe every word I hear-

                    TIM (CONT'D)
        specially not from no inbred central
        Alabama sharecropper.

John notices Tim isn't chewing, then glances to the comic. He
throws it down and laughs. He glances back to the mounds.

                    TIM (CONT'D)
          And you say they ain't creepy.

                    JOHN
          Just don't go diggin' 'em up.

John leaves for the barracks.

Tim watches. He removes a wad of gum from behind his ear and
puts it in his mouth.

INT GARDNER & KELSEY'S APT - LIVING ROOM - DAY

Gardner awakes, still on the couch, *Buried in the Mounds* spread
open on his chest.

He holds his place and grabs a photo off the coffee table-- it's of
him and Kelsey.

He smiles. He closes it in the book as a bookmark.

INT GARDNER & KELSEY'S APT - BEDROOM - CONT

Gardner enters. He sees the bed is empty, and the door to the
bathroom closed. He knocks.

                    GARDNER
Kelsey? You okay?

                    KELSEY
                     (OS)
        I'm fine.

INT GARDNER & KELSEY'S APT - KITCHEN - LATER

Gardner, fully dressed, sits across from Kelsey, also fully dressed.
Both nurse bowls of cereal.

                    GARDNER
        I think I'm gonna head out to
        Moundville early-- maybe help Bart
        prep his shoot.

                    KELSEY
        Don't you have geography?

                    GARDNER
        So I'll go later-- kind of a frivolous thing
        to learn nowadays anyway.

                    KELSEY
        You say that about every class.

                    GARDNER
        Well, especially geography. 'Sides, it's a
        big day. Wanna come with me?

Kelsey shakes her head.

KELSEY
I'd rather pass this semester. I'll just ride with the carpool.

GARDNER
You sure you don't wanna just stay in bed?

KELSEY
Why? Do I look tired?

GARDNER
You look sick.

KELSEY
Thanks.

GARDNER
I mean, if you're still--

BURIED IN THE MOUNDS

                    KELSEY
    I said I'm fine.

Gardner shrugs. He resumes eating breakfast.

EXT MOUNDVILLE - MOUND A - DAY

Ben, Levi and Gardner work a small jib crane with a camera
attached. Bart and McClean, who holds a clipboard, watch the
video feed on a nearby (albeit crappy) monitor.

                    BART
    Beautiful. Keep it steady-- a bit further
    now.

The jib doesn't have weights, so Gardner controls the counter
weight at the rear. He notices something move on his arm-- a tick.

He blows at it; it doesn't stop.

He glances to Bart. He begins to let go of the jib with one hand.

                    BART (CONT'D)
    Keep her steady, kid.

He stops. He watches the tick.

The tick stops moving. Gardner panics. He grabs at it.

                    BART (CONT'D)
    Damn it-- cut!

> GARDNER
>
> Look, I'm sorry--

> BART
>
> You better be-- I think that's Kelsey in
> the one out front.

Gardner looks to the road. A caravan of cars enters the park, led
by a white truck.

> BART (CONT'D)
>
> Right through my shot.

Gardner looks to his arm. The tick is still attached.

> GARDNER
>
> Damn it!

Gardner lets go of the jib and grabs the tick. The camera drops
suddenly. Ben catches it.

> BEN
>
> Whoa!

> BART
>
> Gardner! Watch what you're doing!

Gardner squishes the tick.

> GARDNER
>
> What?

> BART
> You 'bout broke the camera. Come on,
> we'll get this shot later– leave the jib.

Bart and McClean begin to leave, as does Levi, who eyes
Gardner. Bart stops.

> BART (CONT'D)
> And Gardner– leave around back.

Gardner nods. He sees Ben holding the camera off the ground.
He levels out the rear.

> GARDNER
> Sorry.

> BEN
> Ah, don't worry about it. Bart's broke
> ass sold the weights.

EXT MOUNDVILLE - NEAR MOUND F - CONT

Bart and McClean approach the white truck, which has parked
near the mound. Dr. Sims and Kelsey stand outside it. The rest of
the caravan has continued to a parking lot down the road.

> BART
> Dr. Kerry Sims?

Dr. Sims looks to Bart.

BART (CONT'D)
I'm Bart Thompson. This is Dr. Kevin
McClean, my producer–

SIMS
Yes, we spoke over the phone.

All three men shake hands.

KELSEY
Hi, Bart.

Bart just nods to her.

BART
We got some waivers, here, we need
your class to sign, 'fore the end of the
day.

BURIED IN THE MOUNDS

McClean hands him the waivers.

> ### SIMS
> No problem. Now, do you need us to
> do anything specific--?

> ### BART
> Just do what you're gonna do-- we'll get
> what we need.

Several students approach, collecting equipment from the truck
bed.

> ### SIMS
> Kelsey, if you wanna go ahead and get
> started.

Kelsey nods. She takes a final glance at Bart.

Sims notices something behind Bart.

> ### SIMS (CONT'D)
> So, you've already met one of my
> students.

Bart turns to see Gardner, walking down Mound A with Ben,
carrying some equipment.

> ### BART
> Oh yeah. He, uh, showed up early-- we
> let him help us with some things. That
> a problem?

Sims shakes his head.

> **SIMS**
> It's none of my business. I just-- well.

> **BART**
> Yeah?

> **SIMS**
> It's unfair. But, his grandfather was John Patton Jr. I assume you've heard of him?

> **BART**
> I think so, in some of my research.

> **SIMS**
> Well... This mound we're excavating, it was important to him. Let's just say, I hope Gardner's involvement doesn't have an ulterior motive. I hope he doesn't expect to find what his grandfather claimed he did.

> **BART**
> And what was that?

> **SIMS**
> You don't know?

> **BART**
> Not a clue, sir.

> **SIMS**
> I'm sure you'll stumble across it. It's caused some problems here in the past. Problems I'd like to avoid.

> **BART**
> So why dig here then? Why not just avoid it all together?

> **SIMS**
> We've been avoiding it. It's time to put some things to rest.

Bart just nods and smiles.

EXT MOUNDVILLE - NEAR MOUND F - CONT

Gardner walks with Ben to the canopy, which has been moved nearby. Levi stands at a table, readying a boom, his sleeves rolled up. He eyes Gardner.

> **LEVI**
> You were s'posed to go 'round back.

Gardner just looks at Levi. He sees a rash at the top of his arm. Levi notices this and rolls down his sleeve. Bart and McClean approach.

> **BART**
> We got it, Gardner. Go help your class.

> **GARDNER**
> All right.

He exits as Bart and Levi watch.

> BART
> (to Levi)
> Don't worry about it.

Bart walks past Levi to the table.

EXT MOUNDVILLE - MOUND F EXCAVATION - DAY

SEAN digs a trial hole and dumps the dirt in a bucket. He uncovers a skeleton hand.

Dr. Sims approaches and sees it.

> SIMS
> Remains. Cover it and flag it.

Ben films the exchange. Dr. Sims nods and smiles at the camera. He walks to other digging students.

> SIMS (CONT'D)
> What's going on over here, guys?

Ben follows.

Sean carries the bucket to a dirt screen where Kelsey and Gardner work. Gardner dumps it. They sift it, not talking.

> GARDNER
> You're being quiet.

> KELSEY
> So are you.

Gardner smirks. He sees Bart, who films a "wide" shot far off. Levi holds the boom beside him.

> KELSEY (CONT'D)
> What?

> GARDNER
> I don't care for Bart in work mode.

> KELSEY
> I don't really care for him ever.

> GARDNER
> Am I ever like that?

Kelsey shakes her head.

                    KELSEY
I think he picked that up on his own--
not everything comes with being a
Patton.

Gardner smirks.

                    GARDNER
Yeah. Just bad vision and insanity. And
a plot at Tuscaloosa memorial if we
never get hitched.

Kelsey smirks.

                    KELSEY
        Gardner.

                    GARDNER
        Hm?

                    KELSEY
I-- if you're waiting until you can afford
a ring, you don't have to.

Gardner just looks at her.

                KELSEY (CONT'D)
I, just wanted you to know that.

                    GARDNER
        Okay.

Gardner notices a curved piece of hardened clay in the screen. He examines it closer. It's over two-thirds of a painted eye.

> KELSEY
> Find something?

Gardner glances to her, then back to the object.

EXT MOUNDVILLE - MOUND F EXCAVATION - CONT

Gardner walks to the excavation area. He approaches Sean, who digs a new trial hole.

> GARDNER
> Sean, you seen anything else like this?
> It was in your dirt.

Sean shakes his head.

> SEAN
> I was diggin' over there, though--
> probably where it came from.

> GARDNER
> Where exactly?

> SEAN
> Near the flag.

Gardner sees it. He grabs a shovel from a wheelbarrow.

> SEAN (CONT'D)
> Uh... we found remains there.

> GARDNER

Yeah.

Gardner removes the flag. He glances around and digs.

He uncovers finger bones, buried shallow.

He kneels and brushes dirt back with his hands. He uncovers another piece of hardened clay. He matches it to the "eye." It fits.

Bart sees Gardner digging. He glances to Levi. The two approach, still filming.

Gardner uncovers the hand. He notices dirt caked into the palm. He takes a toothbrush and scrubs out the dirt, revealing an indention in the bone-- like an eye socket.

> BART

Find somethin'?

Gardner sees Bart. He conceals the indention. He shakes his head and hands Bart the "eye."

> GARDNER

Just lookin' for the rest of this.

Bart stops filming. He examines it and hands it to Levi. Gardner watches this.

> BART

What ya think it came off of?

GARDNER
A burial disc, probably, or somethin'
ceremonial. The kind of thing we're
supposed to be looking for-- wouldn't
know it, though, way Sims got us
dodgin' remains.

Gardner resumes, though in the opposite direction. Bart resumes
filming. Gardner notices.

SIMS
(OS)
Gardner?!

Gardner sees Sims, who approaches.

SIMS (CONT'D)
Did you not hear a word I said
yesterday?

GARDNER
I found part of an artifact--

SIMS
I don't care. We stay away from
remains.

Gardner scoffs.

GARDNER
How are we gonna find anything, sir, if
we re-cover every piece of bone we

> GARDNER (CONT'D)
> stumble across? For a complete excavation--

> SIMS
> This isn't a complete excavation, it's an exercise. And unless you think the tribes are gonna give you special permission to dig up their ancestors, we're staying away from remains. Understand?

Bart glances to Levi.

> GARDNER
> Yes sir.

> SIMS
> All right. Re-cover this.

Sims walks off. He almost runs into Bart and Levi, who still film. Sims notices the camera.

> SIMS (CONT'D)
> (cooling down)
> Excuse me.

Sims exits.

Gardner refills the hole.

> BART
> Why are y'all avoidin' remains, exactly?

GARDNER
You heard him. It's an exercise.

BART
Sure that's the only reason?

GARDNER
Why. There another one?

Bart stops filming.

BART
What are you doin' tonight?

Gardner just shrugs.

BART (CONT'D)
I think you oughtta stay out here with
us.

GARDNER
Why?

Bart looks back at the "eye."

BART
'Cause I think you mighta found
somethin'.

He flips the "eye" to Gardner, who looks at him.

BURIED IN THE MOUNDS

EXT MOUNDVILLE - PARKING LOT - DUSK

Gardner and Kelsey, both dirty and carrying backpacks, walk to their car in a crowd of their classmates.

> ### GARDNER
> You'll be okay?

Kelsey nods.

> ### KELSEY
> I'll come back in the morning though--
> you don't have to skip all your classes
> this week.

> ### GARDNER
> It's okay. I'll just see you back here at
> the dig.

Kelsey sniffs him.

> ### KELSEY
> I'm at least bringing you a change of
> clothes.

Gardner laughs.

> ### GARDNER
> Don't worry about it--

> ### KELSEY
> And what about your contacts Four
> Eyes--?

> GARDNER

I'll be fine-- I can rough it for one night.
'Sides--

Gardner takes out the dirty toothbrush.

> GARDNER (CONT'D)

They say all you need's a toothbrush.

Kelsey smirks.

> KELSEY

Okay. You got your phone?

> GARDNER

Of course.

They hug. They start to kiss.

A beat up truck pulls in behind them. Levi drives; Bart hangs out the window in the passenger seat beside him; Ben and McClean sit in the bed with their equipment.

> BART

Come on kid!

Gardner motions "a moment."

> GARDNER

You're sure you'll be all right? I mean you're feelin' okay?

                    KELSEY
          I'm not gonna be your excuse out of
          this.

Gardner laughs.

                 KELSEY (CONT'D)
          And you need to spend time with him,
          while you can.

Gardner nods. He leaves for the truck. Kelsey watches as it drives off.

INT CAMPER - LATER

Bart, McClean, Levi, Ben and Gardner enter the camper.

                     BART
          All right, everybody, grab a seat.

Everyone does, except Bart. Gardner sits on the bed.

                  BART (CONT'D)
          Gardner, you got that piece on ya?

Gardner nods.

                  BART (CONT'D)
          You know it's a federal crime to steal
          an artifact from a dig?

Gardner just looks at him. Bart laughs.

BART (CONT'D)
Let's see it.

Gardner hands Bart the "eye", who passes it to McClean.

MCCLEAN
Wow... this-- you might be right, Bart.

McClean flips to a specific page in John Patton Jr.'s journal. On it is a drawing of a disc with the "eye in hand" motif.

MCCLEAN (CONT'D)
This certainly looks like a match.

Gardner watches silently.

MCCLEAN (CONT'D)
Remember where you found it, Gardner?

GARDNER
This ain't about a movie, is it Bart.

Bart doesn't respond.

GARDNER (CONT'D)
What are you looking for?

BART
You got that book I gave you?

GARDNER
What--?

BART
Do you got the book?

Gardner takes it out of his backpack.

BART (CONT'D)
Turn to 49 and start readin'.

GARDNER
Why?

BART
Just do it.

GARDNER
What do I read to?

BURIED IN THE MOUNDS

BART
You'll know. Once you finish, we'll talk.

Gardner starts reading.

INT BARRACKS - 1938 - DAY

John Patton Jr. wakes to the CLATTER of cadets making beds and preparing for the day. He stands.

He notices Tim's bed isn't made, untouched from the previous night. He glances to Patrick Dobbs' bed-- it too is empty and untouched.

DeJarnette enters. The cadets scramble to attention.

DEJARNETTE
Patton-- I need to see you right away.

INT DEJARNETTE'S CAMP OFFICE - 1938 - DAY

John sits across from Dr. Jones, who sits at DeJarnette's desk. DeJarnette stands nearby.

DR. JONES
Do you know either of these cadets John?

Dr. Jones hands John a photograph of several CCC Cadets working. Circled are Tim Shaw and Patrick Dobbs.

John nods.

                    JOHN
Um, Tim, I do.

                    DR. JONES
What about Dobbs?

John shakes his head.

                    DR. JONES (CONT'D)
Did you see either of them leave the
barracks last night?

                    JOHN
Um... no, no sir.

                    DEJARNETTE
You sure?

John looks to DeJarnette.

                    JOHN
Am I in trouble, Dr. Jones?

Dr. Jones shakes his head.

                    DR. JONES
Not you, John. Last night, the
museum's repository was broken into.
Several, choice artifacts were stolen.
Since both Tim Shaw and Patrick
Dobbs have turned up missing-- well,
you can imagine who we thinks

DR. JONES (CONT'D)
responsible. We're just not sure if there
were other cadets involved.

DEJARNETTE
You were there last night, weren't you?

Dr. Jones glances to DeJarnette.

DR. JONES
We just have to question everyone who
might know something. Now, before
their disappearance, did you notice
either Shaw or Dobbs acting suspicious,
in anyway?

John shakes his head.

DR. JONES (CONT'D)
Did you see them interact with anyone
else regularly?

JOHN
Shaw had the bed next to mine. He
only talked to me.

Dr. Jones nods.

EXT MOUNDVILLE - NEAR MOUND F - 1938 - DAY

John digs a trial hole at the base of a mound. He notices
something stuck to his shoe-- a piece of spat out bubble gum.

John sees some broken grass and mud near the top of the mound.
He approaches and examines it closer.

He looks to **SUPERVISOR CHUCK** at the excavation below.

JOHN
Say, what mound is this, Chuck?

Chuck checks his clipboard.

SUPERVISOR CHUCK
F. Why, did ya find somethin'?

John looks to the patch of dirt.

JOHN

Nah.

He stands.

BURIED IN THE MOUNDS

INT BARRACKS - 1938 - NIGHT

John reads a chapter on Mound F from *Certain Aboriginal Finds on the Black Warrior River.*

He looks to Tim's bed. He notices his *Scientific American* wedged between the mattress and the wall.

He retrieves it. He notices something else pinned behind it-- a Bible.

He picks it up. He eyes a folded sheet of paper wedged in "Genesis." He unfolds it.

It's a portion of a map, featuring the Black Warrior River valley surrounding Moundville. He eyes an "x" marked onto a symbol in the woods. He glances to the key. The symbol is for a cave.

He stares at the "x."

EXT BARRACKS - MOUNDVILLE CCC CAMP - 1938 - NIGHT

John exits, fully dressed and holding a flashlight.

He looks to the mounds. State Trooper and Sheriff Deputy patrol cars are stationed around the perimeter. Search teams patrol the distant woods.

John traces the map with his finger. He turns to the woods behind him. They are undisturbed.

He follows the map in that direction.

BURIED IN THE MOUNDS

EXT WOODS - OUTSIDE MOUNDVILLE - 1938 - CONT

John studies the map as he walks. He stops and compares it with what's around him. He scans the woods with his flashlight. It's a thick, dark labyrinth.

He sighs-- then notices something on the ground. It's a gooey black substance that leads off in a sparse "trail."

John follows the trail with his flashlight.

EXT WOODS - OUTSIDE CAVE - 1938 - CONT

John follows the trail. It stops at a rocky area under a bluff.

He eyes a large wooden crate. It is still sealed and labeled "Property of Alabama Museum of Natural History."

On the side, John notices something else-- blood.

He notices a shovel on the ground. He sees the tip is dirty and also stained with blood. The blood is mixed with the mud on the ground. He digs.

He uncovers something buried shallow-- a hand. It's pale, stiff, and covered with ticks.

John turns and puts his fist to his mouth.

He pulls back more mud with his hands. He uncovers the face of Patrick Dobbs. Dobbs has a large gash near his left temple, and his left eye is missing.

John collapses.

He eyes the entrance to the cave at the base of the bluff.

INT CAVE - 1938 - CONT

John enters. He scans the chamber with his flashlight.

He sees Tim, who sits against the wall. He is shirtless and his head is sunk.

John hesitates.

> JOHN
> Jesus, Tim... what the hell... what did
> you do?

No response. John walks closer. He steps on something-- Tim's bloody knife.

John sees both of Tim's wrists have been slit. He kneels and takes deep breaths.

JOHN (CONT'D)
Jesus.

John notices Tim is covered in a rash. He looks closer. Tim, like Dobbs, is covered with ticks.

Further in the chamber, John eyes a collection of stolen artifacts spread on a canvas sheet. There must be fifty.

He approaches. In the far corner, he eyes a shovel stuck in the ground. He picks it up and notices some of the black goo on the tip. The goo also spills from the ground.

He digs.

He uncovers another artifact-- a ceremonial disc. On it is a variation of the "eye in the hand." By the hand is a mirrored, oblong face-- humanoid, but not human.

He eyes something buried beneath it. He uncovers a pile of bones, covered in the goo.

He examines them. On the palm of the hand is an indention, like an eye socket.

He looks to the skull.

It is small and oblong, with no mouth and shallow eye sockets.

It's not human.

He looks back to Tim. He sees something on the wall behind him. There, crudely scratched, are the words: "I Found the Genesis."

John looks to the ceremonial disc. He stares at the oblong face.

EXT MOUNDVILLE - MOUND F - 1938 - NIGHT

John climbs on the mound from the woods, now soaking wet. He no longer wears his shirt, but carries it, as well as a shovel. His shirt is full of the bones and the ceremonial disc.

He digs. He sees the skull.

> JOHN
> (whispering)

God.

EXT MOUNDVILLE - MOUND F - 1938 - CONT

John finishes. He throws his shirt and its contents in the hole.

He wipes the goo off his hands. He buries the bones.

EXT MOUNDVILLE - OUTSIDE CCC CAMP - 1938 - DAY

John exits the woods. His hands bleed; he moves slow.

Dr. Jones and DeJarnette stand near the work truck. They study a map on the hood with several state troopers. Dr. Jones sees John.

> DR. JONES

John?

John collapses. All rush to him. Dr. Jones kneels beside him.

John fights exhaustion. He sees Dr. Jones.

> JOHN
> I... know where they are.

INT CAMPER - NIGHT

Gardner stares at the open book. He looks to Bart.

> BART
> Finish?

Gardner reads.

> GARDNER
> "I could only ask why God had cursed
> me, and I prayed for the first time--
> God, oh God, what does finding that
> here, in the womb of a first civilization,
> imply? Ironic; I found God when I
> found proof He could not exist."

He closes the book.

> GARDNER (CONT'D)
> Why'd you want me to read that, Bart?

> BART
> It ain't obvious?

GARDNER

You wanna find this, thing. So that's
why you came back.

BART

It's the first time you've read it, huh?
Still sound crazy?

GARDNER

You sound crazy, as crazy as he was.
How can you-- how can any of you--
think this actually happened--

Bart grabs a folder from a stack and flips through it.

BART

Tim Shaw and Patrick Dobbs' deaths
were documented. They were found
exactly as grandpa described 'em.

He hands Gardner a newspaper clipping.

BART (CONT'D)
This was published the day after.

The headline reads: "Mound State Monument Thieves Found
Dead in Murder & Suicide." Accompanying it is a photograph of
the investigators at the crime scene.

BART (CONT'D)
It even mentions the goo. You know,
they had train tickets on 'em. Now what
that don't explain-- what they couldn't

138

                    BART (CONT'D)
explain-- is what made somebody who
planned somethin' that precise go
apeshit the day before the big pay off.
All they could blame was the fever.

                    GARDNER
Says here they could've been murdered
by whoever they were gonna sell to.

                    BART
Yeah-- could've. 'Cept I don't know
what for. Shaw and Dobbs' were lootin'
for weeks, but there's no way in hell
they got much more than fifty pieces
out of those mounds, workin' in the
dark. Fifty-five were recovered-- not
counting Dobbs' crate. In other words,
there ain't a motive. 'Cept, of course.

Gardner shakes his head.

                    GARDNER
This doesn't prove anything. He coulda
just used this.

                    BART
True. 'Cept he's mentioned in the
article--

                    GARDNER
"Undisclosed cadet?"

BART

Then how do you explain this?

Bart holds up the "eye."

BART (CONT'D)

You're the one who found it, right where he said he buried it.

GARDNER

It was a popular motif-- it could be from another--

BART

Oh yeah. And Sims won't let you touch remains 'cause he's ethically opposed–

GARDNER

Why would he even carry it back to the mound-- it makes no sense unless he made it up, this is ridiculous--

BART

No way, kid! And you know it's not.

GARDNER

Do I?

BART

You've been scared of him you're whole life. And not 'cause what John the third told ya-- he might've told you

BART (CONT'D)
a lotta shit-- but 'cause you wanna believe it.

GARDNER
Don't--!

Gardner glances to the others in the room.

BART
Guys?

Ben, Levi and McClean exit.

GARDNER
Don't act like you know me, Bart-- you ain't-- haven't been around in a long time.

BART
You ain't hard to figure, Gardner. You're just like you were when we were kids playin' space man. You got an imagination on you-- and you think if you don't kill it, you're gonna wind up like him. Don't let it blind ya.

GARDNER
Oh, I'm blind--?

BART

That's right. You think I'd be wastin' my time back here if I didn't think this was a sure thing? If we didn't have some kinda lead?

Gardner doesn't respond.

BART (CONT'D)

You know the Christian creation story, right? There was water, God made land, then Adam outta dirt. Same goes for the Jewish one, the Muslim-- most of the major religions have some variation. Course that's not too surprisin', most comin' from the same place-- but folks over here had stories too. You heard the Creek? It's the same, 'cept there was a mound first. Same goes for the Seminole, the Chickasaw-- all the major tribes they think came from this place. Most have a story about a flood-- the Choctaw even have one about a "mound of Babel."

GARDNER

So?

                    BART
        History becomes myth, stories. Shared
        myths are evidence of a common
        heritage-- an unconscious memory of
        the same past.

Bart takes a ripped magazine article from the folder and hands it
to Gardner. It's titled: "The Hand of God-- Found?"
Accompanying it is a photo of an unearthed fossilized hand with
an indention in the palm.

                BART (CONT'D)
        That was found in Mesopotamia-- what
        they call the "cradle of civilization."

                 GARDNER
        Celestial Connections? Couldn't afford
        Weekly World News?

                    BART
        Check the date.

Gardner does-- "2001."

                BART (CONT'D)
        You think Grandpa used that too?
        What if he was right, that this thing is
        hard evidence of some sorta missin'
        link between the world's cultures. A
        metaphorical Adam.

GARDNER
He said we came from aliens.

BART
Just 'cause it's alien don't mean its from
another planet. All civilizations began
with a leap-- usually a spiritual one.
What if this thing was a messenger?
One the rest of us forgot a long time
ago.

Gardner shakes his head.

GARDNER
Religious iconography didn't appear
here until a century after the mounds
were built--

BART

And what replaces the soul? So they forgot too.

GARDNER

If that's true... if... what good would finding it do?

BART

I don't know. But I want to. And so do you. What if grandpa was wrong-- what if this is proof that God does exist. It'd make ya rethink everything they shoved down your throat in Sunday school, wouldn't it?

GARDNER

Is that what you really want? What this is about-- your vendetta?

BART

What this is about is provin' grandpa wasn't a liar.

GARDNER

What do you want from me?

BART

Help us look for it.

GARDNER

When? Tomorrow?

Bart shakes his head. Gardner just looks at him.

> BART
> Why else you think we're campin' out?

> GARDNER
> I can't help you. I don't know any-
> thing--

> BART
> You know where you found that piece.

Gardner shakes his head.

> GARDNER
> No. It's a crime, it's wrong-- and it's
> pointless.

> BART
> You believe that? I mean what do you
> really believe, Gardner?

Gardner looks away.

> BART (CONT'D)
> Trooper makes his rounds about 2 and
> 7. We'll be out there, between then,
> when you change your mind.

Bart begins to leave.

> BART (CONT'D)
> And Gardner. This stays here.

Gardner nods. Bart exits.

INT CAMPER - STOVE - NIGHT

Gardner fills a glass with water from a water cooler. He chugs.

His cell phone BUZZES. The screen reads: "New Voicemail." He listens-- there is barely a signal; the message is nearly inaudible.

> KELSEY
> Gardner-- there's-- I need to tell you-- if you could-- I can't really-- message, so, please-- as soon as--

Gardner presses "call back." The phone BEEPS. The screen reads "No Service." He moves the phone and tries to get a signal. He turns it off.

He eyes a folder labeled "Grandpa Research" on the table. It's full of copied newspaper articles.

He stops at one dated "1953", which reads: "Archaeologist's Work Breathes New Life Into Search for Mounds' Origin." A photo of John Patton Jr., now middle aged, accompanies it.

Gardner flips past it. He stops at one, dated "1965": "New University Requirements Cost Jobs for Unqualified."

He flips to another, dated "1973": "Patton's Claims Dismissed by Experts-- Book still tops best-seller list."

Then another, dated "1974": "Hearing to Determine if Patton Falsified Past Research."

Gardner flips past it, to a collection of photographs.

One catches his eye. It's of his grandfather, now an old man, holding an infant, who holds an "ET" plush toy. Gardner flips the picture over; a caption on the back reads: "John and Gardner Patton, 6 Mnths, 1988."

Gardner stares at the photo.

INT CAMPER - CONT

Gardner sits on the bed. He again looks for a signal with his phone. He sighs and sets it down.

He sees Levi's book about the *War of the Worlds* broadcast in a nearby duffle bag. He drags it to him and removes the book.

Underneath it he sees a small handgun. He returns the book and the bag.

He grabs his backpack and removes his copy of *War of the Worlds*. He glances back to the bag, then reads.

INT CAMPER - LATER

Gardner is asleep on the cot, *War of the Worlds* spread on his chest.

His phone BUZZES. He awakes. The screen reads: "New Text Message-- from Kelsey."

He rubs the sleep from his eyes. He grabs at one. He grunts and drops the phone.

He walks to the stove and checks the eye in the mirror. He removes a torn contact.

> **GARDNER**
> (whisper)
>
> Great.

He throws it away. He covers his good eye and looks at himself, blurry, in the mirror. He turns to the rest of the room.

He sees the *Celestial Connections* article on the table. He opens both eyes. He examines the indention in the hand.

He glances to the 1938 newspaper clipping. He notices something-- he squints and holds it closer. In the photo, on the wall, are the words, barely legible: "I Found the Genesis."

Gardner stares. He looks to the photo of his grandfather as a young man.

EXT CAMPER - NIGHT

Gardner, fully dressed, exits the camper. The others sit under the canopy. All look to Gardner.

> **GARDNER**
> I think I know where it is.

Bart smiles and nods.

BURIED IN THE MOUNDS

EXT MOUNDVILLE - NEAR MOUND F - NIGHT

Gardner, Bart, McClean, Levi and Ben walk to Mound F. All carry flashlights and digging equipment, except Ben, who films. They stop at the rear base. Bart checks his cell phone clock.

> BART
> All right, should be all alone.

> GARDNER
> Then let's do it.

Gardner removes a plastic tarp on the mound and walks to the flag, shovel in hand.

> GARDNER (CONT'D)
> Here.

He digs. The others watch.

Gardner uncovers bone and keeps digging. He stops.

Levi approaches with a brush, dusting something in the hole. Ben moves closer with the camera. The others just watch.

Levi cuts dirty fabric from the hole with his knife. He stops. He glances to the others and moves back.

All see it.

> MCCLEAN
> Jesus Christ....

It's a partial skeleton, wrapped in dirty fabric. It's lined with a black "goo"-- and its features aren't human. It's surrounded by broken pieces of the "ceremonial disc."

> BART
> Some people'd say it is, Doc.

Gardner stares. He sits.

McClean puts on vinyl gloves and approaches. Bart leans in beside him.

> BART (CONT'D)
> Whadda ya think?

> MCCLEAN
> I think we have something.

Gardner considers.

GARDNER

I'm not so sure.

Bart and McClean turn to him.

GARDNER (CONT'D)

It might just be, deformed. There's nothing that proves this... didn't come from here.

Bart laughs.

BART

They got you good, didn't they? You can't even see it in front of your face.

Gardner doesn't respond.

MCCLEAN

Now that's strange.

BART

Whatcha got Doc?

MCCLEAN

There looks like a, discrepancy, in the ages of different areas. Areas with this, uh, "goo", seem... younger. It must be some kind of preserving agent?

BART

Why would it need that?

McClean shrugs.

> **MCCLEAN**
> I'm not so sure it's natural. What if this
> was... purposely preserved?

> **BART**
> Make a guess at an age?

> **MCCLEAN**
> It's certainly ancient. The, discrepancy
> makes it hard to determine
> indiscriminately, but, from the exposed
> areas... it, looks more than eight
> hundred years old.

> **GARDNER**
> You mean it was here before the
> mounds?

McClean nods.

> **GARDNER (CONT'D)**
> How can you tell--?

> **MCCLEAN**
> Just look at the condition these are in--
> Bart, this is phenomenal, this, really
> is....

Gardner looks to Ben and Levi. Levi sits silent, looking off. Ben
films a static shot. He yawns. He notices Gardner and covers his
mouth.

Gardner eyes something in a bag of gear beside him.

> MCCLEAN (CONT'D)
> One thing that is troubling me... if this
> was buried that long ago, how could
> Shaw have stumbled across it looting?
> He wouldn't have gotten in that far,
> would he?

> BART
> Just 'cause it died then, Doc, don't
> mean it was buried then.

Gardner considers. He turns to the bag. He uncovers what caught
his eye-- a bottle of lawn fertilizer.

Levi sees an approaching light.

> LEVI
> The hell?

> BART
> That's not the trooper. That's
> University Police. Gardner, did you
> know about this?

> GARDNER
> It's a hoax.

> BART
> What?

154

GARDNER
Everything's too easy. Hell, I'd only buy it in a movie, Bart.

Bart stares at him. He glances to the police car.

BART
Damn it, Gardner-- did you know about this? Do they know what we're doing?

GARDNER
It is a hoax, isn't it?

BART
Damn it Gardner, answer me--

Gardner stands.

GARDNER
No, I want an answer--!

Levi steps behind him and puts the knife to his side.

LEVI
There. Now what about the cop?

Gardner stares at Bart.

GARDNER
I didn't tell anyone... it's, probably a routine patrol, 'cause of the dig.

> BART
>
> Then let's stay outta sight.

Bart returns the tarp. All rush to the woods. Levi keeps the knife on Gardner.

The police car stops at the mound. It scans the spotlight once-- then continues on its way.

EXT MOUNDVILLE - NEAR MOUND F - CONT

Bart, McClean, Ben, Levi and Gardner squat in the woods. They watch as the police car drives off. All relax.

> BART
>
> Turn the camera off Ben. All right, Doc, you and me'll clean up here. We wait half an hour, then move it under the excavation. They're findin' it tomorrow.

McClean nods. Bart looks to Ben and Levi.

> BART (CONT'D)
>
> You guys are goin' campin', like we talked about. (to Ben) Go ahead and get the files and gear-- but stay clear of that cop. And remember, as soon as you hear it on the news-- we gotta have a camera on the outside after the lock down.

Ben nods and exits. Bart looks to Gardner.

> BART (CONT'D)
> (to Levi)
> Get his cell phone.

Levi removes it from Gardner's pocket.

> BART (CONT'D)
> Sorry kid. But you're just gonna have to hang tight a few days.

Gardner smirks.

> GARDNER
> Why do it Bart? All this trouble to convince me... I mean if all that crap about legacy and Grandpa was bullshit to you, why even bother?

Bart just looks at him. He nods to Levi. Levi leads Gardner away.

> BART
> Oh, and Gardner. Thanks for the advice. Won't be so easy next time.

Gardner stares at him. Levi pushes him onward. They exit.

> BART (CONT'D)
> (to McClean)
> You were right.

> MCCLEAN
> I've done this before.

BURIED IN THE MOUNDS

                    BART
        Well... least he's outta the way.

Bart sits. He opens Gardner's phone. The screen still reads: "New Text Message-- from Kelsey."

Bart selects "read." It states: "Im Pregnant."

Bart presses: "Reply."

INT GARDNER & KELSEY'S APT - BEDROOM - NIGHT

Kelsey sleeps in bed. Her phone BUZZES and wakes her. She reads the screen: "New Text Message– from Gardner."

The message reads: "Need time. Im sorry."

Kelsey stares at it.

EXT MOUNDVILLE - NEAR BLACK WARRIOR RIVER - NIGHT

Gardner stands at the fence and stares at the river and surrounding woods. Levi stands nearby. Gardner glances to him. He notices the knife.

Ben approaches, flashlight in hand. He also carries two backpacks, one with a sleeping bag attached, and wears his own, also with a sleeping bag.

                    BEN
        Looks clear, but we better get going.
        We wanna be in the cave by dawn.

> LEVI

You get the gun?

Ben glances to Gardner, then shakes his head.

> BEN

We're not gonna need that, dude.

Levi grabs his backpack (with the sleeping bag). Ben starts to hand Gardner the other one.

> BEN (CONT'D)

I think this was everything--

Levi stops him. He searches the pack, then hands it to Gardner.

Gardner glares at Levi. He looks through it himself.

Ben walks to the bank. Gardner looks to Levi, who waits on him. He follows.

Ben grabs an inflated raft hidden near the river.

> BEN (CONT'D)
> (to Gardner)

Come on.

Gardner glances to Levi, who pockets his knife, then sits at the front of the raft.

He sees his reflection in the river-- then notices the reflection of the stars. He reaches in and removes a rock. He conceals it.

Levi sits behind him. Ben pushes the raft in. He lights the way as Levi paddles.

They reach mid-river. Gardner hesitates-- then attacks Levi with the rock, cutting his face. Both fall overboard.

BEN (CONT'D)
Whoa! What's going on?

Gardner grabs Levi's sleeping bag and pulls him underwater. The sleeping bag breaks loose; he loses his grip. He swims for the bank. Ben spotlights him with a flashlight.

BEN (CONT'D)
This doesn't have to get violent!

Levi recovers and swims after Gardner. He catches his backpack and drags him underwater. Gardner emerges and Levi punches him-- then dunks him again.

Gardner again emerges, struggling for breath. He rubs water out of his eyes. He squints, his vision now completely blurry. In the fight, he lost his other contact.

                          GARDNER
         Wonderful.

Levi drags Gardner to the raft.

EXT WOODS - OUTSIDE MOUNDVILLE - DAWN

Ben and Gardner walk, followed by Levi, who now has a bandage on the side of his eye. Gardner's hands have been tied with rope.

Ben holds the blackberry and follows their position on an electronic map. It BEEPS.

                          BEN
         There it is.

He nods. In front of them is the entrance to the cave John Patton Jr. found years earlier.

INT CAVE - CONT

Gardner, Levi and Ben enter, the latter carrying a flashlight. The cave has changed a lot since 1938-- trash and graffiti are everywhere. Most of the graffiti are lewd phrases-- though some are flying saucers, or statements like "I believe" and "The Truth is in Moundville."

Levi notices a stained sleeping bag in the corner.

> LEVI
> (to Gardner)
There's ya a bed.

Gardner glares at him. He sits down at the opposite wall. Levi grabs a rope and attaches it to the one around Gardner's wrist. He ties the other end around his own waist.

> LEVI (CONT'D)
> When you move, I'll know. Meanin'
> don't.

The blackberry BEEPS. It reads: "New Text Message-- from Bart."

> BEN
Good, we got a signal.

He reads the message.

> BEN (CONT'D)
> (to Levi)
> Everything's set. All we do is wait.

Gardner considers the blackberry.

Ben gets in his sleeping bag. Levi eyes the broken straps on his backpack that had attached his, then glances to Gardner. He grabs a portable television from Ben's pack and flips through the channels.

> BEN (CONT'D)
> Get any channels?

162

Levi nods. He touches his bandage.

                    BEN (CONT'D)
          You don't need anything else for that
          eye?

                    LEVI
          I'm fine.

                    BEN
          Can't help with--

                    LEVI
          I'm fine.

Ben shrugs and lays down. Levi flips channels to a rebroadcast of Orson Welles' post-*War of the Worlds* apology.

                    WELLES
                    (On TV)
          I am extremely surprised... that a story
          which has come familiar to children...
          should have such an immediate and
          profound effect....

Gardner just laughs.

EXT MOUNDVILLE - NEAR MOUND F - DAY

Students from the field school unload equipment and prep the excavation. Bart and McClean stand under a canopy. They ready their equipment.

Kelsey approaches from the crowd.

> KELSEY
> Where's Gardner?

Bart turns to her.

> BART
> I don't know. Sent me a message tellin'
> me he was leavin' a few days. He didn't
> tell you?

> KELSEY
> Leaving? Where did he go?

> BART

No idea. I reckon he got a ride somewhere-- I figured he knew what he was doin'.

> KELSEY

You seem real concerned.

> BART

What, "am I my brother's keeper?" If he wanted me to know, he woulda told me. Hell, I figured he'd tell you more than me.

> KELSEY

Well he didn't. And I don't know why.

> BART

Well, are y'all having some problems?

Kelsey glares at him. She turns and leaves. She touches her stomach.

EXT MOUNDVILLE - MOUND F EXCAVATION - LATER

The class stands around the excavation, which is roped in a grid. Dr. Sims lectures center stage.

> SIMS

From this point on, it's going to get real boring. But it's gonna be rewarding too; nothing beats that thrill of finding something lost for hundreds of years.

SIMS (CONT'D)
And by that I don't just mean artifacts.
Out here, we're connected to them-- to
the people who lived here. Through
what they left us-- sure. But also
through their dirt, and through our
sweat-- and through our search. It's
good not to forget that. You all should
be very proud. You're now part of a
search-- the search-- that's been there
since the beginning. Good luck.

Sims steps down and approaches Bart and McClean. The class
begins.

BART
Hell of a speech, Doc.

Sims smiles.

SIMS
Sorry if this gets a little monotonous.
But I guess we can't always be looking
for the Ark of the Covenant or the
Holy Grail.

Bart smiles. He approaches the mound and films. Kelsey, who
works a dirt screen, sees him.

Bart looks to her. He turns the camera on her. Kelsey looks away.

Sean digs in one of the squares. He stops. The other students stop
and look into his square.

166

Bart approaches. He looks to Sims.

                    BART
            You said it'd be borin'?

Sims looks to Bart, as does the rest of the class, including Kelsey.
A crowd forms around the square. Sims approaches.

                    SIMS
            What's going on?

Sims sees in the square. Inside is the alien skeleton.

                    SIMS (CONT'D)
            It's just remains. Let's re-cover and
            work around them. Everyone, please.

Sims begins to leave-- no one else moves. He looks back to Sean.

                    SIMS (CONT'D)
            Did you hear me, Sean?

                    SEAN
            I heard you.

Sims glances to the rest of the class, who stare in the hole. He
laughs.

                    SIMS
            What are you all gawking for?

SEAN
They may be remains... but I don't
know of what.

There's a MURMUR. Kelsey approaches.

SIMS
Ridiculous, they're obviously human--

He stops.

Kelsey sees the remains. Her eyes widen.

SIMS (CONT'D)
Before this gets out of hand, I think it's
best if we kept this quiet. You all know
the, story-- we don't want people
thinking this--

Sims looks to the class. Most are either talking on or taking pictures with their cell phones.

Kelsey is among them. She starts to call Gardner-- then stops. She looks to Bart. He sees her. He smiles and shrugs. Kelsey closes her phone, considering.

Bart turns to Sims.

> BART
> Still want 'em to bury it, Doc?

> SIMS
> I don't know.

McClean approaches.

> MCCLEAN
> I may have a suggestion.

INT CAVE - DAY

Gardner and Levi sit. The latter drinks from a canteen, slouched and sweating. Ben gathers his gear. All listen to a television broadcast.

> FIELD NEWSCASTER
> ...The lock down occurred just after one o'clock. At that time, the field class was moved to the site's David L. DeJarnette Research facility, where they are reportedly still being held, along with the remains in question. Though

FIELD NEWSCASTER (CONT'D)
there are concerns as to why such
extreme measures have been taken,
representatives for both the Alabama
Museum of Natural History and the
University of Alabama have stated that
these precautions are largely due to
concern that the quote "irregular
remains might be widely misidentified"....

Ben glances to the TV.

BEN
Oh hey-- there it is. (to Gardner) How
you think it looks on camera?

He turns the TV to Gardner. On it is a photo of the corpse.
Gardner squints.

BEN (CONT'D)
Pretty good, huh?

Gardner just shrugs and nods.

BEN (CONT'D)
Ooh, look at that.

FIELD NEWSCASTER
Now, with the activity we're seeing
outside the site right now, these
concerns certainly seem founded.

FIELD NEWSCASTER (CONT'D)
A crowd has already begun to form
here....

Ben smiles.

BEN
I think it's gonna be bigger than we
thought.

Ben grabs his pack. He notices Levi chug the canteen.

BEN (CONT'D)
You guys are gonna be outta water
soon. Here--

Ben hands Levi the blackberry.

BEN (CONT'D)
There should be a spring somewhere
nearby.

LEVI
Where are those games you're always
playin'?

BEN
I wouldn't. It's already pretty drained.
If you can get a signal, it won't do you
any good without a battery.

Ben opens his backpack. He notices a small rash on his arm--
Gardner notices it as well.

Ben ignores it. He takes folders out of his pack.

                    BEN (CONT'D)
          Better leave these with you, too.

He tosses them on the ground. The picture of young John Patton Jr. falls out.

Ben smiles and heads for the door.

                    BEN (CONT'D)
          Look for me on the news.

He exits. Levi turns off the television. He opens the blackberry and plays a game.

                    GARDNER
          Didn't you hear him?

Levi just looks at him.

                    GARDNER (CONT'D)
          You're sick and I'm blind. We're
          gonna need that thing.

Levi turns it off.

                    LEVI
          I ain't sick.

He takes a swig from the canteen. Gardner nods to the TV.

> GARDNER
> Can you turn it back on? Or at least the
> radio?

> LEVI
> The noise bugs me.

Gardner just looks at him. Levi grabs a magazine from a folder and tosses it to Gardner. It's a *Scientific American*, with a photograph of a fetus in the womb on the cover.

> GARDNER
> I can't see.

Levi ignores this. He picks up the photo of John Patton Jr. as a young man.

> LEVI
> He really think he found somethin'?

> GARDNER
> I don't know. I think he was just crazy.

> LEVI
> You kinda look like him.

> GARDNER
> Well I can't help that.

Levi grabs the folder containing John Patton Jr.'s journal. He flips through it.

GARDNER (CONT'D)
Can I ask you somethin'?

Levi just glances to him.

GARDNER (CONT'D)
What the hell are we doing here? I
mean y'all already pulled it off-- I can't
stop it. You're committin' a felony for
no good reason.

Levi doesn't respond.

GARDNER (CONT'D)
Y'all can't get away with it anyway. I
don't care how good you made it, that
thing won't pass any tests. And even if
you forge 'em, I mean no one serious is
gonna believe it. (laughs) They

>   GARDNER (CONT'D)
> wouldn't even if you found the real
> thing.

Levi tosses down the folder.

>   LEVI
> Got anythin' in there I can look at? I'm
> 'bout tired a aliens.

Gardner stares at him.

>   GARDNER
>   Sure.

He opens his backpack and removes *Buried in the Mounds*. It's soaked. He notices the photograph bookmark and removes it. He tosses Levi the book. Levi just looks at him.

He stares at Kelsey on the photo. He notices the fetus on the *Scientific American*.

>   GARDNER (CONT'D)
>   (quiet)
>   Oh God.

INT MOUNDVILLE ARCHAEOLOGY LAB - WORK ROOM - DAY

Bart, McClean and Sims stand near the remains, which are spread on a table. McClean wears gloves and examines them; Bart films; Sims is on the phone.

175

SIMS

Yes sir, getting them home is my top priority-- but until I get that escort I can't do anything. The staff wasn't a target, and then there wasn't anyone out there. I understand, but we've already kept them so long it's gonna raise questions regardless-- and I'm worried about that crowd. All right. Yes sir, we'll keep working-- I'll be ready to make a statement in a few hours.

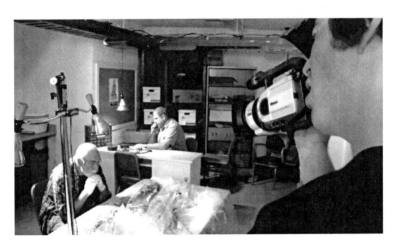

Sims hangs up.

SIMS (CONT'D)

Jesus Christ... it's just getting worse. We have to get some kind of proof that things human, real soon.

BART
And if you can't?

Sims just looks at him.

SIMS
(to McClean)
What do you have, doctor?

MCCLEAN
It's so, unique-- I don't really want to make a guess on an age without radiocarbon dating. But-- several centuries at least. Its disfigurement looks natural, wouldn't you say?

SIMS
Sure. But that doesn't mean it's from outer space.

MCCLEAN
I agree. I can't see anything that would classify this as solely extra terrestrial, not that I'd know it if I saw it. But the gelatin, the small bone length and irregular density-- the dolichocephaly, the shallow orbits-- the, abnormalities-- they don't necessarily discredit that possibility either.

SIMS
Well how can we discredit it? What do we need to prove that, beyond a doubt, this is human?

MCCLEAN

Honestly? Forensics. Genetic Fingerprinting. That's the only way, beyond a
doubt.

Sims sighs.

SIMS

Well, we can't do that here.

MCCLEAN

I know.

SIMS

This has already gotten out of hand. If
we can't prove it in 48 hours-- 72 tops--
it'll be John Patton Jr. all over again.

MCCLEAN

Then we're going to have to move to
another facility.

SIMS

You have one in mind?

MCCLEAN

I have everything I need at Berkeley.

SIMS

Berkeley? That's too far—

                    MCCLEAN
If I make arrangements immediately, I
can get to work as soon as tomorrow
morning. There's not a lot of facilities
with the kind of equipment we need-- it
could take us longer than that just to
find one closer, not to mention getting
access.

Sims considers this.

                    SIMS
Tomorrow morning. You're sure?

McClean nods.

Bart's phone RINGS. The screen reads: "Ben Calling."

                    BART
Excuse me.

He exits.

INT MOUNDVILLE ARCHAEOLOGY LAB - LOBBY -
CONT

The field school students sit, talking.

Kelsey watches the news; on it is a photo of the alien skeleton.

She grabs her phone. She stares at Gardner's name. She closes it.

Bart enters from the lab, phone in hand. He ignores the class.
Kelsey watches him exit down the hallway.

INT MOUNDVILLE ARCHAEOLOGY LAB - HALLWAY -
CONT

Bart answers the phone.

> BART
>
> You back? All right, yeah, get
> everything you can outside-- b-roll,
> interviews-- I want everybody's opinion
> on this thing, the nuttier the better. Oh,
> and use the hotel room tonight. 'Cause
> I think I'm headin' back to Berkeley.
> Yeah, I know. Maybe it's too easy.

Bart hangs up. He notices Kelsey's reflection in the window.

> KELSEY
>
> Was that Gardner?

> BART
>
> I don't think it's your business who that
> was.

> KELSEY
>
> Just tell me, Bart.

> BART
>
> No.

KELSEY

Is this some kind of prank? Is Gardner involved?

BART

What?

KELSEY

You're not being totally honest with me-- and this is too big a coincidence--

BART

Hold on! What are you talkin' about?

KELSEY

I-- I have to know why he's not here, Bart.

BART

Okay. You're right, Kels, I ain't been fully honest with you. Gardner did tell me why he left. He told me you were pregnant, and that he was scared. That he felt guilty, but he needed time. He said he kinda suspected it, why he wanted to come out here in the first place. Now I'm sorry if that hurts you, I didn't wanna have to tell ya-- but you don't need to be thinkin' we had anything to do with this.

Kelsey sits.

                    KELSEY
He told you?

Bart nods.

                KELSEY (CONT'D)
How could... How could he leave me,
when I need him the most?

Bart looks away.

                    BART
Well... he is just a kid.

INT CAVE - DAY

Gardner reads an article on pregnancy in *Scientific American*.

Levi snores. Gardner looks to him-- he's asleep. He notices the blackberry on the ground. He glances to Kelsey's photo.

He rises to a squat. He almost loses his balance; he catches himself on the wall. Levi doesn't notice the tug.

On the wall, Gardner sees the scratched "I Found the Genesis." He continues and squat-walks towards the blackberry.

The blackberry BEEPS. The screen reads: "Low Battery!" This wakes Levi. He sees Gardner.

                    LEVI
You moved.

GARDNER
I was, just gettin' the folder.

Levi tosses it to him. He takes out his knife.

LEVI
Told you not to move.

Gardner nods. He sits back against the wall. He opens the folder. He glances to Levi, who stares at him.

He glances back to "I Found the Genesis." In the folder, he notices the photo of John Patton Jr. as a young man.

Gardner flips through the folder. He stops at an entry: "A Genesis Found." He scans it and notices the caption: "This is the Truth I've ran from most of my life...."

Something else catches his eye, near the corner of the page-- a sequence of numbers: "1330026^-873745>."

Gardner flips to the drawings of the rattlesnake disc and the burial configuration. He eyes the number "-873743>."

He flips to the map of Moundville. He eyes the North arrow point on the compass. He compares it to the "^" in the "A Genesis Found" entry.

The blackberry BEEPS again. Gardner sees it. He glances to Levi- he has fallen back asleep, though still clutches the knife.

Gardner again rises to a squat. He creeps to the blackberry. He stares at Levi and his knife.

He reaches the blackberry. He picks it up and creeps back to the wall. He conceals it with the folder.

He opens the "Menu" and scrolls down the options. He stops at "Send Text Message." He begins to select it and stops. He notices another option: "Open GPS GeoNavigator."

He glances to Kelsey's photo-- then his grandfather's. He selects it.

As the program begins, it reads: "Enter Coordinates-- Latitude and Longitude." Gardner enters the numbers on the "A Genesis Found" entry and selects "Map It."

The program locates the coordinates-- "Nacaome, El Salvador."

Gardner double checks the coordinates. He counts them-- then stops. He removes a pen from the front pocket of his backpack. The pen is busted, however-- he wipes the ink off his hand. He uses it anyway.

On the "A Genesis Found" entry, he writes a "7" under the latitude, and "6" under the longitude.

He marks a ")" between the "1" and the rest of the number, leaving: "330026^-873745>." He enters the new number as the coordinates, and presses "Map It."

The program reveals the location. It reads: "You are Here."

Gardner flips through the journal, circling hidden coordinates in the same notation. He copies down the numbers.

BURIED IN THE MOUNDS

INT CAVE - MOMENTS LATER

Gardner looks at the completed list of coordinates. He plots them into the blackberry-- there's nothing distinguishable about any one, and most are less than a mile apart. He stops.

He sees the map in the journal. He considers it-- then notices something: a notation for a cave. He draws an "x" over it.

He glances back to the list of coordinates. His eyes widen.

He plots a dot over the "x."

INT MOUNDVILLE ARCHAEOLOGY LAB - WORK ROOM - DAY

Bart, McClean and Sims sit around the room. Again, Sims is on the phone.

> SIMS
> Yes sir, I'll tell him.

Sims hangs up and turns to McClean.

> SIMS (CONT'D)
> You can take it to Berkeley.

McClean nods.

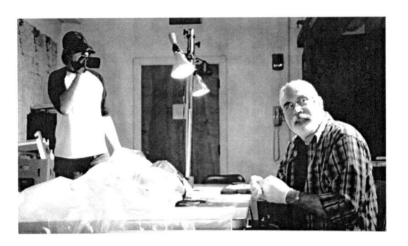

MCCLEAN
I'll start making arrangements.

McClean walks to the phone. Sims looks to the door.

SIMS
I'll dismiss the class.

INT MOUNDVILLE ARCHAEOLOGY LAB - LOBBY - CONT

Kelsey sits. She stares at Gardner's name in her cell phone. She presses "call."

She hears a faint BUZZ in the lab that coincides with the phone ring. She looks in the window-- and sees Bart take out a phone. Bart presses a button-- and Kelsey's call is ended.

She stares at Bart. Sims enters.

> SIMS
> All right guys, everyone listen up, please. I've got some bad news for some of you-- it's a false alarm-- it's human. Good news is you're all free to go. Tomorrow we'll meet back in the classroom.

There is a GRUMBLE as the students prepare to leave.

> SIMS (CONT'D)
> Now, as you're probably aware, there's a pretty big crowd out there, so several University Police officers are waiting to escort you safely out of the site. So everyone, please, stay together.

Kelsey sits still. Sims notices her.

> SIMS (CONT'D)
> Gardner's not here?

Kelsey looks to him. She just shakes her head. Sims considers this. He returns to the lab.

Kelsey stares at Bart through the window.

EXT MOUNDVILLE - PARKING LOT PERIMETER - DAY

Kelsey walks with the rest of the class to the parking lot. She notices the University Police cars in position for the escort.

She stops near the woods and enters.

BURIED IN THE MOUNDS

EXT CAMPER - DAY

Kelsey emerges from the woods. She approaches the camper and knocks on the door. It's unlocked-- she enters.

INT CAMPER - CONT

Kelsey turns on the light. She eyes the photograph of Gardner and his grandfather, still on the kitchen table.

She sees the bed. Something beside it catches her eye-- Gardner's copy of *War of the Worlds*. She approaches.

She eyes Levi's book on the *War of the Worlds* broadcast in the duffle bag. She flips through it. She notices a folded sheet of paper wedged inside. She opens it. She smiles.

It's a blue print for the alien remains.

She pockets the blue prints and returns the book to the duffle bag. There, she notices something else inside.

INT MOUNDVILLE ARCHAEOLOGY LAB - WORK ROOM - CONT

Bart, Sims and McClean are in the room. McClean is on the phone. Bart and Sims sit quietly.

Bart's phone BUZZES. It reads: "New Text Message-- From Kelsey": "Found plans for bones. Meet at camper."

McClean hangs up the phone.

                    MCCLEAN
It's all arranged-- I'll be flying out in a
few hours. I can take the remains with
me.

                     BART
Excuse me.

Bart exits. Sims watches, looks to McClean.

                     SIMS
He sure gets a lot of phone calls.

                    MCCLEAN
That's Hollywood for you.

Sims considers this. He nods.

                     SIMS
I'll get everything ready for you. Excuse
me.

Sims exits.

INT CAVE - DAY

Gardner stares at the map. Multiple points are plotted on it,
spread out over the woods in no pattern.

He looks to the list of coordinates. He notices the first numbers,
separated by a ")." No number repeats.

Starting at zero, he connects the points in numerical order. The shape of the constellation Orion is revealed.

> GARDNER
> (whispering)
> Orion?

Gardner draws the "eye in the hand" over the constellation. He circles a plot point as he draws the eye. It makes a "pupil."

He stares at it.

EXT CAVE - 1938 - NIGHT

John Patton Jr. exits the cave, carrying the shirt full of bones. He stops. He turns and looks up the bluff.

INT CAVE - CONT

Gardner traces a line from the "x" to the "pupil" on the map.

EXT WOODS - OUTSIDE MOUNDVILLE - 1938 - NIGHT

John Patton Jr. runs, carrying a shovel along with the bones. He stops at the base of a tree. He digs.

INT CAVE - CONT

Gardner stares at the map.

BURIED IN THE MOUNDS

EXT WOODS - OUTSIDE MOUNDVILLE - 1938 - NIGHT

John Patton Jr. finishes a hole. He throws the shirt full of bones inside.

INT CAVE - CONT

Gardner leans back, considering.

INT BARRACKS - MOUNDVILLE CCC CAMP - 1938 - DAY

John Patton Jr. sits in bed. He works in his journal. DeJarnette walks past him, eyeing him. John nods and resumes.

In the journal he copies a portion of the map of the Black Warrior River Valley. On the original he has already plotted coordinates, connected by an "eye in the hand" configuration.

He circles "Mound F" in his journal.

INT CAVE - CONT

Gardner considers.

Levi coughs and wakes. He grabs the canteen and finishes it. Gardner conceals the blackberry.

Levi tosses the canteen to the ground.

> LEVI
> We gotta get water.... So, hot... can't keep it in me.

Levi takes off his shirt. His body is covered with a heavy rash.

GARDNER
Oh my God.

Levi picks up his knife.

LEVI
We gotta... where's that thing?

Levi feels for the blackberry. Gardner hides it under his leg.

Levi feels something on his neck. He pulls it off– it's an attached tick. He squishes it.

LEVI (CONT'D)
Goddam, parasites... suck ya dry, if ya
let 'em... make ya bad sick, take all the
water.

Levi pulls on the rope connecting him to Gardner.

> LEVI (CONT'D)
> I betcha, they're suckin' on you. (raises
> knife) Or you suckin' on me?

Levi shuts his eyes. Gardner stares at him.

EXT CAMPER - DUSK

Bart approaches. He knocks on the door.

> KELSEY
> (OS)
> I'm tired of asking you, Bart–

Bart turns and sees Kelsey. She points a gun at him.

> BART
> Jesus, Kelsey--!

> KELSEY
> Where's Gardner?

INT MOUNDVILLE ARCHAEOLOGY LAB - OFFICE - DUSK

Sims works at a computer. He types "Bart Thompson" in a newspaper search engine.

There are many results, most movie reviews or related articles. He scrolls through the page. He sighs.

He types: "Dr. Kevin McClean."

His eyes widen. He prints an article from the "Cahokia-Dupo Herald", accompanied by a photo of McClean: "Excavation Finds Cahokia Giant-- Mound Builder, Anakite, or Hoax?"

INT CAVE - DUSK

Gardner watches Levi, who's still asleep. He picks up the blackberry.

He types a text message: "kels its hoax trapped in cave bart knows where send help."

His thumb hovers over "send." He notices the "pupil" on the map.

He glances to Levi; he notices the knife. He eyes the rope around his wrists. He glances to the empty canteen. He selects "cancel."

He tugs hard at the rope.

GARDNER
Hey-- hey wake up-- we need more
water! Hey--!

Levi doesn't move. Gardner sighs. He looks back to the blackberry.

It BEEPS: "Low Battery!"

Gardner looks to Levi, who wakes. He sees Gardner.

Levi staggers towards Gardner with the knife. Gardner tugs hard at the rope, pulling Levi down. He collapses onto him.

Gardner struggles free. He grabs Levi's knife and cuts himself loose. He scurries to his feet and heads for the exit.

He stops. He looks to Levi, who hasn't moved. He checks his pulse. He sees the dirty sleeping bag in the corner.

INT CAVE - MOMENTS LATER

Gardner drags the sleeping bag around Levi. His shirt is rolled under his head as a pillow.

> GARDNER
> (Quoting *Empire Strikes Back*)
> Sorry if this smells bad, kid.

Gardner zips the bag. He picks up the blackberry. It's dead. He drops it.

He grabs his grandfather's map. He heads for the exit.

EXT CAVE - CONT

Gardner exits the cave, map in hand. He scans the area. Everything is blurry.

He turns and faces the direction of the "pupil." He looks to the map. He places his finger on the line between the "x" and the "pupil." He squints and walks the same direction.

BURIED IN THE MOUNDS

INT MOUNDVILLE ARCHAEOLOGY LAB - WORK ROOM - DUSK

McClean reads a newspaper. The remains are beside him in a box.

He rubs his wrist under his magnetic bracelet. He pulls it back, revealing a rash.

Dr. Sims enters, along with a UNIVERSITY POLICE OFFICER.

> SIMS
> Dr. McClean?

Sims holds out the article.

> SIMS (CONT'D)
> We need you to clear something up for
> us.

McClean just looks at him.

EXT WOODS - OUTSIDE MOUNDVILLE - DUSK

Bart walks in front of Kelsey, who still holds the gun.

> BART
> Jesus, Kelsey, I get the point. You can
> put that away.

Kelsey doesn't respond. Bart's phone BUZZES. He reaches for it.

                    KELSEY
        Hold it. I wanna see it.

Bart sighs and hands her the phone. On the screen is a text message, reading: "10301938."

                    KELSEY (CONT'D)
        It's just a bunch of numbers.

Kelsey hands it back to Bart.

                    KELSEY (CONT'D)
        What does it mean? Does it have to do
        with Gardner?

Bart reads the message.

                    BART
        It's the day martians invaded earth.

Kelsey glares at him.

                    BART (CONT'D)
        It's from McClean. They caught him.

                    KELSEY
        Then it's over.

                    BART
        Not yet. Not if they don't find me.
        They do, it's over for all of us--
        includin' Gardner.

KELSEY
Are you threatening me?

BART
No. I'm makin' a deal.

He holds up his phone.

BART (CONT'D)
One call gets the cops out here. Now I
don't think you believe Gardner's
totally uninvolved. Why ya think he
ignored your message?

KELSEY
What are you trying to say?

198

> BART

I'm the only one who can guarantee he
gets outta this clean. I think that's worth
somethin'.

> KELSEY

I don't see how you can help him if I
let you get away.

Bart laughs.

> BART

I ain't "gettin' away." I just need a few
days-- then I turn myself in and clean
up the whole mess. Just a few days.

> KELSEY

Why?

Bart reaches in his pocket. Kelsey puts two hands on the gun. Bart
removes a Mini DV videotape.

> BART

I gotta get this to somebody.

> KELSEY

And I can trust you?

Bart smiles.

> BART

I might be a liar, a scalawag, and a son
of a bitch... but I'm still family.

He nods to her stomach. She stares at him.

EXT WOODS - NEAR CREEK - DUSK

Gardner traces his steps on the map. He squints and scans the woods. He stops.

A creek is in front of him. He looks to the map. There is no sign for one between the "x" and the "pupil."

Gardner sits by the bank. He laughs. He stares at himself in the water.

He notices the reflection of a star, already out.

He examines the map closer. He notices a wavy line sprouting from the Black Warrior. He traces it; it becomes fainter, barely copied. It runs directly after the "pupil", skimming the coordinate.

Gardner smiles.

INT CAVE - DUSK

Bart and Kelsey enter. They see Levi on the ground.

BART
Christ.

Bart kneels beside him.

KELSEY
Where's Gardner?

BART
(sarcastic)
Well, I reckon he's gone.

Kelsey notices the folder and backpack. She picks up the photo of her and Gardner.

KELSEY
Why'd he leave all his stuff?

BART
(sarcastic)
I reckon he was in a hurry. Escapes usually are.

She gathers the strewn papers and puts the folder in the backpack. She notices the photo of John Patton Jr. as a young man. She considers it, then pockets it.

She sees Levi, who's still unconscious.

> KELSEY
> (sarcastic, forcing accent)
> Sure looks spry. I reckon he was right
> on his heels.

Kelsey grabs the backpack and exits.

EXT CAVE - CONT

Kelsey exits the cave, putting on the backpack. She looks around.
Bart exits behind her.

> BART
> I'm tellin' you Kels, he's probably
> already back. Better get a move on.

Kelsey turns and considers the bluff. She glances to the photo of
John Patton Jr. as a young man.

> KELSEY
> Don't worry, Bart-- you've got your
> head start. But when I find Gardner,
> I'm calling the cops.

Kelsey exits up the hill.

EXT WOODS - CREEK - DUSK

Gardner searches. He scrambles around the bank. He rips back
dirt, then examines rocks and roots, then rips back more dirt.

GARDNER
No... come on. Come on!

He loses his footing on the edge of the bank, almost tripping into the creek. He catches himself on a large root.

He runs his hand through his hair. He stands.

GARDNER (CONT'D)
Damn it.

He feels something on his neck. He removes it-- it's a tick. He looks to the tree.

He sees an "x" carved in the bark.

EXT WOODS - CREEK - 1938 - NIGHT

John Patton Jr. smashes an "x" into the tree with his shovel.

EXT WOODS - CREEK - CONT

Gardner stares at the "x." He smiles.

He rips at the dirt at the base of the tree.

EXT WOODS - CREEK - 1938 - NIGHT

John Patton Jr. digs with a shovel.

EXT WOODS - CREEK - CONT

Gardner digs deeper and deeper.

BURIED IN THE MOUNDS

EXT WOODS - CREEK - 1938 - NIGHT

John Patton Jr. shovels dirt on the shirt full of bones.

EXT WOODS - CREEK - CONT

Gardner rips at the dirt.

EXT WOODS - OUTSIDE CAVE - CONT

Kelsey scans the area. She hears the creek, and the faint sound of Gardner digging. She walks toward it.

EXT WOODS - CREEK - CONT

Gardner digs. His fingers begin to bleed.

EXT WOODS - CREEK - 1938 - NIGHT

John Patton Jr. shovels dirt over the shirt full of bones.

EXT WOODS - CREEK - CONT

Gardner's blood mixes with the dirt. He throws back handful after handful. He stops.

EXT WOODS - CREEK - 1938 - NIGHT

John Patton Jr. stares at the bones. He holds the last shovel full.

EXT WOODS - CREEK - CONT

Gardner stares in the hole. Something protrudes from the ground. He squints and looks closer. It looks like bone.

Kelsey approaches.

                    KELSEY
          Gardner?

Gardner turns to her.

                    GARDNER
          I see it.

                    KELSEY
          What?

Gardner looks to the hole.

EXT WOODS - CREEK - 1938 - NIGHT

John Patton Jr. stares at the bones.

EXT WOODS - CREEK - CONT

Gardner stares in the hole. Kelsey approaches. She notices Gardner is bleeding.

                    KELSEY
          Gardner--

Gardner grabs her hand.

GARDNER

You see it?

Kelsey looks in the hole. She sees Gardner, who squints at the hole. She reaches into her pocket.

KELSEY

Gardner...

She hands him his glasses.

KELSEY (CONT'D)

I think you need to look closer.

Gardner puts them on. He sees in the hole.
It's nothing but roots.

He collapses to the ground. Kelsey kneels beside him.

                    GARDNER
    I fell for it again.

                    KELSEY
    What were you looking for?

He shakes his head.

                KELSEY (CONT'D)
    The skeleton?

Gardner laughs at himself.

                    GARDNER
    Bart was wrong. I wasn't afraid it was
    out here... I was afraid it wasn't.

                    KELSEY
    Why?

                    GARDNER
    'Cause it'd prove there is something
    else. That it's not all just facts and
    fiction. That we're more than just dirt.

Gardner sees Kelsey's stomach. He looks to her. He touches it.

Kelsey hands him the photo of his grandfather as a young man.

                    KELSEY
    You dropped this.

Gardner considers it.

KELSEY (CONT'D)
You look like him.

GARDNER
Yeah, I do.

Kelsey smiles. Gardner sees the gun in her back pocket.

GARDNER (CONT'D)
How did you find me anyway?

The leaves CRACK behind them. Both turn to see Bart.

BART
If Kelsey ain't told you Gardner, it's over. I'm goin'... just thought you'd want this back.

He tosses Gardner his cell phone.

BART (CONT'D)
Look, for what it's worth, I didn't think it'd come to this--

GARDNER
You don't gotta apologize, Bart-- I ain't- I'm not pressin' charges. Just get the hell outta here.

Bart begins to leave.

GARDNER (CONT'D)
Was it worth it Bart? Your revolution?

Bart stops. He nods.

>   BART
> Sorry I had to lie to ya, kid. But some
> things are more important than you and
> me. People gotta see how they
> manipulate themselves, lookin' for
> answers. That it's all perception, all
> stories... that there's nothing beyond
> that. That we're just a culture of myths
> desperate for justification.

>   GARDNER
> That's the last time you call me kid.

Kelsey dials on her phone.

>   KELSEY
> You're losing your head start.

Bart exits. Gardner watches. He shakes his head.

> GARDNER
> He may be a sonofabitch, but he's a
> hell of a storyteller.

> KELSEY
> We need to get some help out here.

Gardner opens his phone. He glances at the "previous calls."

> GARDNER
> I think that's already taken care of.

He hands it to Kelsey. It lists: "Emergency 911."

> KELSEY
> He probably thinks this makes up for
> everything.

> GARDNER
> Let it. We oughtta wait with Levi.

Both stand. Gardner starts for the cave. Kelsey notices something on the ground. She picks it up.

> GARDNER (CONT'D)
> You comin'?

Kelsey nods. She puts the object in the front pocket of the backpack and follows.

EXT WOODS - NEAR CREEK - CONT

Bart walks. He scratches his arm. He pulls up his sleeve, revealing a rash.

He smiles.

INT GARDNER & KELSEY'S APT - LIVING ROOM - NIGHT

Gardner reads his grandfather's journal, from an entry titled: "The Endless Search-- Unlocking the Mounds' Origin."

He holds his place and looks in the front pocket of his backpack. He removes a pen-- then stops. He takes out a piece of dirty fabric and examines it. It's part of a patch, with the letters "CCC" inscribed.

Kelsey enters. She carries a newspaper. Gardner puts down the patch.

> KELSEY
> Hey.

> GARDNER
> Hey. How was Sims?

> KELSEY
> He said if you miss again he'll have you arrested.

> GARDNER
> Sounds about normal.

> **KELSEY**
> I think he's still convinced you masterminded the whole thing.

> **GARDNER**
> Well good– should get me some bonus points, much as it's helped his career.

> **KELSEY**
> Not just his.

Kelsey hands Gardner the newspaper. It reads: "Halloween Hoaxers Face Law Suit– Could see jail time."

> **KELSEY (CONT'D)**
> Now that's his kind of headline.

> **GARDNER**
> Yeah... well I'll believe it when I see it. He'll get out of it someway–

> **KELSEY**
> He already has.

> **GARDNER**
> Huh?

> **KELSEY**
> He's in the hospital– they all are.

> **GARDNER**
> For?

                    KELSEY
Rocky Mountain Spotted Fever. Levi
was just the first to show symptoms--
you're lucky you weren't infected.

                    GARDNER
But they're lucky they were.

Kelsey nods.

                    KELSEY
People are sayin' it's punishment
enough.

Gardner grins.

                    GARDNER
That's what Shaw had.

                    KELSEY
        What?

Gardner shakes his head. His phone BUZZES. It reads: "New
Text Message-- from Bart."

                    GARDNER
        Speak of the devil.

He reads it: "celestialconnections.com."

Gardner and Kelsey share a look. Gardner grabs a laptop and
enters the address. The page reads: "Moundville "Hoax" Cover
Up-- Video leaked to Youtube reveals Truth!"

Gardner selects the link to the video. It's of Bart and McClean the night the skeleton was first unearthed with Gardner. It's description reads: "Was the real thing found before the fake?"

Gardner notices the views: "16,783." He skims the comments-- "this is the proof we need!"; "can't wait to see the movie!"; "it was a cover up"; "the truth is in moundville."

One stops him. It's from "tickfiend666": "a culture of myths gar...."

Gardner looks to Kelsey. He just laughs.

GARDNER (CONT'D)
Least he didn't call me kid.

Kelsey smiles. She walks towards the hallway. She stops by a box labeled "storage" on the kitchen table. She pulls out Gardner's ET plush toy.

                    KELSEY
          Little early.

Gardner just shrugs. Kelsey heads back for the hallway. She stops.

                    KELSEY (CONT'D)
          Gardner?

                    GARDNER
          Yeah?

                    KELSEY
          Do you believe it?

                    GARDNER
          Believe what?

                    KELSEY
          Like all those people-- that, something,
          could really still be out there?

                    GARDNER
          Even if there is... it doesn't have all the
          answers.

Kelsey nods. She continues.

                    GARDNER (CONT'D)
          Oh, Kels, by the way-- did you find this
          in the cave?

He holds up the patch. She shakes her head.

BURIED IN THE MOUNDS

KELSEY
In the woods-- I figured you dropped it.

GARDNER
Near the creek?

Kelsey nods. She exits.

Gardner considers the patch. On the back is a black substance; it's also all over the backpack's front pocket.

He notices the pen on the table. It's busted and covered in ink. He laughs.

He notices a small object protruding from the back of the patch. He peels back the ink-- it's a dead tick.

He flips to the "A Genesis Found" entry. He stops, seeing the photo of his grandfather as a young man.

He sees his own reflection in the table.

He flips back to the "Endless Search" entry.

He looks back to the patch.

He stands and buries it in the trash.

END

A G e n e s i s F o u n d

Written & Directed by Lee Fanning
Produced by Benjamin Stark & Lee Fanning

Gardner Patton	Elliot Moon
Kelsey West	Elise Zieman
Bart Thompson	Luke Weaver
John Patton Jr.	Bennett Parker
Dr. Kerry Sims	Rob Wilds
Dr. Kevin McClean	Steven Burch
Tim Shaw	Tyler Gibson
Ben Watson	Julian "Jay" Burton
Levi Thompson	Philip Barnes
Dr. Jones	Jackson Pyle
DeJarnette	Murray Nicholson
Patrick Dobbs	Jonathan Bradford
Supervisor Chuck	Andrew Hall
Chris	Chris Hicks
Eddie	Eddie Olazaran
Director of Photography	Stephen Martel Lucas
Assistant Director	Markus Matei
Assistant Camera	Joey Brown
2ᵈ Assistant Camera	Greg Taylor
Sound Recordist	Troy Fuqua
Workflow Engineer	Hope Lavelle
Costume Designer	Peyton Fanning
Hair & Make-up	Jackie Hadwin
Set Decor	Danielle Stark
Art Design & Props	Sam Hernandez
Set Construction	Jerrell Bowden
Special Prop Construction	Zac Lawson
Special Effects	David Possien, Ian McCalister
Graphic Design	Jessica Twilbeck
Publicist	Jesse Ewing
Music	Brett Robinson & Christopher Whitney

218

Southern Truths

Featuring John Patton Jr.

"Hoover Hedgehogs"

Art/Ink by Kevin Maggard
Script by Lee Fanning